AMBROSIA

Ann Benson

ISBN: 978-0-9996230-0-8

Library of Congress Control Number: 2019914324

Printed in the U.S.A.

Cover design by Ann Benson

Greek pottery image by Marie-Lan Nguyen

Author photo ©2019 Meryl Glassman

For Jack and Ella with Love

Prologue
Prologis

The ragged man shaded his eyes from the sting of the wind and peered into the February sky. A pale glow of sun hovered in a slit between two tall buildings, where, five years before, it would not have been visible.

"Damn. Didn't you just come up?"

Sheesh. Always in such a hurry.

He shuffled along the icy sidewalks of downtown Manhattan, pausing now and then to panhandle. He secured his jingling fortune in one pocket with a yank on the twisty-tie Gina had installed when the zipper pull fell off.

How many months ago? He couldn't recall. *When I get back on my feet again, I'll get a real good jacket. And I'll be handing out money myself.*

He organized his handful of coins into neat little piles in front of the liquor store clerk. "I'm an accountant."

"Good for you, Pal." The stone-faced clerk swooped the piles into his hand and dropped the coins into the drawer.

A few minutes past sunset, bottle in hand, Freddie turned into his alley. "Honey, I'm home! I picked up dinner!" His slurred laughter echoed off brick walls.

He'd been proclaimed Mayor of this alley because he'd been there longest, and when the lady in the north-side building got her new refrigerator, the crate went to him, by eminent domain. On one inside wall was scribbled, "Home sweet homeless," around which he'd drawn a frame with curlicues. He had a candle in a mayonnaise jar, and an old but decent blanket, another gift from Gina.

Halfway down the alley he stopped.

'Sonuvabitch." The top of the box was dented. He recalled, albeit fuzzily, the previous night's exchange with McCarthy.

I-na-wanna-ko.

I know, Your Honor. You're so full of antifreeze you can't tell how cold it is. It's tax season, your busiest time of year, the cop had explained, *and Gina's worried about you. So get in the cruiser.*

He'd spent one reluctant night in Gina's center, and the wolves had pounced. Where was the honor among thieves?

"Toss that sucker right out on his ass."

But the thought of ousting an intruder was every bit as unsettling to him as the rest of reality. He stood there shivering in agonized uncertainty. Finally, he inched forward through the crunchy slush and stood just shy of the box, his ear slightly cocked.

All he heard was a thin growl. Overcome with relief, Freddie grabbed the back of the box and tried to tip it forward, expecting a small scared dog to come sliding out.

But out of the box came a man-sized being who barreled into the slush and righted himself with fists up and ready. The glowering opponent flexed like the Hulk, and snapped out a string of what Freddie assumed to be threats, but he couldn't be sure, because they weren't English. And then Freddie heard the whining growl again, coming from somewhere *on* the stranger, *not* from his mouth. The drapes of this man's—*dress?* were undulating, as if a snake was writhing within.

The stranger unclenched one fist, then patted the front of his garment. He spoke soothing words in his unknown language to whatever was hiding in there, then yanked a brittle-looking twig angrily out of his hair and tossed it away. There were more; Freddie was tempted to point and say, *you missed a couple,* but thought better of it.

He regarded the man with cautious curiosity. Sandals, in February. No socks. A white dress. Talks to his chest in gobble-de-gook. A funny kind of necklace with something hanging from it. Leaves and twigs on him when there's snow on the ground.

And they say I'm *crazy.*

Chapter 1
Alpha

Regina Bugbee passed under the sweeping arches of the new facade and into the main lobby of Bellevue Hospital. She smiled and waved to security, and headed for the hallway, wondering why no one ever seemed to walk completely upright at Bellevue; everyone was urgent, tilted into some imaginary head wind.

Sliding and dodging through the crowd, Gina cruised by carriages, walkers, and orange plastic chairs, where young mothers cooed sweetly to wonder-eyed babies, and old couples conspired in quiet anxiety. Fresh young doctors, their self-assurance not yet tested by what they would come to witness at Bellevue, strode resolutely toward the clinics, to sharpen their skills on the acquiescent poor before moving on to saner pastures.

She rounded the last corner and skidded into the Bellevue Hospital Police Station, where an alien calm prevailed.

Sergeant Miranda Raspberry kept her gaze on the bank of monitors. "You made it through another running of the bulls, good for you."

"Unbloodied, thank the Force." Gina pointed toward one monitor. "Anything good on tonight?"

Miranda swiveled around, her cascade of braids whooshing behind her. "Leave it to Beaver. June and Ward are about to take a walk on the wild side. At least they won't have to go far to pick up their penicillin. Hopefully that'll be all they need. So, as if I couldn't guess, how's it going down there?"

"I've got guys I haven't seen in months, it's so cold. I actually took a cab over today."

"Unbelievable that you got one. And I guess I'm wondering why you'd leave your snug little cave to come upstairs on a night like this."

"I'm still trying to round up a couple of the guys. Could you get a hold of McCarthy and give him a message?"

Miranda raised one eyebrow. "He doesn't bite."

"I don't have much of a signal."

Miranda held up her own cell. "Four bars."

"I mean downstairs."

"You're upstairs now."

A few empty seconds passed. "Ask him to bring in the Mayor again, I know he won't go to the big shelter. Listen, I better get back downstairs before the mice get their toy box open—I'm just gonna, you know—"

"Yeah. Use *our* bathroom."

Before Miranda could ask, *how's David*, Gina turned and sprinted in the direction of the station bathroom, which always had toilet paper and a light bulb.

No matter, the answer would have been *okay, about the same*, as always. And as she tapped through the numbers on her phone, she mused, "The Mayor. Don't we all just wish the *real* one would turn up missing."

Ω Ω Ω

The man in the undulating dress seemed determined to stand his ground, so Freddie delayed the physical defense of his box until he gathered further intelligence. To which end, he slurred, *Whodafuckeryoo?*

The interloper stood straighter, raised his chin. "Do you not recognize me?" His accent was thick, eastern. "I am Dionysus, son of the immortal patriarch Zeus and the mortal woman Semele. I am the god of . . ." He stopped abruptly and clasped one hand over his mouth.

"Whatsa matter?" Freddie asked, his voice suspicious.

"I—oh, sweet Apollo, this is not Greek, but some awful foreign tongue. . ."

"Sounds like English to me."

"I do not understand this *English*," the stranger said.

"Yeah, well you're talkin' it pretty good. And I don't really give a shit. What I *do* give a shit about is what you are doin' in my box. Didn't anybody here tell you it's already taken?"

The stranger glanced quickly about the squalid alley and took on an even more bewildered look. "I have no idea what I am doing here. I arrived here—it cannot have been long ago—no one came either to greet me or to warn me away. This object, this box, as you call it—broke my fall."

Freddie glanced at the creased box, then pointed upward. "The only place you coulda fallen from was that roof up there. And even this box, *my* box, which you were in *without* my permission, ain't gonna save you from that kinda fall. You'd be dead. I seen what happens when someone jumps from a big building. I was there that day, at my work. I seen it first-hand."

The stranger should have responded with an expression of reverence; jumping from a tall building in New York had become a sacred matter. But he was silent.

Freddie narrowed his eyes. "So maybe you jumped out one of those windows,

4

closer down so you didn't get hurt too bad."

"No, I—oh, sweet Athena, help me to explain—I fell, and from very far away."

"Then how come you're not dead?"

The stranger puffed out his chest. "I am immortal."

Forgetting both his anger and his fear, Freddie laughed aloud. The sound reverberated on cold brick walls.

"*Aieee!*" the stranger wailed. He squeezed his eyes shut and pressed his hands over his ears. The high-pitched yips of a small dog came out of the front of his dress. "*Please*, Mortal, cease your braying! Gods hear things quite a bit more keenly than you!"

"Then hear this, and hear it really freakin' keenly." Freddie planted himself firmly in front of the trespasser. "This is *my* box, *my* home, and *you* are not welcome. And you know what? You look like some kinda terrorist to me."

"By all the gods," the stranger hissed, "you are an abysmal host."

"A guy in a white dress and sandals with twigs in his hair and a dog in his chest is telling me I'm a bad host." He slapped his thigh and laughed. "I musta misplaced my Miss Manners."

The stranger clenched his fist again. "Your disrespect is intolerable! I shall call upon my father Zeus to smite you, and if that is not sufficient to put you in your proper place, then I shall beat you with my own fists until—"

"Smite, *schmite*." Freddie lunged forward and tackled the intruder; they went down struggling in the cold slush. Freddie came out on top and started to pummel his captive, who groaned—not from Freddie's weight, but from his rancid breath. Freddie pounded and punched, repeating over and over, "A man's home is his castle!" The alley was filled with the discordant sounds of a brawl and piercing canine yelps.

Ω Ω Ω

Officer A. Z. McCarthy was parked outside an all-night grocery on Second Avenue when Miranda reached him on his cell with Gina's request.

His partner groused, "Oh, for cryin' out loud. Are we picking up bums again tonight?"

"Yes, sir, Officer Stein," McCarthy answered. "A man's gotta do what a man's gotta do."

"More like a man's gotta do what a certain woman wants him to."

"Don't you be giving me shit about this, Stein. Protect and serve, remember?"

"Even bums?"

He shook a finger in Stein's face. "It's *indigents* now."

5

"Yeah, yeah."

Then a radio call come through, asking for someone in the vicinity to check out fight sounds and dog-in distress sounds. An alley on one of the crosstown streets was named.

"Hey, that's the Freezer."

"Two calls in one," McCarthy said. His foot hit the accelerator. "Hopefully that'll translate to less paperwork."

"Anyone in there got a dog?" Stein asked.

"I don't think so."

"Shit. I hope no one's trying to cook up a stray."

They sped down the next cross street, then cut over again until they reached the Freezer. There they found an unexpected sight: Mayor Freddie, a half-empty bottle in his hand, sat grinning triumphantly on the face-down body of an oddly-attired man who was cursing and blubbering in some clipped language and struggling to get up. As they stood over the pair of combatants in bemused wonder, Stein crossed his arms on his chest. "Officer McCarthy, it looks to me like we have ourselves a case of domestic discord."

Stifling laughter, McCarthy concurred. "You are correct, Sir."

Freddie raised the bottle up in triumph. *Uh manshome iziz cashel.*

"Yeah, Your Honor," McCarthy said, "and you're putting up a very commendable defense. But you know what? It's illegal to beat the crap out of someone, even if they're trying to move in on you. Don't ask me why, but it is. Now, get up!"

Freddie tried, but failed. "*Oof!*" the unfortunate victim groaned as Freddie flopped back down on him.

There was a small, muted growl and they were looking around for a dog when a supervisor pulled up to the alley. A female sergeant called out, "You guys need any help?"

McCarthy and Stein glanced at each other, agreeing in silent *Partnerese* that none was required. "Nah," Stein called out, "we're good, neighborhood tiff over territory. Thanks."

The woman yelled back, "Call in if you need something."

"Wait . . ." Freddie slurred, thumbing in the intruder's direction, "You *might* need help. I think this guy's a terrorist. Look at him."

They did.

"There's that BOLO on a bomb maker," Stein said quietly. "Guy looks a little old, bomb makers don't usually live that long."

McCarthy reached out with a gloved hand. "ID, please."

"What do you mean by this *ID.*"

"Identification. Driver's license, passport, green card?"

"See here. A god does not require such things."

They came to quick accord on the BOLO. "Thanks, Fred," Stein said, "but I don't think we need to call in the Feds just yet."

And with that, the intruder renewed his struggle. Stein lifted Freddie up by the armpits and took him to the cruiser. McCarthy handcuffed the "victim" and rolled him onto his back, then shined the flashlight into his face.

"You'll be sorry if you move."

The stranger squeezed his eyes tightly shut as Stein patted him along his sides and legs. "Great Apollo!" he cried, "I am blinded by your brilliance!"

On Stein's nod, McCarthy grabbed the strange man by the shoulders and dragged him to sitting. "Hear that? Guy thinks I'm brilliant. That's why I'm out in this freezing alley when I could be home watching the Knicks."

The stranger leaned forward. "You are not a woman, are you? I heard the voice of a woman."

McCarthy laughed. "No, Pal, not me." He hitched his thumb over his shoulder in Stein's direction. "You might want to ask Stein." He turned around and grinned at his partner. "Guy wants to know if you're a woman."

"He wants to buy me a diamond, I'm a woman. He wants to kiss me, I'm not."

The stranger regarded Stein with suspicion. "You would be a vile-looking woman," he muttered. Then, louder, "Praise all Gods that you are *not* women! Neither of you is to my liking."

McCarthy laughed again. "And you being in such a good position to choose, too!"

Stein came closer. "A terrorist if ever I saw one." He looked the stranger over again, focusing finally on his forehead.

"Whew, that's a nice little cut you got there, Mister." Then, to McCarthy, "Looks like old Fred got in a coupla good hits. Think this guy might have a head injury?"

McCarthy focused his flashlight on the cut, then shook a finger in the stranger's face. He sighed. "Stay right here."

He pulled his partner aside. "Stein, get a grip. It's a cut."

"Come on, McCarthy, you know me ten years, right? These guys had a fight and Freddie cut the other guy. That's assault, not to mention disturbing the peace. We don't know who started it, so we gotta take them both in."

McCarthy rolled his eyes. "They'll be back out here in six hours and we'll still be filling out forms. They're harmless. Let it go."

Stein glanced from Freddie to the stranger and then back at McCarthy. "You know how this goes lately, we could get sued."

"Every kid in Brooklyn gets a cut over his eye. Before his onions drop!"

As Stein fumed, McCarthy added, "Tell you what, we gotta take Freddie to the center anyway, so how about we take them both? Maybe Gina'll clean up the new guy, this, uh—" He turned back and said, "Sir, what's your name?"

The stranger seemed to like the salutation. "By the Greeks I am properly called Dionysus. Though the Romans,"—he spat into the snow, "call their impostor Bacchus."

McCarthy turned back to Stein. "*So* dangerous. After she looks them over, we cut them *both* loose again. Maybe she'll send the new guy to the shelter."

"Upstairs to the psych ward, maybe."

"Yeah, well, we'll let Gina figure that out. Freddie doesn't need another beef on his sheet. He's already got one he doesn't deserve."

Stein finally acquiesced. "Let's get these two disadvantaged citizens in the car, then."

But Freddie had taken on a very *un*-disadvantaged cast, surprising his escorts. *Combat victory afterglow,* Stein thought, *pure testosterone.*

"Get that shit-eating grin off your face, Freddie," he said. Stein guessed that Freddie's gonads were high and tight, pumping out the big T by the quart. *Must be a nice change for him.* As he guided the grinning man toward the cruiser, McCarthy followed close behind with the strange new guy, who he thought might possibly come up with a credible explanation for himself, given adequate time. He couldn't wait to hear it.

Ω Ω Ω

McCarthy drove; now and then Stein looked back to see how their handcuffed passengers were faring. He noticed the stranger's vacant look. "He's staring straight ahead like he's in some kinda daze, McCarthy. So I'm kinda worried that he might, you know, have a, um . . ."

"Maybe he's high. On LSD, from the way he's talking. Why don't you ask him, Stein?"

"Yeah, good idea." He turned his head toward the back seat. "Hey, mister, you're looking kinda funny and I was wondering if your head hurts."

"It has felt better, but I am not badly harmed."

"Then maybe you can tell me why you're staring at the back of Officer McCarthy's head."

He leaned forward, eyes shifting fearfully. "I am afraid I will see a woman if I look elsewhere."

McCarthy stifled a laugh. "Guy's got a point. A big concern in New York, seeing a woman. Some of them can be pretty scary. Speaking of scary women, we should probably call the good Sergeant Raspberry and ask her to let Gina know we've got incomings."

"What, Gina's phone's out?"

"The signal wasn't good last time I was there."

"Which was how long, an hour ago, maybe?"

McCarthy smirked and picked up the radio handset. He pressed the button and spoke briefly to Miranda, who replied, "Yeah, I'll grab a doctor from the hallway and send him down."

McCarthy could almost hear her grinning. "Good idea. You hate to waste a cop on that kinda work."

"No wasted cops, that's my motto."

"And a good one it is," McCarthy said.

Ω Ω Ω

The frightened stranger closed his eyes and leaned back. He stared upward through the rear window into the Manhattan night sky. "There is little chance that I will see a woman while looking straight up." He choked down his rising bile. "One thing I am sure of is that mortal women cannot fly."

One hundred or more women had proved that statement true, not that long ago, ten blocks from this very location, when all other hope was gone.

"Not without their broomsticks," McCarthy said quietly. And for the rest of the ride there was silence.

"Well, guess what, gentlemen, we're here." McCarthy guided the shaky stranger out of the back seat. Stein clamped one of Freddie's cuffs to a metal loop. "I'd advise you to stay put, Freddie. You'll have to drag the car with you, and you don't really look up to it. I'll be back in a little bit."

They escorted their captive down the steps to the basement facility. McCarthy stomped the slush off his feet and sang out, "Oh, Gina, we brought you a new guy!"

"So I heard," Gina called back. "Miranda sent down this kid with an M.D. on his name tag."

She really did it, he thought, smiling. The kid was probably scared to death. He heard a cabinet door close, then Gina's words, "Take him to my office. I'll be right there."

Ω Ω Ω

"A woman!" the stranger moaned. As they dragged him along, his knees buckled.

"Hey, Bud, hang in there," Stein said. He looked over the stranger's drooping head. "Jesus Christ, McCarthy, and he ain't even my guy, we are gonna get in a big fat pickle over this."

9

The captive stiffened between them and raised his head. "I know of this Jesus Christ. *My* father Zeus was once stronger than *his* father." He began to struggle.

As they strained to contain him, the two cops exchanged worried glances over his dark curls. "Head injury," Stein said. "Just remember I told you so."

They hoisted him up on the examining table, where McCarthy took him by the arm and squeezed hard. "Wait here, don't move." He regarded his captive for a moment, then removed the cuffs. "I'm trusting you, not sure why, but I am. A nice lady is going to come in here shortly and bandage that cut. You better be *very* polite to her. I'll be just down the hall taking a wiz. I'll be really unhappy if I don't get to shake off because you start acting up, understand? Stein here has to go back out to the unit to get Freddie. So behave."

"Of *course* I will be nice to her," the stranger said with a scowl. "I must win her trust to break a curse."

This brought raised eyebrows and a grin from McCarthy. "Like Beauty and the Beast, huh?" He walked out of the room chuckling to himself. "Hope you have better luck than I do."

Ω Ω Ω

As he waited nervously in Gina's office, the stranger smoothed his tattered garment and ran his fingers through his hair. He whispered a hurried prayer: *Zeus grant that I appear godlike, strong, worthy of worship.* Looking around the small room, he saw a cup half full of clear liquid on a counter.

He grabbed it, offered it upward. *"I am wine,"* he whispered, *"let this water become one with me."* He closed his eyes and concentrated; footsteps approached. He tensed and gripped; soft humming neared. He surged all his will into the liquid.

And as Gina stepped through the door, the contents of the cup erupted in a shower of droplets. The stranger's attire, already wet-spotted, was soaked even further; the same damp fate befell her lab coat.

She looked at him in shock. "Oh, God . . ." then flailed her arms to shake off the drops.

Ω Ω Ω

She had said it so clearly. He raised the broken cup in salute.

"Oh, *Woman*," he cooed, "your sweet voice rings in my ears like the wondrous tones of Apollo's lyre . . ."

She stared back at him, then shook her arms again. More drops flew off. Then she smiled. "Wet, nasty-looking woman, I think."

"Do not say such things," he said, easing closer. "Aphrodite will be offended."

"Who?"

"*Aphrodite*. You do not sacrifice to her?"

Gina raised her eyebrows, shook her head. "Nope."

"Why, I am surprised! It is obvious that you are much favored by her, for you are among the fairest flowers of womanhood."

She dismissed the typical newcomer flattery with a wave of her hand. "Sheer *hyperbole*," she said, and then, as if a foreigner might not understand, "You're exaggerating."

He smiled flirtatiously. "You need not have explained, I know this word; it is from my own dear Greek. Well, perhaps I exaggerate a bit, but that is my right, after all, for I am Dionysus, the god of excess!" He beamed proudly.

Regina Bugbee put her hands on her ample hips and stared at him. "Is that so?"

"The men who escorted me here, they did not tell you?"

"We're not in the habit of announcing pedigrees."

He seemed bewildered by her ignorance. "Well, it is of no consequence. We will speak of that later. Now we must continue to speak of you."

He looked her up and down. Gina half expected him to open her mouth and examine the wear on her teeth. She followed him with suspicious eyes as he slid down off the table and walked around her in a circle.

"I do no dishonor to Aphrodite in praising your beauty," he said, "for you are well rounded, soft . . ." He mimicked her womanly shape with his hands. "Your skin has a fine texture. Your hair is the beautiful color of corn; among Greek women, this happens only when there is a Norse ancestor, and we are vigilant in keeping those savages at bay. Your bosom is—admirable. And your eyes are the fine blue of the Aegean Sea. The Fates could have sent me to a crone, but praise Hera, you are not even approaching cronehood! Perhaps you could be a *bit* younger, but—"

"That's enough. And by the way, I'm thir—uh—well, I'm not exactly ancient."

"You are right!" he said quickly. "I see this. And regardless, there have been many ancient women who came to understand the sweetness of my worship—"

"Thanks, really," she interrupted him. "But you should probably get back up on the table now so I can take a look at *you*."

This notion confused him. "But why must you look at *me*?"

In mock-radio voice she announced, "Here at this facility we thoroughly appraise our clients to ascertain their best treatment options, both physical and emotional." Then, more normally, "It's my job to assess your situation for placement and keep you safe until we find something for you."

She warmed the flat metal end of her stethoscope between her palms. "I'd like to do a quick physical exam, just to make sure you have no major health problems.

I keep all the information confidential, of course, so you don't need to worry about anyone learning your secrets, that is, if you have any." She gave him a little wink. "Most of the men who come in here have at least one thing they don't want me to tell anyone else." She hesitated, presenting the opportunity for him to speak. When he did not, she said, "You can tell me anything you want."

When he did speak, the stranger sounded nervous. "How many men come in here?"

"Oh, on a bad night, sometimes twenty or more."

"And why do they come?"

Because, she thought, *the big shelter scares the crap out of them.* "To get out of the bad weather," she finally said. "Why else?"

"I—um—thought perhaps they came here to see *you*. You are a fair specimen of womanhood, it is only natural you would have many suitors."

He picked up the broken cup of liquid and offered it again in her direction. "I tried to make this into wine for you," he said sheepishly. "It is one of the things I rule. But I seem to have little power here. I am sorry."

"No problem," she said. She reached into a pocket and took out a pair of latex gloves, then made a great show of snapping them on, finger by finger. Her steady blue eyes never wavered from his. She gave the broken cup a light push back, then motioned in the direction of the table, indicating that he should sit.

But the stranger was not discouraged. Still holding the cup, he smiled dreamily into her eyes. "Ah, Woman . . . now your worship can begin." With his free hand he grabbed the lower edge of his robe and pulled it up slowly. "See how my godly member rises in your honor . . . regard its divine glory . . ."

In her pocket was the small but effective taser Miranda had given her. *Just enough, just in case.*

But instead of pulling it out, Gina took the remains of the jagged plastic cup from his hand and poured its contents onto the rising cloth. He drew in a gasp as the fabric began to foam and hiss.

She grinned. "Peroxide. Won't hurt you. And your, uh, *member* will be nice and clean. Now, I seem to recall Officer McCarthy made it *quite* clear to you that you should behave. She pointed toward his groin. "So put that—*thing* away and get back on the table, please, or I'll have to get him. I promise you he will not be amused."

His cheeks flushed red. He looked down at the flattening front of his garment with dismay. "Ah, well, even a god cannot withstand the effects of such a rejection . . ."

"Yeah, life is tough," Gina said. "Now, are you going to get up on the table for me, like a good little god?"

"How cruel you mortals can be," he said, looking hurt. But he did as she asked and *scootched* his derriere up onto the table. As he stretched upward, he grimaced.

Gina handed him a towel. "Here, dry off. What hurts?"

He adjusted his position gingerly. "Forgive my ungodly weakness. My buttocks, I fear. They have recently been injured."

"Did you fall?"

He hesitated for a moment. "That could be said truthfully, yes."

"Landed on your backside?"

"Indeed."

"From a—height?"

"It could be so described."

"Well, lucky for you there aren't too many bones in your ass. Very rarely do the docs upstairs put them in casts."

When he failed to laugh, she cleared her throat. "So tell me about yourself. And say your name again."

He sat up proudly. "As I said, I am Dionysus, son of Zeus. My father has given me dominion over wine and the pursuit of ecstasy. I have come to Earth for—uh, I am here to—" He stopped, and seemed not to know how to continue.

Gina examined the cut, struggling to keep the amusement out of her voice. "It's a pleasure to meet you, and I'm sorry we got off to such a bad start. Welcome to Earth, Dion—how do you pronounce it—*I-sus?* What an unusual name." She touched his cut lightly. "But I'm confused. I thought Bacchus was the god of wine."

He stiffened, cursed, frowned. "As I told the soldiers who brought me here, Bacchus is an impostor, a *Roman.* They have copied everything we Greeks did and claimed it as their own. Our gods, our art, sculpture, architecture, even our modes of dress . . ."

On and on. What Gina had hoped would be a simple exchange of pleasantries while she checked him over had disintegrated into a droning recitation of delusions. "You must be some sort of scholar to know so much about ancient culture."

"Well, of course, I would be well suited to such work. But Gods do not work. And I know of these ancient things because I was there."

Deeply held delusions, rapid mood swing, attempts to convince the conversant to buy into the constructed reality. It would be an interesting file when she compiled it.

"Really!" she said. "That must have been very exciting."

He seemed encouraged and sat even taller. "Oh, there is very much to tell! Allow me to call upon the Muse Clio to help me, for it is she who rules—"

She interrupted him. "First I want you to stay very still for just a minute," she said, "so don't talk. I want to get a closer look at your wound."

Though plainly miffed, he complied. She cleaned the cut with gauze dipped in Betadine, wiped out a bit of dirt, then wiped away the excess with a fresh pad.

eless head should

"Okay, now stay even more still, just another minute. . ." She steadied one gloved hand on the side of his head, and felt a slight lump where the skull should have been smoothly rounded. She applied a butterfly closure to the cut.

He hardly flinched. Perhaps he *was* under the influence of some opioid, but if so it hadn't slowed his ability to speak. At all.

"You're very brave." She covered the butterfly strip with a larger bandage. "I thought that would hurt."

"I have lived among Spartans and learned from them. One must cut out a Spartan's *liver* before he will admit to pain."

"Well, I'm impressed. It confirms my belief that they don't make men like they used to. Now I just want to check something on your head, something I noticed while I was putting on the bandage . . . hold still again, please." She placed her hands one on each side of his head, and was astonished to find two nearly identical lumps, an old, well-healed head injury of some sort. *Maybe that "long fall" was a while ago . . . head first.* She shivered at the thought.

But he'd said he landed on his butt, and *that* pain he had conceded. She parted his curls with gloved fingers to look at the skin on his scalp. The lumpy areas were darker and rougher than the rest, which was pink and healthy.

Bracing herself for the standard rancid odor, she was almost shocked to find that his hair smelled sweet and fresh. She ran her fingers through his black mane; her hand came away with a small twig and a few bits of dry bark.

Twigs and bark were all over the littered courtyard area of the nearby 800-bed shelter; there would be little or no snow cover under the overhangs. But this man's hair was clean, shiny, and free of the usual encampments of fauna that invaded outside-dwellers.

Freddie seems to think he's a terrorist, Stein had told her.

He's got the right look, she thought. But she wondered if he might instead be a local head-trauma case with relatively high-functions who'd managed to escape his keeper. He was too well-fed to be a street guy.

"How old are you, Sir?"

"I was born well before the Great War," he said. "And you must call me Dionysus."

"Sorry. *Dye*-on-*I*-suss. It's hard name to say, though. We like to use nicknames around here. I'm sort of in that habit. I could call you Mr. Isus if you prefer."

He sighed. "You may suit yourself."

She brightened. "Well, in that case, I'll give you a nickname. Who do you remind me of?" She stepped back and regarded him. "I know!" she said, clasping her hands together. "Harpo Marx. Wrong color hair, but the same kind of curls, the baggy clothing is right . . ." Then she laughed and said, "Only the original Harpo didn't talk much. But that's OK, it'll give you something to work toward.

Anyway, you were born before The Great War. I assume that means you were born before World War II. But I'm confused because I thought the Great War was World War I. If that's what you're talking about, you look pretty damn good for your age."

He seemed genuinely surprised. "I mean, of course, the War of Ilium."

"What?"

"The one canonized in *The Iliad,* the poem, by the illustrious Homer? The greatest of all wars. Some called it the Trojan War. How can one not know of it?"

She almost laughed again. *Reality, schmeality.* "Of course. We all read it in high school. A little joke. I'm just trying to assess your health relative to your age."

"I assure you I am quite well."

She thought, *except for that sawdust between your ears.* "You probably are, but I'm going to check you anyway." She placed the tips of the stethoscope in her ears; he eyed the gleaming instrument with curiosity. She moved the flat end around his back, listening intently. "You have a strong, steady heartbeat," she said. "Now let me check your breathing. I'm just going to open up your—" She hesitated, searching for a word, finally settling for "garment". No sooner had she touched the drapes of fabric than she heard a small growl.

She pulled her hand back. He crossed his arms quickly over his chest.

"Will I get bitten if I put my stethoscope in there?"

The stranger slowly reached down into the front of his garment and pulled out a fluffy white dog with a black nose. As he held the male dog hanging by his collar, the tiny pooch struggled.

"He's adorable! But be careful . . ." She reached forward and supported the tiny dog with cupped hands. "I don't think he weighs more than an apple," she said, smiling. "Can I hold him for a minute?"

Reluctantly, he loosened his grip on the dog. Gina cradled the trembling thing close to her face and scratched his stomach. The dog responded by stretching out so she would have more to scratch. "You're so cute!" she said, the pitch of her voice rising. "What's your name?"

"His name is Midas," the stranger said. "*Mee-dthas.* Though I fear you would say it differently. Perhaps *mie-das.*"

"Ah, like the guy who turned everything he touched into gold."

"Indeed. It was I who gave him that cursed ability. It worked out poorly. Though I told him he ought to be careful what he wished for."

"Too bad he didn't listen. It's an interesting name for a dog, anyway.

"Indeed! Midas was once a—"

And he stopped.

"What was he once?"

"It is unimportant."

15

"Well, okay. You can tell me some other time."

The little dog relaxed in her grip. "What a cuddly sweet thing you are!" she said. He licked her nose and she scratched his neck. "And you've got this pretty little collar . . ."

She moved aside the white fur with two fingers. Out of the corner of her eye, she saw the man stiffen and move toward her with a look of growing distress.

On closer inspection, she understood. "Jesus, Mary and Joseph. Is this real gold?"

There was a long, strained moment in which Gina knew he was sizing her up.

"Yes," he said finally. "How can there be *unreal* gold."

She turned the collar around the dog's neck. It was adorned with a rainbow assortment of glittering cut stones. "Then I assume these are also real jewels."

His eyes were still locked suspiciously on hers. "Indeed."

"Harpo, do you know what this is worth?"

He winced at the name but did not protest. "Not precisely," he said, "but I understand that mortals value such things greatly."

"Yeah. We do. *Greatly.*"

"It was a gift from Aphrodite. We spoke of her earlier. She still lives in Olympus while I am here now, banished, at *her* insistence."

"You mean Venus, right?"

"Venus was a Roman goddess, and has faded into a well-deserved oblivion," he said angrily. He turned his head and made a mock spitting gesture. "I have no use for Romans. Nor should you."

"Sorry, Aphrodite, then. I didn't realize they were different."

"Few mortals do," he said with disdain. "Perhaps that is why she has so little power now." He looked down sadly and said, in quiet voice, "That is why we *all* have so little power."

Then he shook off his melancholy and continued, as if the explanation were a task requiring completion. "There was a time when she and I were, uh, *friendlier* than now. She gave it to me in gratitude for a divine vintage I once made just for her."

McCarthy should see this, Gina thought as she regarded it. *Could be stolen. But maybe not and he just doesn't have a secure place to put it.*

She knew that some Middle Eastern immigrants depended on portable wealth; the women came laden with gold jewelry under the watchful eyes of their men, who later converted it to cash. Neat, simple, often untaxed.

Perhaps this was *Harpo's* portable wealth.

"Well, I'm sorry to hear you're not friends anymore. But I don't think you should be carrying that collar around, especially if it's important to you. There are guys out there who will try to steal anything, and if they see that collar and you resist, you might get hurt, even killed."

"I cannot be killed," he said defiantly. "I am immortal."

She cracked a little smile. "OK then. *Not* killed. But you could still get messed up."

He said nothing but reached out for the dog. Gina handed it back. The dog's little tail wagged in a blur.

"I could put the collar in my safe for you," she offered.

After a moment, he handed the collar to her. She slipped it over her wrist, admiring the look, thinking, *Maybe in another life*. She crossed the small room and knelt down. A few metallic clicks, then back at his side.

She put a hand on his arm. "If you decide to go back where you came from, just come back here and get it. But in the mean-time it'll be safe." Then she pointed toward his neck. "Maybe you want me to put your necklace in there, too."

He covered the amulet with his hand and shook his head vehemently. "I would sooner give up my blood," he said firmly.

"Well, you might, if someone decides he wants that necklace. And you could find yourself going home, wherever home is, without it."

"Oh, most assuredly not," he said.

Chapter 2
Beta

Officer A. Z. McCarthy strode into Gina's office, assessed the situation with a cop's critical eyes, found it acceptable. When he turned to Gina, his expression softened.

As did hers. The stranger observed their interplay, his eyes nervously darting back and forth between them.

"Stein brought Freddie in," McCarthy said.

She nodded approval. "Let's hope he stays." She turned to her new client. "Harpo, could you wait outside in the hallway for a few moments? You and I aren't done, but I have some business to do with Officer McCarthy first. He has to get back to his car and I don't want to keep him too long."

As he left the room, Gina patted him reassuringly on the shoulder. He stopped after only a few steps and turned back toward the room as the door slowly swung shut.

He pressed his ear against the wood.

There were shuffling footfalls behind him, then a none-too-gentle tap on his shoulder.

"If you got such keen hearing, how come you got your head pressed up on the door?"

He turned around and stared at Freddie. "I do not much like you."

Freddie grinned. "Too bad. I'm in *love* with you." Then, laughing, he turned and walked away.

Ω Ω Ω

McCarthy leaned his six-foot-four-inch frame back against the counter in Gina's office and crossed his arms, making everything around him look small and drab. "Well, am I gonna get sued?"

"Jury's still out, but I don't think so."

Her heart was almost pounding. *He's just one of those guys . . . and he doesn't even know he has that effect on me.*

Does—did—David have that effect on you? Miranda had asked.

Well, not exactly that *effect . . .*

"Think he'll bolt?" McCarthy asked.

"Probably not. He loves me already."

"Who wouldn't?" he said, and before she could react, "*Harpo?* Why?"

"The name he gave me is just too weird to pronounce. *Die-on* something."

"I know. Went right over my head. I didn't pay much attention, though, because Stein and I were trying to figure out what to do with him and Freddie. You know, after the fight."

"That's how he got cut?"

McCarthy nodded. "Maybe we should stop calling Freddie 'Mayor' and start calling him 'Rocky'."

"He'd probably like that. But Harpo suits this other guy, don't you think?"

"Except for the color of his hair, yeah. Same goofy grin, that's for sure." Then his tone of voice became more anxious. "But really, what do you think about his head?"

Gina chuckled. "The *outside* cleaned up nicely. I asked him to come back so I could check it for infection and he didn't object, but I think it would be good if we managed to keep an eye on him over the next few days. Sometimes it takes a little while before the effects of a good whack show up. But I have to tell you, McCarthy, the inside of his head . . . he's probably not psychotic, but *delusional?* You betcha. Whacked out, but still lucid. I don't know how one guy can manage all that. But he *does.* What was going on between him and Freddie, anyway?"

"We got there when it was already over; Freddie was sitting on top of him, grinning like a fox. Looks like he was trying to move in on Freddie's box."

Tsk. "So he's *not* local, or he'd know better."

"When I asked where he was from he gave me mumbo jumbo about Greece."

"You probably wouldn't have gotten much farther with him, anyway. He was pretty evasive when I hit him with the usuals. When he did give answers they were sarcastic, like he was—*playing* with me."

"Yeah, he did that with me and Stein, too. He and Freddie weren't behaving like best friends when we found them. And I've never seen him around here before." He shifted his weight from one foot to the other. "But why are you so interested? He's not really that different from anyone else who comes in here. And it's not like we're running short of them lately."

She scowled. "You're right. Too bad."

McCarthy stammered. "I'm sorry, I didn't mean—"

She put her hand up, stopping him, then tapped a finger on his chest. "I know about all the stuff you do for these guys, and for the families."

He said nothing for a moment. "Well, I am sort of a—family."

It was an uncomfortable subject for him; he almost never mentioned his wife.

"But you should be careful. You're developing a reputation for softheartedness out there."

"Just so long as the real crooks don't get wind of it, I don't mind."

She drew in a long breath and folded her arms cross her midsection. "Good. You shouldn't. It's important stuff. Thing is, though, I don't think this guy is just another bum."

"Gina. Can't say bum. Indigent."

"Whatever. There are a number of things that don't add up. No tracks, good nose, sound health, so he's probably not a hype. He has none of the symptoms of alcoholism, either. And if he's a displaced mental patient, he must have been released within the hour, he smells so good. Didn't you guys notice that when you were bringing him in?"

"Freddie was in the car."

"Oh, well, enough said. But there are some other things I wonder about. The head injury—"

McCarthy raised his arms in frustration.

"Relax," Gina said. "An old one. Nicely healed. But it's almost perfectly equilateral, and symmetrical, like his head was put in a vise or something."

"Christ," McCarthy whispered. "Didn't they have a refugee upstairs with that kind of injury a little while ago?"

"Yeah, but I don't think *this* guy was tortured. The scars from a vise would be lower on his head. I have no idea what could have caused that type of scarring. But whatever it was, it probably wasn't very pleasant for him."

"I guess not."

"And he thinks he's immortal, has a huge ego. *Chutzpah*, Aaron would say. He tried to charm me into 'worshiping' him."

McCarthy recalled Harpo's statement about winning Gina's trust, dismissed at the time as a passing comment, and briefly considered telling her about it. Instead, he grinned. "Can't say as I blame him."

Gina blushed against her will. "Anyway," she continued as she pointlessly shuffled chrome instruments around her countertop, "there's more. He seems to be extremely well educated, not that higher education's a terribly unusual thing to find in some of the guys over there." She nodded in the direction of the 30th street shelter. "But if you add it to the cleanliness and his overall good health, I'd have to say I don't think he's homeless, or if he is, it's extremely recent. He's got no bugs, McCarthy. At least none that I can see with his clothes on."

"That must've been a nice change."

"It was," she said, "but it's really strange. I'm beginning to think he parachuted in. I bet if I look I'll find him in the system somewhere. And if I can't, I'll ask

Aaron Richman next time I see him. He's got some pretty good tricks up his sleeve."

McCarthy had never met the renowned psychoneurologist. "You see him often?"

"Often enough," she said. "Mostly with David. Sometimes by myself."

"I heard he's a good man."

Ω Ω Ω

She slipped into a memory of Aaron's goodness, five years back, three weeks after, when the dust was just beginning to settle and the extent of David's injuries had become more evident.

You know I'll do whatever I can to try to try to bring him back. David was on my rotation, Gina. I miss him, too.

And Aaron had kept his word, treating David's physical injury and the emotional trauma of his tower experience as if David were his own son. Called in a star surgeon, oversaw a parade of medications, cocktail after cocktail, seeking the combination that would allow David's personality to reemerge. But the damage had been done; and after a while, what had started as a search and rescue mission inside David's head morphed to search and recovery.

I've said from the start, he'd told her, *we need to be realistic.*

Ω Ω Ω

She came back to the moment. "Yeah, he is. A very *decent* man."

McCarthy drew in a long breath. "So. How are you gonna keep track of our new friend? He'll have to leave in the morning."

"I think I'll tell him I need to check his cut again. And I've got something of his for safekeeping, which is another reason I don't think he's homeless. Take a look at this."

She opened the safe and pulled out the small gold collar.

McCarthy examined it carefully. "Holy Mother of God . . ." he said. "Where was he hiding it?"

"It was on the little white dog he had tucked into the front of that thing he's wearing."

He handed it back to Gina. "I must be losing my touch. I missed this completely. Stein did, too. I wonder if this thing is hot."

"I don't get the feeling it is. The dog appears to be his. And he seems to understand its value." The gems cast a rainbow onto the ceiling as she turned the collar over in her hand.

"So he'll come back to get it. Problem is, you don't know when. He may disappear for a while and then just show up one day."

"I hope not, McCarthy. I think there's more there than meets the eye. And there is *always* the possibility that he's something we don't want here—Bellevue's a sweet target."

"If you really think that then we have to call the FBI and Homeland Security right now."

She paused. "I don't."

McCarthy weighed the options. "I could hold him for 24 hours on assault. According to Freddie he *did* hit back. But then I'd have to drag Freddie in, too, since he did some of the assaulting."

"God, no. He's had enough trouble."

"Or maybe you could have someone on the outside stay on him and report back to you."

"Yourself, maybe?"

"Hell, no, Stein'll kill me if I volunteer for anything else! I was thinking about one of the other guys who come in and out of here. Maybe even Freddie."

"Talk about the blind leading the blind!"

"Hey," McCarthy said, "it might work. Otherwise we have to get them both into the system in some way tonight. Tomorrow at the latest."

"I suppose it could work," she said, shrugging.

"Worth asking Freddie," McCarthy said. He stood up and zipped his coat. "Well, unless you need something more, I'm off. The night awaits." He tipped his hat to her and turned.

"McCarthy?"

He halted and turned back. "Yeah?"

"Stop in at dinnertime sometime. It's nice to have a sanity break."

He beamed. "I will. And I appreciate your confirmation of my sanity. I wonder sometimes."

Ω Ω Ω

Harpo smiled broadly as he presented himself in response to her summons.

"There you are," she said when he entered. "Just a few more questions. Then you can go back out and bed down for the night. Of course, you're free to go if you want to, but I hope you'll consider staying. It's awfully cold outside."

His smile faded to a pout, and as Gina waited for his answer, she wondered at the change. Finally, he said, "Indeed, the cold is beyond misery."

"So, stay, then," she said. "I don't know if you know how this center works, being new, but we're open overnight for intake assessment. You know, if you need services but don't really know what or where to go. You're welcome to sleep here until I finish processing you. There's a soup kitchen down the street, past the main shelter. A lot of the guys who come here go there first to eat."

"Ah, food . . ." he said. His hand clutched his silver amulet.

Food. Necklace. She thought it an odd association "Now, I *will* need to check that cut again to make sure it hasn't become infected, so if you leave, I'd like you to come back tomorrow."

His eyes met and held her gaze, with unsettling intensity. "I will always come back to you. You need not even have asked."

Her hand went to the taser in her pocket. The smart ones could fool you. Every now and then one showed up with survival instincts so finely honed that they were almost beyond detection, a quiet barracuda, deadly and patient, but quick to strike when prompted. Still, this strange Harpo didn't seem that type, at least not yet. Would she recognize the line, if he crossed it? Time would tell.

The form on her computer screen had the usual blanks for *curriculum vitae*, but she didn't think an ordinary grilling would draw him out. Subtlety would be required.

He was still staring at her. She turned her focus to the screen. "So," she said, "where is home, anyway?"

"Far away," he said, with a tinge of sadness. "Farther than you can imagine."

"But you *do* have one," she said.

"Oh, indeed, a most magnificent home. But right now I am not welcome. There is something I must do before I can be accepted back again." For a few moments, he was quiet and pensive. When he spoke, his tone was bitter. "Some of my 'family' want me home again, but more do not."

"Your family's large?"

"Oh, very. My father has sired many children. My family might even be described as *huge.*"

She wondered how many children Usama Bin Laden's father had, by how many wives.

"What's your father's name?"

"Zeus, of course, as I have already told you. And as regards my siblings, my father has presented me with a *pantheon*: Athena, the Muses, too many to count! In Olympus it seems that every other deity was sired by the Great One himself."

"Sounds like a randy old bugger to me."

He gave her a wry smile. "Indeed. That could be said of him."

"It's too bad you're not on good terms," she commiserated, thinking, *Lots of layers . . . maybe if I share something of myself . . .* "Families can be tough stuff. My own included. And then there's my boyfriend. He can be *really* hard to understand."

"I do not understand this word 'boyfriend.'"

Without revealing her surprise, Gina explained. "Um, that's a male friend with whom I have a romantic attachment. More than a friend, but less than a husband."

"Aha!" he said. "I understand. Yes, he does seem to be a troublesome character. Why, when he brought me here he was rather ungentle . . ."

She found herself smiling, almost laughing. "McCarthy's not my boyfriend. He's just a good friend, a colleague, really. I've been—romantically involved with a man named David for many years." Her expression sobered. "Unfortunately, he hasn't been well lately."

"Where I come from . . ." Harpo began.

"Which is where?" *Come on, blurt it out.*

"As I said, very far away . . ."

"It's a big world . . ."

He raised his voice. "Where *I* come from," he said, "a man would consider himself lucky to possess such a woman as you."

She sat back, stiffened, her arms crossed. "You must come from some other *planet*. Around these parts men no longer *possess* women, though you may find that hard to believe from the way some of them behave."

She paused. "But perhaps in your country women are treated differently? Which country was it again?"

His shoulders slumped. "Ah, I have offended you." He took on the expression of a chastised puppy. "I feel—distressingly mortal." He bowed in supplication. "Please forgive me. I am unfamiliar with your modern customs and I meant only admiration."

When he began to teeter she tapped him on the shoulder. "You can stand up now, Harpo."

He stood, swaying, before regaining his equilibrium. "May the bleating of a thousand goats shriek in my ears for offending you."

When he saw her amusement, he moved closer and added, "May my fondest wish be granted to my most despised enemy."

She began to laugh and he smiled, moving closer again. "May I be mistaken for a Roman god."

She was giggling freely when he said, "May the stench of a thousand mating yaks be visited upon my breath."

"Okay, okay, Harpo . . ." She held up her hand. "Stop! *Please* stop. I get that you're sorry." She wiped away tears of laughter. "So, now that we've established that you've got a sense of humor," she said, "what's your social security number?"

He shrugged. "I do not know."

"Visa? Green card? Passport?"

"*What are these things?* The soldier who brought me here asked of them as well."

He was so good at his charade. "They're things we use here to determine who you are. Because, well, you know, all mortals are unique. So, anyway, are you staying or going tonight?"

He bowed with a courtly flourish. "It would be a most ungodly discourtesy to reject your hospitality."

Ω Ω Ω

The alarm sounded. "Rise and shine," Gina chirped, in a cheerful maternal voice, and most of the men did just that, smacking, scratching and yawning in a sleepy baritone chorus. As she walked to her office, it gave her guilty pleasure to see men line up for a turn at the oval target.

Seeing Freddie in line, she tapped him on the arm. "When you get a minute, I'd like to speak with you. I'll be down in my office."

Freddie abandoned his place in line immediately and followed her, his chest puffed in pride, leaving his line-mates staring in awed envy that only intensified as she waved him into her inner sanctum and closed the door.

"I'd like to ask you a favor."

He was nearly giddy. "Anything."

"Don't be so fast to agree. You know that new guy who came in with you last night? Die-on-something or other?"

She noticed his immediate change in expression. "What's the matter?"

Freddie's eyes shifted like a naughty child's. "I don't like him."

Just what I expected. "Why not?"

Freddie shrugged. "I don't know, something about him ain't right. He looks like a fucking terrorist." He paused, looked down. "Sorry. I shouldn'a swore."

He'd been a decent man, in his previous iteration; he spoke of his work and his family reverently. On the rare occasions when he spoke of his faraway wife, he never besmirched her.

"It's okay, Freddie. I hear a lot of language down here, don't worry. I talked with McCarthy about this guy and he's going to check into him for me. In the meantime, I need your help. I'm worried that he might have a head injury. If we send him to the shelter or upstairs in the hospital I'll have to tell them who he was fighting with."

"Aw, no, don't—"

"It's okay, Freddie, I wouldn't do that to you. I couldn't." She paused again, hoping he would understand her genuine concern. "But the cops are on me about this and I need to throw them a bone. I can't keep an eye on him when he's back on the street, and I don't know where he comes from so I can't call anyone to come and get him. He looks kind of soft to me. Not like you."

Freddie soaked up the compliment with visible pride. "Oh, he's soft all right. I pounded him good."

"I know. I patched him up after. But I was hoping you could get past that and help me out. I'm afraid he might not know how to get back here by himself, and he *does* need to get back here."

He said nothing, but stared downward.

"Please?"

He silently counted the scuffmarks on his boots.

"How about we barter this one?" she said. "Is there something you need or want that I might be able to get for you in exchange? A lantern, maybe another blanket?"

Freddie straightened up. "What month is it?"

Wondering the significance, Gina said, "February."

"You file your taxes yet?"

"No, but—"

"Let me do your taxes."

"Freddie, I—"

"That's what I want. Let me do your taxes and I'll take care of him for you."

Visions of an IRS audit danced uncomfortably through her head. *I could always have a practicing accountant look it over,* she thought . . . "Okay. Deal."

Ω Ω Ω

She unlocked her cabinet door with one twist of a small key, and within seconds had the contents plumb and parallel, in keeping with her compulsion for order. *See, Aaron? I'm the crazy one, not David.* She stood there, staring at evidence of her own rigidity, when she heard someone behind her.

"I suppose you have some explanation for how that cabinet looks."

She turned around, already smiling, knowing the voice.

"Good morning, Officer McCarthy." It sounded more flirtatious than she wanted. She turned away to hide her blush.

"I'm sorry, Gina, looks like I interrupted you in the middle of something. I'll—I'll come back another time."

"No, don't leave." *Oh, God, that came out too fast.* "I just had a couple of things to tuck away," she lied. "I'm glad you're here. Listen, if you can wait about twenty minutes, I'll get these guys organized, then do you want to go out and grab some breakfast?"

"Yeah," he said, grinning widely. "I'd like that."

"Good. I won't be long."

Ω Ω Ω

Harpo was just outside the room, pretending to be in line with the rest of the men. He overheard their conversation through the open office door.

Soon they will be leaving these premises, and I shall have to follow them. He touched his chest and felt Midas quiver, then pulled out the front of the draped garment and spoke softly. "We'll be going back outside again soon, my friend. It will be cold, so prepare yourself."

Several of the men standing nearby looked at him in surprise, for although talking to oneself in the facility was a common practice, talking to one's nipple was rare.

He stared back defiantly. "What? Are you all so sane, then?" One man made a timid but curious attempt to touch the front of the toga; Harpo promptly slapped his hand away. The man skulked off, losing his place in line.

Harpo puffed out his chest and glared at the remaining gawkers. They responded in the same manner as their departed comrade by leaving the line as well. Those behind them shuffled forward.

He felt a tug on his sleeve. He turned around and saw Freddie.

"Oh. *You.*"

"Yeah, don't look so happy about it."

"Why would I be happy? I have already told you, I don't like you."

"It was me that told *you.*"

"As I recall, it was a mutual sentiment."

"Yeah, but I said it first."

"I suppose then you are the victor in this pitched battle of dislike. My sincere congratulations." He turned away.

Freddie tugged again. "I'm supposed to baby-sit you."

Harpo turned back again and gave him an odd look. "I am not a babe," he said, "I am a god. And if I recall correctly, you have already sat on me. Perhaps it brings you some exotic form of pleasure. I found it a most *un*pleasant experience, one I would not recommend to my followers. If you expect me to lay still for it again, you will be sorely disappointed."

For a moment, Freddie was flustered. "No, no," he stammered. "What are you, *thick*? I'm supposed to take care of you. Not *sit* on you."

Harpo scowled. "Even if I were incapable of caring for myself, I would not place myself in the hands of a lout such as you." Then he turned his back on Freddie again.

"You snobby jerk," Freddie said, wanting to add, *I can pound you again.* But with the cherished prize of Gina's taxes for inspiration, he checked himself. "Gina says she wants me to look after you."

Harpo whirled around. "She did?"

"Yeah," Freddie said. "I told her I don't like you, but she still wants me to take care of you. She said it was important that you come back here again, and I'm supposed to show you the way."

A hopeful smile came over Harpo's face. "I see now that you are a man of honor, and that you feel bound to keep your word to her." He hid his excitement. "Very well, I will not refuse your assistance. It would be a most ungodly thing to do."

Ω Ω Ω

"Looks like you two have made your peace," Gina said. "Good for you guys. So I guess I'll see you both tonight?"

Harpo smiled wanly. "Indeed." Having no more reasons to stall, he turned and headed toward the exit door, intending to lay in wait outside to see where she would go. Then he heard her calling after him. "Harpo, wait a minute. You need some warmer clothes."

He and Freddie waited there until Gina came back with a bundle in her arms. "I think these'll fit."

Reluctantly, he took them. She pointed to a small room. "You can go in there and change. I won't be locking the door for a few more minutes. I have to make a phone call before I close up for the morning."

She disappeared back into her office. Harpo went to the side room and inspected the rags the woman had given him one by one, cursing vilely under his breath.

Ω Ω Ω

"I just have to check in with David," Gina said to McCarthy.

"Take your time."

With a nod, she slipped back into the office and tapped in the familiar number on her cell, which miraculously had a signal.

"Hi, Honey, it's me." After a moment, "I'm still at work, where else would I be?"

The call was only seconds old before McCarthy, waiting outside, understood that it was not going well.

"No." She was defensive. "But I'm about to leave and I just wanted to let you know I'll be a little later than usual. I have some things to do."

A brief silence was followed by, "You know, *things*. Errands."

And after that, there came a softer exchange, barely intelligible, from which the word "medicine" could be deciphered, little else. The call concluded with a louder

28

declaration: "I'll see you in a little while."

Ω Ω Ω

Gina stood staring at her well-carved desk top for a few quiet moments, distracting herself with the consideration that it ought to be in the Expletive Hall of Fame. She inched toward *calm* with slow, deep breaths. *I hate lying to him,* she thought, *but what else can I do?* David's overnight medication wouldn't wear off for a while, so he'd probably watch television, or keep himself distracted in some other way until she got home. *Maybe he'll refold all the towels again,* she thought, *and with a little luck, I can get him to go to Randy's.* She hoped desperately that he wouldn't be standing behind the door, waiting for her with a million questions as he had when she last returned later than usual. Going home to him was getting scarier.

She closed the office door and locked it as McCarthy waited just outside. She forced a small smile.

"Harpo? Are you ready?"

As he stepped forward and his image clarified, they shared a quick, sly grin, passing the silent message, *don't laugh, whatever you do.*

"I find the breeches too restrictive, too undignified," he explained to their looks of amusement. "But these other items seem quite useful." He wore a sooty parka over his white robe and his sandals were now strapped on over multicolored argyles. A fur-lined flap-eared hat was on his head, with the tie strings hanging down. The mid-portions of both legs were still glaringly bare.

"Very spiffy, Harpo." Gina struggled not to laugh. "All you need is a pair of dark glasses and you'll be totally cool. You come back tonight, please, and I'll check your cut again." Then, including Freddie in the wish, she said, "Have a warm day, you two."

Ω Ω Ω

As they walked away, Harpo asked Freddie, "If I am to be cool, why is it that she wishes me to have a warm day?"

Freddie shook his head. "You just don't get it, do you?"

"Apparently I do not." He turned back in the direction of the shelter, as if looking for something. Then, with a small curse, he pulled his companion into a door well.

"Hey, what are you doing?" Freddie said. He tried to shake free.

"I must follow the woman," Harpo said urgently, "and you must help me. She is just coming out now, and I do not wish her to see me."

"You can't follow her! That's stalking!"

"I do not understand this 'stalking,' and I *must* follow her!"

29

"*Why?*"

He pulled Freddie back further into the shadows just as Gina and McCarthy walked past, too absorbed in their conversation to notice the hiding pair. After a few moments, Harpo poked his head out, and when he was satisfied it was safe for them to follow, he pulled Freddie out as well.

Freddie tried to push him away. "I'm not following her till you tell me why."

"I do not have time to explain now," Harpo said, his eyes glued on Gina's rapidly disappearing form. "I will tell you later."

"Then I'm not gonna follow her!"

"You gave your word to the woman that you would take care of me. Following her is vital to my well-being. And if I lose track of her, you will guide me back here later."

Freddie scowled. "I don't like it. And I don't like you."

"I share your sentiments equally, my friend," Harpo said. "Nevertheless, this is what must be done."

Ω Ω Ω

The kosher deli was sandwiched between a dry cleaner and a rare book dealer. A short, wide woman of later-than-middle age stomped up to their table with a steaming pot of coffee and two menus. She plopped the menus down, saying, "You'll take a minute." Then she poured coffee and pounded off on bent ankles encased in support hose.

McCarthy followed the departing harpy with his eyes. "Why, yes, please, Ma'am, I'd love some coffee. Thanks very much for asking."

Gina waved in dismissal. "She's always like that." She pointed to a small thin man behind the counter. "He's the owner." The waitress was fussing with one critical curl in her lacquered, Lucy-red hair. "I think Carrot Top is his wife, based on how often they *don't* speak to each other. So I don't think she has to worry too much about getting fired."

"But why would anyone want to build that kind of—*structure* from human hair?"

"It's a hair wall. A girl thing, much as I hate to admit that there are girl things and boy things." She drew her thick blond ponytail over her shoulder and waved it playfully. "She's probably had that hairstyle for thirty years."

"It does have a sort of vintage look, now that you mention it," McCarthy observed. "Speaking of habits," he said with a smile, "you were going to explain that neat cabinet."

"Ah," she said, "another girl thing, sort of. A holdover from the Sister Wars, as my mother called them."

30

"I failed history."

Her laugh was warm and genuine. "It's *personal* history. My mother coined that phrase when Diane was fourteen and I was sixteen. We used to needle each other in various creative ways."

"Sounds like the raging hormones we had. My brothers and I were always nailing each other."

"Yeah," she said. "It was something like that, just the female version. There was one incident that was really funny, although at the time it was infuriating. I've always been a neat freak, as you might have guessed from that cabinet. I like my hangers spaced evenly and my shoes lined up in pairs. My throw rug is always parallel to the floorboards."

McCarthy gave her a raised-eyebrow look.

"I know how it sounds," she said, "but I just always felt that there was safety in detail. Anyway, one day my little sister—and by the way, *little* is a relative term—she got pissed off at me for something, I can't remember what, and when I came home later, she'd tangled up a bunch of hangers and hung the entire mess from the closet pole. And to do that she had to un-space all my *other* hangers. Then the little shit angled the rug and hid one shoe from each pair."

"*Whoa*, how did you *ever* recover?"

"Do I *look* recovered? It's still going on. Every time my sister comes to visit she does *something* to one of my closets."

"Did you do something to get back at her? I mean, there's really no war without *two* adversaries. And revenge is sweet. Me, I would've punched out one of my brothers if they pulled that kind of stuff on me. Frequently did."

"You haven't seen my sister," she answered. "She's six feet tall and I think she eats plywood for breakfast."

"Oh, well then," he said. "That explains your reluctance."

"Right. But I got her good. I poured all forty-seven bottles of her nail polish onto one big piece of cardboard and made swirl art out of them."

McCarthy laughed heartily. "Did she make you eat it?"

"Nope," Gina beamed. "Framed it. Gave it to me just before I went away to college. I still have it hanging on my living room wall. Big as life and just as ugly."

"You see her much now?"

"Pretty regularly. She and her husband live on the yupper West Side. She slums her way down here every now and then. I don't go up there too much, though, air's a bit thin."

Their waitress, having restored her *coiffure*, stomped toward them. "Uh, oh," McCarthy said, "here comes the bride."

"Order blintzes," Gina advised in a whisper.

Neither one had time to crack the menu before the grumpy goodwife appeared at the edge of the table, pad and pencil in hand.

"Blintzes," Gina said.

"Blintzes," said McCarthy.

Then, "Blueberry," Gina declared.

"Blueberry," McCarthy followed.

"Hmph," the woman observed stiffly as she reclaimed the menus. She departed in the direction of her cowering husband to issue the appropriate cooking directives.

"*Oy,*" McCarthy commented as he watched her. He turned back to Gina. "You've still got it on the wall, huh?"

"Yep."

"That reminds me of the time my brother decided he would take my baseball cards to school for Show and Tell . . ."

They traded stories until the blintzes arrived, at which time they dutifully picked up their utensils and consumed the entirety under the occasional scrutiny of Carrot Top, who tolerated no unlicked plates in her little realm.

Chapter 3
Gamma

From across the street, Harpo could see them laughing and smiling, enjoying each other in the unmistakable way men and women did when there was comfort between them.

Midas interrupted his surveillance with a few bored yips, so Harpo pulled the little dog out and set him on the sidewalk. The dog scampered around, all nervous energy. When he'd sniffed out a spot to his liking, he lifted his leg and peed. The stream meandered toward one of Freddie's boots.

Freddie jerked his foot away. "Hey, don't piss on my boot!"

The little dog raised his head and barked, then let out a string of snorting sounds and scraped the concrete with one of his paws. He powered up his legs, and, claws clicking on the concrete, thudded head-first into Freddie's boot. He bounced back and landed spread-legged on the ground. He shook his head a few times, got up, and started barking again.

Freddie stared down at the tiny white animal. "The little shit attacked my fucking foot!"

Harpo smiled. "You should be grateful that Fate did not bring you together before today. Not long ago, Midas was a bull."

"Oh, please."

"Why else would he come at you with his head? It is a very un*dog*like thing to do, is it not? He was transformed, for how was I to fall to Earth with a bull? *Impossible*."

"But it was possible for you to get here with a dog in your, uh, *dress?*"

"*Toga*, or *chiton*, if you will, and I did it, did I not? How then, would it be possible for it not to be possible?"

As Freddie pondered that question of logic, Harpo tucked the dog away again and closed the jacket, patting his chest in reassurance. "At least you are safe and warm, Midas, which is a far better state than my own."

For a few moments, he watched the hurried passersby; no one paid him or Freddie the slightest attention; indeed, it was as if they tried not to. And when McCarthy and Gina came out of the deli, he watched their parting ritual with a glimmer of relief. *No touches*, he observed, *just a kiss on the cheek. Worthless as spit.*

Ω Ω Ω

Gina turned the key in the lower lock of her apartment door; the deadbolt slid out of its catch with a clunk, which would alert David to her return. *Right about now he should be just on the other side of the door . . .*

Before she'd have time to hang up her coat he'd ask a question. *Today*, she thought as she stepped inside with her bags, it will be, *"Where did you go?"*

"Where did you go?" he demanded.

You're not being mean to him if you wait until you're settled. Aaron had repeatedly assured her of this. *He needs to remember that he won't always get an immediate answer, that his gratification might be delayed.* This was among the skills the *after* David had needed to relearn, with sketchy success. They hadn't gotten it completely worked out, in . . .

Five years.

Had it really been that long?

Her winter gear stored away, Gina got up on tiptoes and gave David a kiss on the cheek. He remained motionless by the door, a tall, thin pillar of green striped flannel, his feet bare, the questioning look still etched on his face. He did not return her kiss.

"Hi, David, how did you sleep last night? And where are your slippers? Your feet must be cold."

"Where did you go?" he repeated.

Gina steeled herself, felt the ache of wanting, *needing* to reply immediately. She walked toward the small narrow kitchen. "Did Mrs. Miller come by with your dinner?" Seeing a plate and fork in the sink, she knew the answer, but she wanted to coax it out of him, to make him process, and then respond appropriately, however mundane the subject.

He seemed confused for a moment, stood stiffly with a puzzled look on his face. Finally, he said, "Mrs. Miller brought meat loaf."

One small step for David. "I like her meatloaf. Diane's is better, but Mrs. Miller's is very good, don't you think?"

"Good," he parroted. Then, with great eagerness, "Where did you go?"

Okay, now you can talk about it. "I had some things to do after work." She nodded toward her bags. "Nothing terribly interesting." She hated the lie, but the truth about her need for meaningful human interaction would not be well received or understood. Aaron had been careful to warn her. *He can still feel so many emotions, including jealousy . . .*

"Oh, okay," David said. "Okay." He seemed distracted, but was apparently satisfied. "I forgot."

She smiled and took his hand. "It's all right. I forget things sometimes too. We must be getting old. But let's not worry about that. It warmed up a little and the sun is bright. I think we should walk to the bookstore instead of taking the bus today. Let's go get you dressed so you can get to work on time."

His only cousin owned a West Village bookstore; Randy paid David for
sweeping, recycling, the rote tasks eschewed by his clearheaded employees. David
went five days a week if Gina could get him to go, and when there were no tasks
for him, he would sit with a book in his lap, often staring ahead, not really reading.
Gina would come home and sleep. The money for his minimal paycheck came
from a trust fund, which had kicked in almost four years prior. On that sad day,
when his mother died of what was essentially a broken heart, David had been in
restraints at Bellevue, recovering from a post-traumatic psychotic break, not his
first.

Gina watched as he began to slip his lean body into the clothes she had laid
out for him. She helped him with the shirt buttons before reminding him to zip his
fly. Then he started to pull the wool sweater over his head.

"No, wait a minute," she said, "that's backwards."

He ignored her.

"Stop," she said. "You're putting it on with the tag in the front. It's supposed
to go at the back of your neck, remember? Otherwise you'll look like a dork."

But he kept trying to pull the sweater down, struggling with the arms, and
soon Gina was unable to keep herself from reaching out. She grabbed hold of one
sleeve and started to pull it off his arm, and as soon as she touched him, he pulled
away.

"David, you've got it on backwards and you can't go to work that way. I'm
going to help you turn it around. Now, stay still, please . . ."

She reached up, straining for height, and started to pull the sweater up over his
head, but David would have none of it. Soon he was helplessly tangled, with his
arms stuck over his head in the grip of a nubby wool straitjacket.

He twisted his body from side to side, but could not break free. Gina leapt
upward but couldn't get purchase on the sweater. "Oh, for God's sake, will you just
stay still?" she shrieked. "Bend over! I can't reach over your head!"

He continued his frantic dance, coming perilously close to a lamp, but no
matter what Gina did, she couldn't calm him. *"David!"* she finally screamed. *"Why
can't you just do what I tell you?"*

In desperation, she jumped up onto the bed. And in the midst of the wild
thrashing, his elbow collided with her face.

She was momentarily stunned, but recovered.

In a minute I'll melt down.

Balancing precariously, just missing the overhead light, she yanked upward and
freed David from his woolen prison.

She threw the sweater on the floor in anger. David stared down blankly at it
for a moment, and then looked up again, regarding Gina with a strained look on
his face. His fine, silky hair stood on end from the static of the sweater, and when

he ran his hand through it, the air crackled. He gave her a weird little half-smirk and said, "No jumping on the bed."

She gawked at him in astonishment, holding one hand to her eye. As the shock of contact wore off, pain set in.

And anger. It rose up like hot lava. She leapt down onto the floor with a *thud*. "You don't remember how to put your sweater on, but you can remember that you're not supposed to jump on the bed?"

He shrugged as if that were a given.

"You hardly ever talk to me, but you can get it together to say *don't jump on the fucking bed?*"

He cowered backward.

"How about, 'Thanks for helping me with my sweater,' or, 'I'm sorry I gave you a hard time? And maybe a black eye?'"

He shrank away, and she moved closer.

"How about, 'I love you?'"

Ω Ω Ω

There would be no "on time" today. She stood before the mirror with an ice pack on her eye, hating herself.

How many times had Aaron said to her, anger is stage two? That it's only natural and right? *I felt it myself,* he'd said, *and so did the rest of the staff, after David was hurt. And all the others we knew.*

She still fought it, five years on, so many times raging heavenward, *Why?*

No god ever answered.

She toweled her eye with tender pats and saw with dismay a blossoming shiner. Digging through her makeup, she found a concealer, and used it liberally in the bruised area. It did nothing to hide the swelling, but the bruise looked—acceptable.

She went back to the bedroom. David was still standing bed-side. When he saw her, he bent down and picked up the sweater. He shook it a few times to untangle it, his expression a mix of fear and uncertainty, then held the sweater toward her, a peace offering.

His childlike contrition brought her rage to its knees. She flopped down on the bed and let out a long sigh, then put her face in her hands and stayed quiet for a few moments.

"I'm sorry, I'm so sorry," she finally said. "I shouldn't have said those awful things." She took the sweater from his hand and stood up slowly, aching all the way. "I feel like a total shit. I'm really, really sorry."

As she moved toward him, he backed away again. "It's all right," she said quietly, "I'm not angry anymore." She reached out one hand very slowly; he stayed still and allowed her to stroke his hair.

"You've still got a hell of a right, you know."

She opened the bottom of the sweater, and after checking that the label was in the proper position, stood up on tiptoes and slipped it over his head. With great effort, he worked his arms into the sleeves.

"It's like Velcro, I think, pulling wool over flannel." She laughed a little, trying to dispel her shakiness. "Okay, let's do your hair. Hopefully that'll go a little better than the sweater did."

David seemed relieved and sat down immediately on a small chair in front of a dressing table. He regarded himself in the mirror, but gave away nothing of what he might be thinking. He had always been careful about his grooming, neatly shaved, well dressed, an attractive young man poised on the edge of his prime.

Not that young any more, Gina thought. *Me, either.* She positioned herself behind him and loosened his disarrayed locks with her fingers. She pressed the back of his head against her belly and massaged his forehead, then brushed his shiny brown hair with long, slow strokes. The unevenness of his head, while not new to her, was—as always—disconcerting. There were fine lines where his skull had been opened along which his hair no longer grew. But to look at him, you wouldn't know, if you *didn't* know.

You wouldn't know about the symmetrical scars on Harpo's head, either, but they were still there.

When she had finished tying the leather thong around his ponytail, she leaned over and planted a small kiss on the top of his head.

"There. Gorgeous again." He looked upward and locked eyes with her, gave her a slight smile. The old fire flashed and retreated, leaving her wanting more.

Well, it's better than nothing.

She sat down and wiggled her feet back into her walking boots, looping each lace into the proper hook, topped off in a good solid double knot, with one last compulsive tug.

"It's still cold outside," she said as she stood. "I'm going to get my coat. I think I'll wear my hat and gloves, too."

It's a high-level parenting skill to demonstrate something that stimulates his behavior, better than just ordering him to do something, Aaron had said. *Make him think, make him process.*

Looking at the handsome, kind man she'd fallen in love with nearly a decade earlier, she saw a child in desperate need of such manipulation. Five years into their love, a cog had been cruelly chipped off David's mental transmission. When he tried to shift gears, the result was only grinding and screeching. He no longer even attempted to go from first to second; his preference was reverse, back to some place in his past where he'd felt safer. He rarely let Gina or anyone else in there with him.

As they entered the daylight, she put on sunglasses to hide her eye, recalling her earlier remark to the new arrival about being cool, which she definitely was *not*.

Ω Ω Ω

They walked at David's unsteady, slow pace. The vagabond pair followed them nearly to Randy's bookstore, until Freddie had refused to go farther.

"She'll come out," he'd insisted, and she had, alone. Her pace traveling home was brisk, unfettered, *free*. As she disappeared back into her building, they resettled themselves on the same other-side stoop.

But after a while, Freddie became agitated. He tapped Harpo on the shoulder. "Hey, Pal, how long we gotta stay here?"

"My name is *not* Pal."

Freddie sat up and raised his chin indignantly. "Okay, trying again. Hey, *Shithead*, how long are we gotta stay here?

"Great Zeus, you mortals are annoying." He waved Freddie back with his hand. "Do not bother me now! I must watch for the woman."

"She probably isn't coming out for a while yet," Freddie said.

Harpo regarded him warily. "And how do you know this? Are you an oracle?"

Freddie poked a finger to Harpo's chest. "*Don't. Get. Personal.* She's probably asleep. Works all night, sleeps all day."

"But this is a ridiculous way to live!" Harpo said. "Has she no children to tend?"

"I dunno. I don't think so."

Harpo scratched his head. "A woman with no children, who has a profession, who sleeps all day, and toils by night." he said. "Unthinkable!"

"Ah, it's not so unusual," Freddie said, "lots of 'em do it."

Harpo shook his head. "Then womanhood has surely undergone a dramatic and terrible change! In my home, we would never allow such a thing. At least this one has the *look* of a woman, soft, voluptuous and—*welcoming*. Some of the others we saw on our way to this place were sullen, emaciated, with those garish colors on their faces, dragging their sacks of Zeus-knows what."

"That's just the style now."

"Why, to bed such a woman would seem like tumbling over and over again into a bush of thorns. What would be the pleasure in it?"

"Beats me," Freddie said. "I don't do much business with women these days. Now, come on, let's get outta here."

"In good time," Harpo countered.

But Freddie persisted. "*I'm* supposed to be the guide. Well, I'm gonna guide you away from here."

"Had I the power to change you into a camel . . ." He stopped. "But I need you in your human form. It is a matter of some importance to me to watch for the woman."

Grumbling, Freddie let it rest. They sat together in suspicious truce until Freddie said, "You're *really* not from around here, are you? You talk kinda strange."

"And you, of course, speak so perfectly."

"*Noo Yawk*. That's how we talk here. So where *do* you come from?"

"Normally," he sighed, "I dwell in Olympus."

"Wait. I thought that was O-lym-pi-*ah*. The town in Washington, right?"

"Sweet Athena," he muttered, gesturing skyward. "O-lym-*pus*! A beautiful sphere of ether atop a mountain in Greece, where the air is always warm and fragrant. All the gods dwell there, except, of course, Poseidon and Hades, who—"

"You mean like heaven?"

"Where else would a god dwell but some heavenly place?"

Freddie laughed. "Oh, yeah, right, you're a god. I forgot. Oh, and by the way, I'm Julius *See-zhur.*"

Harpo spat on the ground. "A mortal Roman! He did not complete the tasks his *own* gods gave him. You would do better to choose another to emulate. But I *am* a god. Do you doubt me?"

"Yeah," Freddie said. "I fuckin' doubt you, all right. But go ahead, prove it. Make it warm outside."

"Only Zeus can do that! Weather is within *his* realm of power. And it would be an ostentatious act, very ungodlike." Then his voice quieted. "In any case, none of us has much power anymore, with so few believers."

"Excuses, excuses," Freddie sneered. "You must be a pretty fucking wimpy little god if you can't get believers."

His eyes widened. "A truly mortal thing to say, for which you will eternally be sorry! *I shall smite you with a madness you will not enjoy!*"

"Hah," Freddie said with a flip of his hand. "The Roman guy got here first." And by way of proof, he laughed hysterically.

Midas began to howl in accompaniment, prompting, "Be still!" from his master, who turned to Freddie and said, "You, too."

"No. I want to go home *now*. Back to my box. I don't feel so good. "

Harpo cursed under his breath. "Will nothing else satisfy you?"

Freddie shook his head vehemently.

"And you know how to get back to the woman's place?"

"I could get there with my eyes closed. Sometimes do."

"Cursed wrath of Hera," Harpo fumed, "you are a wretch, but I need you." He let out a long sigh, then grabbed Freddie under the arms and raised him up. "Very well, my *friend*, to your home we shall go. But you must lead the way. I am lost in this despicable place, and I cannot navigate for myself."

Ω Ω Ω

By the time they reached the Freezer in late morning, Freddie was quite uncomfortably sober. "Wine," he croaked as he slipped into his box. "I gotta have some wine. I think McCarthy threw the bottle I had last night back into the box before he took us to Gina's, but I can't remember."

Harpo searched around in the corners. "Cursed box of Pandora!" he swore. "I am the god of wine, damn the irony!" Then his hands came to rest on the coveted bottle. "Eureka!" he cried. "See here, impatient one, I have found it."

With shaking hands, Freddie brought it to his lips and guzzled. Small rivulets of deep red liquid slipped down the sides of his face.

"By all the gods! Can you not savor it?"

"Save it?" Freddie said.

"*Savor* it!"

"*Save* it?" Freddie cried again, "*Hell, no!*" Then he wiped his lips with his sleeve, belched loudly, and rolled into a ball in the corner of the box. In a few minutes, he was snoring loudly.

Chapter 4
Delta

Half asleep, with a dream lingering, Gina reached over and pressed the alarm button. She looked at the clock through slit eyes. *Half an hour earlier than usual,* she thought dully, wanting more sleep.

Images of stairs, vertigo and confusion hung on the edge of her consciousness, the remnants of her reverie. The stairs had ended at a blank wall with no door for further passage, no place to go but back down again in search of a different route. That story had been told over and over in interviews with survivors and had crept unbidden into her psyche. She wondered what nameless thing she'd been pursuing in her dream. *That bright elusive butterfly of love again . . .*

In the bathroom she caught her own reflection; her eye was deep blue all around. She sat for a few moments with an ice pack, wishing for more time, but there were things that needed doing. She carried her coffee cup with her as she moved around the small apartment tending to this and that; pillows were fluffed, dust banished, crumbs captured and tossed into the trash can. The first jolt of caffeine kicked in as she was getting dressed.

She brushed her hair, then, for a change, plaited it into one long braid, and wondered again, *Am I too old for this length?* She rejected the idea of cutting it. *David always loved it long.* As she went through the preparations for David's return, making sure his pajamas were in the usual place, his toothbrush in the holder and the toothpaste plainly visible nearby, she made a mental list of the things she wanted to tell his neuropsychologist that afternoon. Another *State of the David* speech with Aaron; it was all becoming so routine.

But today would be un-routine for David. His normal rhythm would be disrupted by an early departure from the bookstore. *Maybe that breakfast with McCarthy wasn't such a good idea,* she reprimanded herself. Sometimes when she was really jammed up, cousin Randy would bring David back and get him settled, but Randy had a previously scheduled meeting, one that he couldn't change. *Or wouldn't,* Gina thought.

She regretted that unspoken indictment before it even finished flashing through her mind. She couldn't fault Randy for his impatience; his love for David was understandably different from hers, something more brotherly. She herself was motivated, or had been at the start, by something deeply primal. She was tending to the needs of the man with whom she once assumed she would spend the rest of her life.

Now what she felt for David was moving steadily in the direction of *pragma* on the love curve, a sobering realization. No longer was it the love between a man and a woman; it was universal, obligatory, the *right* thing, beyond her ability to shape it. The love just somehow understood what it needed to be and shape-shifted to that form to keep itself going, without regard for the desires of the lover. *Love Darwinism*, she thought.

Ω Ω Ω

Entering his office, Gina tucked away her self-pity, knowing that *woe is me* did not compute with Aaron Richman. He'd been a competitive diver in college, a driven, disciplined perfectionist. She'd met him many years later when he came on staff at Bellevue, while she was still training. One day she'd been on her way to some blossoming crisis, tilted into that Bellevue head wind, when he came around the corner. She very nearly toppled him, and spent a few spectacularly awkward moments apologizing. His piercing blue eyes had locked onto hers before they'd parted.

"Slow down," he admonished her, adding the universal truth: "You might miss something."

"He was giving a demonstration to his daughter's school diving team," Miranda later told her. "Hit the back of his head on the board. Broke his neck, with his daughter right there watching."

Aaron's assistant Mike was seated behind a desk when Gina entered the office, his thick fingers clicking away on a keyboard. He looked slightly surprised but said nothing about her eye; instead he nodded and pressed an intercom button to announce Gina's arrival. Then he fell quickly back into his previous typing rhythm. After a short wait, Gina heard the single summoning buzz.

Gina found Aaron seated in his wheelchair behind the desk, dressed in a silk suit and a beautiful tie, shirt blazingly white, dark hair neatly combed, his tanned and handsome face smiling in sincere welcome. *Chair or no chair,* Miranda had once confessed, *the man curls my toes.*

She slipped into the chair on the other side of the desk.

"Hello, Gina. You look great, as usual."

"Right." She pointed to her shiner. "It was an accident. David's elbow collided with my face when I was getting him dressed."

For a moment Aaron said nothing. "I'm a mandated reporter, I'm sure you know."

"So am I, in case you forgot. Really, Aaron, it was totally accidental. He got stuck in his sweater and couldn't get his arms out. He couldn't see me and we just ran into each other."

"Well, okay then. Otherwise you do look great, but you also look unhappy. What's making you unhappy today?"

"Oh, just the usual." She found herself unexpectedly on the edge of tears. She smiled and tried to laugh as she wiped her eyes. "All this makeup is going to run. But I must be making progress. It usually takes longer before I start to cry."

Aaron smiled back. "Actually, that *is* progress. You're opening up faster. Tell me what's making you cry. Beyond the obvious."

"It was an absolutely awful morning. He just wasn't cooperating and it made me so angry . . ."

"Good."

She stopped speaking and looked at him quite pointedly. "Good? I was shrieking. He doesn't understand—"

"Balderdash," he said. "What David understands in any given moment is unclear. Unless he chooses to tell us, which he hasn't been doing lately. And you're *supposed* to feel anger because something that used to be a wonderful part of your life is going through a prolonged death. We've talked about this; you're cycling through the Kubler-Ross stages. You're past *denial* of David's illness. Now you're in anger. *Finally.*"

"Oh, God, couldn't we talk about it in some other way? I mean, *death. Grief.* It's so final. He might still get—at least *somewhat* better."

"Oh, well, back to denial," Aaron said. Then his voice went very quiet. "I'd be questioning your sanity if you weren't upset a good deal of the time. Your life is not what you expected it to be. But you should try to laugh every once in a while; it'll help you heal."

"I know, but sometimes I just feel so overwhelmed . . ."

"Of course you do. But remember our talk about how your situation isn't entirely about David? Why is it so easy for you to do for him, and so hard for you to do for yourself? If David does happen to get better—and you know that I doubt he will—but you get ruined in the process, that's not a very good outcome, is it?"

She shook her head.

"There are lots of simple ways to help yourself, things you probably did without thinking during your relationship with the *before* David. Go out *without* him. Get exercise. Read trashy novels if that's what you like. Get your nails done, eat chocolate. Shop. Surely you've heard of retail therapy? I'm living proof that it works. They love me at Barney's."

Finally, she gave him a weak smile.

"Do *whatever* works. You're *still* essentially the person you were before all this started. It's David who got hit in the head. He's the one who's gone through the change. Through no fault of his own *or* yours."

Was that true? She wondered, as she always did, if she had tried hard enough to keep him from going to the towers that morning.

Tears welled. "There isn't anyone in New York who hasn't changed because of that day."

Aaron let her cry for a few moments, then said, "True. But David is bearing a greater burden of change than most. As are you. So make sure you take full advantage of your support system."

Gina blew her nose and dabbed at her eyes. "I've drifted from a lot of my friends, or they've drifted from me, maybe. I feel like that woman in *Love Actually* whose brother keeps calling her. I wish there were a few more people in my 'support system.'"

"There are never enough. And to be charitable, friendships change, quite naturally, as people move through their lives. But you're quite fortunate in one regard. Imagine what it would be like if David had no financial resources."

"I don't think I want to." She looked up. "He must've picked me out a mile away, I'm such a caretaker. But I always felt like it was more me picking *him* out. He was just—*everything* I ever wanted."

Aaron smiled. "He fit right in with your compulsion for care-taking. For creating *order*. The David I knew back then had a fairly chaotic life, what with being a medical student. They're pretty much all a wreck if they don't have someone in a support position. Miriam took care of all *our* loose ends."

And has shared the rewards of your success, which I will never get to do.

Gina slapped herself mentally for that thought.

"Is Randy still wanting to place him in a facility?"

She nodded yes. "He could just do it, he has all the legal power, being the blood relative. But he's been—generous in letting me make most of the decisions about care. Still, he and I are always negotiating over something . . ."

"Bargaining."

"I suppose."

"And I'm not sure I'd call that generous. *Kind*, maybe." He smiled. "Tell me again what *you* want to do."

Gina released a long, weary sigh and rote-repeated her goal mantra: "I want David to regain his healthy personality and previous intellect. I want David to be able to connect with me again in a meaningful way. I want to remain healthy while David is healing."

"Good," he said. "It's important to continually re-examine what you want. One day you might be surprised to discover that what you want has changed. Then you won't spin your wheels over something you think you *should* want, but actually don't."

Gina looked at the wadded tissue in her hands, now several wet shades darker, then looked up at the very self-possessed man across the desk, wishing she could have one small portion of his confidence. She sighed again and tried to smile.

"Do you want to talk about David now?" he asked.

She shifted in the chair, unmasking her discomfort. "He seems to destabilize when his schedule gets disrupted. It takes a day or so before he seems calm again. When he gets upset, he has this edge to him. You've seen it; that pent-up nervous energy. Randy says he has occasional moments of being ornery at the bookstore, though they are rare. But truth be told, I'd rather have him edgy than the catatonic state he was in before we switched medications last time."

"You told me last session that he seemed more alert in general after the switch."

"Compared to the statue-man he was? Absolutely. But he's still in the ozone most of the time. This new ozone is just a little less murky. I get flashes that he understands who I am to him, had one today after our 'incident,' in fact, but it's happening less and less. On the up side, he can get through most days without having any 'incidents' if we're careful."

"Does he still react negatively to the microwave noise?"

"I put it away."

Aaron wrinkled his brow. "I hate to have you removing things. He'll start trying to control everything so it's all exactly as he wants. We're trying to keep him in a 'normal' situation. Do you know anyone who 'normally' gets exactly what he wants all the time? I certainly don't."

"I don't either," she admitted.

"On the other hand, if he's going to stay at home, his behavior has to be in control. I don't think there will ever be a situation where he *tries* to hurt you, but he is still strong as you found out this morning, so I need to keep an eye on that, and I can only do it through *your* eyes."

The concerns for her own safety that had been creeping into her mental process more frequently in the last couple of months had been heightened by the morning's fracas. Images of what might happen if David went wild floated horribly through her consciousness. She shoved them aside with a brief memory of how it used to feel when he slipped his arms around her.

Ω Ω Ω

He had just put on his long white coat, the one he was so proud of; it had "Bellevue Hospital" embroidered on the chest pocket. His name tag was pinned to that pocket, just below the embroidery.

"I don't think I'll need anything heavier, it's so nice out."

She had turned on the television to a local news channel a few minutes earlier. "Seventy-two, they're saying."

He slipped his Bellevue ID badge into a side pocket, along with his wallet. Another intern had had his badge grabbed off his neck walking to work, so they were all waiting until they got there to put them on their necks.

"The last blast of summer. It makes me nervous when it's this nice now. Law of averages. I wonder if we'll be trekking through mountains of snow this winter."

"You never know," she said. "Can't predict the weather or the future."

And in that moment, the future arrived.

The red streaming banner appeared at the base of the television screen.

BREAKING NEWS BREAKING NEWS BREAKING NEWS

"We're going now to the World Trade Center . . ."

They both moved closer to the television, watching silently for a few stunned moments. They saw the black cloud and blossoming flames, heard the announcer's confused narrative.

"Holy shit. Gina, what the hell . . ."

"That was an airplane. A big one. Dear God."

David turned abruptly and headed for the door.

"Wait." She grabbed his arm. "Where are you going?"

"*There*. We're fifteen blocks away. People will be hurt. You know how many people there are in that building."

"David, please . . . go to the hospital. They'll need you in the ER."

"Not as much as they'll need me there."

He shook off her grip, but before going out the door, he turned back, reached out and drew her in. He held her tightly, almost painfully, against him.

"It's okay. I'll be careful, promise." And then he went out the door.

It was the last time his embrace had felt real to her.

Ω Ω Ω

She heard Aaron's voice and looked up as he was completing some question. "What?" she said. "Sorry; I was drifting there for a minute."

"I was asking, any more digestive problems from the medication?"

Gina looked at Aaron, felt that *there but for the grace of God go I* twinge of able-bodied guilt. Diaper. Colostomy. *Unimaginable to someone who hasn't experienced it.*

"No. No more accidents."

"Good. Well, then." His wrapping-it-up tone signaled the close of their session. "David's externals seem to be in pretty good order. We'll look at his internals next time you bring him—uh, let's see now—"

He touched a button on the arm of his chair. "Friday. I see no reason to suggest any changes for the moment. But that's your call, and you know I'll support whatever decision you make."

She didn't hesitate in declaring her preference. "I still want him home. We're getting by. I don't see how he'll get any better if he's not at home."

She had given him the opening. "Gina," he said, "he *hasn't* gotten any better at home. We may need to start considering whether it would be better for him to be somewhere else."

Ω Ω Ω

Freddie came out of his stupor around sunset. He yawned once, then turned on his side, colliding with his forgotten house-guest. In his haze, he planted his feet in the middle of Harpo's back and pushed, sending him skidding out of the box into the cold.

"Aiyeee!" wailed the stunned evictee, who righted himself and brushed the slush off the back of his legs. "You are fortunate my followers are nowhere about, for they would tear you limb from limb for this insult." He stood up, shook his finger and cursed firmly into the box, "May your nose hairs tickle your chin!"

Freddie found that notion amusing, and laughed.

"*Arghhh!* Your impertinence is not to be borne. Invite me back into your hovel."

Freddie shook his head no.

"The woman will be unhappy."

"I told her I would get you back there. I didn't say nothin' about sharing my box."

Harpo scowled. "In Greece, a man is shamed if he refuses hospitality to even the lowest wanderer. Why, my father Zeus was very fond of assuming a different identity and appearing at the gate of some poor unsuspecting mortal, simply to test him for observation of that custom. I myself appeared many times in the filthiest rags—"

"Kinda like what you're wearing now?"

Harpo paused and surveyed his attire, then took a deep breath. "I was never refused a place at the hearth of any man who had even the smallest crust of bread to break with me. But *you* would cast me out like a stone from your shoe, with no thought to my comfort! No Greek would *dare* to do so."

Freddie shrugged his shoulders and belched. "Sorry, pal, I didn't know. I'm Italian."

"I take this word *Italian* to mean rude, inhospitable, and stupid."

"Hey! What kinda thing is that to say? Da Vinci and Galileo were Italian.

Marconi, too. They were world-class smart guys. And you can't say *stupid* no more. You have to say *challenged*."

"It is a pity, then, that you could not be more like them." He patted his chest. "Midas, do you also find this behavior deplorable?" He waved his hand in the air. "If so, please tell the good mortals hereabout."

The dog yipped and howled. Windows screeched upward and irate neighbors renewed their threats from the night before. And within a few minutes, the blue flashing light appeared at the end of the alley.

Harpo was standing just outside the box when McCarthy reached it.

"I greet you!" He grinned at McCarthy with the expectation that his salutation would be returned.

Without a word, McCarthy shined his light inside the box and saw Freddie tucked in the far corner looking very unhappy, but otherwise sound. Then he shined the light back at Harpo.

"Are you guys really having another fight, or are you just trying to piss off the neighbors? Someone called in about a lot of barking. Are you beating that dog?"

Harpo was the epitome of sugary innocence. "Never! Midas is unhappy, as we have been treated most inhospitably." He flashed an angry glance at Freddie. "We were shoved rudely out of the box. Midas whines in protest. I tried to stop him, but as my powers are diminished here on Earth, I have been unsuccessful."

"So I see."

"Perhaps you should take us to that warmer place with the kind woman who dressed my wound yesterday."

The wound, McCarthy thought, furrowing his brow. Notions of career-ending IAD investigations sneaked unnervingly into his consciousness. "Let me see the dog," he said.

"As you wish," He reached inside his toga and pulled out the small white dog by the neck fur, then held him up. Midas trembled pathetically and peed a straight line into the cold air. When he was finished, Harpo shook him off and tucked him back inside the warm toga.

"Though he is fine for the moment, he might start barking again at any time. However, if you take us to the woman's place, I am relatively certain that he will be silent."

Head injury, McCarthy thought. *Well, Gina wants to see him anyway.* He looked at the unkempt pair and sighed in resignation. "Christ Almighty. Look at the two of you. Prime examples of what not to be when you grow up. Come on, let's go get in the car." Then he turned and stomped through the slush to the cruiser. His would-be passengers followed, stepping in the footprints he left behind.

Chapter 5
Epsilon

In the hot dry air of the basement, Gina's swollen eyes felt as gritty as sandpaper. She popped open an ice pack and applied it to her face, then sat back in the chair and put her feet up on the desk. McCarthy found her in that position when he strolled in.

"Busted," he teased her. "I always wondered how you ladies of leisure spend your time."

Without moving, Gina said, "Just like this. Feet up. Getting a facial."

"Hey, I brought in a couple of customers, just so you wouldn't get bored. Freddie's back, and that new guy Harpo. I know you wanted him back anyway."

She took the ice pack off her face and sat up. "Right enough. But Freddie came along? That's three nights in a row. I think I'm honored."

McCarthy winced when saw her face. "Ouch," he said. "How does the other guy look?"

"Five-eleven, one-seventy, long brown ponytail. Vacant stare."

"Did he hit you?"

"No. *No.* I walked into his elbow in a getting-dressed accident. He would *never* hit me."

And though McCarthy didn't know how she could be so sure, he let it go. "I don't think coming back was Freddie's idea. They were heading for another beef over the box, and Harpo wanted to come here. Freddie didn't seem too happy about it."

"He probably wasn't. First thing he said when I asked him to keep an eye on Harpo was, 'I don't like him.'"

"I wonder why he went along with it."

"I offered him a bribe. You want to know what he asked for? He wants me to let him do my taxes."

"Well he *was* an accountant."

"But you'd think he'd want something like a new jacket or a pillow."

"Sounds to me like what he really wants is to work."

"Maybe I should let him do the books for this whole place. I have to keep track of everything I spend so I can fill out these ridiculously detailed audit forms. The City of New York wants to make sure I'm not wasting their grant money."

McCarthy snorted. "Now there's irony."

"You said it. It really wouldn't break my heart to have someone else do that bookkeeping for me. I'm not very good at it, so it takes me forever."

"Can you afford to pay him?"

"I could probably scratch up something. Not much, though."

"Still, sounds like it might be a good deal for everybody."

"Yeah. It might." She sniffed quietly.

There was a brief moment of silence, then McCarthy looked into her eyes. "You want to talk about it?"

Her gaze shifted guiltily away from his. "It was just an accident."

"No. Your eyes are all swollen, like you've been crying."

"Oh," she said, "*that*." She gave him an unconvincing little smile. "I mean, thanks for being concerned, but I was hoping the shiner would keep it from being so obvious."

He tried to lighten the strained moment. "Law enforcement officers are rigorously trained to notice even the smallest hint of trauma."

"Well, that makes me feel better," she said. "Is it still really bad?"

"You wouldn't want to pose for your passport picture right now."

She tried to laugh, but it came out sounding forced and a troubled look resettled quickly onto her face. "Sometimes I feel like all I do these days is talk about 'it'. I'm all talked out right now. But you're sweet to offer, McCarthy, I mean that sincerely."

"Well, the offer was sincerely tendered. It helps to have someone to talk to."

"So I've heard." She knew she sounded bitter. "David never had that. *We* never had that, not like you guys and the firefighters. Med students don't have that ongoing brotherhood. And he was fairly new at Bellevue. He didn't have that automatic association." She looked up at him. "He had me."

Has you, McCarthy thought. "Well, then, I hope you'll take me up on it should the need arise." He shifted his position nervously. "Now here's an offer I hope you can't refuse. How about I buy you dinner? I thought I'd pick something up and bring it here, you know, maybe Mexican or Szechuan. You choose."

"Hmm," she said, "Szechuan sounds good. Just make sure you bring some antacid."

"What kind?"

"Pink," she said.

"A woman after my own heart." He wished silently it were true. "How's midnight sound?"

"Like a good time to eat dinner, in our crazy world."

He gave her a thumbs-up. "I'll be back."

The overhead light glinted on his gold name badge as he turned.

A. Z. McCarthy.

Curiously, in all the years she'd known him, she had never asked him about the letters. "Hey, McCarthy—"

He turned back. "Yeah?"

"You never said, and I guess I never asked. What do your initials stand for?"

"Absolute Zero," he said, and winked.

$$\Omega \; \Omega \; \Omega$$

Harpo tiptoed from one of the side rooms to a concealed spot just outside Gina's office and listened for a few moments. It was quiet, so he entered and presented himself.

"Oh, hello, Harpo, I was hoping you'd came back."

He moved closer and gave her a seductive, half-lid gaze. "I will always come back to you. For you have the most beautiful—great Zeus!" he said with alarm. "What injury has befallen your eyes?"

Already, the story was becoming tiresome to her. "It was an accident, I ran into something. And I've been crying. I'm having kind of a tough day. Not my first, and definitely not my last."

"If someone has caused this to happen to you, I swear to seek revenge on your behalf. Only name him, and I will see that he suffers." His eyes narrowed and he lowered his voice. "Was it McCarthy?"

She reacted with prompt indignation. "Good heavens, *no*. McCarthy's a cop, an extremely good one. He *keeps* people from being hurt, in case you haven't figured that out yet."

"Yes, of course, how foolish of me to think that of him. I've said the wrong thing and now you are angry with me." He bowed in supplication. "May fire ants kiss my fingertips for speaking such an insult."

"*Ugh, Harpo* . . ." she said, making a squeamish face. "Where do you come *up* with this stuff?"

"Ah," he said proudly, "among Olympians I am the cleverest of those who compete in the sport of cursing. But it is Hera who is best at making those curses come about. She has an arrangement with Nemesis, and is viciously persistent in seeking revenge."

"Remind me to avoid her." Gina said.

"That will not be a problem," he said, "for she is trapped in Olympus with the rest of the gods. Except myself, of course, and Eros, who has wings and can fly to

Earth whenever he wishes."

"Lucky him, or her," Gina said.

"Him, or so we think."

Gina arched one eyebrow. "You *think?*"

"Well, I suppose we are sure."

The exchange was oddly amusing to her. "Are you sure or not sure?"

"Well, he *does* have the necessary, uh, equipment to qualify as a male. And his mother Aphrodite swears that he is. But it's just that he is pink, and—"

"Pink?"

"Yes, an unmanly color, certainly. Except the tips of his wings and his hair, which is golden, much like yours, only lighter. And very curly. And he is quite small, so he can squeeze himself through the thinnest cracks like a rat. Surely you must know of him. He comes to Earth often, especially when it is time for his festival. A terrible pest, always shooting arrows into everyone—"

She almost laughed. "You mean *Cupid?*"

He crossed his arms indignantly and lifted his chin. "*Eros.* Cupid is another Roman artifice for one of our fine Greek inventions."

"Oh, really," she said. "I didn't realize." Then she turned back to face the counter again, trying to hide her giggles.

"Before you resume your work," he said gently, "perhaps I can help you with your eyes."

She turned back toward him. "How are you going to do that?"

"Remain perfectly still," he said, moving closer, "and shut your eyes. I shall touch your lids with my fingers and send health into them again."

Strangely, Gina found herself unwilling to object, or maybe—it crossed her mind—*unable.* She did as he'd told her and stood motionless. She felt comforting warmth in his smooth fingertips as they rested gently on her closed eyes.

But then, reality. *Fool! A mentally unbalanced and probably strong man, who may just hate you and your kind, has his fingernails less than a millimeter from your eyeballs.*

She reached up with a quick but smooth motion and took hold of his wrists, then guided his hands away from her eyes, slowly so as not to upset him. "Thank you, Harpo," she said, "I feel better already."

He looked back and forth between her two eyes, assessing his work. "I curse my lack of power. I would like to have done more. But there is some improvement, I think."

"I'm sure you're right. And I'm very grateful. Now why don't I take a look at that cut over *your* eye? Sit up here on the table so I can take off the bandage."

He did as she asked.

"This will probably hurt a bit," she warned, "but not for long." She took hold of one corner of the square patch and pulled it off, expecting him to shudder or wince. But he remained still. And where there should have been split skin held together by an adhesive closure, she found instead a closed pink line with no apparent infection or scab. She stepped back in surprise and tried to remember just what the cut had looked like when she'd first treated it.

Surely it was worse than this . . . She envisioned the original wound, and saw in her mind a two-inch diagonal gash over his eyebrow, at least one-third of an inch into the skin, close to bone. "Wow," she said. "Do you want to tell me what kind of vitamins you're taking? This wound is healing incredibly fast."

"I do not understand this word 'vitamin.'"

She stared at him for a moment. "Never mind, then," she finally said. "But I'm impressed. I've never seen a man heal so fast."

"As I told you," he said quietly, "I am a god."

Aha. What was that phenomenon, she studied it in school: *psychoneuroimmunology,* where people who wished very strongly to be well literally psyched themselves into improved health. She regretted not taking a photograph of the cut the night before.

But why would *I* have done that? If anything, McCarthy or Stein might have done so, for potential evidence. She would ask.

And it had seemed so—ordinary. Deep, but—ordinary.

"That's right, I forgot," she said. "A god. That explains it."

Ω Ω Ω

Freddie scowled at Harpo when he sat down next to him in the center's waiting area.

"And what have *you* to scowl about?" Harpo said. "You have not just been mocked by a mortal woman as I have."

"Hey, Pal, that's because I don't deserve to get mocked."

"Great Zeus," . . ." he muttered. "I do not understand why you dislike me. Examine your own likability first! You will find that you are everything deplorable in a mortal. Rude, dirty, completely inhospitable. But it seems that the Fates have thrown us together, though to what end, I am not entirely sure. This is something we can do nothing about." He leaned closer still. "So it is useless to fight. Perhaps we should try to be kind to one another, eh?"

Freddie regarded him suspiciously. "You're weird."

"Ah, yes," Harpo said. "*I* am weird. You, of course, are a magnificent example of human perfection."

"That's right, Pal, *human.* I don't go around telling people I'm a god."

"Midas! You know that I am a god. Speak for me."

Midas poked his head out of the front of the toga and panted happily, his little pink tongue hanging out. He stretched himself up and licked his master's nose then grabbed hold of the amulet necklace and began tugging playfully.

Harpo laughed. "Take care, Small One! We *need* this." He pulled the dog off the necklace and put him down on the floor.

The tiny dog scooted up into Freddie's lap and forced his head under one of Freddie's hands, wanting to be petted. Freddie looked down at him in surprise and started to pull his hand away. The dog stayed in his lap, his tail wagging happily. So Freddie reached out and cautiously stroked the dog's head.

"You see? He likes you. You like him. This is a start."

Freddie *hmphed*, still suspicious. But the dog nuzzled him affectionately, and he could not help but respond. "I guess it is a start," he said. He scratched the dog's neck. "Don't know where it's going, but it's a start."

Gina appeared suddenly in the doorway of the common room. "Hello, boys," she smirked. In one hand was a plastic bottle of milky light green soap, in the other a long-handled brush. Over one shoulder was draped a tattered-looking white towel, its fibers worn down from repeated bleaching.

"Oh, shit," Freddie mumbled under his breath. He started to get up. "She's got the shower stuff. The guys who get sent up to the hospital have to be showered before they go up. It's nice and warm and they got good food, so guys are always trying to trick her into sending them up. You get a bed in the ward, clean sheets, a bathroom, meds, television; it's kinda like the Holy Grail."

"Spider Man!" Gina said firmly. "If you want that bed, you better get in here!"

They sat and watched in silence as the thin, dark man with long limbs rose and headed toward the door where Gina stood.

Harpo said, "He looks as if he is walking to the altar of sacrifice."

"He'd probably be happier if he was. She's brutal with that hose."

Spider Man followed Gina to a small room on the opposite side of the shelter. As soon as they disappeared from view, Harpo took Midas from Freddie's lap and tucked him away. "I will observe this ritual," he said.

"You don't wanna watch," Freddie said. "Trust me."

"Nevertheless, I *will*." He went out into the hallway and stood just outside the small shower room.

He watched silently as she pulled a white plastic bag from the pocket of her coat and gave it to the cowering Spider Man. "OK," he heard Gina say, "Put your clothes in this bag." He saw her pull a long green hose down from its hook on the wall.

"Ready?

A moment later, she turned a spigot with her free hand and a spray of water came out. The naked man shrieked.

He could hear her voice over the hiss of the spray and the howls of her unhappy victim. "Quit complaining, the water's nice and warm. You know the drill, hair, pits, and crotch, every crevice. The nurses want you coming up *clean*."

Scowling at his tormentor, the dripping man came out of the small room, and yanked the towel rudely from her outstretched hand.

Gina smiled. "Once a year whether you need it or not." The man arranged the towel around himself, took his bag of clothes, and grumbled away.

Freddie came up behind Harpo and tapped him nervously on the shoulder. "Come on, we're getting outta here." He started walking toward the door. "She might just decide to do us for fun."

Harpo turned around and grabbed him by the sleeve of his jacket. "No! We must stay."

"Whatsa matter, you scared? Gods don't get scared." He pulled free.

Harpo grabbed him again. "But you are to help me!"

"Then you better come along," Freddie said as he yanked his arm away, "cuz I ain't staying."

"But I must remain near the woman—"

"We'll come back later." Then he ran toward the exit door, dragging Harpo behind him.

Ω Ω Ω

They walked along First Avenue, heading north from 29th. At 30th, Harpo stopped and looked into a littered courtyard. Along the perimeter, where snow had not accumulated, the ground was strewn with dead brush and brown leaves.

"Why do we stop at this edifice?" Harpo asked.

"It's the old hospital building," Freddie said. He shivered. "They turned it into the shelter Gina talks about. Tough place."

It was surrounded by a tall chain link fence that enclosed a shorter wrought-iron fence; along the top four feet of the chain link there was a continuous length of plywood, the same dark green as highway signs.

"Look up under here," Harpo said. "You can see the old sign."

The bottoms of the cast iron letters were barely visible.

"It says Bellevue Hospital," Freddie told him. "This is where it used to be. Way back when."

"Many poor mortals must have come here to die."

"How'd you know that?"

Harpo stopped and considered the question. "I do not know," he said. He closed his eyes briefly, then opened them. "I see—renditions of them, all in a row."

"*Wow,*" Freddie said. "The Wall of Prayers used to be all along here," he said. "Pictures of all the people who were missing."

"But why were they missing?"

Freddie stared at him. "You're kidding."

"No. From where were they missing?"

"Now I *really* don't like you."

He led onward. They turned, zigzagged, meandered farther. On a crosstown block they came upon a small grocery store.

"You hungry?" Freddie said.

"I do not know. In Olympus we eat only ambrosia, when it pleases us. Of course, when I wandered the earth many centuries ago, I ate mortal foods, often grapes, since they are in my domain." He sighed wistfully. "I never tire of grapes."

"How do you like that," Freddie chimed in. "Me neither. Especially when they're squished and fermented." He chuckled.

"And goat," Harpo continued, "which was often sacrificed to me. My Menaeids would tear a young animal limb from limb in the frenzy of worshiping me, and we would eat it freshly killed, bloody and raw, warm, still dripping with the essence of life. But as I have told you, that was many centuries—"

Freddie interrupted him. "You ate raw *goat?*"

"Indeed. Well, only the very young ones. The older ones are—unpleasant."

"I'd have to be half dead before I ate raw goat," Freddie said, scrunching up his face in disgust. "Probably taste like a rat. I mean *normal* food. Are you hungry or not?"

"As I said, I am unaccustomed to mortal ways where food is concerned. I do not know what it *feels* like to be hungry."

"Damn. You must live like some kind of prince or something."

"God," he corrected him.

"Right. I forgot. So, Mr. God, you want some Earth food? I think I got some vouchers left."

"Vouchers?"

Freddie opened his mouth to begin an explanation, but stopped. "Never mind," he said, "just come with me. And keep your mouth shut. I don't want you pissing off the chick who runs this place."

They were barely inside the door before the Korean proprietress was on them. "Show money."

Freddie pulled open the zipper on his side pocket and extracted a handful of folded notes. He smacked them down on the counter. "There," he said. "You happy?"

She gave him a small forced smile, followed by a stiff little nod of her head.

"So," Freddie said, the matter of payment settled, "you see anything you want?"

Harpo was carefully examining a plastic-wrapped sandwich. "We may choose?"

"Yeah. But put that back cuz we don't have enough money. Stick with some kinda chips."

He looked confused. "I do not understand these chips."

"Whew," Freddie said. "You eat raw goat and you don't know what chips are. Incredible. But okay, I'll play. We'll get some chips." He grinned. "I'm gonna take your chip virginity."

"Virginity?" Harpo said, his eyes widening. "Please! Do not speak to me of virgins! It is all because of a virgin that I was forced to leave Olympus. It was a dreadful situation, and—"

Freddie held up a hand to silence him. "Hey, Pal," he said, "I'm sure this is a great story, but I'm trying to make a decision here, so you'll have to save it for later. Let's see," he said, poking through the bags on a standing display, "we'll get some Doritos and some barbecue potato chips. That oughta give you a pretty good idea." He pulled two bags off their hooks and went to the counter. "We'll have these," he said to the woman. He smiled at his confused companion. "Chip lesson one."

Outside on a nearby stoop, Freddie tore open one of the bags. He popped a chip into his mouth and crunched down on it.

"Hah, *hah!*" he said with a grin. "Bet raw goat doesn't crunch like that. Grapes don't, neither."

"Most assuredly not! The noise these chips make is most unholy—"

"You get used to it."

Harpo extracted a chip from the bag and bit into it. He chewed slowly at first, but was soon chomping away. He turned toward Freddie with a look of amazement. "Why, these are marvelous!"

"And all this time you've been eating goat. *Sheesh.*"

Harpo grabbed the bag and began shoving potato chips into his mouth at a frantic pace. Freddie grabbed it back. "Whoa! Slow down. We'll finish 'em too soon."

"But I saw that there are more . . ."

"I only got a dollar's worth of vouchers left."

"Then you must acquire more vouchers."

"I'll have to panhandle to do that. I don't feel like it right now."

"What is this 'panhandle'?"

After a long, dark sigh, Freddie explained. "You stand on the street and ask people going by to give you something. I usually say, 'got any change,' or 'got a quarter'. . ."

"A quarter of what?"

Freddie threw up his hands in exasperation. "Do I have to explain everything to you? A quarter of a dollar! What did you think I meant?"

"I did not know. As I have said before, I do not understand your mortal customs."

"I guess you don't." He sat, fuming, and tossed the unopened bag of chips back and forth between his two hands.

Harpo eyed the bouncing bag longingly. "But I am eager to understand," he said. "Please go on."

"Okay. So people either give me something or they don't."

"But this is really only begging. Why do you not feel like doing it?"

Freddie stopped tossing the bag and set it on his knees. He stared down at the sidewalk. "Because it makes me feel kinda bad, you know, ashamed."

"But it is no shame to beg if you are in need. Why, there are peoples to whom beggars are sacred and cherished."

Freddie let out a cynical *hmph*. "Not the *peoples* around here. Most of them won't even look at me. They throw money, but they won't look me in the face."

There was a brief but weighty lull in their exchange, then Harpo said, "So you gather these vouchers . . ."

"Yeah, they're only good for food. Some stores don't accept them, because they don't want guys like me coming in all the time."

Harpo pondered the things Freddie had told him for a few moments. "Then it was an act of great hospitality for you to share your chips with me. Worthy of a Greek, even. I am grateful."

"Hey," Freddie said with a shrug, "no problem. We all gotta eat. Problem is, I gotta drink, too. So I like it when some people give me cash. I try to save it up so I can buy some wine every couple of days. Then I don't get sick."

"I fail to understand how that can make you sick. Unhappy, yes . . ."

"I get a real bad headache and I tremble all over. Sometimes I puke, even if I don't have anything in my stomach." Freddie hung his head. "And you want to know what's strange about that? I used to work for a guy who sells wine."

"It offends me as the god of wine that these things should happen." He patted Freddie on the shoulder. "When I have my power once again, I will see to it that you have all the wine you desire."

Freddie smiled wanly. "Great. I think." He stood up and stretched his thin body. "Gina's probably all done with the showers now. I guess it's safe to go back. Come on, we'll eat these Doritos on the way."

Ω Ω Ω

Gina had magically transformed from the mad hoser back into a kind and caring woman. She was seated at her desk laboring over the shelter's annual grant proposal when McCarthy returned at midnight with two brown paper bags in his arms. She looked up at him from a desk strewn with half-completed forms and stubby pencils, a few with points, a few with erasers, none with both.

"Excuse me, Miss," he said, all authority, "but could you clear the area, please? We've got a culinary installation coming in here."

Happily gathering up her work, she said, "Certainly, Sir, anything to be of assistance to a law enforcement officer."

"Then kindly assist me with this bag," he groaned, "cuz I think it's gonna blow."

She leapt up and helped, narrowly averting a Chinese food disaster. "I don't know, McCarthy," she said as she took the bulging bag. "Do you think you got enough for the two of us?"

She set it down on a counter, closed her eyes and drew in the aroma. "God, that smells good. I'm hungrier than I thought. And that's a surprise after working on this *nauseating* City grant application all night. The stupid thing is about fifteen pages long. I didn't even finish one page tonight."

"Tough night, then, I guess," McCarthy said.

"Not entirely. Earlier tonight I got to send a few billion cooties screaming down the shower drain." She opened the steaming white containers. "But no worries. Cooties regroup in the sewers and plan their return. It's all part of a communist plot to keep social workers in business." She handed him a paper plate. "I've got chopsticks here if you want some."

"Never used them, I'm ashamed to admit."

She smiled wickedly. "I'll just have to teach you, then. First time for everything."

She opened a side drawer in her desk, and as she was poking around for the chopsticks, she saw McCarthy unfold a yellow paper tablecloth and spread it over the cleared surface.

"Oh, McCarthy, how nice!"

"Yeah, you do want just a hint of color." He grinned. Then he pulled out a fat white candle with a glass base and set it in the middle of the tablecloth. "Got a match?"

She found an old musty pack with a driving school ad on the inside cover in the same drawer as the chopsticks. After a few unsuccessful tries, McCarthy finally managed to light one.

Gina surveyed the impromptu banquet with delight. "Well, I'm impressed. I don't think you forgot anything." She looked up at him and smiled. "Shall we?"

"By all means. Just let me lower the lights." He reached over and flipped the wall switch, killing the glare of the overhead.

It took a few moments for their eyes to adjust to the dimness. "I have no idea what I'm spooning out of these boxes," Gina said as she served herself. "I suppose I'll just have to trust you."

"I don't even remember what I ordered. My memory's not what it used to be. Goes with the age, I guess. My eyes, either. Speaking of eyes," he said, "Yours look a whole lot better."

"I think the ice pack really did the trick."

"How long did you use it after I left?"

"Not too long. A little while, I guess."

He leaned closer, examining her eyes in the candlelight. "Really? They look perfectly normal." Leaning closer still, he added, in a softer voice, "They look wonderful, in fact."

She could feel herself being drawn over the candle, pulled forward by some giant kiss magnet. She surprised herself by thinking, *good*.

Then the guilt popped on like a red light and she thought of David.

She shoved the thought away. *Just this once.*

And next time you'll tell yourself you can stop any time you want to. You just won't want to.

But it was too late, the kiss was in progress; they each moved closer, almost there, she could feel his breath mixing with hers . . .

And from somewhere beyond the office door a massive fart rang out like the Liberty Bell, shattering the moment.

Gina covered her mouth with her hand and convulsed with laughter. "Oh my God I'm gonna wet my pants . . ."

McCarthy was laughing so hard that no sound came out of his open mouth. Snippets of praise could be heard from the communal room where the melodious methane had originated.

McCarthy said, "Boy, talk about a mood crusher . . ."

Still laughing, Gina said, "Okay. Wow. So now that the moment has been completely massacred, do you want to learn how to use chop sticks? I promise I won't laugh. I'm just about laughed out."

"Yeah, what the hell, I'll give it a shot. It can't be all that hard." He picked up one of the sets Gina had laid out and removed them from the red paper sleeve. "I always thought the writing on the sleeve said, 'not for use by morons.'"

Gina picked up her own set. "No excuses, McCarthy. This is the multicultural age." She manipulated them expertly and tapped the tips together a few times to demonstrate the proper technique.

McCarthy did as she showed him. After a couple of unsuccessful tries, he managed to pick up a cube-shaped piece of chicken. As he brought it toward his mouth he said, "Hey, this is easier than I thought . . ." and it dropped into his lap.

Ω Ω Ω

Freddie pinched his nostrils together and turned to Harpo, who was seated next to him. "Whew!" he said nasally. "No more chips for you."

Whispers of approval passed around the room. One man said, "How'd you *do* that?"

Harpo smiled. "Hardly a Heraklean task. I am a god. I merely willed it to happen."

The man elbowed the fellow next to him. "Hey, wake up. You're not gonna believe this. We got the Fart God. Right here."

Inspired by the praise and congratulations, Harpo made a few courtly bows, accepting the praise of his cohorts. But as the odor dissipated, so did the entertainment value of the event, and soon everyone settled back down and went to sleep.

Everyone but Harpo, who sneaked out of the room and edged along the wall toward Gina's office, staying in the shadows.

From a covert position outside Gina's office, he had heard their gentle laughter, smelled the scent of the candle, sensed the intensity radiating out of the room. He knew their lips would come together. So he'd ducked back into the sleeping room and powered up the most obnoxious interruption to a kiss he could imagine, and it had worked splendidly.

But only for a moment. Now back at his listening and looking post, he saw their gaiety resume.

"Look at them," he muttered to Midas. "Neither sees anything but the other."

But in the dim candlelight, *he* thought he saw a shadow, moving above a tall cabinet. He stood very still, his eyes glued to the spot of the disruption. His heart began to pound. "It cannot be," he whispered urgently. "By all the Gods. That meddlesome imp."

Ω Ω Ω

McCarthy pushed back his chair and stood up. "Ah, crap," he said as the runaway tidbit tumbled from his leg to the floor. "It landed on my pants. Do you think this stuff stains?"

Gina stood up, ever ready to help. "Here, let me get you another napkin. Wipe off as much of it as you can. The rest should wash out." She turned around and reached toward the counter.

Something whizzed by the side of her head.

"Damn," she said, ducking. "I thought we got all the bats out of here."

Still watching from behind the door, Harpo looked back and forth between her exposed body and the top of the cabinet. The shadow moved again, and he felt the hot bile of fear flooding into his belly. "Great Zeus," he whispered frantically, "he is about to shoot . . ."

"Cursed rock of Sysiphus!" he shrieked aloud. "No!" He leapt forward into the room with a wild and wide-eyed look on his face. He raised his hand in front of Gina's chest as he lurched crazily toward her.

"Harpo?" she said, drawing back in alarm. "What the—?"

He did not hear her. He was caught in a futile effort to maintain equilibrium. He tumbled to the floor, unconscious.

Out of the corner of one eye, McCarthy saw something whiz by over *his* head and with cop's logic, tried to process what he'd seen. *Not a bat*, he concluded. *Bullet*, was his natural reaction.

But there was no sound, not even the quiet tap of a silencer. He shook off his confusion. "No way," he muttered.

"Give me a hand here," he heard Gina say.

He knelt next to the fallen Harpo. Gina had her hand on the underside of his chin and was checking his pulse. "He hit his head. He might be in shock. There's a blanket on the bottom shelf of my cabinet."

McCarthy nodded and turned toward it, looking upward as he did, seeing nothing there at all. Gina was taking Harpo's temperature when he turned back to her. "Cover him," she said. She looked critically at the digital temperature display. A look of grave concern came over her face. "Wow," she said quietly. "He's spiked a high fever."

Harpo groaned and tried to roll over.

"He's coming to," Gina said. "Hold him still if you can."

Harpo's hand rose limply and he tried to point at something, but the uncooperative limb flopped back down and landed palm-up next to his head on the floor. In the middle of his hand was a large red welt.

"It almost looks like an insect bite," Gina said as she took hold of the hand, "but what kind of biting bugs are out in the winter? I mean, we have *armies* of other bugs down here, but not the kind that leave bites that big."

"Horsefly?"

"This time of year? I don't think so."

She'll think I'm crazy. "I thought I saw a bird just now. And I could swear it was pink."

Gina looked up at him with worry on her face. "Should I be taking your temperature, too, McCarthy?"

He said nothing for a moment. "No. Hey, maybe it was a spider that got him. They're around in the winter, aren't they? I'll bet that's a spider bite."

"Well, one thing it *wasn't* is a pink-bird bite. If it was a spider, he's having an allergic reaction. A pretty severe one."

Ω Ω Ω

Harpo floated in a dream, saw himself drifting slowly through a crowd of white-robed women. They reached out in adoration and laid tender hands on him as he passed. He was gloriously attired in a toga of the finest linen, secured at the shoulder with a bunch of grapes, beautifully rendered in gold. Across the other shoulder was draped the soft skin of a leopard, its head resting squarely on his chest, yellow teeth bared to strike, its eyes rich amber rounds polished to smooth translucence. He strode majestically forward toward the ritual altar on the hillside, where the goat waited, bleating plaintively, unaware of its impending Fate. Beyond the altar were ancient olive groves and lush, fruit-laden vines. In a distance he saw the hazy horizon dotted with more small hills. Birds circled lazily in the blue and white sky, black dots against the soft clouds. The sun eased downward, approaching its daily death with glowing grace.

A great white bull, his collar gold and jeweled, followed behind him, led by a smiling young girl with a garland of blue flowers woven into her long black hair. The beaters sounded their drums, slowly at first, but increasing in tempo as the celebrants surged forward. Pipes joined in, and small cymbals, their mesmerizing sounds inspiring the worshipers to dance. The crowd of women, arms upraised in adoration, swayed back and forth sinuously, and suddenly he found himself encircled by them. They pressed closer, their warmth wrapping him, the moisture of their lips slippery on his skin . . . he groaned with the pleasure of their attentions . . .

"Nhhh" . . . He opened his eyes and saw the woman kneeling close to him. Her brow was furrowed in worry.

"Harpo, can you hear me?"

"Nhhh . . ."

"Blink your eyes if you can hear me."

He heard her, but faintly, as if from a distance. He blinked, then opened his eyes fully. The harsh overhead light was back on again and he shielded his eyes with one hand, blinking repeatedly as he slowly came back to consciousness. He saw Gina and McCarthy exchange worried glances, and then Gina spoke, though her words were dim and muffled.

"I think you were bitten by a spider," she said gravely. "You seem to have had a pretty serious reaction to it." She checked his temperature again. "You're not as hot as you were a few minutes ago, but your temperature is still elevated."

McCarthy knelt by his side. "Do you think we oughta take him upstairs? Maybe he should go to the ER."

Gina let out a breath and straightened up. "He seems to be coming around. I think he'll be okay. And he'll just end up sitting in some hard chair watching them dig bullets out of teenagers." She looked back down at him, and was encouraged to see some of the color returning to his cheeks. "He might be better off if we keep an eye on him down here. I'm going to give him an antihistamine. That'll suppress the buildup of additional histamine in his bloodstream. Then I'm going to hose him down with the hottest water he can stand for as long as he'll let me. We can bring him upstairs if he gets worse."

McCarthy let out a relieved breath. "Sounds more like a treat than a treatment," he said. "I think I might be jealous."

It lightened the moment. "Don't be," she said. "He's gonna itch like crazy for about five minutes. The heat of the water will release all the remaining histamine in his system. But then he won't itch again for several hours. One of those wives' tales that actually works." She got up and went to the under-counter drawer and found a foil packet of antihistamine tablets. She broke two out of their sealed holder and handed them to McCarthy. Then she found a glass and filled it with water from the sink. "Give me a hand with him, will you?" she said.

They got him up and sitting, and after a good deal of convincing, watched him swallow the two pills.

"*Ugh.*" He grimaced as the bitter-tasting pills went down his throat. Then they stood him up fully and half-dragged, half-carried him to the small drain room, where together they stripped off his toga, socks and sandals. McCarthy took Midas, who whined pitifully on being separated from his master. He stood outside the drain room door, cradling the trembling little dog, looking away while Gina hosed the scratching Harpo from top to bottom with steaming hot water. The only thing remaining on his body was the necklace. When McCarthy had tried to remove it before the hosing, Harpo nearly went mad on him, so McCarthy had let it be.

Ω Ω Ω

Harpo sat on a stack of mats in one of the sleeping rooms, rocking slowly back and forth. The red welt was now a small pink dot. He remembered the bemused looks that Gina and McCarthy had exchanged as he explained to them that the arrows were an aphrodisiac to mortals, but poisonous to a god. Gina had dismissed it all as nonsense, with cynical words about there being no gods. McCarthy, he recalled, had just stood there, shaking his head.

The dog shivered at his chest, and Harpo rubbed him comfortingly. "I have made a mess of things, Small One," he said. "No one believes a thing I say. Why, one would think I were Kassandra."

He looked around at the dirty walls and the cracked concrete floor of the shelter. "But it seems a very small mess compared to what *they* have done here . . . I cannot understand what has happened to Earth."

He tucked the dog back into his toga. "And this woman is a mystery to me. Of one thing I am sure—we can no longer stay here in this dungeon. We must go back to the box again, no matter how foul. Here we are trapped in these small rooms, this darkness, this squalor. With that pink menace to attack us with his hateful arrows! And it is useless to try to bring her into the fold here, for she is much too distracted."

He did not speak of his dismay on hearing her declaration of non-belief.

"But we will follow her," he said, "and we will try our best to bring her to enlightenment. And when I get my hands on the Fair One's irritating little flea of a son, I will pluck out his wings, one feather at a time."

$$\Omega\ \Omega\ \Omega$$

McCarthy wet the tips of two fingers and squashed the glowing wick of the melted candle; the "party's over" smell filled the room. Their spilled plates were on the floor next to the desk and Gina was on her hands and knees with paper towels trying to clean up the mess. McCarthy joined her, and in a few minutes the floor was once again restored to its previous state of quasi-cleanliness.

When the yellow paper tablecloth was crumpled into the wastebasket, Gina slumped down in her chair. "Never a dull moment in this place, even when I think things are under control."

McCarthy agreed. "Yep, just like being a cop. Always something to distract you."

"Did you notice anything unusual about Harpo?" she said.

"That's a loaded question. Got a day?"

"No, seriously. About his—*body*. I don't know, maybe a man wouldn't notice."

"What wouldn't we notice?"

"That he was a little too—what's the word I want here—*perfect*?"

He tilted his head. "I'm not sure I follow you."

"Well, to begin, he's so white."

"Gina," McCarthy said, "he's a white guy. I can speak with some authority on that. We're white all over."

"Don't be a smart ass, McCarthy. When I say white, I don't really mean skin color—he's pretty olive. He looks Middle Eastern. I mean, I get that sense when I look at him with his clothes *on*. It's more about essence than color. Undressed he seems—almost alabaster, like marble. His skin is more consistently perfect than anyone I've ever seen."

"My grandfather was so white he was almost blue."

"But did he have freckles or moles or anything like that?"

"Are you kidding? I think he invented freckles."

"Well, Harpo didn't have *one*. Not a mole, not a freckle, not a blemish of any kind. Except the bite mark on his hand. And that's already mostly gone. When I'm showering the guys who come in here, I pay attention to their skin because it reveals a lot about their general health. I'm telling you, McCarthy, this guy lives somewhere, probably some kind of palace. These men are generally frail, with lots of open sores, because in cold weather they don't heal. Their feet are almost always cracked and bleeding. This guy looks like a goddamned statue, he's so perfect. He has the tightest *tush* I've seen on a bum yet."

Feigning offense, McCarthy said, "I *didn't* notice that."

"I couldn't tell whether he's circumcised, he had his hands in the way."

"Did not notice that either, don't really want to know."

"Understandable. But it's my job to notice that stuff, in context, anyway. And something else is very weird here. That gash he got only a little over twenty-four hours ago is almost completely healed."

"Cut it out."

"I'm not kidding. Did you take a picture before you brought him here?"

"No."

"Damn. I didn't either before I dressed the wound. But it's already healed. He's way too healthy for someone you'd find living in the Freezer."

"So what are you going to do?"

"I don't know. He doesn't have any papers at all. I can do some computer work. I might be able to find something on him."

"Maybe you should ask Miranda to take a look."

"I plan to. It really wouldn't surprise me if someone's looking for *him*, maybe there's already a listing in Missing Persons. And I think I should probably do it pretty quickly. He's too soft to survive out there."

"Attila the Hun is too soft to survive out there."

The radio clipped onto his epaulet started beeping and vibrating. McCarthy reached up and pressed a button, then listened.

Gina watched his expression morph as they heard a code announced, and then the words *officer down*. Losing not a second, McCarthy pushed himself up off the chair.

"I'm outta here." He leaned over and surprised her with a quick kiss on the cheek.

"McCarthy . . ." she called after him. "Be careful . . ."

But her words disappeared down the hallway. He was already out the door.

Chapter 6
Zeta

Harpo shuffled compliantly behind Freddie, allowing himself to be led. "*Unghhh*," he moaned as they ascended the stairs into the stark daylight. "I feel a great pounding, as though Hephaestus were using my skull for his forge."

"Raw goat withdrawal," Freddie said with a smirk.

Harpo pressed one hand to his forehead. "Please! The thought of food, even such a delicacy, only makes it worse. And I cannot even describe how my belly feels. Is this the feeling of hunger? If so, it is to be avoided."

"Sounds like you mighta just had too many chips last night. Judging by that fart you let. Stomach aches aren't my thing, anyway. Now headaches—there I can help you. Tell you what, I'd douse it with a booze."

"With what?'"

"*Sheesh*," Freddie said. "You're supposed to be the god of wine and you don't understand booze? You know, liquor. Beer or wine."

"Douse? Do you mean to say that you pour wine on your head?"

"No, *no*," he said, exasperated. "Down my *throat*. It gets to my head on its own after that. You know, through the stomach."

"*Ugh*. A tortured journey, no doubt."

The air outside was crisp and after a number of good, deep breaths he felt tolerably sound again. They stood in the same door well two buildings away from the intake center, waiting for Gina to pass. In a few moments she walked briskly by, burdened with her customary canvas bags. They fell in behind her, adjusting the pace of their pursuit until she was far enough ahead of them that she would not hear them, but never far enough away to risk losing her.

"There is so much about you mortals that I do not understand!" They crossed at a corner, then he continued. "This woman: why does she spend so much time with these—these *indigents?*"

"Hey, watch it, *Harpo*," Freddie said, "you're hanging out with one of those indigents."

"There. You see? You admit it yourself. And you cannot even remember my real name!"

"Your real name is stupid. Ah, crap, I mean *challenged*. And I seem to be good enough for *you*."

"For the moment."

Freddie muttered under his breath. "All this just so I can do a damn tax return."

They settled in on a stoop across from Gina's apartment building.

"We shall follow her again if she leaves with the man," Harpo said.

"Aw," Freddie protested, "didn't we already settle this? You know she's just gonna come back."

"I wish to know more about this place she goes with him."

Their negotiation came to abrupt end when Gina emerged from the building, once again in the company of the blank-faced man they'd seen the day before.

"She is leading him more than walking beside him," Harpo observed. "He walks unsteadily." He took it all in, the slight shuffle in his gait, his blank look, Gina's careful supervision of his rigid movements. It was plain to him that the man depended on her entirely for guidance.

"Does this woman do nothing but care for others?" he asked.

"Dunno."

"And who cares for her?"

"I dunno that either."

A number of blocks later the woman led her companion into the same building as the day before. Harpo stared up at the sign. "I cannot understand the letters," he said. "Beta, omicron, omicron, kappa . . ." Through the clear front he could see hundreds upon hundreds of squarish objects bound in colorful flat shells, all with lettering, some with images. "Perhaps these things provide some form of nourishment," he speculated.

Freddie laughed and explained what they were.

"Ah!" Harpo said. "Then I was right."

Ω Ω Ω

When Gina had David settled into the first tasks of his routine, she walked slowly through the colorful stacks of books toward Randy's office. She found David's cousin already poring over a spreadsheet with such concentration that he didn't see her. She tapped on his open office door and gave him a little wave when he looked up. "Just wanted to say hi."

"Good morning," Randy said. "Did you guys walk over?"

"We did. It's cold out, but it's beautiful, a lot nicer than yesterday."

Randy changed his focused expression to something that might pass for a smile. "I assume David's already hard at work on the wastebaskets."

"That he is," Gina said.

"How were things with him today? You know, I mean after . . . the disruption yesterday."

"He was a little fidgety this morning, but it wasn't as bad as I expected. By the way, on Friday he has an earlier appointment. I'll be taking him out of here about 3:30."

Randy sat back in his chair and cupped his hands behind his head. "So how's it going with his doctor?"

"He's as—*meticulous* as ever," she said. "He'll be doing a series of outpatient tests Friday, no brain scans this time. Mostly verbal tests, word associations, that sort of thing. He'll also take some blood to check the medication levels. He says it takes a while to get him up to speed."

Randy commented, "So far he seems to be tolerating this med pretty well."

Her expression darkened. "Physically, yeah. We'll get the numbers a few days after the tests and then we'll know what's up."

"Well, keep me posted. I'm always keeping my fingers crossed."

"I know, Randy. Me, too." She smiled at him and stifled a small yawn. "Well, I'd better go get some sleep. I'll see you later."

"The usual time today?"

"The usual." She waved good-bye and left the office, walking through the stacks in reverse alphabetical order, picking out familiar, beloved names as she progressed. *Lessing, Kafka, James, Ishiguro. Next time I'll take a different row,* she thought, *maybe the bottom end of the alphabet.*

She moved through fiction and found herself suddenly in the MYTH section. She stopped and perused the offerings for a few moments. Her hand settled on a thick tome.

Her finger worked down the index pages through the D's, and finally stopped at the section for Dionysus. There were several sub-listings, each with its own column of chapter numbers. *Too much to look at now,* she thought, and for a moment she considered buying the book. With the discount Randy gave her, it wouldn't break her week's budget. *But it would be just my luck to buy it and find out who he really is the next day.* She tucked the book back in the stack, and decided on the library should it be needed.

She found David and gave him a kiss good bye. David seemed almost bothered, as if it were an unwelcome interruption in his strict routine. *No time for a kiss, got a whole store full of baskets to empty.* It made Gina sad.

Ω Ω Ω

They followed her back home, stopping for a bag of chips on the way, and settled back into their vigil.

"You stay far enough away so I don't have to catch your farts," he said. "And let's sit on the other side, it's sunny. Warmer."

"This is wise," Harpo said. "The rays of Helios seem to come only rarely to this city. You know, I am led to wonder if perhaps the inhabitants have not made proper sacrifice to him. If they did, he might be more inclined to visit."

"It used to be worse," Freddie said. "Less sunlight, when the towers were there."

Harpo looked around. "And these towers are no longer here?"

Freddie sat upright. "You keep saying stuff like this. Like you don't know about the Twin Towers."

"Sadly, I am ignorant."

"You'd *have* to be. Two huge buildings, side by side, way up into the clouds. They're gone." He glanced in the direction of where the towers once stood. "They started building again, but it's only gonna be one this time. I never thought I'd say this, but the thing I miss most about them is the shadows. You could almost tell the time of day by where the shadows fell."

"These were temples?"

"I guess they were, sort of, but not like a church or anything. They were temples to business and hard working-people."

Then his eyes narrowed. "It was a whole bunch of guys looked *just like you* that took 'em down. Dark hair, you know, oily, accent. Yeah. *Just like you.* Only when they did it they dressed up like normal people. And they killed a whole lot of *really* normal people."

"But surely you must know that I as a god could never do such an unholy thing—"

"I don't know nothing." He sat back, as if composing himself. He seemed lost in memories. "I used to work in the North tower. My company was lucky, cuz everybody got out. But I knew a lot of people that *didn't.* I knew some of the guys who took care of the place. They mostly died." His head drooped down and he rubbed his forehead.

It was clear, even to Harpo, that comments and questions were not appropriate in that moment.

Finally, Freddie emerged from his darkness. "Oh, well. Life goes on, I guess."

"Indeed. For some of us, it goes on forever. But I would ask—these were men from another country?"

"From a couple of countries. Mostly they were Arabs."

"Ah. A nomadic people. Bedouins, in my time. They had the finest large tents. Very well appointed."

"Not so much anymore. Now they got skyscrapers and jets and all sorts of stuff. And they got money, lots of it. But it's not enough for them. They want the whole world. At least the bad ones do. Most of them, they're good people. They just want to be left alone, live their lives, work, raise families. But there's some of them . . . they kill everyone who disagrees with them. Three thousand people died. Just cuz they hate us."

"But why should they hate you?"

Freddie paused. "Because we have our own religions. They want us to have *their* religion. Pray to their god. And the thing is, *their* god says he's their government. Makes laws they have to follow. We don't do it like that here. Our government can't tell you how to pray. They don't like it that we can pray any way we want. Or not at all, I we don't wanna pray."

And for a moment, it was Harpo who remained silent, considering the implications of Freddie's statement. Finally, he said, "Surely your rulers have sought retribution."

"They're tryin'. In all the wrong places. So far they got nothing."

"Then it must be difficult for you to clear the memory of these towers from your psyche."

"You don't even want to know."

Freddie went pensive, but after a time, he shook it off. "I got a question for you, Mr. God." He tore open the bag of chips and popped one into his mouth. "Who do I have to sacrifice to if I want to get another job?" He offered the open bag to Harpo.

As he chewed a chip himself, Harpo considered the question. "Most likely my sister, holy Athena. She rules over tradesmen and those who work at crafts, all artisans and the like."

"Well, I was pretty artistic with DeMoula Wine Importer's books. So how do I get started? If I can get a god on my side, might help me get my shit back together."

"Goddess," Harpo corrected, "and you would do well not to make light of her influence. She may look upon you with disfavor, and worsen your situation."

"Like it could get any worse." He stood up and stretched. "I don't wanna sit here anymore. Let's go."

Harpo looked back nervously at Gina's door. "I think perhaps I shall wait here."

"Suit yourself," Freddie said. "But you don't have to wait here because you're afraid of losing her. She's not coming out. She does the same thing every day. Day after day."

Harpo pondered for a moment the notion of waiting for Gina alone, and found it distasteful.

"I will accompany you."

"Well, all right."

He got up and ran after Freddie, who was already two buildings ahead.

"Same thing, day after day," he mused. "No wonder they die."

Ω Ω Ω

They came upon a large area with a wrought-iron fence. There were benches; most were free of snow. Freddie led the way and they sat down in sunlight.

"Tompkins Square," Freddie said. "Whole lotta hippies used to camp out here in the sixties and seventies. You shoulda seen it, it was wild. They did these sit-ins and protests all the time, sometimes they had these great big parties where they danced and played music. All the women had these long dresses and flowers in their hair. They danced around like they were crazy sometimes. It was somethin'."

Harpo sat taller. "But—this is precisely how I am worshipped!"

Freddie considered this. "Nah," he said. "We used to live not too far from here. I never saw goats."

"In the same type of abode as you have now?"

"No, an apartment. You know, inside a building. Like Gina does."

For a moment Harpo sat quiet and watched the people passing by. Then he turned to Freddie and said, "If you did not always live like this, how was it that you came into such poverty?"

"It's a long story," Freddie said.

"I may have all of eternity."

"Well, in that case . . ." He stretched out, then began. "When I worked in one of the towers, I used to be an accountant, and I kept . . ."

"Wait," Harpo said, "What is an *accountant*?"

"Oh, come on. You can't be that clueless. You know, a numbers guy. I kept the books for different people."

"Books such as those in the bookstore?"

"Well, sort of, but those books have words. The ones I kept had numbers."

"Strange," Harpo said. "How does one read numbers?"

"No!" Freddie said in frustration. "Not the kind of books you read, the financial kind."

"Financial? I do not—"

"Aargh!" Freddie shrieked. "You're making me *crazy* with these stupid questions! Crap. I mean *challenged*. Okay, I'm gonna try again. Don't interrupt. I might lose my train of thought, and then I'll have to start all over."

Looking vaguely hurt, Harpo said, "Perish the thought."

"Yeah, same to you," Freddie said. "I love it so much when *you* go on and on.

An accountant keeps financial records of all the money transactions for a business. My company had different clients, I got assigned to a liquor importer on First Avenue, the guy I told ya before, DeMoula. I worked on this guy's books for a coupla years and everything was great. I was making good money and he loved my ass, my boss at my company was happy . . . then one day this DeMoula asks if I want to make some extra money on the side. I had a kid in college and things were tight, so I said to myself, 'What the fuck?' you know? Lots of guys moonlighted, so . . . But this guy didn't just want me to do *more* books, he wanted me to change the ones he had. So he could cheat on his taxes. So I said no. Then he says, 'I'm gonna hurt your kids if you don't.' I thought he was connected so . . ."

"Connected to what?"

"Who, not what. *Don't interrupt me.* This is important. So what could I do? I fixed his books. Then when the IRS—"

"What is this IRS?"

"Arghhh! They keep track of all the money so the government can get their share. And you're better off not knowing about them anyway. They're bad news. I know, I was an accountant."

"So you have said."

"And when the IRS finally figured out what he was doing and called him in he told them it was my idea, that I told him I could work it out so he'd get a lot of free money out of the business and we could split it. Lied like a son of a bitch in court. He got off with nothing and I took the whole fall. So my wife left me, took the kids and moved all the way to California. I lost everything."

Harpo stood and began to pace. "But this is very terrible!"

"You betcha."

"And this California, is it another nation?"

"They *act* like it is," Freddie said. "It's just a state, though, out west. Real nice place, too. Warm all the time."

"Then why would anyone choose to live *here?*"

"Beats the hell out of me. Maybe because this place is run by a bunch of liberal fucks and you can get away with almost anything here."

"Please explain lib—"

"Never mind!" He coughed into his half-gloved hand. "Ain't *no* explanation for them. But anyway, here I am. Nice place to land after being on top to the world, huh? It was my own fault, really, I shoulda known what he was talking about when he first came to me. Too good to be true, you know what I mean? My mother always told me, rest in peace, if something seemed too good to be true, then it probably *wasn't* true. Shoulda just moved my family to California *myself.*" He sighed and gave Harpo a haggard-looking smile.

Harpo considered this tale for a few moments. "Let me see if I understand you correctly. You kept the tablets of record for a wine merchant so that he could pay proper tribute to the ruler—"

Freddie corrected him. "We don't have rulers. We just have a government."

"Rulers govern, do they not?"

"Yeah, I suppose they do, but we don't call—"

"This merchant then forced you, by *moonlight,* to cheat the—uh, government out of the proper tribute—"

"Taxes," Freddie corrected him. "And I did it at night after I finished my other work, that's why I called it—"

"Call it what you will! He forced you to do his bidding by taking your children hostage? By all the Gods, you must have been a man of much influence and learning for your children to be so valuable! Were you a noble before you became poor?"

"No, no, *no!"* Freddie said, exasperated by his companion's quirks of comprehension. "He didn't take them hostage. He just threatened to hurt them. And he knew all the right bad guys, so I took him seriously. And you don't have to be a noble to get educated here. Lots of poor people get educated."

"Remarkable," Harpo said, rubbing his chin as he pondered Freddie's revelations. "So when your crime was discovered, you were both called for judgment. The merchant lied to save himself, and those in power allowed him to do so?"

"In a nutshell, yep."

"But this is an outrage! Why did you not swear an oath of your innocence?"

"I did! A hundred times on a stack of Bibles. But the other guy didn't have anything to lose by lying. I had my family to think about. It cost me almost everything to pay a lawyer."

"What is a lawyer?"

Freddie looked at him in disbelief. "Oh, man, your people must be *really* thick. A lawyer speaks to a judge to help convince 'em you didn't do what you're accused of doing. Or convince them that you didn't do it even if you did. Which was sort of the case in my situation. I did fix his books, and like I said, I shoulda known better. Anyway, I don't think my lawyer was too good, since I went to jail anyway."

"You were *imprisoned?* For *someone else's* crime?"

"You got it. Did a year. Got out a little more than a year ago."

Sensing his master's agitation, Midas began to growl. Harpo opened the front of his toga and said, "Indeed, Small One, this is beyond understanding." He looked back at Freddie. "Did no one step forward to champion you? No patron, or priest, or an orator perhaps?"

"Yeah, my priest stood up for me. Told 'em what a fine upstanding citizen I was, good father, taking care of my mother, altar boy, all that shit. It didn't do any good. But, hey, Harpo, like the song says, nobody knows you when you're down and out. And you know what? I'm gonna get back on my feet one of these days. After I get through leading you around, Gina's gonna let me do her tax return. It'll be good practice. I'll sacrifice to this—uh . . ."

"Athena."

"Yeah. Her." He sighed, sadly.

Harpo shook his head. "In my home, such trickery against mortals can only be carried out by the gods, and then it is done as mischief, not the evil plot you have suffered. When mortals do wrong to other mortals, it is the duty of the gods to intervene, and if we have the power, we do. In the end, the truth always comes out, for it is the most important thing."

His expression turned serious. "I have been reminded of its importance only recently. I tried to tell my Lord Father an untruth, and it is because of this that I was banished. I do not know why the Fates decided I should land here, but here I am. Perhaps, in view of your tale, I have been sent here to protect *you*."

"Oh, yeah, you're gonna protect me. It's written in the stars, all right. *It's mandated by your religion*. We still got other kinds of people here who try to make you behave like their religion says. Makes a big mess, let me tell you."

Freddie popped a couple of chips into his mouth and crunched noisily. "So. That's my story. What happened to you?"

Harpo sighed and glanced downward at the sidewalk. "It is an even longer tale. But no less unfortunate. Another time I shall tell you, but I fear you will think me simply mad as all the others do."

"I don't really give a shit if you're nuts," Freddie said. "And anyway, you know what? I'm still hungry."

"But we have no more vouchers."

"I know. I guess I'll have to panhandle. Unless you want to."

Harpo looked again at the people passing by, and decided against it. "Perhaps your experience will give you better success."

Chapter 7
Eta

When she came out later that afternoon, Gina found them sound asleep and leaning against one another at the bottom of the stoop. There was an empty potato chip bag on the sidewalk at Freddie's feet.

Great, she thought, *brain food.* She picked up the bag and crumpled it into a little ball, then stuffed it into her tote bag for later disposal. Oddly, she was only a *bit* disturbed to find them there.

But why had they followed her?

She looked down at Harpo, remembering his implausible perfection from the previous night's hosing. *There's just something about him,* she thought. *There has to be a story here, a good one.*

Or a very bad and dangerous one. She leaned over and tapped him lightly on the shoulder.

"Harpo?"

He came awake instantly and leapt up to his feet.

"*Whoa,* slow down there," she said, stepping back a little. "Sorry, I didn't mean to startle you."

Teetering slightly, he bowed. "I greet you," he said.

"Well, thanks, I greet you, too. But let yourself wake up a little bit. Then maybe you should tell me why you're here."

He was momentarily flustered and seemed to grope for an explanation. "I have come to escort you," he finally said.

"To where?"

Same thing, day after day. "Uh—mm, to your center."

"Ordinarily I would appreciate that but I'm not going there right now."

"Then I will escort you wherever you are going now."

"You're very kind, but I can't accept. I have to bring my boyfriend back home first. But when I go to the center later you can keep me company on the way, if you want to."

Same thing, day after day. "I will wait," he said nervously.

"Okay, good. I'll be back in a little while."

Ω Ω Ω

Every few seconds he glanced in the direction of her departure, as if his nervousness would make her return more quickly. He was at the point of wandering out to find her when she appeared on the next block, accompanied by the same blank-faced man as before. He shook Freddie awake. "They are back."

Freddie stretched and yawned, then leaned up on his elbows. "Told you."

"She smiles and speaks to the man," Harpo said, "yet he seems not to hear her. What do you make of this?"

"Not much," Freddie said. "That's your gig, remember?"

They were only a few steps away, so Harpo held back his annoyance. He watched with curiosity as Gina gently turned David toward them.

"David, this is Harpo," she said, "and Freddie."

They both stood up. The tall, thin man called David looked at Freddie momentarily, collecting his image, but his eyes did not dwell. He turned quickly to Harpo.

"I greet you," Harpo said. David looked at him with great intensity, and seemed poised on the edge of speech, but nothing came. Harpo felt a distinct wave of assessment pass through him as David took his image in, processed it, and then just as quickly discarded it again.

Gina shrugged apologetically. "He's a little tired, I guess. I'm going to take him inside and get him settled for the night. Then after that I'll be going to the center." She led David up the stairs.

"He is mad, this boyfriend of hers," Harpo said to Freddie as the door swung shut behind her.

"No shit," Freddie said. He shook his head sadly. "He got hit by a piece of granite when the towers came down. Too bad."

"And this brought on his madness?"

"Well, he had a head injury from the impact. And lots of the guys who worked there that day had post-traumatic stress syndrome, and before you say you don't understand, it means that he's sad and angry and upset and confused and afraid and he can't get it all out of his brain."

Harpo pondered the explanation, then shrugged. "He cannot clear his psyche."

"Yeah, that."

"She is surrounded by madness, this woman."

"Guess so."

"This is not necessarily a bad thing. Why, my almighty father Zeus visited madness upon a fair number of mortals. Some of them came to view it as a divine gift. It can be a very useful thing."

Freddie *hmphed*. "That hasn't been my experience."

"Bu surely you have heard of the mighty Odysseus! He feigned madness so that he would not have to leave his family to go to war."

"The first draft dodger," Freddie observed with a yawn.

"What?" Harpo said. "I—"

"Never mind. I'm just being a smart ass."

"Indeed, more ass than smart, I think. You know, my own worshipers once drove themselves purposefully into frenzies of *ecstasis* in my adoration, and I can tell you, they were plentiful in number. But here, the demented are loathed and feared. Why?"

The door *whooshed* open behind them and the question hung unanswered. Gina descended the stairs, moving at her own unencumbered pace. But as they started walking away from her building, Harpo noticed that she adjusted her pace again, this time to correspond with what she seemed to think Freddie could match. And as always, she carried things.

"May I help you with your burdens?" Harpo said.

"Oh, thanks," she said. "I get pretty tired of carting all this crap around with me." She handed him one of the two canvas tote bags she carried to and from work every day. He extended his hand, offering to take the other, but she held onto it. "That's my computer," she said. "I think I'll carry it myself."

"I do not understand this computer."

Her expression lightened. "Then you're not alone in this world."

"Would that that were true," he mused. He faced her directly and said, "Earlier I sensed your hesitation to allow me to accompany you. You must not be afraid of me, for I have only the most honorable intentions toward you. And I do not require that you readjust yourself to suit me, as you seem to do for others."

To his great surprise, she smiled and said, "Oh, I'm not afraid of you, Harpo. I can take care of myself. And I assure you, I have no intention of doing any additional 'adjusting'—I do quite enough already. But I'd love to get to know you better."

Her interest excited him, and he failed to notice when she and Freddie both stopped walking. Suddenly he felt himself stumbling. Gina reached out and grabbed hold of him; they teetered on the edge of balance for a moment before settling back onto the curb. A yellow cab whizzed by at deadly speed, just barely missing him.

She steadied him with both hands. *"Watch where you're going!* Look at the walk sign before you cross the street. You could have been killed!"

He reddened with embarrassment, then raised his chin indignantly. "I cannot be killed, for I am immortal."

But she was shaking, her voice angry. "*Fine.* But I'd appreciate it if you didn't tempt fate."

"The Fates—"

"*Don't* try to talk your way out of this. *Look* before you cross the street."

He bowed and apologized. "But what should I look for?"

It was a completely innocent question. She pointed at the rectangular black box on the light post. "If it shows a person walking, you walk. If it shows a yellow hand, you don't."

"Ah," he said, "Indeed."

He looked dutifully up at the sign, and Gina knew from his expression that it all meant nothing to him. By sheer luck, he had managed to avoid being killed. She stunned herself by thinking, for one brief moment, he *is* immortal.

Ω Ω Ω

"Nice haircut," she said to Mike.

"Thanks. I'm flattered you noticed," he said.

"Hey, you're the Keeper of the Shrink. I *have* to flatter you if I want to see him."

"Good point."

"So. When I bring David in on Friday, can I get about five minutes extra? There's another matter I want to discuss with Aaron. About another patient."

"A patient of Aaron's?"

He was so protective. And it was no wonder; once a firefighter, Mike was one of Aaron's most amazing successes. He had been pulled from the rubble of the South Tower, physically intact; over the next two weeks he'd taken his turn on the pile. The things he saw brought him to the edge of suicide, but Aaron had brought him back. And when Aaron's personal assistant moved away to care for aging parents, Mike had begged for the job. And got it.

"He's not his patient yet," Gina said. "But potentially. Someone new at the center. I'm having a hard time placing him, or figuring him out at all."

He typed a few commands into the keyboard and brought up Aaron's schedule. "You're the last appointment already," he said. "I can just add another five minutes onto it." Poised to type again, he said, "Who does the bill go to?"

Oh, that. "I'm not sure yet. If I can't work it out before then, I'll pay and go for reimbursement."

"OK, you're all set, then," he said, tapping a few keys. "See you Friday."

Ω Ω Ω

What a loathsome task, she thought as she opened the envelope in which the grant forms were stored. *Formalized begging,* she'd once said to Miranda.

No one else had wanted the space her intake center occupied. *Well, it was once part of the morgue . . .* There were hoses and small rooms and a decent floor with drains. She'd done a fair amount of the reconstruction herself, with the help of her Amazon sister Diane. And in the short time she'd had it, the place had become more home to her than home. Here she was free to dedicate herself to the well-being of men who were too scared, soft, or introverted to go the eight-hundred bed homeless shelter in Bellevue's original building. On her own terms. Some of them she'd been able to help; some of them she had not. Her failures only made her work harder.

When the night's sacrifice to the grant god was complete, Gina shoved all the papers into the same big envelope and put it away in her desk. Then she plugged in her computer and logged into the City's main social services database. She typed in "Isus", then "Esus", but there were no matches for any person with that name or anything close.

With a sigh of frustration, she typed in a couple of spellings that seemed too bizarre to work, and was not surprised when they didn't. It was completely implausible to her that any person could exist in this world without making it into *some* database, but she was beginning to believe that this man had done it. After a protracted round of fruitless searching, she closed the cover on the laptop, folded her arms on top of it, and fell asleep.

Ω Ω Ω

She heard the jangling of the bracelets before anything else, and then the sultry voice.

"Yo, Cave woman! Anybody home?"

She came awake and saw Miranda standing in the doorway with a very annoyed look on her face.

"I've been trying to call you for an hour."

Gina pulled out her phone and saw the missed calls. "No bars."

"The guy who got shot, he's gonna be okay."

"Wow. Thank God. McCarthy ran out of here like a rocket when he got the call."

"Another gang banger, they said, trying to get his ticket."

There was nothing to be said on that subject; her records were full of men who had failed to make the cut into their "communities." They'd grown older, less cool, less connected, and had nowhere to go when the young Turks took over.

Many of them, she thought, were better off homeless than in those gangs.

"You all right? You're quiet."

"It's quiet *here* tonight. I did a little computer research. I dozed off."

Miranda glanced up at the cracked ceiling and frowned disapprovingly. "If I had an hour to kill, I wouldn't be digging around in the computer."

Gina smiled. "No doubt you'd find something much more intriguing to do."

"You bet your ass I would." She pointed upward. "After I patched that ceiling. Anyway, listen, I took a look at the missing persons list like you asked me to."

Gina sat up in anticipation. "And?"

"Naturally, there were a shitload of them. But I sorted the list and printed out a report for all the men between the ages of thirty-five and fifty-five." She handed over a multi-page printout.

Gina unfolded the list and took a quick look through it, then looked up at Miranda in dismay. "There are *still* a shitload."

"Yeah, but once you get into the particulars, you can probably eliminate a lot of them right away. There are a couple hundred husbands on the hoof on that list. But I didn't want to take anyone off, on the chance that it might be your guy."

Gina's eyes scanned the list hungrily. "I would really like to get into this database myself some time. I mean, think about it—everything is so connected, so available. Just waiting. The web has everything that's everything. You know, I *could* probably get in without too much effort."

Miranda shook her head disapprovingly. "You are a conniving and dangerous woman, Regina Bugbee."

"Don't I wish."

With a dismissive wave, Miranda said, "Since *when* do you wish *that?*"

"Oh, I don't know." Gina put the printout down on her desk. "A lot, lately, I guess. I mean, think about it. Here I am getting all excited about this whacked-out weirdo. Who bears a remarkable resemblance to a lot of known terrorists. And I'm thinking about how much fun it would be to break into a police computer system. Something kids with pimples do when they're not busy jerking off." She crossed her arms in front of her chest and said, "At least it's something I can do without David."

"David or no, you're entitled to have some fun every now and then."

"Yeah, but I always feel like I'm cheating on him if I have fun without him."

"Oh, *please*. It's only really cheating if there's sex. And if you don't mind me asking, how long has it been since you had sex?"

After a brief pause, Gina said, "I *do* mind you asking."

"Okay, sorry, let me rephrase the question. How long has it been since you had sex?"

"Oh, that's a lot better. I like *that* phrasing."

Miranda sat and waited for Gina to answer, her fingers counting out the seconds on the desktop. When no answer came, she said, "That long, *hmm*?"

Gina folded her arms on the desk and put her head down on them, then drew herself back up slowly, with a long sigh. "When he first got out of the hospital, it seemed like all we did was have sex. Night and day, seven days a week. It was a *schtupfest*. I don't know how I managed not to get pregnant. Then when he started taking his first medication, it just stopped. A side effect. I remember feeling a little relieved then. I don't feel that way anymore."

Miranda's voice softened. "Look, Gina, you can't keep living like this. I know it's hard, what you're going through. But it's five years now. *Five years*. One of these nights I'm gonna come down here and find nothing but your feet sticking out of the computer screen. Hopefully I'll be able to yank you back out again."

Gina remained silent, staring intently at a pattern of freckles on her arm.

"Well?" Miranda demanded.

"Well, *what?*" Gina answered, her face back on her folded arms again, her voice muffled.

"Well, do you agree? You *better*. You know I'm right. And I *know* you know. And I'm sure Aaron's telling you the same thing."

"Every time I'm in there."

"Well, I'm not terribly impressed with the way you're listening. Does he also tell you that you cannot let your situation with David suck every bit of life you have out of you?"

"Yes, he does."

"He's right." Then she softened her voice. "And do you really think David's going to know if you have a little fun every now and then?" She reached out and touched Gina's arm and instantly felt the tightness. "Hell, Honey," she said, her voice full of sympathy, "David doesn't even know he's David anymore."

$$\Omega \ \Omega \ \Omega$$

It was David who now sat in the chair in front of Aaron's desk. "Gina told me your stomach is doing a little better."

David's eyes shifted back and forth. He concentrated for a few moments, a look of struggle on his face. "Mrs. Miller brought me meatloaf," he finally said.

Aaron kept the thread going. "Was it good?"

Several seconds passed. "Mrs. Miller makes good meatloaf."

Aaron cast a glance at Gina, whose pained look betrayed the costly effort of restraining herself from plunging in. Then he turned back toward David, probed further. There were brief questions, equally brief answers, sometimes pertinent, sometimes not.

After a short while it became apparent that David was beginning to tire. "I think we've had a good talk today, but I'd like you to go with Mike to a lab down the hall, just a short way. He'll stay with you while the technician takes a sample of your blood from your arm. Gina is going to stay here while you go."

The door opened and Mike came inside, answering the buzz.

Miraculously, David did not resist. Gina watched anxiously as the pair left the office, and only after she'd heard the outer door close did she relax.

"One of the things I like about Mike is that he inspires trust, despite his size."

"Somehow it doesn't jibe with the linebacker image."

"That just gives more credence to the notion that one can't judge a book by its cover. Anyway, getting back to David. I think there's good news and bad news here."

Without waiting for him to ask, Gina said, "Bad."

Aaron smiled, then got serious. "His response level is not what I'd hoped for. Either his depression is stagnant or perhaps worsening a bit. We'll know when the blood tests come back if the meds are at the correct level. I also want him to have another CT scan to make sure the clot is stable."

Ω Ω Ω

It would not be his first CT scan; that had happened on the day the future arrived.

As she watched the door close behind David at 8:55 that morning, a plea hung on her lips: *Please. Don't go.*

But he was preparing himself to specialize in trauma, and there would be no stopping him. When he got to the site, the Towers were still standing, but the pavement was already littered with bodies; it was blood that marked the landing spots; the bodies themselves were nearly beyond recognition.

And when one landed ten feet from him, the unholy sound and the twisted red smear stunned him. He turned away, vomited, dropped to his knees. Crawling through the shards, David made his way to the victim. Part by part, limb by limb, he reverently reassembled that poor soul, then covered it all with his own white coat.

Ω Ω Ω

As time went by, and the worst came to pass, Gina heard nothing from David.

Her face masked, she headed toward the site, walking through the crowds of dust-covered escapees, so many of whom tried to turn her around. Her Bellevue ID did her no good; she was finally halted several blocks north.

83

Please, my fiancée— New York Downtown, she was told, *that's where they're taking them.* She ran there, through swirling clouds of debris, screaming sirens, unimaginable chaos, into the dusty lobby. She went from gurney to gurney through the triage area, not finding him, and tried desperately to locate someone who could tell her if victims were already in surgery. No one could tell her anything.

Is there a list of the known dead?

That, there was. And David's name was on it. They'd found the body with his ID in the pocket of the coat. For more than twenty hours, Gina believed that David was dead, that he had died in the most horrific way possible. Positive identification procedures were the farthest thing from anyone's mind in those early hours. *Get them out first, save them if you can, then figure out who they really are.* That was the *modus operandi.*

She stayed at New York Downtown, side by side with true heroes, helping where she could, through a veil of tears that would not stop. Hours later, exhausted, covered in blood and dust, she trudged home, and found the light flashing on her answering machine.

Oh dear God please . . .

It was one of his fellow Bellevue interns. *He's here, he's alive . . .*

A firefighter later told her, as David could not tell her anything himself, not immediately, that when the South Tower collapsed, a jagged football of concrete had hit him in the head.

To Gina, the Bellevue neurosurgeon who opened his skull, removed the initial blood clot, and then reassembled his dented skull again, was nothing short of a god.

So many times, she had asked herself why *any* god would let this horrible thing happen. Wiser people than she had never been able to answer that question.

Ω Ω Ω

Aaron drew in a very long breath, one that a yoga teacher might refer to as a "cleansing" breath. The first time she'd seen him do it, Gina had wanted to ask if everything was all right, if she should call for help. He'd perceived her discomfort and reassured her. "Most of the time my brain goes faster than my breath will allow me to speak."

The breath completed, he spoke again. "Now the good news. He's making *some* appropriate connections, as with my question about his stomach and his reference to Mrs. Miller's meatloaf. So we know for sure that he's hooking into what's being said around him, on some level. And if the blood tests show more than a certain threshold of the medication, we can notch it down a bit. We'll know the numbers Monday afternoon, likely. Now, before they get back, Mike said you wanted to talk to me about something else. We've got a few minutes right now, so maybe we can take care of it without having to bill for an extended session."

She brightened and sat up straighter. "Right. There's a new man one of the cops brought into the center, and I feel like I should be placing him somewhere, but I can't figure out where. There are a whole bunch of things about him that really make me curious."

Aaron noted her excitement, but disguised his concern. "Tell me about him."

"I almost don't know where to begin," she said. "He had a fight with one of my regulars and got a gash over his eyebrow so they brought him to me for a quick patch up. I cleaned the cut and gave him a routine exam. All the while I'm doing it, he's coming on to me like I was Venus."

"I would imagine that happens a lot."

"More than I'd like, but I think he would have hit on me if I looked like Magilla Gorilla. And he seemed—I don't know how to describe this—out of context, do you know what I mean? Displaced in time or something."

She detailed his accent, his odd clothing, his apparent education, and his uncannily perfect body, the strange bilateral head scars.

"He sounds like someone you'd want at your next dinner party. What is his mental health status, as close as you can judge?"

"Delusional. He claims to be some Greek god, Di -on -I something."

"Dionysus," he said. "Hmm. I did a paper on him in college."

She smiled eagerly. "So you know what I'm talking about, then."

"Well, it was a really long time ago, I hate to say how long . . . I'd have to bring myself up to speed on him."

"But you know the character. So just imagine. He comes in wearing a robe and sandals—"

"Clearly externalizing . . ."

"Stays completely in character, all the time. That gash on his forehead healed in one day, literally. And then the other night there was a seizure of some kind, I think he may have been bitten by a spider and had a bad reaction. He was physically fine in less than an hour and he's been fine since. Anyway, I had to hose him down to lower his temperature. I've never seen a body like that on a homeless guy. He had a very small roll of flesh around the middle, but otherwise, he was as perfect as a marble statue."

"How old would you say he is?"

"I asked him, but he went into this song and dance about being born before the Trojan War. He's got some lines on his face, probably late forties to early fifties."

"Middle aged, in general."

"Yeah. I asked him where he's from, but he just told me it was far away. I spent an hour poking through the City database and a couple of others, and didn't find him anywhere in the system, so he might be telling the truth about that. Maybe you could look in the broader mental health system. You can get in deeper than I can."

"I could, and I'd be happy to do it, but I'll guarantee you that Dionysus is not his real name. It might be his first name, so I *could* get a hit that way. But don't get your hopes up."

"I suspect he's from a very wealthy family and that he's been receiving private treatment of some kind and he just got loose. Or he's a Saudi prince and he's working his way inside so he can blow up Bellevue."

"Please. Don't even whisper that."

"Sorry." She paused for a moment, chastised. "That wasn't funny. Anyway, he has a small dog with him and this dog has a solid gold and jewel studded collar, which is now in my safe, by the way, and a silver and gold necklace that he refuses to allow anyone to remove."

"Hmm," Aaron said. "I wonder why he'd let you take away one item of such obvious value, but insist on keeping something else. He might reveal a few things about himself if we can get him talking about it. Does he show any tendency toward violence?"

"After his initial scuffle with another client, none whatsoever. He's quite polite, almost courtly, even. He can be sarcastic, and sometimes he's very funny. The only thing that has me even slightly worried is the sexual thing, but he backs off immediately when I tell him to."

"I'd like to meet him."

"I was hoping you'd say that," Gina said. "But there's still more I should tell you before you do."

She heard the outer office door. "Remember the other day when I left your office with the shiner and both eyes as swollen as basketballs?"

Aaron nodded. "Sorry."

She was almost frothing in her attempt to get everything out before David reentered. "He placed his fingertips on my eyes for a few seconds and someone told me later they looked perfect. And Aaron, this is the strangest thing of all— he's pretending that he can't read, at least not English. But he speaks it."

The door opened behind them and she turned around. She didn't see the look of growing concern on Aaron's face. As Mike guided David through the door, she became patient, accommodating Gina again, with no signs of the animated interest she'd shown a few seconds earlier. "You're back so soon!" she said, forcing enthusiasm. "How did it go?"

Mike didn't wait for David to answer. "Just fine. David was very cooperative."

"Excellent," Aaron said. "Well, David, are there any questions you want to ask me?"

There were none. There was only the vacant stare, and a small shake of the head.

"Okay, then, I think we're through for today." Aaron nodded, his own equivalent of extending a hand for a farewell shake. "It's been a pleasure seeing you again. Gina will call me for the test results, and we'll know how to proceed then. Take care of yourself."

Gina stood up, and Aaron said quietly, "You need to make two appointments for next week, one for yourself and one for your new client. See you soon."

She hadn't expected to need an appointment for herself for another month. "Nothing for David?"

"No," Aaron said simply. "Not until we have the test results. Mike will schedule the CT scan. After that we'll talk about David."

"OK, you're the shrink."

Ω Ω Ω

Alone in the privacy of his office, Aaron dictated his notes on David into a voice recorder. He made a series of comments about David's responsiveness and what should be done once the tests results were in.

Then he said, "The following comments should be transcribed into Regina Bugbee's record."

He paused for a few moments to put his thoughts in order. "The patient's anxiety level has increased since her last visit. She's developed a personal curiosity about one of her clients, which she knows better than to do. I'm allowing her to bring this new client in for a session to see the two of them together. I'm afraid there may be some reverse transference going on and it's important to get a grip on it early if that's what's happening."

He tapped a key with one of his fingers and the recorder shut itself off. Then he pressed the buzzer, and waited for Mike to come and begin his complex ritual of departure.

Ω Ω Ω

Harpo's about David's height, she thought to herself as she scanned the list Miranda had given her. *But heavier. Five-ten to five-eleven. Weighs maybe one seventy-five, one-eighty.* She went from name to name, assessing the details of each missing man, crossing out those who were too old, too young, too fat, or too short with a heavy line. She made a light pencil line through those whose personal histories indicated that they might be deadbeat dads. She was left with about forty middle-aged, medium-sized, well-educated, dark-haired men.

A third of the way through the remainders she hit what looked to be pay dirt. Klein, was the man's name, a good physical match, and he was a professor at Columbia. *Classics*, she read with a grin. *Missing only a short time.* It was a very neat fit, almost too neat.

There was a phone number for his wife, one Judith Klein. Gina looked up at the clock on the wall. *Too late to call tonight,* she thought. *I'll call first thing in the morning.*

It would be good to have this behind her.

Maybe.

Chapter 8
Theta

Gina's mood brightened as she and her sister exchanged telephone greetings.

"You want to go on a little expedition with me?"

"Where?"

"Columbia. I have to check out a missing person."

An hour later Gina watched her large sister bound through the door of the upper west side bakery where they'd agreed to meet. Diane's bear hug left Gina wheezing for breath. They sat at a small round table and shared a sinful pastry.

"So what's this mystery you have to solve all the way up in the hinterlands?"

Gina put down her coffee cup. "There's this new guy who just started coming into the center, and there might be a Columbia connection. I'm trying to come up with a placement for him but he's being cagey."

"Uh, oh," Diane said. "Watch out, New Guy."

"I don't know . . . he's got me stumped."

She explained his delusional behavior briefly in terms her non-social worker sister would grasp. "Miranda got me the missing persons list for guys of similar age, and there was this Professor of Classics from Columbia on it. I tried to get a hold of his wife, but all I got was a housekeeper who speaks about three words of English. I did manage to figure out that the wife is away, maybe on vacation."

"Your husband is missing and you go on vacation?"

Gina shrugged. "Apparently that's what they do now. I left a message but I don't know if she'll ever get it. I thought if I went up there someone who works with him might be able to give me better information than the MP report has."

"Sounds like something you could accomplish in a phone call. Or on the web. You're so good on the web."

"Yeah, maybe. I've been looking at images with as many descriptors as I can, but nothing really matches. Checked a few databases, but no hits. And anyway I needed to get out. The walls are starting to close in on me."

Diane kept the comments she might have made to herself, knowing they would not be helpful or well received. She wanted to enjoy their visit without delivering the David lecture that was aching to get out.

"Well, I'm glad you called me. I've been craving a dose of sister love."

They paid their small bill, then, arm in arm, headed for the train, chatting about simple things.

Ω Ω Ω

They wound through the halls of the nineteenth century brick building and found themselves at the Classics Department office. They stepped inside and were greeted by a pleasant, grandmotherly receptionist.

"I'd like to speak with someone about Professor Klein," Gina explained as she handed the woman her card.

The receptionist took on a troubled, almost guilty look. "I think you'd better speak to the Department Head," she said. "Dr. Poulos. I'll see if he's available."

A few moments later they were ushered into a small office, lined with wall-to-wall, floor-to-ceiling shelves, all crammed to bursting with books and artifacts. Two large suitcases were shoved into one corner. On one side of the desk was a stack of papers held firmly in place by a large segment of a pottery vase that included a perfectly intact handle. Gina's hand went out instinctively to touch it.

A small, dark, wiry man of late middle age came through the door. "Etruscan," he said, and Gina pulled her hand back. "You can touch it. I've got a ton of them. They were originally made to be used, so I use them." Then he nodded his head almost formally. "I'm Peter Poulos. Please forgive the mess in here. I'm leaving on a research trip tomorrow. I understand you're interested in Professor Klein."

"Regina Bugbee," she responded. "This is my sister, Diane Lynch."

"Just along for the ride," Diane said.

"I'll try not to take up too much of your time," Gina said as she handed him her card. "I run an intake center for homeless men at Bellevue, and I'm trying to discover the true identity of a new man who's been coming into the center recently. He's a high-function delusional who thinks he's the Greek god Di-on . . ."

"Dionysus," Poulos said.

"Right. An associate of mine who's a sergeant on the police force told me there was a report filed that Professor Klein was missing."

"*Is* missing," Poulos corrected her. "We're covering his classes, of course."

Gina read more annoyance than worry in that comment, but also a bit of pride. David's shifts at Bellevue were "covered" at first . . . "Of *course*. There are a lot of rather convenient similarities between Professor Klein and my client. I wasn't able to contact Mrs. Klein, so I was hoping that someone who worked with him might be able to tell me a little more about him."

"Judy's away on an extended vacation," Professor Poulos said. His voice was gossipy, and he seemed almost eager to talk. "I must say, I find it rather odd that she'd put herself so out of touch while he's still missing." He lowered his voice and added, "Joe's disappearance has been a very disturbing event here. There have been rumors, rather unsavory ones, I'm afraid . . ."

Gina refrained from asking him to elaborate, though she would have loved to hear the racy dirt. "Can you describe Professor Klein for me?"

"I wish I had a picture," Dr. Poulos said, looking in vain around the littered surface of his desk. "He came on board not all that long ago." He shuffled a few papers aside, as if he were looking for a photograph. "He's handsome in a rugged sort of way. Weathered, olive skin. About five-eleven, medium build, very good shape for a man his age . . ."

"The report said he's fifty-one."

"He doesn't look it. He's one of those people for whom you have difficulty estimating the age on a glance. He has dark curly hair with a very small touch of gray, looks sort of Greek himself. Intense eyes, close-set, and a long, rather aquiline nose. He's got a very regal bearing." He leaned closer, confiding. "His students *worship* him. Especially the women." He winked and grinned.

She hid her dislike of this man with a sugary smile. "I'm sure," she said. "I wonder if you could tell me about this god—"

"Die-on-*I*-sus," he pronounced it. "He's one of the most complex and well-developed of the Greek myths." He glanced at his watch, then smiled back and forth between Gina and Diane. "I don't think I could do him justice without a very long discussion. Perhaps you might have time this afternoon for a—"

She stopped him in mid-play. "How about just the high points?"

"All right. Dionysus ruled wine specifically, and in general, rapture. And notably enough, for your purposes, madness. His followers drank a lot and worked themselves into this sort of ecstatic frenzy where they became one with the god— *enthusiasmos*, is the Greek word. The rituals were almost orgiastic, especially in the later stages of his popularity. The vast majority of his worshipers were women. It caused a lot of resentment with the men in charge; they didn't like seeing their women slip into someone else's control, even if it was a god."

"Go figure," Gina said sarcastically.

Poulos *hmphed.* "They had some good reasons to object. There are some parts of Dionysiac ritual that would curl your hair, literally."

"Well, if Professor Klein was popular with women students, might he not want to play that sort of role?"

"I have to admit, Joe enjoyed the, uh, *admiration* of his students. But I'm not prepared to speculate whether he'd go *that* far."

Gina wished silently that he would, but didn't push. "Is there anything else you can tell me?"

"Not much, about Joe, anyway. He could be rather standoffish to the rest of us in the Department. Frankly I can't imagine him taking on that persona. Of course, anything is possible."

He paused, reflecting. "There are a few more things you should know about Dionysus, maybe they'll help. He is supposedly the son of Zeus and the mortal woman Semele, so he's half-mortal himself."

Gina noted with some interest that Poulos was speaking in the present tense.

"He has a stronger connection with Earth than almost any other Greek deity, with the possible exception of the goddess Demeter, who rules grains and the harvest in general. In fact, the myth holds that he was married to a mortal woman named Ariadne and had several children with her. He is reputed actually to have died, which was an unusual thing for an immortal to do." Then he smiled and laughed. "But if you've got him in your facility, that can't be true, now, can it?"

Gina smiled in return. "Another myth, shot to hell."

"Ah, yes," Professor Poulos said, "we do try to get to the bottom of these pesky myths as often as possible around here. Enhances the academic reputation."

"What was Professor Klein's specific field of expertise?"

"Ancient Greek religion, what else?"

Gina exchanged a quick glance with Diane, who shrugged noncommittally. She stood up. "Well, thank you for your time. I don't know where this will all lead, but it's been very illuminating."

Poulos slipped out of his academic reverie long enough to say, "We'd be glad to have him back, you know."

"No doubt. So would his wife, I suspect."

The professor smiled slyly. "Perhaps."

Outside on the street, Diane said to Gina, "Well?"

"Could be him. Everything fits. The physical appearance, the Greek myth thing. All the 'personal' information is in line with what he's told me. It's worth pursuing, but I don't know quite where to go with it. I mean, proper protocol would dictate that I locate the wife and ask her to ID the guy.

"You're talking like a cop, not a social worker."

Gina made a small chuckle. "Yeah. It's kinda fun, in a lascivious sort of way. Anyway, if we get to her first, her feathers won't get ruffled because someone finds out before she does that her husband is back."

"Then why would she go away leaving his whereabouts unsolved?"

"Good question."

Ω Ω Ω

"I'd like you to meet a friend of mine," Gina said to Harpo as they walked along. "I told him all about you and he's eager to meet you."

He hustled along beside her, carrying her bag again. Freddie shuffled a few steps behind.

"Though I still wonder why it is that you have so many friends who are men, it would be my honor to meet another of them."

"Good," she said. "He could meet you on Wednesday afternoon." She'd already arranged with Randy to bring David home that day, but in polite deference to the very remote possibility that her strange client might actually have something scheduled, she asked, "How does that work for you?"

He looked puzzled. "I do not understand this Wednesday."

She laughed a little to cover her astonishment. "You're a person of distinctly antique sensibilities, Harpo. You know, *Wednesday,* the day of the week. Sunday, Monday, Tuesday, Wednesday, etc. Today is Monday, in case you haven't seen a calendar lately."

Again, the puzzled look came over him. "In Olympus we have little need to mark the days, but when we do it is by the change in the sun, how it strikes a sundial. I do not know your calendar."

She stared at him, seeing nothing but innocence. "Well, in that case," she said, "I'll guess I'll just have to explain it to you."

He hesitated at the top of the stairs, but finally, with a good deal of coaxing, she got him to follow her inside the center. He poked his head into every room, looking around suspiciously before passing by. When he reached her office, he would barely take his eyes off the ceiling.

Can't say as I blame him after that bite. "You have to look down to see this," she said. He did so, but warily. She picked up a small calendar from her desk and went through the days of the week, pointing at each day as she said its name. She patiently explained the entire concept of months, weeks, days, hours, minutes, and seconds.

He paid strict attention to her brief lecture. "It is *brilliant,*" he said with hushed reverence when she'd finished, "simply brilliant. Much more useful than our sundials."

She pointed again to one of the Mondays and said, "This is today." She moved her finger two squares ahead and said, "This is *Wednesday.* Wednesday is the day my friend wants to meet you."

"Two more comings of the daylight," he said.

"Exactly."

He shook his head in wonder. "Brilliant."

$$\Omega \; \Omega \; \Omega$$

McCarthy sauntered unannounced into Gina's office the following night toting a bag of assorted Mexican delicacies.

"*Buenos nochas*, senorita," he said, faking a Mexican accent. "I sure hope this works out better than the Szechuan. Don't need chopsticks so I thought it might be safe to eat it. I've got enough for two if you care to join me."

She laughed. "Superfluous question. But I don't know how safe that stuff is. I've cracked a taco or two in my day."

"I got soft tacos. And burritos. And some refried beans. All knife and fork foods."

"Smart man."

"A man who knows his limits, that's what."

She touched his arm. "Hey. I was really happy to hear that the guy who got shot is going to be okay. Do you know him personally?"

"No," he said. "Not in my precinct. But he's a brother no matter what."

"You don't need the same blood for that, I guess." She picked up her papers, tapped them into a neat pile, thinking once again that Bellevue interns, though a very select lot, did not have an innate brotherhood, as cops and firefighters had. Some of David's colleagues had come to his bedside to visit in the first days and weeks, but the demands of their internships were so great that it was difficult for many of them to tear away.

And difficult for them to maintain touch. When the common bonds of profession, education, and privilege that had existed between them were gone, they slipped away, over time, one by one.

She stored the papers in the big manila envelope as McCarthy loaded the desktop with containers. "Just don't let Harpo in here; he might *explode* if he eats anything this spicy."

McCarthy laughed. "Speaking of which, I saw him outside with Freddie. How's he doing?"

"Pretty well, I think. He keeps coming around, still loves me apparently, but it's tough to get him inside since the night of the spider. I think he's afraid he'll get bitten again. His head seems to be okay, though, if that's what you're wondering."

"Well, indirectly, I guess. How are he and Freddie getting along?"

"Surprisingly enough, pretty well."

"Really? You wouldn't think those two have much in common."

She dropped a hot burrito onto her plate, then blew on the tips of her fingers. "I'm not sure their alliance is much more than one of convenience. Soon as I let him do my taxes, Freddie'll probably drop Harpo like I just dropped this burrito. I think Harpo really annoys him."

"Who *doesn't* he annoy?"

"He is a *presence*. I'm intrigued with him. But I haven't had any luck in tracking him, I mean his *real* identity." She related the details of her inconclusive trip to Columbia. "I can usually nail these guys down in a couple of hours at most. I also took a look in Immigration and Naturalization yesterday, but there was nothing there."

"What do you mean, 'took a look?'"

"I logged into their database."

"Is that legal?"

She smiled slyly. "Marginally. I had a password." She held up a hand. "Don't ask. But I didn't find anything."

He gave her a *you bad girl* look. "Did you ever manage to get all the digs on Freddie's family?"

"Are you kidding? In about ten minutes."

"Ever call them?"

"Once. I got a fast brush off. The woman who answered, I assume his wife, basically told me to mind my own business. And not too politely."

McCarthy shook his head and sighed. "It's a shame, what happened to him. Talk about bad luck."

After another bite, Gina said, "Yeah. But Harpo doesn't seem too down on his luck. Out of his element, maybe, but from what I remember about that dog collar, he probably doesn't need to panhandle a whole lot."

McCarthy agreed. "Probably not. He seems pretty smart. Maybe he's just one of those guys who don't *want* to be fenced in. You know they're out there."

"Oh, yeah." Then, recalling the calendar story, she became more animated. "You know, something really interesting just happened with him. I did make an appointment for him to see Aaron Richman. He had a slot open for Wednesday, so I asked Harpo, on the off-chance that he might return to his home planet in the meantime, if he could go then. He didn't know what Wednesday is."

McCarthy looked up from his food. "What? Is it a holiday? I thought the Police Union knew about every holiday that ever happened."

"No, that's not what I mean. He had no concept of the *calendar*. He understands days and years and even months because they're defined by observable physical occurrences. But he doesn't know anything about the days of the week. At least he says he doesn't. And if you think about it, how's Friday different from Tuesday, if you don't know they've been labeled that way?"

"Friday's payday. Tuesday is the day of the following week when I run out of money. That's a pretty significant difference."

She laughed. "Not if you're not getting paid. I mean, don't you think that's pretty bizarre? He's obviously educated, but he doesn't know the days of the week?"

"Yeah," McCarthy owned, "it *is* weird."

"I'll be very interested to see what happens when Aaron gets a hold of him."

After a brief pause, McCarthy said, "Speaking of shrinks, how are things going with David? I mean, if you don't mind me asking."

He'd always skirted the issue delicately, as she had skirted the issue of his wife, and Gina had only volunteered what was necessary. That said, she was sure that Miranda, Queen of Matchmakers, was feeding McCarthy bits of information. And everything she herself knew about McCarthy's wife had come from the same source.

Someday I'll ask him, but not tonight.

"I don't mind," she said quietly. "He's holding his own, but he's having some difficulty with the dosage on his medication and we're going through a process of adjustment. It seems to take a long time to get it right."

McCarthy watched as she spoke, looking for clues in her face. "This is tough stuff, I know," he said.

"Yeah, it is."

"I never really know what to say. I hate to see you be unhappy, but I just don't know what to do."

She reached out and touched his arm. "You're doing just the right thing. I really appreciate your kindness. Your friendship is very important to me, especially now."

Emboldened by her willingness to talk, he pressed further. "So, does it look like this medicine will work?"

She let out a long sigh. "They all do at first. Then the effect seems to wear down, and we have to try something new. This is his fourth medication this year."

"That can't be making him too happy."

"Or me." She made no effort to hide her bitterness. "I'm not sure he knows he's unhappy. I'm not sure he *is* unhappy. Maybe he was unhappy before and this—catatonic state is a way to avoid feeling it."

"Aw, come on, Gina, he had a significant injury, he was *there* that day. He was in it as thick as anyone, but he didn't have any training or any equipment. Tons of guys who *did* have equipment experienced the same thing. It was a nightmare. And please, be nice to yourself. I mean, how could any guy be unhappy with you?"

He'd said it so innocently. She squeaked out a thin 'thanks' and stuffed her mouth with a bite of burrito. When she could speak normally again, she changed the subject. "And thanks for this food. Since it's coming up on Tuesday and you're about to run out of money, can I get this one? You got the Chinese."

"That was just a joke," he said, smiling. "I do okay for money. Overtime helps. And there's lots of it these days with all the shootings. Makes me feel bad to cash my check sometimes, knowing why the extra's there."

He paused, then smiled. "But I do notice that we seem to be spending all our time around food. How about we try catch a matinee some time? Take a break from the bums?"

Her willing heart and her cautious brain duked it out. As it almost always did, the brain won. "Indigents," she said softly, with a little smile. "And not yet. It's not a good time for that now."

He took the rejection with surprising calm. "Well, it never hurts to ask." He shrugged his shoulders. "Maybe I'll ask again sometime."

"You could do that."

He pushed himself away from the desk and stood up, wiping his mouth on a napkin. "Well, I better go back out into the void." He reached out his hand, and with one finger, drew a light line down the side of her cheek. "See ya," he said.

"Soon," she said. And as the tingle coursed through her, she thought, *not soon enough*.

Ω Ω Ω

She brought Harpo up to Aaron's office using the stairs. On the second floor landing there was a jam-up of people, and while they waited for a clear path, her eye was drawn to the informational slide show on a wall-mounted monitor.

Flu shot? Had it.

Hep B vaccination series? Naturally.

Then came a beautiful photo of smiling people, all different colors, shapes and sizes, much like the throngs that crowded the streets of New York daily. Mixed in with the hard hats, flannel shirts and pea coats were turbans, veils, and saris. Their skin colors were legion: black, white, brown, olive, freckled. And the caption read:

We don't care about their immigration status, we care about their health.

And even though she hadn't gotten a hit on him in the database, Gina wondered anew, knowing that Harpo would have fit right into that photo, if his immigration status was the factor he didn't want to reveal.

But why?

As they passed each floor, Gina was, as always, struck by the contrast between the original brick building, so stately, venerable, and storied, and the sweeping new façade that now enveloped it. The offices and clinics housed within the façade were bright, clean, and new.

But they had yet to earn their history.

Harpo's appearance garnered a few stares in the waiting area. And though he wasn't that much more *outré* than many of the Bellevue's patients, those patients were not normally seen in these clinic areas, but more often in the wards for acute psychiatric care.

Gina signed them in with the outer receptionist. After a few moments, Mike came out and led them into Aaron's private waiting area, all the while keeping an eye on this new patient. Gina understood, with no real surprise, that Mike was assessing his danger potential. When they were settled, he handed Harpo a clipboard with several pages secured in the clamp. Resting at the top of the clip was a ball-point pen.

Gina watched quietly as Harpo examined the things he had just been given, searching for any sign that he understood their purpose. After a few moments, obviously flummoxed, he put the clipboard down on the table and picked up a magazine.

Mike observed their lack of progress on the patient questionnaire. "I hate to spoil your fun," he said, "but Aaron's going to be ready for you in just a minute. You might want to work on that form."

"Right," Gina said, taking the magazine from Harpo's hand. He began to protest.

"We can look at them later. Right now we have to fill out these blasted forms." She picked up the clipboard and placed it on her lap. "I'll help you."

He seemed confused. "What precisely is one supposed to do with this?"

"These are some questions we have to answer before we meet my friend."

"How *inhospitable*." He leaned closer to her and whispered, "And why does he have a guard?"

She leaned close as well. "Mike's not really a guard, he's more like an assistant. And Aaron's a very important man, but he has some—problems. It helps him if we give him information ahead of time."

"What sort of problems?"

"You'll see soon enough. We need to do this now." She took the pen, clicked it a few times, and scribbled in the margin of the paper to flow the ink. Harpo immediately grabbed the pen from her hand and repeated her action. He scribbled furiously, and before Gina could get the pen away from him, he'd drawn across a few areas where information was supposed to be written.

"Harpo, it's just a pen."

He started clicking again. "What an intriguing noise! We have no such devices in Olympus."

She was about to ask the sarcastic question, *then how do you write*, but stopped herself. "Let me show you." She took the pen from his hand and held it in her own. "Like this. First we have to write in your name."

He said, quite firmly, "Dionysus. *Not* Harpo."

"Is that your first name or your last name? We usually have two names, one first, and one last, like—Joe Klein, for example."

No reaction.

"It is my *only* name," he said finally. "At least in Greece. In other lands I am called other names. But please, use my Greek name."

Oy, she thought. "OK, we'll put it in for last name. Tell me the letters."

He reeled off a list of Greek letters, the first of which she recognized as delta. The rest disappeared into the air as rapidly as he spoke them.

What to do with this? she wondered. Finally, she handed him the clipboard and said, "You try writing your name. Right here." She made an X-mark on the proper line. "Write it in Greek."

He held the pen too tightly and painstakingly drew a series of symbols on the line. He handed the board back to her, with the expression of a child seeking praise.

Gina studied the letters for a few moments and said, "It's so beautiful! My name looks so plain." She flipped the page over, found the line where payment guarantors were to sign, and wrote her name.

"But you are wrong," he said. "Your markings have grace and fluidity, and you make them so effortlessly." He touched her hand with his own, patting it gently and said, "See how this 'pen' obeys your commands."

She laughed and drew her hand away, thinking, *Nice move, Harpo.* "OK. Next question. Where do you live?"

"I have told you before. In Olympus."

So you're still not going to play. I'll just plow right ahead anyway. She quickly wrote OLYMPUS in the space for his street address. "That's in Greece, right?"

"More or less . . ." he said. "It has drifted away over time, and now it floats somewhere out in the Cosmos, or the Ether, some call it. Others might say the 'Universe'. But it is all the same place. It is everything that is."

Woooo, she thought. *Just like the World Wide Web. Everything that is everything.* She had never before run into someone who claimed to *live* there.

"You're going a little over my head with this stuff, Harpo." She penned the word COSMOS in that space. Then, nonchalantly, hoping to catch him in an unguarded response, she said, "And where do you work?"

He seemed miffed. "As I have told you before, gods do *not* 'work.'"

"Well, you must do something with your time. Are you sure you aren't a, um, teacher, maybe? Some sort of professor? Maybe at one of the local schools, like—Columbia?"

He gave her a frosty look. "Certainly not."

"Sorry, but I have to ask." She scribbled the word "god" in that space. "They like to know these things. Now, how about your marital status? Are you married?"

He seemed to dwell on that question; there came no *how-can-you-not-know-this* answer.

For a moment, Gina considered bringing up the supposed wife Ariadne, about

99

whom Professor Poulos had spoken, albeit briefly.

"I am not," Harpo finally said.

She scanned through the remaining questions quickly. Medical history, significant illnesses, family history, there was nothing more she could fill in, except the emergency notification space, where she put her own name and phone number.

She got up and handed the clipboard back to Mike, who glanced at it, then looked back up at her with a very puzzled expression.

She shrugged. "It's all I can get out of him now. But I'm sure Aaron will get more."

"Count on it," Mike said as the buzzer sounded.

Ω Ω Ω

Mike stood to one side of the office, in a less lit area, next to the comfortable-looking chair where he generally sat when she and David were there.

He never stayed in the office when she was there alone; she had no threat potential. But a middle-aged man, in good physical but questionable mental health? That was another story.

His two hands were held together in front of his buttoned suit jacket, his feet spaced slightly apart. Black shoes, neat haircut. Ninety percent Secret Service; all that was missing was the curly ear wire.

She watched, fascinated, as practitioner and patient sized each other up, but it was quickly apparent that she had not prepared Harpo well enough, for he peered curiously at Aaron's wheelchair and asked, "What strange armor is this that you wear? Are you some kind of warrior?"

As Gina blanched, Aaron laughed. "My wife thinks so sometimes."

Gina started to explain. "It's a wheelchair, Harpo. Dr. Richman had an accident a number of years ago and he's paralyzed."

"Ah!" Harpo said. "This is a Greek word—*paralysis*—which means that something has come to a complete stop, such as a military campaign, or perhaps a journey. Have you come to a stop here?"

What have I done . . . "It's the same word," Gina said, "but today we use it to mean that a person is unable to move." She looked nervously at Aaron, who listened with bemused interest to the exchange.

"I am pleased that so many of our words are used in your language," Harpo said. "Perhaps as time passes you will manage to rid yourselves of the Roman words." He paused and smiled, as if expecting them to laugh. When the desired reaction did not occur, he looked again at Aaron. "But why are you unable to move?"

Aaron nodded slightly at Gina, which she understood as permission to continue discussing his condition. As she spoke, he observed.

"Aaron's neck was broken in an accident, and his spine was damaged."

Harpo turned his head and stared at Aaron in disbelief. "And you were strapped to this chair as a punishment for your clumsiness?"

Gina rose up from her chair, gushing apologies. "Aaron, I had no idea . . ."

"It's all right, Gina. Sit down."

Red-faced, she sat.

When he spoke again, he showed no obvious signs of offense. "Please call me Aaron, Harpo. That's my first name."

"And you must call me Dionysus. That is my *proper* name."

"Dionysus. Of course. I'd be curious to know what happens when someone in your country loses the ability to move."

"In Olympus, such an event has never occurred."

"What about in Greece? Surely injuries like mine have occurred in Greece. What happens there?"

"When I was last in Greece, it depended on the city in which the person lived, for the customs from one to the next were very different. In Sparta there were many such injuries, because the people who lived there made much war. Should a soldier become so maimed, he would choose a swift and honorable dispatch by the sword of his captain, after sacrifice to Athena and Ares, of course. In Athens, such people might be helped by their physicians to die in other ways. Sometimes small children were exposed to hasten the end of their misery, when the parents would not do it."

Gina looked at him, aghast. "You mean left outside to die?"

"Why, yes."

She looked back at Aaron. "I'm so sorry," she said to him, "I guess I didn't think this through very carefully."

"It's all right." He turned his attention back to his new patient. "You come from a very ancient time, then, don't you?"

Harpo scratched his head. "Yes, I suppose to a mortal it would seem ancient . . . I was born many thousands of years ago, and the world was very different."

"It's been a while since you've visited Earth, then?"

Harpo sat up taller in his chair. He leaned closer and whispered, "You are perhaps a believer?"

Aaron smiled knowingly, but said nothing. Gina marveled at how easily he had managed to manipulate a very intelligent patient into thinking precisely what he wanted him to think without actually lying to him. It was clear that Harpo took Aaron's smile as an affirmative response, but it was also a pretty safe bet that Aaron did not actually believe in this patient's purported divinity.

And she wondered nervously how often he did that with her or David.

"Then it will pain you to know that I left Earth not long after the arrival of the one called Jesus Christ. Since then, our view of Earth has been—uh, *clouded.*"

"So you wouldn't know that our doctors have gotten much better at taking care of people like me. There was a time when not too many of us lived. Now almost *all* of us live."

With complete innocence Harpo said, "But why would one choose to live such a life?"

There was a pause, during which Aaron took one of his cleansing breaths. Gina was staring at her fingernails in horror, hoping to melt through the chair.

Finally Aaron answered. "I cannot speak for others like me, but for myself, I have many reasons to live, among them a lovely wife and daughter, both of whom seem miraculously to need and want me. Some other time I'll tell you about them. But now I'm very eager to learn more about you. Gina's told me some interesting things already."

For the next half hour, Gina listened in quiet fascination as Aaron skillfully drew much more information from him than she could ever have hoped to get. He managed to create a meaningful dialogue between himself and Gina's delusional client, to the point that some of the wild tales seemed plausible. When they spoke of Alexander the Great, Harpo said, "I had great regard for him as a leader, despite his personal flaws." Hippocrates, he said, was "a great healer and physician, perhaps the best of all time, though I mean no offense to you in this regard." Of Socrates, he said, "A brilliant rhetorician, and a fair sculptor. I posed once for him personally, and he made a good likeness of me. But he was wrong to conclude in the end that we gods do not exist." When Aaron brought up the subject of Sophocles, Harpo could barely contain himself. "He won the prize at my festivals more often than any other dramatist. His gifts were marvelously diverse, and he was a fine statesman, too."

The exchanges were quite animated at times, as much as Aaron could manage. During one of Aaron's long breaths, Harpo rose up from his seat and walked around to the side of the desk where Aaron sat, and began to examine various parts of the chair.

Mike moved closer immediately. Aaron gave him a quick glance; he stopped, but he was poised and ready.

Harpo poked and prodded at the shiny stainless steel like a child in a science museum.

"It might be a good idea to ask permission before you touch the chair," Gina said.

Aaron overrode her objections. "It's no problem. I'm sure it seems like quite a novelty, especially since our new friend is from a time when nothing like it existed."

Harpo ran his fingers over the smooth metal surfaces, and stared intently at the small computer by which it was all operated. As he was peering closely at the controls, Aaron pressed one of them lightly, and the chair moved a few inches forward. Harpo reacted to the unexpected movement with a quick backward hop.

When he saw Aaron grinning, Harpo laughed and said, "Marvelous! This is truly a wonderful device. Why, you have no need of one of those horrible *big* moving machines!"

The psychiatrist laughed, too. "I wish that were true. A horrible small moving machine is bad enough, thank you! But I do still need a big one; this whole chair has to fit inside it. I have something called a minivan with the rear seats taken out."

Harpo pondered this idea momentarily. "A moving machine inside a moving machine. *Fascinating.* This is something I must experience. I will ride with you one time."

Gina buried her face in her hands. *First he insults him, then he gives him a history lesson, then he invites himself for a ride.* The receptionist buzzed as she looked up again. Her torture was at an end.

Ω Ω Ω

She stomped angrily through the Bellevue halls with Harpo trotting close at her heels. He seemed terribly excited, in complete contrast to her own overwhelming shame.

"Truly," he said, "I am indebted to you for bringing me to meet such a remarkable man. He and I shall become the best of companions."

Gina came to an abrupt stop in the middle of the corridor and turned around to face him. "I have never been so mortified in my life." Her words echoed off the white walls of the façade, and people stared as they passed.

Harpo was taken aback by her anger. "I do not understand why you should feel this way."

"You don't understand *anything!*"

Traffic began to jam up all around them. People twisted themselves into odd positions to sidle past the bickering pair.

"But—"

Gina cut him off. "I will *explain* it so you *will.* Maybe on the planet *you* come from, it's considered OK to question a handicapped person about the cause and nature of his injuries, but on *Earth* we don't do it. We try not to remind people of their problems. We try to treat them with unconditional acceptance."

"But how can a man forget that he cannot move, except with the help of that armor?"

"He told you, it's not armor, it's a wheelchair. And I'm quite sure that Aaron never forgets about his limitations for even one minute. And that's *precisely* why he doesn't need you and all the rest of us to remind him."

"He cannot forget for even—one-sixtieth of—twelve times—"

"Yeah, *that* amount of time," she fumed. "*Please* try to be more careful about what you say to people. You're going to hurt a lot of feelings if you don't."

She pounded off. It would not have surprised him to see steam rising from her head. He followed dutifully, but hung back, confused and dejected.

Chapter 9
Iota

The stranger who called himself Dionysus opened the top of his toga, took out the small white dog, and plopped him into his lap. The dog jumped around playfully. "I envy your carefree happiness, Midas," he said, "for all joy has deserted me. These mortal women! They are not what they used to be. You should thank the Cosmos that you are—"

He paused, then laughed. "Ah, I was about to say that as a bull you must only understand cows, but now you are a dog. So you must only understand bitches. Still, they are women, are they not?"

"Heh, heh, heh," Freddie croaked. "Women, of *any* species. All the same. Confusing as hell. They got those hormones all the time. But they all think *we're* nuts. My wife used to say to me, 'Fredo,' she said, 'you're *molto loco*.' She was right. And you know what? You and me, we ain't the only ones. The whole fucking world is crazy."

"Ah, my friend, how I wish! Things would be so much simpler. But you mortals *revel* in your complications. Why, when I roamed the earth before, women were obedient, humble, submissive . . . now they seem to have acquired a confounding free will, in direct opposition to the pleasing nature Zeus gave them! It seems that the more they know of the world, the worse things get. The women are ruined, completely ruined."

"Ruined," Freddie echoed philosophically. He sighed and shook his head.

Harpo waved away the smelly cloud of Freddie's breath. "Once mortal women would willingly rend their finest garments to make their flesh available to me. And this was in a time when clothing was not so easily acquired as now."

His hands worked the air energetically, demonstrating the toil. "The beating of the flax, the combing, the spinning, the weaving . . . but I needed only to speak a wish, and the garments would rend."

"Wow, you musta been *something*," Freddie said. "I'm *impressed*."

"Oh, I was *very* impressive," Harpo said wistfully. "I was magnificent. When my worship was at its peak of glory, women sought me out without being summoned, because in the frenzy of adoring me, they could bring themselves to a state of completion and—"

Freddie sat up a little taller. "Wait a minute," he said, "what do you mean by *completion*?"

"I mean complete ecstasy, full rapture, total oneness with divinity. *Eros.*"

"Oh," Freddie said, much less impressed. "*Divinity.* You're talking about religion." He let out a small nervous laugh. "For a minute there I thought you were talking about a different kinda completion."

Harpo gave him a curious look. "What, pray tell, did you think I meant?"

The blush was visible even through Freddie's weathered skin. "I thought you mighta meant—uh, you know, um, the kind of completion when you have—"

He made a suggestive gesture with two of his fingers. "You know, *ah-boompah-boompah.*"

Harpo leaned back and laughed heartily. "Ah, my friend, that is *precisely* what I meant. *Ecstasis* in its purest form. *Orgasmos.* Perfect joy, unblemished rapture, complete and total surrender to the will of the Cosmos. And it is so much sweeter under the blessing of a divinity."

"Whoa," Freddie said, "hold your horses, there! This is *heavy*. How come you never told me about this before?"

"The opportunity did not present itself," he said, matter-of-factly. "Of course, the men of those times were not terribly pleased; some of them reacted quite bitterly at being left out of the process and—"

Freddie sat up even straighter and grabbed Harpo's arm. "They—um, *completed* themselves without men?"

"They did," Harpo said. His grin was almost devilish.

"They, uh, didn't use any, uh, *devices*?"

Harpo gave Freddie's question a long moment's thought. "What do you mean by—"

"Never mind," Freddie said, waving his hands in front of his chest. "It's not important. I gotta tell you, I'm having a tough time buying this. You got a, uh, credibility gap happening here. Either you're lying or you're even crazier than I thought."

"While I confess to a substantial madness, I assure you, I speak the truth!" Harpo said indignantly. Then he slumped down. "But I cannot prove myself, for I have not had such power in a very long time. No one believes."

"What's that got to do with anything? Lots of people don't believe in God and they get—completed. I used to be a believer, but I can't say I do anymore. I don't think Gina does, she never says she does. But even if someone doesn't believe in a god, that doesn't make the god not be god. You're God, you don't have to give a shit what anyone else thinks."

"You are wrong, my confused mortal friend. I, for one, care deeply. For what is a god, but something holy that a mortal has constructed? Without belief, there is no divinity, and therefore no divine power."

Freddie crossed his arms over his chest and gave him a look of undisguised skepticism. "I gotta think about this for a minute," he said.

Harpo shrugged his shoulders. "By all means, feel free to do so. You are only the latest in a long line of—*distinguished philosophers* who have felt themselves qualified to describe us. I am always amused by what they come up with. No doubt your contribution to theology will be novel, in view of your unique circumstances."

Freddie shot him a look of resentment. "So, tell me, Mr. God—you're here in this box with me, so how are your circumstances different from mine?"

"*My* circumstances will change soon."

"Oh, yeah? So will mine. I got a plan. Soon as I get through escorting your sorry ass all over the City I'm gonna start thinking about getting a job. It'll be *good-bye, Freezer!*" His expression was full of resolve. "So what's *your* plan? *If* you have one, that is."

Harpo suddenly grew quite somber. "My plan is to return to my home in Olympus," he said quietly.

"Well, I know *that*, but how?"

Harpo said nothing.

"You don't have a plan at all, do you?" Freddie said.

He received a long sigh in response, and then the quiet admission. "Well . . ."

"Oh, man, I knew it! This is just my crappy luck. I gotta drag you around this city until you figure it out but you aren't trying to figure it out because you think you're gonna just flap those wings you're gonna sprout one of these days and—"

Harpo interrupted him. "Contain yourself! I am not a winged god. But a plan does exist. There are—*conditions* by which I may return."

Harpo cradled the little dog to his chest and said, "Shall we tell him, Small One?"

The dog licked his master's chin and jumped up and down, wagging his tail enthusiastically.

"I take that to be a positive answer," he said, scratching the dog's neck and wiping the saliva from his own chin. "And once again I am glad you are no longer a bull."

He looked at Freddie. "But first I must tell you how I came to be here. We delayed this discussion, as I recall."

"Shoot," Freddie said, "I'm all ears."

"Indeed," Harpo said, one eyebrow arched. "Except for the part of you that snores. Well. I suppose the best place to begin would be with the girl, the virgin I mentioned before." His face took on a dreamy look. "Ah, such a girl she was!"

He leaned back and closed his eyes, then let out a long, pining sigh. "Exquisite, in every detail! Aphrodite—"

"Hey!" Freddie said. "I saw a movie about her! The goddess of love, right?"

He nodded. "And beauty. She brought the girl to Olympus for use in a ritual she hoped would restore some of her power. She was always trying these things, for of all the deities, she has suffered most by our decline. And since Aphrodite is in charge of overseeing beauty, she was once perfectly beautiful. And though we are immortal, we have aged. Slowly, of course; Cronos alone knows what we would be now if we aged as mortals do! Oozing puddles of rancid slime!" He shuddered.

"Every century or so, a new wrinkle appears, and a wisp of gray, and a sag in her bosom She is desperate to keep it from getting any worse. Now, this virgin had great potential to become a believer. It must have been a difficult task for Aphrodite to bring her to Olympus, for it has drifted very far from Earth these last centuries . . . I suspect she had considerable help from her lover Ares. He is a great brute, though he does have sporadic moments of cleverness. But his most notable quality is a desire to please Aphrodite. He will do anything she asks, if only she promises to bring her honeyed self to him in return."

"Hmph. Sounds like a typical guy. You sure he's a god?"

"Regrettably," Harpo said. "Very bellicose. He has been present at all your mortal wars, hovering, and while he still had his power, he determined the most suitable outcome. Now, well . . . you are on your own, I suppose, to determine the victor.

"One day I came upon this virgin as she was bathing herself in a holy stream. I was quite surprised that Aphrodite brought her into our presence, for the girl was of such quality that she nearly rivaled her patroness. Naturally, I was taken by her. And I knew almost instantly that she was a virgin."

He leaned closer to Freddie and whispered, "The scent, you know."

"What scent?"

"Of virginity, of course. It was intoxicating, so pure and fresh and unspoiled. I had not smelled it for centuries! It is not my fault that I was helpless to resist her. And she did not object when I made myself known to her! I took her on the bank of the stream, in the fragrant grass, with the sound of the ripples to accompany us. Ah, what sweetness we made!"

He lowered his head. "But Aphrodite must have heard the music of our love, for she came to us on a raging whirlwind, heard all through Olympus. When she found that the girl had been spoiled, she went before Zeus to demand retribution. Unfortunately, he assented to her request."

"Your *old man*? Why?"

"Because I lied to him about it. And because he has always suffered from guilt where I am concerned. My birth was—unusual."

Freddie looked at him and laughed. "Gee, but you turned out so terrific!"

Harpo wrinkled his brow. "You had best not take this tale lightly. You are the first mortal to hear it told by a god. I cannot tell you what Sophocles or Euripides would have given to be the first to hear a myth told by its origin."

"Breaking news! I'm scooping the Universe!" He laughed heartily, then hiccuped.

"Shall I save this tale for a more appreciative listener?"

Freddie's laughter hitched down to small chuckles. "Sorry. I get a little carried away sometimes. I actually kinda like this story."

"As well you ought," Harpo said. "Now. . . ah, yes. I am the son of Zeus and the mortal woman Semele. Zeus saw her one night and was so enthralled that he simply had to have her. But of course, he is married to Hera, who is eternally jealous, for he is the greatest of all philanderers in history."

"Nah. Bill Clinton. And you shoulda seen how Hillary reacted."

"Who is this—"

"Not important. Keep goin'."

"Very well. Semele was blessed by Aphrodite, and as a follower of the moon, her beauty was of a most pearly, wonderful quality . . ."

Freddie sat higher. "What did she look like? My mother, she was pretty, too."

"I do not know," Harpo said sadly, "I never saw her."

"I thought you said she was your mother. She either was or wasn't your mother. Which is it?"

"Patience!" Harpo exploded.

"Well, you're not making sense—"

"I am speaking of *gods*. But you are hearing me with mortal ears. I would advise you to consider adopting a more universal view. Then perhaps your puny mind will grasp what I am trying to tell you."

"Well, excuse the fuck outta *me*."

"Perhaps. We shall see. Semele was my mother because I was conceived in her womb. But Hera became so jealous that she could not abide her continued existence. She devised a plan by which to trick her."

"I'm glad to hear that *some* of your people have plans."

"Oh, some of us have plans that are *too* clever. Semele had never seen my father, because he was so brilliant that he could not show himself to her, or she would perish in the flames of his glory. He always came to her at night in the form of a dream.

"But one day Hera came to her on a breeze and planted the notion that she should see her phantom lover. 'How do you know who he is?' she whispered to Semele. 'What if he is some horrible monster?' So Sem—my mother—became confused. She withheld her favors from Zeus and finally he was compelled by his desire to promise her anything she wanted. And when she asked to see him, he had to comply. He is a god, you understand, and we always keep our word."

"So she sees him. Big deal."

"Oh, indeed it was. The same thing happened to her that happens to every mortal who sees Zeus in his full glory. She was immediately consumed by flames."

In the brief silence that followed, Freddie closed his eyes and envisioned the charred bodies he had stepped over in the lobby of the North Tower.

"Go on," he said quietly. "Please."

Harpo's voice grew equally quiet. "Before she was fully consumed, Zeus ripped me from her womb and implanted me into his own thigh, so I could be safe until I was ready to be born."

Freddie rubbed his chin in contemplation. "Wow. This is heavy. Your father was your father *and* your mother."

"Indeed."

"Wow," Freddie said again. "*Sheesh*. So he saved your life, then. I don't get why he'd feel guilty."

"Because Semele paid for his love with *her* life, and because he was caught once again being unfaithful to Hera."

"Oh," Freddie said, "The old man-gets-caught thing."

"Zeus originated this practice."

"Not a terrific invention."

"Indeed *not*," Harpo said. "So when Aphrodite came to him to demand my punishment, she reminded him of his misdeeds and he gave in to her. He called all the gods together to decide my Fate. And to make matters worse, Zeus allowed Aphrodite to choose my punishment. She demanded that I be banished to Earth."

Freddie crossed his arms over his chest. "So this is how you landed on my box."

"Indeed. But my father softened my punishment before it could be enacted, praise be to his august self. He gave me the means to return."

Harpo grabbed hold of his necklace and held it out for Freddie to see. "This vial contains ambrosia. Zeus blessed it so it will enable me to return to Olympus when I complete a certain task."

Freddie's eyes narrowed. "Which is?"

"More fit for Herakles than myself, I'm afraid. I must make the first woman I meet on Earth believe in me. Accept my divinity. That was the only way Aphrodite would agree to the change."

"Wait a minute," Freddie said, "*that's* why you wouldn't look outside the car. So you wouldn't see a woman till you wanted to." His look darkened. "Hey! The first woman you met was Gina." He clamped his hand over his eyes, then wiped it down across his face. "Oh, man, I don't believe this."

"Do you doubt what I say?"

Freddie sat up straight and stared at him. "No. I mean, well, maybe I doubt you, maybe I don't, but what I really mean is I don't believe my luck. I promised Gina I'd sashay around with you until we found out where you live and send you back there. And she ain't *never* gonna believe you're a god."

"But she must! Or I will be stuck here for all eternity. And you must not tell her what I have told you! I must win her trust and belief in me, and it will not help me if you tell her what I am trying to do!"

"*Shit.* I made a deal with her. I can't go back on that. I got principles, too, you know. Now, *I'm* certifiably nuts, so I'm gonna give you the benefit of the doubt about all this crazy stuff you just told me. But she's not. She's logical, and smart, and . . . and . . . like you said, *complicated.* So I'm gonna be stuck with you. No tax return. *Shit.*"

"With your constant references to excrement, you make it sound like it is an onerous task to be my companion," Harpo said indignantly.

"Oh, it's a piece of cake. I just like to *pretend* it stinks."

"Then perhaps you should consider how it is for me, a god, a divine and once perfect being, to be in the company of a filthy mortal such as yourself." He raised his chin. "Imagine my shame if any of my Olympian associates were to see me in this state—"

"But they can't see you, right? They're up there, and you're down here. Can you see them?"

"No."

"Well, then, why should they be able to see you?"

Harpo sat quietly for a moment. "I think there is another god on Earth who can."

Freddie threw his head back and laughed aloud. "Oh, man, this shit pile just keeps getting bigger . . ."

"I saw him the other night at the center! Surely you have seen this winged one yourself. Why, he still has his own festival, before the spring mating season, and is worshiped by many mortals. That is why he can still go back and forth so readily."

"What the *fuck* are you talking about?"

"Eros! Small, pink, winged, shoots arrows into the hearts of mortals . . ." He traced a small rounded shape in the air with his hands.

"You mean *Cupid?*"

Harpo yanked open the drape and spat furiously out into the snow. The wind howled into the box, and he drew it shut again. "His proper Greek name is Eros! He is Aphrodite's son. She has given him reign over all passionate love. He is here spying on me; he tried to shoot an arrow into Gina's heart; she would have been distracted with love for this McCarthy and it would have spoiled my chances to gain her belief. I stood in the way of his arrow. It nearly killed me, but at least I prevented it from entering her. That would have been a complete disaster!"

Freddie just stared at him, dumbfounded. "She said you got bit by a spider. That you're allergic. Now you're telling me Cupid—"

"*Eros!*"

"*Okay*, for Christ sakes, *Eros* is spying on you and reporting back to his mother."

Harpo nodded. "And to make matters worse, he is meddling in my situation so that it will be more difficult for me to do what I must do."

"*Shit*," Freddie said quietly. "I'm *never* gonna get rid of you."

"Oh, please," Harpo said, almost pleading, "do not tempt the Fates with such a statement! They may hear you and *make* it come true!"

"I'm gonna have to figure out something," Freddie said. "I'm not gonna be your damned babysitter any longer than I have to." He gave Harpo a disgusted look, but after a few moments, it softened to pity. "I guess I'm gonna have to help you."

Harpo tossed Midas unceremoniously off his lap and got up on his knees. "Oh," he said, his hands clasped together, "thank you! Praise be to Zeus for sending you to me! Surely Hades will make your journey in the underworld easier in gratitude for this great thing you do for me!"

"I'm not planning to hang out in Hades," Freddie said. "Hopefully I'll go *upstairs* when the time comes." Then he rubbed his hands together and said, "But never mind all that religious stuff, we got some work to do on Earth before this Eros guy messes things up too much. This is not gonna be easy." He picked up his bottle of wine and took a long pull, then handed the bottle to Harpo. "Here," he said, "fortify yourself. We're gonna need it."

The harsh wine burned his tongue and Harpo swallowed quickly to rid his mouth of the foul stuff. "*Bah.* Swill."

"Yeah, well, my cellar's running a little slim these days," Freddie quipped. "Okay, let's get to work here. First thing, we have to get you back in her good graces. She has to like you if she's gonna believe in you. We gotta think about what women like."

Harpo brightened. "Why, that is simple! I will simply bring her to *ecstasis*. To completion, and then she will *adore* me—"

"Whoa, whoa, wait a minute," Freddie said, waving his hand disapprovingly. "It doesn't work that way these days. You gotta get her to like you first, then you can *maybe* think about the completion stuff, but not with you. Women these days wanna be in love with the guys they—complete with."

"This is *very* distressing," Harpo said. "Against the natural order of things."

"Lotsa guys would agree with that, I think. But now women like to be wooed.

You know, courted. You ain't never gonna get there with her, but some of the same stuff will get her to maybe like you enough to think you're, you know, a god."

"How does one court women in these wretched times?"

"Let's see," Freddie said, rubbing his chin. "My wife used to like flowers. And she loved it when I wore aftershave."

Harpo looked stymied, so Freddie explained.

"I require no such olfactory enhancements."

Freddie leaned over and sniffed him. "You got no smell at all. We better get you some aftershave, just to be on the safe side."

"And where does one obtain this magical stuff?"

"I know a store where they have samples. Then we'll stop at a market and get some flowers. She'll love it."

"As long as she will not reject *me*, it will suffice."

Freddie laughed. "Okay," he said. "Let's get going. Freddie and Harpo's excellent adventure. *Heh, heh, heh.*"

Ω Ω Ω

They headed through the revolving doors at Macy's, with Harpo clinging white-faced to the inside corner of his rotating wedge-space. He dashed out of the opening and slammed into Freddie, who was awaiting him on the other side with a big sassy grin.

"You must love elevators."

"I do not know this 'elevators.'"

Freddie grabbed him by the arm. "You mean you're an elevator virgin?"

"See here!" Harpo said, trying to shake himself free. "I am no kind of—"

But Freddie was already hauling him roughly toward the center of the store. They joined a crowd of people in front of a pair of shiny metal doors. One by one, the members of the waiting crowd slipped further away from Freddie, whose rancid smell did not invite close contact. When the elevator doors slid open, they stepped forward quite alone.

The doors closed behind them, and they were imprisoned in the small space. "It is much like your box in size," Harpo observed, looking around. "Though more lavishly appointed."

"My box doesn't go up and down," Freddie said. He reached forward and pressed a button.

The lavish box began to rise. "Great Poseidon," Harpo cried, "The very Earth is moving!" He stared in horror at Freddie, who was grinning widely. Freddie stepped closer and began to sniff the air.

"What are you *doing?*"

"I'm smelling your elevator virginity. Like you said, you can always tell by the scent. Smells kinda like you're scared to me."

The car came to an abrupt stop before Harpo could respond and he found himself being dragged out by Freddie, who was laughing heartily. People waiting outside the door stepped aside to give the ragged pair room to pass.

"Damn," Freddie said, looking around. "I thought it was on the second floor. Oh, well, come on."

A few seconds later they were teetering at the top edge of a moving staircase.

"Great Zeus!" Harpo cried.

"Nope," Freddie said, "just an escalator. But hey, we're almost at the aftershave counter, so don't worry."

His face alternating between green and white, Harpo closed his eyes until the angle of descent lessened, then leapt gratefully out onto the solid tiles of Macy's ground floor.

"Fun, hmm?" Freddie said.

"Most decidedly not!" Harpo fumed. "These devices are worse than your infernal moving machines!"

Ah, you'll get used to it," Freddie said.

"I do not intend to be here long enough to get *used* to it."

"Yeah, yeah. Come on, we gotta keep moving or they'll throw us out of here." He dragged Harpo toward the men's fragrance counter.

They wound through the handbags, the glittering jewelry, the oversized photos of perfectly painted women. The lights were bright and cheerful, casting a warm glow on everything and everyone. Soft music filled the air. And within seconds of their arrival at the sample display, Freddie had splashed Harpo with several concoctions,

"Stop!" Harpo gasped. "Do you actually assert that women *like* this?"

"It'll start to wear off in a few minutes," Freddie insisted. "It'll get more subtle. By the time you go see Gina, you'll smell pretty good."

Out of the corner of one eye, Freddie saw a security guard approaching. "Oops," he said, "time to split. Damn. I shoulda gone to the bathroom." He took hold of Harpo's collar and led him away, while his captive coughed and sputtered.

Out the revolving door they went, with Harpo taking baby steps between the glass panels. Emerging into the outside air, Harpo gulped in great hungry breaths. "We must never go there again," he wheezed. "I cannot put myself in such danger."

Freddie dragged him onward, saying, "You should see it when there's a sale."

They headed west on 34th, then south on Seventh, passing in their trek myriad racks of garments being pushed north by groaning handlers.

A few blocks further, the worst of the odors had dissipated. "You're starting to smell pretty good," Freddie said. "Now we just need to get some flowers."

The wind gusted and blew open the front of Harpo's coat. He wrapped it tighter against himself. "But where are we to obtain flowers?" he asked. He looked down at the gritty sidewalk and stomped down on it with one sandaled foot. "Nothing grows here in this hard stuff."

"We're gonna buy them," Freddie said. "Follow me."

Soon they stood in front of a small market. Just inside the door were several white buckets of small bouquets, which the proprietor was busily arranging to enhance their appeal.

Freddie pointed through the window. "Give her one of those bunches of flowers." He dug into his pants pocket and pulled out a big handful of silver change. "Here's some money."

"This is a great kindness," Harpo said as he took it. "You are improving. For a mortal." He stepped inside the market as Freddie waited outside and stood over the buckets, pondering the choices. The proprietor gave him a scathing look of assessment followed by a sniff test. She made no attempt to hide her disapproval. "You got money?" she said.

He opened his hand; her eyes scanned the assortment of coins. She scowled upon calculating the sum and said, "What you buy?"

"I am in need of some flowers. For a woman. I must win her trust."

"Not enough money," the woman said coldly. "Flowers eight dollar. Have two." Then she scrutinized him once again and pronounced a more deadly opinion. "You need more than flowers." She turned away and busied herself with stock-keeping tasks.

Harpo raised his voice and said, "Why are you all so miserably rude and inhospitable here? When I am powerful once more—"

The woman turned back toward him. "You go now," she said.

"I came here to engage in honest trade, and you have treated me miserably. Why, in Greece—"

The woman reached over to one side and grabbed a long broom, then spun around and wielded it towards Harpo. Spouting a stream of gibberish, she threatened him with the handle. He retreated backward out the door.

When his charge emerged flowerless, Freddie said, "I guess it didn't go too well in there."

He handed the change back to Freddie. "In Greece," he complained, "I would have been given the flowers without the coins in exchange, and I would have had the best wishes of the merchant for success in my pursuit." He slapped his hands down at his sides in frustration. "Here I get insults. And an invitation to depart."

"Ah, don't pay her no mind," Freddie said. "These places are always gettin' robbed. I don't blame her, way we look. You can't take it too personal." He patted Harpo on the shoulder to console him. Then his face brightened. "Hey, I got an idea. Let's go look in the dumpster. Maybe there'll be some flowers in there that she tossed out. We might find a couple of good ones."

A few steps further down the street he entered an alley, with Harpo close at his heels.

Ω Ω Ω

Gina had been updating client records for nearly an hour when Harpo arrived outside the door of her office, his hands held oddly behind his back. He poked his head inside and looked around, warily inspecting the ceiling and the top of the cabinet for unauthorized beings. When he was satisfied that nothing would jump out and bite him, he looked at her with doleful, puppy-dog eyes.

"I greet you," he said softly.

Gina sighed and put down her pencil. "I greet you, too, Harpo."

"I have brought you an offering," he said. He brought one arm forward from behind his back and held the flowers out for her to see. They were a sad-looking assortment of semi-wilted blossoms; bits of green and small flashes of color struggled to be seen in the brownish mass. He smiled weakly and offered them toward her. "They are no match for your beauty. But I wish to appease your anger at me."

Two scents collided, assaulting her. *Did he dip himself in aftershave?* The other was less pleasant. *Earthy, rotting.* She took the proffered bouquet from him and brought it cautiously to her nose. The rank odor was coming from the flowers, or what was left of them.

But so touching. *Who are you and what have you done with Harpo?* She made a show of inspecting them. "Thank you so much!" She poked around in a cabinet and took out a tall glass, then compared the size of the bouquet, and judged that it would fit.

"I wish there were more," he said.

She filled the glass with water, then tried to put the bouquet into it. The stems would not all fit, and she held the bouquet out at arms' length.

I wish there were more, he'd said.

She stared up at Harpo. He grinned goofily.

Nah, she thought, dismissing her own incomprehensible thought. She spent a moment picking off wilted blossoms, but stopped when she realized that she'd have little left if she continued. She crammed the lot into the glass and set it on the counter. "There," she said. "I really needed something to cheer me up." She turned to him and smiled.

"I curse myself for disturbing your harmony earlier. I am nothing more than a stupid oaf. May I drown in a pool of my own urine. May worms nest between my toes. May . . ."

She cut him short. "Okay, okay," she said. "You're sorry. So am I. I was way out of line to give you such a hard time. After thinking over what happened this afternoon, I've come to the conclusion that you didn't know how offensive the things you said were, and I shouldn't have berated you. Please accept my apology. I didn't mean to hurt your feelings."

"Nor I yours," he said.

She smiled. "Friends?"

"Friends," he agreed.

"Good," she said. "Speaking of friends," she added, "How are you and Freddie getting along? Okay?"

"Oh, very well indeed."

She seemed relieved. "I'm glad. I thought you two might end up liking each other. And I want you to keep coming back here. I'm very interested in what happens to you."

She was sorely tempted to add, *Professor Klein.* Instead, she smiled sweetly. "Now, if you'll excuse me, I have some work to finish tonight."

He wanted to be agreeable, so he gave up the notion of engaging her further and bid her good-bye. He went back outside to where Freddie waited.

"The flowers worked reasonably well," he said as they started back toward the Freezer. "Now with Zeus's blessing, perhaps we can acquire some wine. I do not wish to be sober just now."

Chapter 10
Kappa

Amid the daily barrage of book club offers, coupon packets, catalogs, and bills was a large, squarish envelope made of very fine cream-colored paper. It looked terribly out of place, as if it should be dropped through the polished brass mail slot of some ornately carved wooden door, and picked up immediately by the gloved hand of a butler who would deliver it to the addressee on a silver tray.

Gina turned it over in her hands, taking great care. The envelope was weighty, promising multiple layers. Her name and address were written with elegant flourishes in calligraphy. There was a beautiful wildflower stamp in the right corner, canceled with a circle of red.

I simply remember my favorite things, flashed through her mind for a sweet moment. "Hey, David, take a gander at this. Looks important." She held it up in front of him, allowing him to stare at it for a few seconds. Then, feeling greedy, she took it back. *He's not going to read it anyway.*

She opened it and separated the contents, laying each piece carefully on the table so the proper order could be restored later.

"The Directors of Bellevue Hospital, in cooperation with the City of New York, cordially invite you to attend the 57th annual Community Service Awards Banquet."

The remainder of the letter listed the particulars of the event. There was a return card with envelope, an onion skin liner, and a pair of tickets to the event itself.

The return card had a line for a guest. There were *two* tickets.

Ugh.

Enclosed with the invitation was a handwritten note from one of the directors informing Gina that she would be receiving an award for outstanding community service that night, and that she would also be given a $1000 cash grant along with a plaque, both of which the director sincerely hoped she would see fit to accept.

"Are you kidding me?" she said aloud. "A thousand dollars! What kind of moron wouldn't accept it?"

David sat fidgeting on the couch nearby, his jacket unzipped, a slight look of anxiety on his face.

In her heart's ear, she heard him say, *Gina, that's great!* Her shoulders ached for the feel of his arms around them.

It's about time, don't you think? the before David said in her reverie. *They should have given you an award years ago, with all the stuff you do in that center. Hey! We should use that money for a nice long vacation. I'll see if I can get someone to take over my patients for a week, and we'll go together. Tell you what, here's an even better idea, let's get married first and that'll be our honeymoon! What do you say? We can pull it all together pretty quickly . . .*

He was staring straight past her, with the fixed gaze of a statue. *Does this never go away? What do I have to do?*

Bargaining.

She folded the director's note in half again. The familiar frustration of having no one on hand to share good news, *any* news, settled over her with stunning quickness. She picked up the phone and called her mother in New Jersey, but there was no answer. *God forbid they should have an answering machine or anything equally decadent,* she thought in disappointment. She called her sister, remembered she was away, and left a lengthy message. The urge to share still unsatisfied, she considered her other possibilities.

McCarthy? Vague discomfort filled her. That left Miranda. She reassembled the invitation carefully and tucked it back into its envelope, then started to prepare David for the night. The sharing would have to wait until she got to Bellevue.

Ω Ω Ω

The strong aroma of thickening coffee filled the small police office. Gina walked in with her nose in the air, sniffing as if she were following a scent trail, the envelope in her hand. She untilted herself as she settled in front of the counter.

Miranda poured a cup of the aromatic coffee from the pot behind her and handed it to Gina. Then she grinned slyly and crossed her arms on the countertop. "So," she said, "who are you going to take to the banquet as your date?"

Gina scowled and slapped the envelope down on the counter. "Dammit, Miranda, you were my last chance to surprise someone with the good news!"

"Sorry," she said. "I already knew. I'm on the nominating committee."

"You never told me that! Cut it out!"

"A politically active African American female sergeant? Are you kidding? I GOT THE POWER! I'm on every committee in New York. They *love* my opinion. And I'm always happy to give it."

"So are you responsible for me getting this award?" Her expression was tinged with disappointment.

"Oh, no," Miranda said with a broad grin. "We're not allowed to nominate those folks with whom we have a 'personal' relationship. Your name was brought up by someone else, though I'm not at liberty to say who it was."

Gina looked relieved, and the eagerness reappeared. "Oh, come *on*. Tell me. *Please*."

"Un *unh!* Forget it. But I will tell you that it's not the first time you've been considered. Last year you missed it by only one vote. This year you sailed right through."

"Wow. I'm dumbfounded. I didn't think anyone noticed me down in the dungeon."

"Oh, they notice, all right. Congratulations."

"Thanks." Then quietly, "Wow."

Miranda reached out and pulled lightly on Gina's ponytail. "I'll tell you one other thing they'll notice. The way you look when you show up to collect your fancy award. You are going to have to do some *major* shopping beforehand." She peeked over the counter and pointed at Gina's feet, which were clad in her customary laced-up brown leather. "None of your damned Earth shoes." She flipped the ponytail back over Gina's shoulder. "And fancier hair."

She leaned closer as if conveying a confidence. "I think that's why they give you the money. They want you to show up looking prosperous. Keeps the deep pockets open when they see all those shining faces who work here. So you, my dear, with a little helpful advice from yours truly, will look *good*." She drew out the last word sinuously. "We are going to do some truly Olympic shopping."

A carryover of the favorite-things feeling Gina had felt when she opened the invitation started to filter in, warming her. She smiled and said, "It'll be like getting ready for the prom."

Miranda beamed approvingly. "Only better."

"Well, I should get going," Gina said, still flushed. She finished the last of her coffee in a long gulp, then crushed the empty Styrofoam cup in her hand and dropped it into a wastebasket. She hesitated, then said, "Wow. This is great." Then she turned and tilted off into the hallway traffic, heading upstairs.

As soon as Gina was out the door, Miranda said to her departing figure, "Not like any prom *I* ever went to. Won't *you* be surprised." She snickered and turned back to her paperwork.

Ω Ω Ω

Gina squirmed in the chair opposite Aaron. She looked directly into his eyes and ate crow.

"I'm still mortified after that fiasco on Wednesday."

"It was nothing."

"Oh, *please*. Even *you* don't have that thick a skin."

"You'd be surprised."

"In this case, Aaron, I think I really would. I mean, some of his behavior was just horrifying to me. I can't imagine how it must have felt to you."

"He was just being inquisitive. He played the innocent well enough to appear genuine, and to tell you the truth, I find him fascinating—refreshing, even. He has himself unnervingly convinced that he is who he says he is. But there's a lot of case history on people deluding themselves to the degree that they believe their own falsehoods. Richard Nixon thought those tapes were going to exonerate him. Then there's O. J. Simpson. And Colin Ferguson. Not to mention a whole host of former Nazis who keep claiming the Fuhrer made them do it. So forget it. I don't hold you responsible for what he said."

"Whew," she sighed. "I have to admit it's a load off my mind to know you feel that way." She glanced down at her hands, tightly clamped together in her lap.

"Now if we could just get rid of a few of your other loads, things might start to resolve a little."

He said it with a beautiful, warm smile, in a tone of voice that would have calmed a charging bull, but Gina knew when Aaron was being serious. She smiled wanly. "You never let me get away with anything." She crossed and uncrossed her legs self-consciously. "Problem is, every time I think I'm ready to drop something, I can't decide what."

"Which makes me wonder why you'd want to take on another burden right now."

She looked at him in surprise. "I don't understand."

"Sure you do. Harpo."

She stiffened and sat up. "He's a professional obligation, not a personal one."

"Having observed your association with this man, I'm not convinced. I don't recall you ever having brought someone in here for a conference. Referrals, yes, and outside services. But you've never actually asked me to see one of them. As a therapist."

"But this is a very unusual case. You said so yourself." She laughed nervously and fiddled with her ponytail. "I just can't get a handle on him."

"And you're digging still, to try to find out more about him?"

"Yes, of course I am."

"Why?"

She sat up straighter still. "What do you mean, why? You and I are birds of a feather in that regard. I think you may actually be even more of a digger than I am."

He smiled. "But I'm *supposed* to get in there and dig. Your work is different.

You assess, you quantify, you move them along. So your digging should be less intense. No less important," he hastened to add, "just different in the scope of the details."

"In this case, I think there's good reason to stretch some of the boundaries. He's unlike any guy that's ever come in to the center. I'm drawn to him in ways I can't begin to describe. These stories of his, I mean, they're just wild, and he's so intelligent . . ."

"Oh, I'll give him that, all right. That and another thing. He's as inside-out as a sock on laundry day. Classically delusional. He's living what he thinks the life of a Greek god should be. I have to admit, he's got it down pretty well. The only thing he seems to lack is the historical meanness of Dionysus." He nodded toward the corner of his desk.

A book. *The Bacchae*. Euripides. She turned it over in her hands, examining the worn paper cover. She flipped through the pages and saw hand-written notations. She glanced up at Aaron.

"Your notes?"

He nodded. "Back when I still could."

It was the first time she had seen his pre-paralysis handwriting. "Aaron, your script, it's—beautiful."

"Blame my mother." He smiled. "Miriam dug it out of one of my old boxes last night. I would suggest you read it. In one of the scenes, a mother rips the head off her own son at the bidding of the god Dionysus."

She blanched. "Yikes. Really?"

"Really. And your Harpo is patterning on this mythical deity," Aaron said. "I don't *think* he has the potential to do that sort of thing, but it's early in my assessment. He may just be working his way up to it."

Gina let a silent moment pass. "We've gotten slightly off track here. We were talking about me having too many loads."

"Yes, we were. But it all fits. Just like the god he's patterning, he's seductive and appealing. He's fascinating, cultured, he's all sorts of interesting things, and most appealing of all to *you*, he needs care. The point I'm trying to make is that it's dangerous for you to form another care attachment right now. You're not supposed to be doing that, remember?"

"Oh, really, Aaron," she protested, "it's part of my job—"

"He's basing his delusional identity on a very unpredictable mythological character, one who could change like the wind from orgasmic sweetness to demonic brutality. Now to be clear, I doubt that he would ever harm you, but I'll guarantee that as he plays out this identity, he will change. And you'll be so heavily invested in him that you'll hang in there to see if you can change him back."

Her head drooped down, she was staring at her fingernails again.

"Sound familiar?" he asked.

After a moment, she whispered, "Yes."

"Harpo's much easier to deal with than David, and—because of his intelligence and approachability—you unconsciously view him as very receptive. You may be doing some reverse transference to feel successful, because you *like* to take care of people."

"Aaron, I'm trying not to do—"

He didn't let her finish. "It's perfectly okay for you to like to take care of people. What's *not* okay is for you to do it to your own detriment. You're not feeling successful with David, and although it's beyond your control, your attempts to bring him back feel like a string of failures to you. It's your job to bring this *client* in, keep him safe for a little while, get him established in the system, and then hand him off like a football to someone who'll try to get him over the goal line."

Gina let out a long breath. "So, what do you suggest I do? Ask him not to come to the center? We both know he's too soft for the big shelter. And he may be nuts, but I actually—have come to like him. He arrives at my building every afternoon to 'escort' me, as he puts it, talks about things that interest him. It's nice to have conversations with someone who actually responds. He brings me, for lack of a better word, a small amount of joy."

"And that's perfectly okay, but don't forget one very important thing: the delivery of joy is an important characteristic of his assumed persona. So don't delude *yourself* into thinking about him as some benign but loony second cousin who tries to get a little too familiar some times. You don't have to push him away entirely, but don't take on the obligation of trying to figure him out. He'll only play with you."

Gina stood up and started pacing behind the chair. Aaron followed her with his eyes.

"Damn it, Aaron, this is one of those rare occasions when I feel like it's really worth it to expend the time. *He isn't completely wrecked yet.* He's one I think I could actually save. I could make a difference in his life."

"And I'd be the first to say that when a positive difference can be made, it *should* be made." He breathed deeply. "So, I have a suggestion. How about if I take him on as a patient?"

She frowned, arms folded across her chest. "Who's gonna pay?"

"I'll do it free."

Her eyes narrowed. *"Why?"*

"Because I agree that he's worth the effort and that he's especially savable. And he fascinates me, too. But I'm in better shape than you are right now—" He paused and smiled from his wheelchair— "and it won't be a burden to me. Maybe I'll write an article about him for a professional journal."

Gina sat down in the chair again, looking whipped. "Okay, I guess." Then she smiled. "But only if I can I get my name on that article."

Aaron laughed. "Of course. You'll get specific credit for the identification of his unique delusion."

"Are you sure you want to do this?"

"Definitely. I can't wait to hear about Cleopatra."

It lightened the heavy mood; they both relaxed and laughed, and the matter of Harpo was closed. Then the matter of David was reopened. All joviality ceased.

"The test results show no excess medication in his bloodstream. We had the dosage right. So I have to conclude that it's probably not the perfect medication for David."

She was quiet for a moment then said, "We're about out of choices, aren't we?"

"From the 'normal' channels, but there *is* an experimental medication in clinical trial that has some potential for David. He fits all the proper subject criteria, especially since this medication is intended to work with people who have baseline permanent physical injuries.

"I took the liberty of calling the director of the study to see if they could take David. I hope you don't mind. She said they'd be happy, even eager to have him. This medication belongs to a different group of chemicals than David's already tried. Most of the participants have shown very few side effects. Some sub—"

He paused. "Some *patients* show dramatic improvement in their depressive symptoms, and a smoothing of the manic symptoms, others with a similar disease profile show none whatsoever. I need to know that you're aware of these things before we get him going in the trial."

Gina nodded her acceptance. "I guess my only real question is the same one I always have: how long will it be before we see any improvement?"

"Same answer," he said. "This is still experimental."

She sighed wearily. "So how do we get started?"

"We'll set up the initial appointments. David will be given a physical before they enroll him. I'll want to see him when he's been taking it for about two weeks. The study people won't talk to you directly, but I'll stay on top of things and let you know how it's progressing."

"Thanks, Aaron. I'd prefer that, anyway."

"I thought you might. Now you have to set up two appointments when you leave, one for yourself in about two weeks, and one for our friend Harpo, whenever."

She stood up. "Aaron, I can't begin to thank you for everything you're doing for David. And now Harpo."

He smiled. "It's my job, but I'd probably do it even if it weren't. Sound familiar?"

Gina smiled. "Yes," she said.

Ω Ω Ω

Diane loped into the shelter and strode into Gina's office, surprising her sister in the middle of a supply inventory. They exchanged light pecks on the cheek and a quick sisterly hug, and Gina put down her note pad.

"I just got back," Diane panted. "I got your message. I needed some exercise so I figured I'd jog down here."

"Fifty blocks?"

"Piece of cake."

"Didn't you guys ski this weekend?"

"We tried," she said with a wave of her hand, "but the snow was lousy. We did some snowmobiling, but that's about all. The only real exercise I get doing that is pushing the damn thing out of the garage and clinging for dear life to Rick. But what a nice message to come home to! Good for you."

"A thousand dollars good."

"No way!" Diane said.

"*Way*! But Miranda says I have to get really dressed up to go to this thing, so I guess I'll be spending some of it before I even get it."

Diane smiled warmly. "I knew you'd come around eventually."

Gina took the invitation out of her purse and gave it to her sister, who handled it with similar reverence. She removed each piece carefully and read the particulars with a look of excitement on her face. She looked up from the cream vellum. "I'm going to be around that weekend. For a change. You want me to take care of David?"

"You're not going upstate?"

"Rick's giving a seminar that Saturday afternoon so we decided it wouldn't be worth the trip for just one day."

"That would be great."

"But you have to promise me you'll try to relax and have a good time. None of your eleven-thirty crap. You stay until the party's over, even if it lasts all night. I'll just sleep on the couch."

"It's an awards banquet. It's not gonna last all night. Midnight, maybe. One at the latest."

"I mean it, Gina. After parties like that there's always a group of people going somewhere else to continue the celebration. Is Miranda going?"

"Yes, but—"

"You stick with her, then. And I don't want to hear any arguments. This is

125

going to be *your* night."

Gina knew the futility of arguing with her headstrong sister. "Okay," she said.

"That's a good girl." Diane put an arm around Gina's shoulder and hugged her with sisterly warmth. A silent moment of happiness followed. And was broken. It was as if she couldn't help herself.

"David just had another evaluation. It wasn't terrible, it just wasn't very good." She told Diane about the clinical trial and the new medication.

Diane shook her head slowly and sighed. "Well, it's better than him getting worse, I suppose."

"It doesn't *feel* better."

Diane put a comforting hand on Gina's arm. "I'm sorry, Gina. We were all hoping for better." Awkwardness prevailed for a moment. "Maybe this experimental stuff will work for him." She glanced down at her sport watch. "I'd better run back before I cool down too much. And I have to pick up Farfel from the neighbor's. I hope he'll remember me."

"Soon as the can opener hits the cat food, he'll remember."

Diane laughed. "No doubt. He's a boy cat." She drew on her mittens, hugged her sister again and left the basement, wishing she felt brave enough to say the things she really wanted to say.

Ω Ω Ω

Upstairs, there was a psychiatric intern who'd just completed her studies at Columbia; Gina asked to see her yearbook. She found Klein's photograph in a group shot of his department. It was no better than the one she'd found online. Joe Klein was standing in the back row, just behind Peter Poulos, looking like a deer in the headlights. His hair was tight to his head and very wavy. She recognized it as the kind of hair that would curl mercilessly if allowed to grow. Just like Harpo's. The height was right, as was the shape of the face, and the general build, based on what she could see in the bad photograph.

For a moment she debated dragging Harpo uptown to show him around. Someone would tell her conclusively if he and Joe Klein were the same person.

But what about the wife? Her behavior didn't make any sense.

And Aaron's probably right, she thought to herself. *Harpo will play along if I press this. Play with my head.*

We all play with each other, she thought, and, with a sigh, she closed the yearbook, admitting to herself as she did that she wasn't through playing with Harpo just yet.

Chapter 11
Lambda

While Freddie slept, he slipped out.

"You see, Midas? We found it without Freddie."

The small dog yipped excitedly; Harpo set him down on the sidewalk in front of Gina's building. "Stay close," he said, as Midas jumped around his ankles. "These mortals can be very clumsy sometimes." He leaned over and tickled the little dog's head. "No doubt you miss your horns," he cooed. "I miss my own terribly. But they would not be appreciated here, eh?"

He walked up the steps and pulled on the door handle; the metal rim of the door grated against the bolt of the lock. He pulled again, got the same frustrating result.

He was sitting on the top step pondering his quandary when an older man came out of the building. Harpo stood up quickly and tried to catch the door with his hand, but the man spun around and grabbed him by the arm.

"You got business in this building, mister?"

He tried to shake his arm free, but the grip was surprisingly strong. "I have come to see Gina," he said. "And kindly remove your hand from my arm."

The man gripped harder. Midas grabbed hold of one of his pant cuffs and pulled, growling through his tiny teeth as he tore at the fabric. The man shook him free; Midas scampered down to the safety of the bottom step, where he barked furiously.

"Yappy little shit," the man muttered. He turned back to Harpo and said, "You wanna see Gina Bugbee?"

"I . . . I think so. I know her only as Gina."

"You a friend of hers?"

"Oh, yes, very much so," he said.

The man gave him a pointed stare. "Then how come you don't know her last name?"

He thought about that for a moment. "I suppose it is because she never told

127

me."

"Not much of a friend." He let go of his captive's arm and straightened his jacket, then hitched his thumb back in the direction of the intercom. "Anyway, she's on the buzzer list. She'll let you in if she wants to." He started to walk down the stairs.

"But I cannot read the letters."

The old man stopped, and when he turned around, his expression was softer. "She's in number 12C. You know your numbers, right?"

"Uh, I would be grateful . . ."

The man sighed and walked up the stairs again, then pressed the correct buzzer. He explained the process, then left to get his *Times*, glaring down at the snarling little dog.

A few seconds later the buzzer sounded, and Dionysus heard Gina's voice. "Who is it?"

He took a step backward. He stuck his finger out, hesitating, then pressed the answering button. "Dionysus," he said.

"Who?" he heard her say again.

"*Dion—*", he started to say, then, "Harpo."

"Harpo? What are you doing here?"

"I, uh, wish to see you."

Though her voice was scratchy, he could hear the hesitation. "It's my day off."

"I do not understand this 'day off' . . ."

There was a moment of silence and he wondered if she had heard his last transmission. Then her voice came back again. "Stay there. We're coming out anyway."

A few minutes later Gina and David appeared in the doorway. "Where's Freddie?" She looked around. "I'm surprised to see you without him."

"He is sleeping. It would have been ungodlike to disturb him."

"Pretty human, though. Mortal, I mean. So why did you want to see me?"

He had not anticipated the need to explain himself. "Because it pleases me to do so."

He could see the battle between curiosity and hesitation in her eyes.

Curiosity won. "David and I are going to the Met now," she said. "You're welcome to join us if you want to."

"What is this 'Met'?"

"A museum, uptown." She was surprised when he did not ask for an explanation. "There's a lot of Greek art there, so you might really enjoy it. It'll be my treat."

"Treat? I do not . . ."

"It means I'll pay the donation."

"We must give a payment to someone to see art?"

"Of course," she said. "How else could they keep the place open?"

Ω Ω Ω

He clung to a vertical pole, green-faced and wavering, as the northbound train rocked its way toward the museum. They walked crosstown from the station to the Met, with David determining the pace as usual, and Gina looking embarrassed as passersby gawked at her male companions. While there was occasional conversation between Gina and Harpo, David remained silent.

"He does not speak much, this boyfriend of yours," Harpo observed.

"He's not terribly comfortable around strangers."

"But I am not a stranger . . . he has seen me before."

"Only a couple of times. He has to really know you before he'll talk to you."

"So he speaks to you often, then?"

A look of great sadness came over Gina's face. "Not as much as he used to. Sometimes, when he's in the mood."

"I have seen this type of madness many times before, it does not surprise me that there should be little said by the one living it." He gave her a look of sympathy. "But you must take heart, and do not despair, for some mortals who experience such madness are, oddly, content in their worlds."

Gina looked at him in surprise. *This is what I'm talking about, Aaron,* she thought. "You may be right. Sometimes he *does* seem content."

Then Harpo said, "But *you* must feel terribly sad, for you are doing the living of two mortals and feeling the pleasures of none, eh?"

She stopped walking and stared at him. David walked on, but she caught him by the arm. "That was an extraordinarily perceptive observation," she said quietly.

He shrugged. "It is nothing less than my divine duty to know such things."

He gave her the usual goofy smile, and gestured in the direction they'd been moving before she stopped. But when they rounded the corner and the museum came into view, he gasped in delight.

"Why, it is magnificent!" he said.

She saw his captivation, so she turned her own eyes toward the building. "I guess I've seen it so many times I'm immune to its magic. But you're right, it's wonderful. And if you like the outside this much, you're really going to like what's inside. Come on," she said. "There's a lot to see."

No sooner had they entered the great hall than Harpo came to an abrupt stop and pointed upward, toward the mezzanine balcony.

"What is it, Harpo?"

"Perseus!" he said. "Up there!" He ran to his right a bit to improve his view of the massive statue, and Gina followed, pulling David along with her.

"You've seen this statue before?"

"No! Not the statue, I have seen Perseus *himself*! The likeness is not perfect, but he holds the snaky head of Medusa, and he slayed her, so it must be him! But—it is wrong!" he cried. "The sculptor has gotten it wrong."

He ran a few steps closer and pointed to the stone head of the slain Gorgon. "Don't you see? He is looking directly at it! Perseus would *never* look at the head—to do so is to die the most horrible death, for the viewer is turned immediately to stone."

"Well, he *is* stone, *now*. And I'm sure the sculptor did it for artistic reasons . . ."

His voice grew louder and more agitated. "And why did the sculptor make his manhood so pitifully small in proportion to the rest of him? Perseus was a mighty hero, and most virile!"

"Maybe when this statue was made it was the fashionable thing to do, you know, sculpturally speaking—"

"Bah!" he said. "How can it be fashionable for a hero to look unmanly? This sculptor did not know what he was doing."

People began to stop and gather around them. Gina looked apologetically into a succession of staring eyes, wordlessly begging indulgence.

"Harpo," she said, "We should be moving along. We're drawing a crowd here. And other people might want to stand here to see the statue, too."

"I do not understand why they would waste time viewing something so imperfectly executed," he said huffily. He leaned toward a member of the crowd and said, "Do not bother. It is grossly inaccurate."

When Gina tugged on his arm, he turned to her and said, "They should see the truth about Perseus: that he was a giant among warriors, and that he was far too wise to cast his gaze in the direction of Medusa's head."

"Okay," Gina said to placate him, "I'm sure you're right. But let's go." She drew him along with one hand, and held onto David with the other.

He craned his neck all around as they stood in the ticket line, gawking at the things he saw. As the moments of waiting passed, he calmed. "This place is like a temple," he observed. "There are many people here, but still it is quiet."

"It is sort of a temple, for art."

"In Greece, we did not pay to enter our temples. We sometimes brought gifts or offerings, a newly slain beast or some sheaves of grain perhaps. But we did not pay with coins."

She laughed. "Don't take it personally," she said. "We don't use, uh—animals for trade here anymore. It's a little cumbersome carrying them around. Money is a lot simpler."

He was just mumbling *money is not simple* when they reached the head of the line. Gina paid for three, wondering as she put the change back how her wallet had become so unaccountably thin. "MasterCard for lunch," she said, turning back to her companions.

As they passed by the ticket lectern, a security guard looked Harpo over, carefully assessing his oddity, and received a scowl in return. Harpo turned toward Gina and said, "The sentries are quite rude here in this—"

He stopped talking in mid-sentence, and stared speechlessly over her shoulder. His mouth was open, and he tried to speak, but only small squeaks came out.

"What is it, Harpo? Are you okay?"

He pointed over her shoulder. "Do you not see it?" he said, his voice trembling.

"See what?" she said. Confused, she turned around. "Oh!" she said. "The statue. Yes. It's terrific."

"No. *No!* You do not understand. Can you not *see* it?"

She looked back at the statue, searching for something unusual. "See what? I *don't* understand."

"The resemblance! Have I aged so much, then, that you do not recognize this statue as one of *me*?"

She looked at the statue, then back at her charge, her patience ebbing. "Oh, for God's sake, Harpo. *Get a grip.* That is not a statue of you. It couldn't be. It's thousands of years old."

"As am I. And I stood for it when it was first made."

Well, Gina thought, *there's a statement I wasn't ready to hear.* "Oh, my." She stepped toward the statue and read the placard. *Dionysus,* was the boldface title. The text was in fine print, and Gina skimmed through it, one hand holding David's sleeve.

"*Dionysus, God of wine and divine intoxication, wears a panther skin over his short chiton and high sandals with animal heads on the overhanging flaps. He stands beside an archaistic female figure whose pose and dress imitate those of Greek statues carved in the 6th century B.C. It is difficult to know whether the original statue of Dionysus, of which this is a copy, included the female figure. Supports in the forms of pillars and herms and small statues were not uncommon in classical art, but the figure may represent Spes, a Roman personification of Hope, who was commonly shown as an archaistic maiden.*"

She stepped back and moved closer to Harpo. "You posed for this?"

"Yes, *yes!*" he said, greatly agitated. "Indeed. It was a tiresome task, but the sculptor—his name I do not recall—had great skill, and it was a worthy effort. But some talentless fool has copied it, and ruined it! The original was different, and far more beautiful."

"How was it different?" Then, she thought, *He's been here before, but he doesn't want me to know. Who do I know that can get me a look at the Met mailing list?*

He stepped forward and reached up, touching the front of the sculpture. "See how the copyist has placed the skin of a panther over my shoulder? In the first work, it was a leopard. And my hair was arranged differently, more like you see it now." He touched the rounded marble curls with one hand. Then he stood next to the statue, assuming the same pose. "Look!" he said. "While I am here next to it, study the likeness."

She glanced from him to the statue, then back to him again. "Well, now that you mention it . . . look, I'll call the curator when we get back later. To express your concerns. But right now—"

"And there is more . . ."

His voice, high pitched with excitement, drew the attention of the guard, who approached the group of three and said, "Excuse me, but is there a problem here?"

Harpo drew close to him. "Indeed, there is! This statue is a false copy of the original." He touched the front of it. "See, here—"

"Sorry, sir, but you have to keep your hands off the art."

"You would dare order me not to touch something that was inspired by my own divine being? *Intolerable.* I have touched the original statue—this is but worthless fakery—many times, long before you were born." He rubbed his hand purposefully along the front of the statue.

"Harpo . . ." Gina pleaded, "calm down. If it's a fake, it's not your problem."

"It is not a problem that false images of me are placed in public temples?" he cried. "How can this not be my problem?" He ranted on despite Gina's pleas that he be calm and the guard's insistence that he quiet down.

David stood to one side, staring at the floor, but as the confusion built up around him, he began to rock back and forth, muttering softly, and when Gina heard him, she disengaged herself from the disagreement. Without her buffering presence, the standoff came to a quick and ugly head.

Harpo poked the guard in the center of his chest. "You are a pathetically ignorant mortal." He stared contemptuously into the man's face from inches away. "You have the beady little eyes and the hawkish nose of a Roman. It is no wonder you act so stupidly."

The guard pointed toward the main entry. "That's it, mister, *out!* You're disturbing the other visitors."

Harpo stood his ground defiantly. "And well they should be disturbed. All mortals should be disturbed by false representations of divinity."

The guard grabbed him by the collar of his jacket and forcibly dragged him in the direction of the front door. The cacophony of their disagreement rose into the heights of the great entry hall, shattering the hallowed atmosphere. Visitors with wary looks stepped aside and let them pass.

Gina followed with David in tow, and when they finally caught up, she put one hand on the guard's shoulder. He turned around and faced her, leaving Harpo almost hanging from his own upheld jacket. "Wait," she said, "please. He didn't mean anything by that."

Harpo flailed his arms in protest. "Indeed, I did!"

Gina tightened her grip on the guard's shoulder and whispered, "He's a little— um, unbalanced."

The guard politely removed her hand and said, "I can see *that*." And with a great grunt of effort, he dragged the struggling, protesting Harpo out the main door and deposited him roughly on the steps. "You and this other gentleman can stay inside, Ma'am, but your friend here," and he pointed to Harpo, "is gonna have to wait for you outside."

The guard turned and went back inside, leaving them alone on the stairs. Gina crouched down next to Harpo, who sat on the top step fuming and swearing in Greek. "Nice little scene you made in there," she said angrily. "Thanks a lot for spoiling this trip. I'm going to take David inside and we're going to look around for a while; maybe I can salvage *some* fun. You can wait here if you want to, or you can leave. I'll either see you when I come out or I won't. Your decision."

He looked up at her with the expression of a hurt, angry child. "Indeed."

Chapter 12
Mu

Freddie scooted over to make room. "Where the hell have you been? I'm supposed to be watching you."

Sighing, Harpo climbed back into the box. "You were asleep, and I thought it ungodly to disturb your rest. I went to someplace called the Met Museum."

"What the fuck were you doing there?"

"I accompanied Gina," he said. "First I went to her abode, following the trails you have shown me. And then I tried to contact her through the talking device at her door. She invited me to accompany her with the man who is insane."

"Well, that's a start. She wouldn't take you if she didn't like you."

"Not so good a start. I have offended her terribly. Again."

"Well, it's a good thing you got back when you did. I was just about to go out and start looking for you." He paused, then admitted, "I was worried when I couldn't find you. So—what'd you do this time?"

"I behaved rather indecorously, or so I'm told." He related the details of his undignified expulsion.

"*Tsk, tsk, tsk*," Freddie said, shaking his head. "You shoulda told me you were going. I woulda gone with you. Then you wouldn'ta done what you did because I coulda told you not to."

"But I did nothing wrong!"

"Hey," Freddie said, "you did *something* wrong, or they wouldn'a thrown you out."

Harpo crossed his arms in front of his chest and let out an indignant *hmph*. "I did only what any other god confronted with a false image of himself would have done. Is it not your Christian god who has an admonition that there shall be no graven images? Suppose you came upon a sculpture of yourself, and the artist had given you a fine big wart on your nose or some other undeserved imperfection. Would you not object?"

Freddie laughed. "No one's gonna make a sculpture of me. And if they did, and they gave me a wart, I'd probably figure it was just a joke."

"But how am I to command the respect of followers, and win the faith of this woman, if I am shown unfavorably?"

"With all the followers you got, or don't got right now, I don't think it's gonna be too much of a problem. I'm the only one who believes *any* of the stuff you been spouting, and I don't give a shit what you look like." He pulled the drape aside for a moment to let in some air. "You're just pissed off because you made an ass of yourself in front of Gina."

Harpo glared at him, his dark eyes flashing anger.

"Come on," Freddie said, "don't give me that look. I *know* what you're up to, remember? You gotta make her believe in you and you're not doing too well."

His hard stare melted into a pained look of utter confusion. "What am I to do?"

"Well, first, you gotta apologize."

"Why? I did nothing wrong!"

"See, that's your problem in a nutshell. You don't understand women at all."

"Well, of course I understand women. It is through me that they complete themselves."

"Yeah, yeah. Forget that completion shit. Right now, you gotta get back on her good side. And with women, even if you didn't do anything wrong, you gotta apologize. Like this: 'Oh, honey, I'm *so* sorry, I was a great big shit and I promise I won't ever do it again.'" He smiled. "There. Just like that."

"Really?"

"Trust me, it works if you suck up to them. And you should probably bring her some sort of gift. A token of your undying love."

Harpo arched one eyebrow suspiciously. "Like the flowers? Their effect seemed rather temporary."

"Maybe something different this time. Hey," Freddie said, his excitement building, "I got an idea. Chocolate. Works like a charm. Problem is we don't have enough money. We'll have to panhandle. What time you got?"

The stranger who called himself Dionysus looked at the wristwatch Gina had given him and muttered softly as he did the necessary computations. He smiled in triumph and said, "It is twenty-five minutes after the hour of two."

"Okay," Freddie said, "that's good, real good. The streets'll be busy right about now. Come on, let's go."

Ω Ω Ω

Gina entered the fitting room at Macy's with a pile of dresses draped over one arm. *Just the thing to get that museum fiasco off my mind,* she thought, *a well-lit, full length view of my own cellulite.* She regarded herself momentarily in the tall mirror, and almost instantly found things to dislike. "Love you, Mom, hate your hips," she whispered to her own image, wishing she had inherited, as Diane had, the length and narrowness of their father. "In my next life," she said, smiling sarcastically at herself, "I will be a goddess."

She took the first dress off its hanger. It was short, with thin straps, and fitted. It zipped up the back, so she stepped into it and pulled the zipper up a little higher than her waist. She flung the curtain aside and stepped resolutely out to the viewing area where Diane and Miranda awaited her, prepared to deliver their opinions on each candidate for the Big Night.

"Help me zip this up, someone, will you? I think it's a little tight in the bust."

"Can you breathe?" Miranda asked.

Gina breathed in and out in front of the mirror, and watched her heaving *décolletage* rise and fall. "Yeah," she said, "but not decently."

"Then it's the right size," Miranda declared.

"But I look so—"

Miranda and Diane clucked out their unison approval, one saying *young*, the other, *sexy*. They pronounced the dress perfectly wonderful. Then came a red one, too short. And a turquoise dress, declared by the saleswoman to be the new black. It was just not cut right for Gina's voluptuous figure.

And fourteen dresses later, the winner was that simple first dress. "I could've saved myself all that bother," Gina said. She stood at the register, flanked by friend and sister, and watched, credit card in hand, as the saleswoman carefully wrapped and bagged the little black treasure.

"Yeah, but you had to try them all. Now you're sure it's the *one*," Miranda said.

"I guess . . ." She looked at the charge slip, gulped silently at the amount, and signed. "But to tell you the truth, I think you guys are more sure about it than I am."

"Hey, that's what you have us for," Diane said with a warm smile. "To help you with the hard stuff."

Ω Ω Ω

Freddie stood on the corner of Third Avenue and 28th Street with his hand extended and droned, "Got any change?" at each passerby. Vouchers would not do today. Nearby, on the stoop of a neat-looking building, Harpo sat beside an empty flower pot and rehearsed his apology.

"Honey," he said, pleading desperately for forgiveness, "I'm *so* sorry." Then came the humble admission of guilt. "I was a great big shit." And the guarantee of rehabilitation. "I promise I won't ever do it again."

The mantra was nearing perfection when Freddie sat down beside him and announced, "I think I got enough."

"Excellent! Now let me show you how well I have learned my apology." He stood up and cleared his throat. He placed one hand dramatically on his heart, raised the other in supplication, and cast his glance heavenward. "Honey," he nearly begged, "I'm so *very* sorry." He looked at Freddie and said, "I added the *very* myself. To show my sincerity."

Freddie nodded his approval, so Harpo resumed his Thespian stance and completed the rehearsed line. He turned back to Freddie. "Well, what do you think?"

Freddie was almost laughing, but managed to stifle it. "It'll do," he said. "*What*, I don't know, but it's bound to do something."

They found a drugstore nearby and received the customary scrutiny from the guard as they passed through the detectors, but Freddie smiled and extended his money-filled hand as proof of their good intent, and they were allowed to pass. They headed straight for the candy aisle.

"Hey," he said happily, "this stuff's all on sale. Just don't tell her we got the chocolates on the cheap."

"Why not?"

"Because she'll think *you're* cheap, and that don't sit well with women. You want to impress her with your *mag-nan-imity*."

They selected a small square box of chocolates and paid for it with Freddie's begged fortune, then left the store.

"Okay, what time is it now?"

After a few moments of tortuous ciphering, Harpo announced, "Four o'clock plus ten minutes."

"Perfect. We can go over to her apartment and wait for her. She should be coming out soon." With Freddie leading the way, they headed out in the fading daylight, to conquer the soul of a woman.

ΩΩΩ

"Thanks again, Mrs. Miller," Gina said to her short, gray-haired neighbor, who disappeared out the door with a twenty clutched in her wrinkled hand. She looked at the clock on the wall near the kitchen and said to Diane, "I'd better get out of here. Miranda will shriek at me if I'm late." She picked up several bags and boxes piled near the front door and said, "Here goes nothing."

"Never mind," Diane said. "You'll knock 'em dead."

Still hesitating by the door, Gina said, "I'm not sure how late I'll be."

"Don't worry about it. I told you before, stay out all night if you want to."

"I won't be out all night, Diane."

"Hey, you never know. Stranger things have happened than you having a good

137

time."

"Very funny."

She picked up her burdens, kissed David and her sister good-bye, and lumbered out the door.

Ω Ω Ω

As Freddie and Harpo were coming around the corner toward Gina's building, she emerged with her boxes.

Freddie put out his hand abruptly. "There she is. Hey, looks like she's going somewhere."

"Then we must follow her!"

They watched as she put one hand's worth of bags down on the sidewalk and raised her hand in the air. A yellow cab pulled to the curb, and she loaded all her bags into it.

"Aw, shit, she's taking a cab!" Freddie said.

"Then we must hurry!"

"Wait a minute, pal, I ain't running after a cab."

Harpo gave him a cold stare and said, "Then I shall do so without you." He took off after the departing cab in a sprint.

"Ah, crap," Freddie said, and he loped after him.

Ω Ω Ω

Gina nearly fell through the door when Miranda opened it. "Sorry I'm late," she panted. "Traffic was brutal for some reason and the cab just crawled over here. I could've walked faster."

"You should've had a U-Haul, by the looks of it." She took a few of the bags out of Gina's hands. "You know, I'm pretty sure I said *come over*, not *move in*. What *is* all this stuff?"

"Oh, just every pair of black shoes I own. I can never decide which shoes to wear. And I brought all my jewelry, too. It's been a long time since I got all duded up." She laughed nervously and handed over the Macy's bag.

"Ah, the dress," Miranda purred. "That's where we start. Then we add the embellishments. All right, let's see what else you've got here."

Gina opened all the containers and laid out her treasures for Miranda's inspection, then stepped back, expecting Miranda to point from one offering to another and say, "*Those* shoes, *those* earrings, and *that* color lipstick." Miranda spent a few moments studying the collection, then turned to Gina with a disappointed frown.

138

"I hope you don't take this wrong, but I think you might have misread that invitation. It said party, not funeral."

Looking hurt and surprised, Gina said, "But this is all my best stuff!"

Miranda picked up the jewelry box and scrutinized the contents. It was full of small precious things, all "good" pieces. "What are you planning to do with your hair?" she said.

Gina fingered her ponytail. "I thought I'd put it up in a bun, you know, so it would be off my neck."

Miranda looked up at her and sighed. "A *bun?* Sweet Jesus." She shook her head back and forth slowly and said, "I bet you iron your sheets, don't you?"

Gina stared at her curiously and said, "Well, only if —"

"Oh, good Lord, Gina, I was *kidding!* Listen, all this stuff you brought says '*tea party*' to me. Don't you have anything *bigger?*"

"I can't afford anything bigger."

Miranda let out a long, resigned sigh and placed her hands on her hips. "I don't mean real stuff, I mean good fakes. I swear to God, you white girls don't know anything about dressing up."

"Miranda! That's so—"

"It isn't *that* if it's true! Especially not between girlfriends. Look at this stuff, it's all little and pretty and sweet. And I know it all looks wonderful on you. But for something like this, you want *big, big, big.* Go for effect. Nobody's gonna be able to see any of this tiny stuff from the back row when you're up there on that stage getting your award. You have to wear something that'll get their attention."

"I don't *want* to get their attention."

"And that's your damned problem. The way you're going, you're just gonna make yourself disappear right off the face of the Earth. You hide all night in the basement at Bellevue, you sleep all day in your apartment with the shades down, and now when you finally get a chance to shine, you're gonna hide behind these sweet little opals." She sang the last three words.

She picked up a simple black leather shoe, well made and expensive for Gina's modest budget, a classic wardrobe staple intended to last years. "I mean, just look at these. They're beautiful but they're recital shoes! You probably don't even own any FMP's."

"Any *what?*"

Miranda gave her a look of disbelief. "Oh, Lord, you don't even know what they are."

"No. I have *no* idea what you're talking about."

"FMP's," she said again with emphasis. "Fuck Me Pumps. Invitation shoes. Also known as Fill My Pussy shoes."

"*Miranda!!!*"

Miranda ignored her. "What size do you wear?"

Somehow, Gina sputtered out, "Nine."

"Well, girl, this is your lucky day. Wait right here."

She left a limp, mute Gina sitting in the living room and returned a few moments later with a pair of black satin shoes with pointed toes, three-inch spiked heels and a big cluster of rhinestones on the vamp. She plunked them down in Gina's lap. "Now *these* are shoes, genuine certified Fuck Me Pumps. Try them on."

Gina looked at her with an expression that said, *are you kidding?*

Miranda laughed. "Come on, they're not bear traps."

Gina dutifully took off her walking shoes and slipped on the satin pumps. She looked down at her feet, morphed suddenly into transplants from someone else's body.

Miranda beamed approval. "Now that's more like it. Those are *serious* shoes."

"They look more like something you'd nail up on the wall to hang a side of beef on," Gina said.

"I've used 'em for something along those lines once or twice."

"I don't want to hear about it."

"Your loss. You might learn a thing or two." With a few flips of one hand she said, "Walk around a little."

Gina wobbled for the first few steps, then found her footing. "I feel like I'm six feet tall in these things," she said. "In the Diane zone."

Miranda stood with her arms crossed and looked Gina up and down. "You just may be. And that gives me a little room to work. Legs are important." She rubbed her hands together and grinned like a Cheshire cat. "Okay, let's see now . . ."

An hour later, after black lace stockings, two pounds of rhinestones, a Miracle Bra, ten total inches of false red fingernails, and about a pint of makeup, Gina sat in Miranda's robe in front of the vanity mirror as the finishing touches were put on her *chignon*. A few stray strands fell onto her shoulder, perfectly.

"There," Miranda said. "Hair and a half. Now put your dress on. *Carefully*, so you don't mess up all my hard work. Then take a look in the big mirror while I finish up on myself."

She stepped into the small black dress and slid it up over her hips. Its satiny lining slipped easily over her hose with a rustle of taffeta. Gina reached around behind herself to pull up the zipper. She had enough time to think, *David used to do this for me*, before the zipper finally obeyed. After a few awkward moments of poking and shifting things around, she finally managed to get her lingerie-enhanced bosom settled into the fitted bodice. Holding her breath, she moved into position in front of the mirror for a look at the whole package of herself.

Staring back at her was a rhinestone Cinderella. And to her great surprise,

Gina didn't dislike that woman. "I expected to hate this," she said. "I don't."

"Told you," Miranda said.

"Wow," Gina said softly. "I almost don't know what to say."

"Say, 'Thank-you, Miranda.'"

"Thank-you, Miranda. I didn't know this much jewelry existed," she added with a laugh. "And I look like Joan Crawford with these eyebrows."

"Good. Joan Crawford was a hell of a handsome woman, despite her— personality. A genuine WWA."

"Dare I ask?"

"Woman With Attitude," Miranda said, pulling on her stockings. "Every time you put on your eyebrows, ask yourself, what would Joan do? Now, you are not going to think about David tonight. You are not going to worry about grant money. Bums will not cross your mind. You will march up on that stage, take that check, ooze out a few sincere words of gratitude, and then you are going to party. Is that perfectly clear?"

What is the big deal about this banquet? Gina wondered suspiciously. "Okay, I promise to be as decadent as possible. But I'm not sure I understand why you're getting so worked up about it. It's not like it's going to change my life or anything."

Miranda grinned slyly. "You never know," she said. She zipped her own dress.

Chapter 13
Nu

Harpo hung back in the shadows of a large column outside the Waldorf Astoria, with Freddie panting at his side. He glanced up at the building's façade, admiring its faded beauty, while Freddie caught his breath.

"Definitely—out—of—my usual territory—" Freddie gasped. "Traffic—thank—God—"

"Yes, yes, Hermes came to our aid. But be quiet or you will give our presence away," Harpo warned. "The place is maddeningly ablaze and there are few spots to hide." He watched as Gina and Miranda were stopped at a door by a well-dressed sentry, who let them pass after they each presented something small and white. The muted sounds of festive music poured out of the door as they went in, and when it shut behind them, the sounds were once again swallowed up.

"They have entered," Harpo observed, "and many more of these glorious mortals are arriving! This looks to be a gathering of nobility, at which the common people may bring them tribute. We must see this!"

"I ain't going in there," Freddie said.

"But surely you must be curious!"

"Not about that stuff. Great big waste of time, in my opinion."

Harpo gave him a disdainful look. "I shall go in without you, then."

"Suit yourself. But they won't let you in. So I'll just hang out here. Catch my breath. Maybe by the time you get back I'll be able to walk again."

He scanned the surrounding environs quickly and settled on a recessed doorway near the corner of the block. "I'll wait over there," he said, pointing. "See you later." He skulked away into the shadows.

Left alone, Harpo searched the front of the building for an unguarded entry, finding none. But off to the right he saw a small single door through which men were going in and out, with boxes from a nearby vehicle.

Crouching low, he ran through the shadows and slipped into the vehicle. He picked up a carton and followed the others, but when they reversed direction and went back outside again, he stayed within. He slunk off toward the center of the building, where he had last seen Gina and her splendid Nubian companion.

He opened a door and cautiously entered a large, hot room, and found himself standing amidst a scurrying battalion of black-clad men, all carrying trays. The air was thick with the smells of cooking. Plates rattled, silverware clanked, doors whooshed open and closed. Steam rose from trays of colorful food. He scuttled quickly through the winding paths of the kitchen, keeping low, and followed the army of men out into the main ballroom.

The room was large and luxurious and filled with glamorous people. "By all the gods!" he muttered under his breath. "What grandeur!" Midas squirmed up to the top of his toga and poked his head out.

Toward the front of the room he saw a stand of tall plants arranged around the base of a column. There was a path along the side of the room by which he could reach it unseen. "That will do for a hiding place, I think," he whispered. He waited until there was no one between him and his destination, then scooted fast and low into the cover of the foliage.

"Safe again," he whispered to Midas. "We shall be able to see quite well from here, I think . . ." He scanned the crowd anxiously, looking for the tall sliver of red and black that would identify Gina's companion, and therefore lead to Gina herself, and after a few moments, he found her.

Ω Ω Ω

Her fingers idly twirling a glass of champagne, Miranda surveyed the scene. "So many penguins, all in one place."

Gina took a sip from her own glass. "I feel like someone dropped me into the vault at Tiffany's. There must be enough diamonds here to fund a couple of third-world countries for a year or two, not to mention a few thousand shelters. You could go blind."

Affecting snobbery, Miranda lifted her chin and said, "The flashes of brilliance are nicely counterbalanced by a soothing Brahman patina."

Gina laughed. "What you said. Hey, maybe we should go find our seats. I was too nervous to eat before I came to your apartment and this champagne's already going to my head."

"You're a cheap date."

"So I've been told."

They made their way through the crowd, politely excusing themselves, smiling and nodding to people Gina had never seen before. Miranda seemed completely at home floating through the crowd of *glitterati*, flashing her perfect white teeth with stunning expertise.

Feeling like that renowned fish out of water, Gina walked behind Miranda, blushing intermittently and wobbling every now and then on her alien shoes, a displaced person, illicit, as if the people who would inevitably accuse her of impersonating a guest just hadn't discovered her yet.

They approached the section of the room reserved for the honorees and those involved in their selection, and the grandeur hiked up another notch. Miranda introduced Gina to several other members of the awards committee. Miranda engaged in brief, bright conversations with each one for a few minutes after the mandatory courtesies. This was not the get-down, trash talking desk sergeant that Gina knew from the night shift at Bellevue, her familiar friend and colleague, but some more polished gem in a setting crafted to enhance her natural brilliance. As they sat down she said, "How do you know all these people?"

"I make it my business to know them. I vote for their pet nominees every year." She waved and winked at a handsome man, who smiled and winked back as he passed their table. "Don't forget I'll have enough time in to retire in a few years, and I want to be sure I have some favors to call in."

The notion of Bellevue without Miranda made Gina feel sad. "I think I'd better have another sip of this fizzy stuff here to console myself over the thought that one of my peers can see retirement already. My biological clock is deafening right now." She tossed down the remainder of her champagne. Before the fizz had even left her tongue, a waiter was there, ready to remove the empty glass from her hand, offering another.

As the next sip was spreading its warmth into her belly, a thin, horse-faced woman appeared at their table, clipboard in hand. A name tag was pinned to her dress, at the base of which Gina saw the words "Awards Coordinator." The woman gave Miranda a crinkly smile and a cute little wave and then turned to Gina. She ran her finger down a list.

Miranda rescued her from uncertainty by saying, "Bugbee. Regina."

"Oh, right! I'm so happy you could be with us tonight, uh, is it Miss or Mrs. Bugbee?"

She wanted to say "*Ms.* Bugbee to you . . .", but she politely said "Miss," relieving the woman of the onerous task of deciphering her marital status. "But please, call me Gina."

"Oh, thank you. Gina, then," she said. "Now, when the awards ceremony starts things will move pretty quickly. We like to keep it short and sweet to make sure there's lots of time left for everyone to dance and enjoy themselves afterward." She paused, expecting a reaction to that *largesse*. When Gina was silent, she said, "You'll go up the stairs on the left side of the stage. After you've been given your award, exit on the right, and then please wait with the rest of the honorees in that area over there."

She pointed to a column rimmed with potted plants. "There's a photographer here from the *Times* and he wants to take a group shot for tomorrow's paper. It shouldn't take too long." She beamed another wide smile.

"Of course," Gina said. "Thank you."

"Well, I'll run along," the woman said. "Enjoy yourself, now."

As the woman departed, Miranda said, "Straight out of *The Age of Innocence*."

It was a world that neither of them would ever inhabit. How would it feel, Gina wondered, to have so much money that you could give away millions? That you could wear the down payment on a house around your neck, or hang a year's tuition in your closet?

I'll never know.

Dinner arrived, and soon the room was filled with the hum of conversation and the sounds of silver on china. A quartet in formal attire played soft jazz, which somehow made the food taste even better. The conversation was brilliant, worldly, sane.

When she had finished eating, Gina touched three fingers to her mouth and stifled a belch. "What a feast," she said to Miranda. "I can't remember when I've been this full. Is my tummy sticking out? It does that when I eat too much."

"You look positively voluptuous, my dear."

"Thanks, I think. I suppose I could actually have another glass of champagne now without getting completely plastered."

"You might want to hold off a few minutes on that," Miranda said. "It's just about time for the awards."

"Oh, *criminy*, better run, then." She pointed. "Ladies'".

As her companion wobbled away, Miranda cast a sly gaze in the opposite direction to the other side of the reserved section. Despite the alien black worsted in which his body was so gorgeously wrapped (though she thought he looked more himself in blue), she found McCarthy with little difficulty. She smiled to herself and wondered how the evening would unfold.

Ω Ω Ω

From his station behind the plant, Harpo watched Gina walk across the room. "Cursed fangs of Cerberus!" he whispered to Midas. "She is off again! Where can she be going now?" He craned his neck, exposing his head farther than he thought wise as he watched her shape grow smaller. For a few unnerving moments he considered leaving the safety of his temporary blind to follow her, but he relaxed again when he saw her push open the door with the symbol of a woman painted on its front.

"Ah," he said with great relief, "I have seen such doors at the Bellevue building. She will return in a few minutes." He let his gaze wander around the huge banquet room, and soon his head was swimming with its intricacies. "It is too much!" he whispered to his pet. "How they fill up their palaces with *things!* So many statues kept inside; why do they not set them outside for all to see? Some are

145

quite handsome . . ."

Something moving near the chandelier caught his attention, and his eyes were drawn in its direction.

A man at the closest table had seen it as well.

A bird? He faintly heard the man say it.

It's a bird it's a plane . . . and then laughter from his table-mates.

He focused loosely on the area of motion, and in a few seconds a small shape materialized on the chandelier, which swayed just slightly from the disturbance, causing the cut drops to sparkle brilliantly. As the crystals tinkled noisily against each other, many heads among the banquet guests looked up to find the source of the noise.

Harpo heard another guest say, "Probably a little draft from the heating system."

"Little, indeed," he hissed to Midas, "but that was no wind."

Ω Ω Ω

By the time Gina returned to her seat, a man in a white dinner jacket and black pants had taken the stage and was adjusting the microphone to the correct height.

"Here we go," Miranda said. "Your fifteen minutes of fame is at hand."

"Fifteen minutes?" Gina cried. "I won't last more than two up there!"

"Relax," Miranda said. "You won't be up there for more than fifteen *seconds*. They move this thing along. So calm down. You've got a couple of minutes before you go up there." She leaned toward Gina and gestured in the speaker's direction. "He gives pretty much the same speech every year. I'll let you know when he's almost done."

It was new for Gina, and she found herself listening with genuine interest as the man described the mission of a public city hospital and the steps the Bellevue Board had taken since the previous banquet to ensure that the mission was accomplished. She was there almost every day, and it was just—*Bellevue* to her. But it was so much more.

The speaker referenced the establishment's long and colorful history:

Oldest continuously-operating public hospital, opened when the states were still colonies. First public ambulance service. Sabin and Salk. First U.S. nursing school. The HIV cocktail. First maternity ward. First legal dissection of cadavers. Perfection of the hypodermic syringe.

Miranda tapped her shoulder. "Here come the goals for the upcoming year." Two sentences before he finished, Miranda said, "Get your hands ready." She counted backwards from ten, and at precisely zero, the speaker looked up from his notes. Applause commenced. As it waned, Miranda said, "Now come the awards."

Gina fidgeted in her seat as each honoree was called. Soon she heard the speaker say, "For some years now, one woman has operated an independent outreach center serving the homeless men of New York. . ." and as the details of Gina's subterranean kingdom were revealed, Miranda tapped her on the arm. *"Go on up."*

She rose from her seat and headed for the stage as the man continued singing her praises from the podium. Somehow, she found her footing, and the wherewithal to smile, take the check, ooze thanks, and descend the stairs again without walking out of Miranda's shoes. Her heart beating nervously, she joined the small smiling group of honorees waiting by the potted plants in front of the column.

Five or six awards later, she heard the familiar name, and for a few seconds her heart seemed to stop completely. *Oh, my God,* she thought as McCarthy climbed the stairs, *he looks good enough to eat* . . . Tiny beads of sweat popped out on her forehead and palms.

"For his long years of service to the community in Precinct 13, and for his wonderful work with the children of 9/11 responders . . ."

He took his award, smiled and waved, then came down the stairs, his steps light and confident for such a big man. Gina watched in admiration as headed toward the small gathering of grinning check recipients, shaking each one's hand in turn, finally to take his place among them. He excused his way through the group and came up beside her, then wrapped his arms around her and gave her a hug.

To those gathered around them, it would seem the sort of warm, comradely greeting that one coworker might give another on such an occasion, but Gina felt the undeniable extra little squeeze that McCarthy added to the brief embrace, and she was absolutely certain that he meant her to feel it.

"I had no idea you would be here . . ."

"Me, either," he said. "I mean that you'd be here. I guess we should talk more." He pulled back from embracing her and held her at arm's length, then looked her up and down. "Jesus, Mary and Joseph. You look *spectacular,*" he said.

The jaded social worker blushed and smiled like a shy virgin. "It's all Miranda's fault," she said. "She did it all. I just sat there and let her do it."

"Well, whatever it was, you are absolutely beautiful." He let go of her waist, then took one of her hands in his.

"And you look . . . you look . . ."

He laughed at her speechlessness. "Yeah, I know, I clean up nice. At least that's what my mother used to say."

"Well, she was right." She lowered her head and looked away, not wanting him to see the confused look on her face.

And then, more quickly than she wanted, the awards were over. The gathered honorees assembled into two lines as directed by the photographer and smiled when told to do so. Lights flashed, and they were dismissed.

But before the photographer could dismantle his tripod, McCarthy went up to him. He said a few quiet words to the man, pressed a bill and one of his cards into his hand. Then he came back to Gina. "He's gonna take a couple of shots of just us," he said with a smile.

And before Gina could say, *meaning what?* McCarthy was at her side with his arm around her and was pulling her close. The camera flashed, and they shifted their positions slightly. It flashed again, and McCarthy waved the man his thanks.

"Maybe you could come sit with me at my table. I didn't bring a date."

The eagerness she heard in her own voice surprised her. "Are there two? I came with Miranda and I don't want to desert her."

"Only one,' he said. "But you could sit on my lap."

She laughed. "I don't think so. One of the hoy-polloy might see me and take my check back."

"They'll have to fight me first," he said. He still had her hand in his, but it soon became apparent to both of them that there was really no reason for him to continue holding it. Reluctantly, he let it slip out of his grasp. "Too bad," he said. "Oh, well, will you save me a couple of dances?"

"Yeah," she said, "As many as you want."

After a breathy good-bye, they separated and headed toward their seats. Gina wove her way through the mass of tables, holding onto the backs of chairs to steady herself, apologizing for her clumsiness continuously.

As she neared her table, she saw a wide grin of triumph on Miranda's face.

"Put those teeth away right now," Gina said. "You are an *evil* person. You are the Great Deceiver."

"That's *Ms.* Great Deceiver to you," Miranda countered with a hearty laugh. "And don't you forget it."

"That's what this was all about, right? All those little giggles between you and Diane at Macy's. This was a setup, all this makeup and jewelry; these legs up to my neck and all these *tits!*" She cupped her hands under her breasts in demonstration and pushed them even further upward. A woman sitting nearby grimaced in disapproval.

Miranda stifled her own laughter with a glittering hand, and with eyebrows raised, said, "You've had a *lot* to drink, haven't you?"

Gina lowered her voice and sat down. "You knew McCarthy was going to be here and you didn't tell me."

"You didn't ask."

"Why would I think to ask?"

When she finally stopped laughing, Miranda said, "Would you have come if you'd known?"

Gina didn't answer.

Ω Ω Ω

Harpo cursed Aphrodite silently when he saw McCarthy and Gina embrace. "Somewhere out there in the Cosmos," he whispered to Midas, "the Fair One has regained power and is using it to torment me. This man will make her happy and she will have no need of a god at all." He glanced up at the swaying chandelier and followed its motion with his eyes.

"He is up there, I know it," he whispered again. "I can feel the little demon just plotting my downfall." He shook his fist upward and seethed, "May your whore of a mother wake up in the arms of a Roman for all of her never-ending days!" He rooted around in the base of one of his camouflaging plants and extracted a small pebble, then lobbed it hard in the direction of the suspected pink tormentor. It missed the intended target but struck a hanging crystal with just enough force to send it tinkling harmoniously into the adjacent drops.

Ω Ω Ω

Passing through the crowd on her way to find McCarthy, Gina was surprised to see Aaron. It entered her mind instantly that he might have been involved in her nomination. *He'll never tell, though,* she thought to herself as she approached him.

"I almost didn't recognize you without the desk in front of you."

"They let me out every now and then. Otherwise I get cranky." He eyed her up and down with obvious admiration. "My, my," he said, "aren't you just a vision tonight."

"It would seem that I am," Gina replied with an embarrassed grin, touching his hand. "You, too," she said, "all tuxed up! Only it's more of a stretch for me." Then she reached up and shook hands over Aaron's shoulder with the handsome willowy woman who stood behind his chair, his wife of many years, Miriam.

"It's my Dolly Parton costume," Gina said. "Miranda made me do it."

"You make that sound like, 'the devil made me do it'," Miriam said.

"You must know Miranda."

"No," Miriam said, "but she sounds like someone I'd *like* to know. I can't seem to let myself wear all that great stuff. At least not in public. But I probably should sometime before I get too old to pull it off."

Aaron laughed. "Now, Mim . . ."

Miriam laughed, too, but Gina saw her hand reach up and lightly stroke Aaron's neck. She thought to herself, *if he could move* . . . She didn't think Aaron

149

had intended for her to notice the excitement in his expression, but neither had he made any effort to hide it. Gina was tempted to thank them for letting her see it.

Out of the corner of her eye she saw McCarthy heading towards her. She broke free of the spell and excused herself, saying, "I hope you have a wonderful evening," thinking, *May you enjoy the best of each other tonight and all nights.* Then, slightly flushed, she left them, and turned toward McCarthy.

When they came together, she extended her arms and said, "I'm all yours."

"Promises, promises." He took her hands and guided her to the dance floor.

Ω Ω Ω

Harpo cast his nervous gaze back and forth between Gina and the crystal chandelier.

"She's walking away now," he whispered anxiously to Midas, "toward the man McCarthy."

He looked back to Aaron. "But of course he would be here," he whispered. "Such a mortal must surely be a noble." He saw that the blond woman with him was now leaning over him, with her arms wrapped around his shoulders, chair included; her curls tumbled over his chest and her lips were on his cheek. She swayed back and forth in time to the music, and they both had their eyes closed.

"Great Zeus," he whispered almost reverently. "Why, they are dancing . . ."

He was captivated by their joy, and compelled by divine ordinance to watch, so he was momentarily distracted from watching his quarry.

Ω Ω Ω

The band played a smooth instrumental rendition of Cole Porter's *All Through the Night.* In her mind's ear Gina heard the velvet voice of *Ella* singing the words: *"You and your love bring me ecstasy . . ."* She was locked in McCarthy's strong grasp and they were dancing, but with such small, contained motions that they barely moved on the polished floor. Gina's head rested on his shoulder; through half-opened eyes she looked around the dance floor and saw Miranda's long red form pressed up against another even longer one in black and white.

She pressed her own body closer yet to McCarthy's and he responded by tightening his grip on her. One strap of her dress slipped off her shoulder, revealing the lacy black strap underneath it, but Gina couldn't bring herself to make the effort required to pull it up again. As they shuffled languorously her mind drifted, for once free of self-incrimination.

Ω Ω Ω

"Oh, Midas, this is very terrible."

He watched them move around the dance floor; their movements were smooth and slow.

"How shall we ever claim her?"

And when that music stopped, a new song began, and they danced again. He watched in complete dismay as McCarthy suddenly touched her shoulder. A few moments later, she touched his cheek.

Ω Ω Ω

Taking his hand from her shoulder, McCarthy touched his hand to his face. "It feels like something bit me, too."

Gina reached up and gently touched the tiny red spot. "Looks like Harpo's spider bite. Don't you go passing out on me now."

"Not a chance," he said, pulling her even closer. "You'd think in a place like this they could clean out the cobwebs."

Gina laughed, but the resulting sound echoed oddly inside her own head, which seemed to have expanded and hollowed. Suddenly she was exquisitely aware of every sensation in her body; she could feel the blood surging through her veins, driven by a merciless primal force to feed every nerve ending. She was locked to McCarthy with the unbreakable grip of a desperate, body-long magnet.

McCarthy used his teeth to pull down the revealed bra strap and when it was out of the way, attached his lips to the skin of her shoulder as if it were the spring from which all life flowed. She whispered encouragement and felt his lips work their way lower. Their movements became more sinuous and pronounced, in rhythm with their breathing, which had synchronized to the beat of the music. She felt herself slipping into a haze of pure sensation, where no rational thought would dare intrude.

Then she opened her eyes and looked around, realizing that the song had come to an end, and that their little *pas-de-deux*—a coupling that would more appropriately be private—was being performed in the middle of a room full of people. Somehow, she had thought she was on a bed of clouds with the only lover she had ever known, and that no one could see them. But all around them people had stopped moving, and were staring with prurient interest. She could feel the critical burn of their eyes.

She became aware of McCarthy's lips sliding lower, but she was helpless to stop him, didn't *want* to stop him. But somehow her mind managed to grasp a last straw of reality and she reached up and placed one hand on the back of McCarthy's head.

"McCarthy . . . wait a minute. . ."

He stopped his urgent exploration and looked up. "Uh . . ." he said as his face reddened. "Oh, my God . . . where are we?"

They stood still amidst of a hundred censorial watchers. They were panting, disheveled, beaded with sweat, and unimaginably embarrassed.

Then blessedly, the next number began. One by one, the other couples turned away and got back to the business of dancing, leaving the objects of their gawking alone in motionless confusion in the middle of the floor. They stared, bewildered, at each other. McCarthy swallowed hard and whispered, "Oh, my God, Gina, I'm so sorry if I embarrassed you, I don't know what I was thinking . . ."

She stared into his eyes. "I think you were thinking the same thing I was thinking."

"What the hell is happening here?"

"I—I don't know . . . I feel so strange all of a sudden . . . almost like I was drugged or something . . ."

"Me, too . . ."

Groping for some logical explanation, Gina said, "Maybe it was the champagne."

"That was *good* champagne. I mean, it never hit me like this before. Never."

She nodded in wide-eyed, hungry agreement.

"Listen," he said, "maybe we should take this somewhere else." Then nervously, he added, "I mean, if you want to. Oh, Jeez, Gina, I didn't mean to assume . . . I mean, if you want to, take it somewhere else, that is . . ."

She could not stop herself from nodding *Yes*.

"How much time do you have?" he asked.

She had given no serious consideration to her sister's directive to stay out all night; now, Gina knew that it was all part of the scheme. All thoughts of propriety had vanished, replaced with an endless and undeniable series of *I-wants* and *I-needs* and *I-will-haves*.

"All night."

Pointing upstairs, he said, "I'll get a room."

"I'll get my purse."

"Meet me in front of the elevator."

They said all of this while still attached at the pelvis by that invisible magnet. With a final push they separated and ran, panting, in opposite directions.

Gina arrived at her table in a state of high flush and found Miranda seated there with the man she'd seen her dancing with a few minutes before. Not wanting to reveal her intentions in the presence of a stranger, she said, "I'm going somewhere now and I'll get home by myself later. I'll call you in the morning about picking up my stuff from your apartment."

"Okay," Miranda said. She cast a knowing glance at Gina then shifted her eyes in the direction of her companion. Gina quickly extended her hand toward Miranda's dance partner and said, "Hi, I'm Gina. It was nice to meet you, I mean see you . . . oh, hell. . ."

Red-faced, she turned and hurried across the room, rhinestones flashing, straps falling, her hips rocking as she tried to run in the high heeled shoes.

Aaron watched her from his table. He glanced up at Miriam, who leaned over. He spoke into her ear. Within a few seconds they both smiled, and then they brought their lips together in a long kiss.

He was still feeling the leftover pleasure of that kiss twenty minutes later when his phone sounded.

Ω Ω Ω

Harpo found Freddie fast asleep in the recessed door. He tapped him gently on the shoulder. Freddie smacked his lips together a few times, stretched and yawned, and then opened his eyes.

"We may depart now," Harpo said. "There is nothing more for me to do here."

"Did you apologize to her and give her the chocolates?"

Harpo sighed dispiritedly. "No. She was otherwise occupied."

"Aw, too bad," Freddie said. "Well, next time you see her you can do it. Least you tried."

"Indeed. I did. And it *is* too bad." He stood. "I wish to return to your box now."

Groaning upward, Freddie said, "Sounds good to me. I never did like this part of town much. Too fancy for me."

"Myself, as well," Harpo said. Then, while Freddie was struggling to stand, he took the box of chocolates out of his pocket and flung them as far as he could.

He spat viciously on the ground. "Honey," was his bitter whisper, "I'm so sorry. I was a great big shit and I promise I'll never do it again."

Chapter 14
Xi

Gina stood looking out the window at the awakening city below, her bare feet sinking into the plush carpet, McCarthy's white tuxedo shirt providing a veneer of modesty. She turned away from the city view and regarded the hotel room. She remembered nothing of how it had looked when they'd entered it the night before, already nearly locked to each other. *Probably a little neater,* she mused with a small smile. *Poor chambermaid. Today might be the day to become a big tipper.*

She went to the bathroom and restored a partial sense of normalcy by washing the assorted colors off her face, then toweled her skin briskly until she had some natural glow again. She swished out her mouth until her breath was tolerable and went back into the room.

McCarthy was still cocooned in the white sheet, one arm hanging off the bed, his fingers just touching the floor.

My oh my, she thought. She surveyed the trail of lacy black things that began just inside the door and ended at the side of the bed.

McCarthy's voice broke the silence. "A penny for your thoughts," he croaked, still half asleep.

"I was just thinking about how I'm going to look hailing a cab in that outfit so early in the morning." She picked up one shoe and tossed it so it landed next to its mate in a limp attempt to create some order. "I didn't realize I was thinking so loud. I hope I didn't wake you up."

"You didn't," he mumbled. "I don't think I ever really slept. I think I've been playing reruns of last night in my head while my eyes were closed." He groaned and rolled over. "*Whew.* Even the reruns are spectacular."

She walked over to the bed and sat down on the edge. She placed her hand lightly on his arm.

He opened one eye and peered at her. "Nice shirt," he said.

Gina smiled. "Thanks. Someone I really like lent it to me."

He reached out and pulled her down into an embrace. "Am I dreaming, or did we do what I think we did last night?"

"It would seem that we did," she said, nuzzling against him.

He kissed her; his mouth still smelled faintly of the scent he'd acquired while nestling it into a certain crevice in her body. When their lips finally separated he said, "I was never that good with any other woman I've ever been with, ever before."

Gina pulled back and giggled. "How do you know you were good?"

He looked momentarily crushed, then realized that she was teasing. He reddened. "I mean, um—I was never that, uh, long, oh, shit. I think I just put my foot in my mouth."

She drew in a long breath through her nose, tasting the air around his mouth. "It doesn't smell like your foot." She licked his lower lip with the tip of her tongue. "And I think you're probably right. You never were that good with any other woman you've been with. You couldn't possibly have been." She gazed into his eyes and smiled. "So, now that we're on such intimate terms, are you gonna tell me what the A and the Z stand for?"

He paused, thinking. "Amorous Zealot," he said as he drew her toward himself.

Ω Ω Ω

Gina protested the notion of ordering Room Service coffee. "It's probably fifty-seven dollars a cup."

"Who gives a damn," McCarthy said. "I've got a grand in my pocket that I didn't have before. I can't think of anything I'd rather do than spend it on having a good time with you."

"You say the nicest things, McCarthy." She breathed in the scent of the coffee and took a long sip.

Bravely, he laid his soul bare. "I mean every one of those nice things. I've wanted this for a very long time."

She forced a small smile, which faded almost instantly. She padded over to the window and looked out. "My life is such a mess, I've got *suitcases* of complications. . ."

He came up behind her, and wrapped his arms around her. "I know, I *know*. I'm not sure I could have handled what you've handled over these years."

She sighed and looked down at her polished nails. "I know you've had some burdens of your own."

"But mine are—past."

She smiled. "I think you just gave me an opening. You want to talk about it?"

He was quiet for a moment. "No. But I will. You should hear it from me."

She sat down. "I saw her picture on the Wall of Prayers. Before they moved it."

"She's still on it. At the museum. They never found her body."

"I'm so sorry. I'm sure you miss her."

155

He looked away for a moment. "I wish I'd known her well enough to miss *her*. We met in January, had this crazy whirlwind thing, got married in July, and in September . . .well . . .

"My captain wouldn't let me go there that day, he assigned me to the Bridge. So I stood there all day, keeping cars away, directing ambulances and firetrucks, watching the ghost people go by, waiting for her to show. Someone from her company came along and told me she'd gone up to Windows to make arrangements for a conference lunch. She was an event coordinator, she loved her job."

His face grew somber. "No one got down from there. You know sometimes I even have trouble picturing her in my mind. I have photos at home, but if they're not right in front of me, it's hard to bring her up.

"So what I think I really miss is what *would* have happened if she hadn't been there. I miss what I wanted to happen. What *should* have happened. You know, anniversaries, kids, school sports, all that stuff. We had one Valentine's Day, that was it. Not even a Christmas. I feel more robbed than anything."

"Yeah," Gina said. "I know that feeling."

He reached out and took her hands in his. "I've been able to move on, at least I think I have. You haven't had a chance to do that. But through everything, you've behaved with total class. Hell, you managed to keep me interested and at bay at the same time. It just makes me—uh, *like* you all the more."

"But that's just it, McCarthy, I haven't *wanted* to keep you at bay. I've been forcing it on myself. I've been denying that David is as sick as he is so I could avoid having to deal with all the messy things I need to do to—put him out of my life."

It was the first time she'd said it aloud; the words burned her tongue. She buried her face in her hands. "Oh, God, when I say it like that I feel like such a shit. And why am I always saying *oh God* when God hasn't done us any favors. *Putting* him out of my life. I mean, who am I to just *put* someone someplace?"

McCarthy placed a comforting hand on her shoulder. "You're someone who still cares about him and knows him well enough to do what's best for him."

"Am I? How do I know I am?"

"Let me put it this way: I've watched you take care of a lot of men for years now . . ."

She looked straight into his eyes, one eyebrow raised.

He paused and gave her a little smile. "Don't even ask." Then, "You've *put* them all in the best places you could find for them. *Placed* is a better word. With limited resources. And if I were in David's situation, I would sure as hell want someone like you making decisions for me."

She was quiet for a few seconds. "I can't make any promises, at least not right now. I want to, but I can't."

"I'm not looking for promises. Just possibilities. I'm a patient man, Gina. Whatever you have to work out, I understand."

She could see the sincerity and hope in his eyes. The overwhelming calmness of the man drew her in. All her anxieties were attracted to his serenity like protons to electrons, and were instantly neutralized. Some bondage inside her was released, a tightness she had been holding for a very long time, although she couldn't remember quite why it was that she'd held it.

Ω Ω Ω

McCarthy did the unthinkable, the unpardonable for a New York cop: he called another cop who he knew would be pushing a cruiser at that moment and asked her to take Gina home from their hotel tryst, which constituted a gross misuse of a City vehicle for personal purposes. "My mother would smite me from heaven if I let you go out to hail a cab," he'd said when she protested.

He kissed her lightly on the cheek and smiled hopefully as he opened the back door of the cruiser for her. "Your carriage, my lady," he said with a flourish of his hand.

"At least it's not a pumpkin," she observed.

He laughed. "There is *that* to be thankful for."

"I'm thankful for a lot more than that this morning," she said. Then with a wistful smile, she slid into the back seat.

Their eyes locked through the window for the briefest of moments, sharing a private little thrill. McCarthy broke free first and tapped the passenger side front window of the cruiser, then stood on the pavement, hands in his pockets, staring at his feet as the car began to inch forward.

Gina followed him with her eyes as she was transported away from the hotel. When McCarthy was a mere speck, she turned forward again. She sank into the back seat, all black lace and embarrassment, trying very hard to become invisible, the delicious memories of her night with McCarthy still simmering in her mind.

As they neared her block she leaned forward and said, "Why don't you let me out here at this corner?"

The rookie dutifully pulled over to the curb, and got out to open the door for her. "No handles in the back," the cop said, smiling as she got out of the car.

"So I noticed," Gina said. "Thanks for the ride. I feel like I should be paying you or something. At least tipping you."

She laughed, her wrinkle-free face lighting up with a youthful innocence that was all *girlfriend* and vaguely annoying. "No problem, Ma'am. Our mission is to protect and serve. This is the serve part."

As she drove away, Gina thought to herself, *Ma'am. Oy.*

Ω Ω Ω

She teetered toward her building and saw Harpo waiting on the stoop. *Oh, great,* she thought with annoyance, *just who I wanted to find here. Museum Man. Professor Emeritus in the Irritation Department of Cosmic University.*

He gazed up at her as she approached, his face the dictionary illustration for "dejection." He looked colorless and hurt, and although all she wanted to do was get inside to the safe invisibility of her own apartment and get out of last night's clothes, she managed to find a small amount of concern in her heart. She sat down beside him on the stoop, wrapping her coat around her legs for warmth. "Are you all right?" she said. "You look terribly unhappy."

He turned toward her. "I greet you," he said somberly.

He always makes a comment of some sort, she thought, wondering why he was so quiet in a moment when she looked so grossly comment-worthy. "I greet you too," she said. Forgetting for the moment her agreement with Aaron to lessen her involvement, she added, "I'm going to go inside now and change. Then I'm going to take David to work. When I get back we can talk about what's bothering you if you want to."

He sighed from the very depths of his soul. "I do not think that will help. The things which worry me are more than a mortal can understand. And anyway," he said, "your David is not in your home."

Your David. She tilted her head and leaned toward him as if she had not heard him correctly. "What?"

"He is not in your home, as I have just said."

Her hand tightened on the railing. "How do you know he's not there? Did you go inside?"

He sighed again. "No, I have been sitting here since the moon was high, waiting for you to return. As you can see, the moon is no longer high."

A series of disturbing questions flashed through Gina's mind, foremost among them: *Was Aaron right? Is the behavior starting to go over the edge?* But she pushed them aside, for they were not as immediate as the next: "Then how do you *know* David's not there?"

"I saw him leave."

She gripped him by the shoulders. *"When?"*

He looked at the watch and moved his lips in concentration. "Eleven rounds of the large stick ago."

Ten PM? She would throttle Diane for taking him out that late. And then the panic hit her. *Oh, God,* she thought, *what if he went out alone? What if Diane's still asleep up there and she doesn't even know he's gone?* "Did anyone go with him?" she asked urgently.

"Oh, yes, he left in a very colorful moving machine, one with large letters in red, and lights flashing on the roof, and he was escorted by some men who seemed very anxious to hold him still . . ."

As the color drained from her face, Gina yanked off Miranda's absurd shoes and bolted up the stairs in stocking feet, fumbled with her keys for a moment, and then dashed inside her building. Harpo stood on the stoop staring after her. Then he turned and headed back to the box.

Ω Ω Ω

Diane was sitting on the couch, looking pale and shaken, the ridiculous nail polish painting behind her. She stood up immediately.

"Gina, something happened last . . ."

"I know," she interrupted. "Someone told me as I was coming in that they took David away." She looked around for a few seconds, stunned by the wreckage of her home. "Oh, my God," she whispered. She looked back at her sister. "Bellevue?"

Diane nodded somberly. "Gina, I'm so sorry, I just couldn't handle—"

"It's all right. I know he's still strong. But I need to get to him right now." She dropped everything on the floor where she stood, her spike-heeled shoes, her coat, and her evening bag. She dashed over to the couch and grabbed her running shoes from under the crooked table, tying them on right over her torn black stockings. She grabbed her parka and purse at the door and grabbed her sister's arm. "Come on. You can tell me what happened on the way."

Ω Ω Ω

The taxi sped forward.

"I was already asleep on the couch when I heard him get up. It was about nine thirty, I think; the news wasn't on yet. David was just muttering and saying, 'I can't sleep,' over and over again . . . I tried to calm him, but he really didn't seem to recognize me."

"Did he ask for me?"

After a hesitation, Diane said, "No. I did finally get him to sit down on the couch and I found something on the television that seemed to hold his attention. He didn't eat much for supper, so I thought he might be hungry and just couldn't—express it . . . I got a yogurt from the fridge and asked him if he wanted some. He still didn't say anything, so I opened it up and started giving it to him, you know, spooning it right into his mouth. He didn't object at first."

159

Diane's hands twisted together in distress. "He started making noises again, so I stopped feeding him. I sang to him for a while; that seemed to help. And then he started making noises *again*. Not talking, just noises. I couldn't get out of him what he wanted."

She hitched in a big breath and bit one of her knuckles, a leftover habit from childhood. Gina reached up and instinctively grabbed Diane's hand to stop her.

"That's when he just started to really lose it; he was tossing stuff and bouncing all over the place like a ping pong ball, grabbing things out of the closet and throwing them around . . . I tried to subdue him, but he was just too much, even for me; you know me, Gina, I'm strong enough, I should have been able to handle him—"

"I know," she said, "It's okay. I'm sorry you got put in the position of having to try." She touched her sister's arm. "He's had meltdowns before, but this . . ."

She looked away from her sister and out the window of the cab, her eyes misting. "How long did they get there after you called 9-1-1..."

"I didn't call 9-11, I called the number you gave me for his doctor. He called back right away, said he would send an ambulance. I asked if I should come along and he said, no, that the attendants would know what to do, that he would speak to them before they came and then meet them at Bellevue. Then he said it would be good if I waited for you so I could tell you what happened when you got home. He called about two AM and said they'd gotten David 'stabilized,' whatever that means."

And why didn't he call me? "It means they sedated him," she said. "Probably pretty heavily."

They fell quiet. There wasn't much more to say until they got to Bellevue. But in her mind, Gina could hear the things David would have said, perhaps screamed, in his maniacal romp of the previous night, had he the means to let it out. He had let it out to her once—only once—in the few hours of clarity he had before the bleeding in his brain started again. And since then he'd been silent about what had happened to him the day the future arrived.

Ω Ω Ω

Sobbing. Hitching breaths. "It was chaos, Gina, mayhem. Indescribable. Most of the people on the ground around me were already dead. There were some people who made it out of the North Tower and they were moving away from the buildings like the walking dead, slow plodding steps, and I couldn't understand why they weren't running because all of a sudden someone was yelling that the south building would collapse, to get out of the way, but they couldn't go faster, they were covered in I don't know *concrete* and maybe they couldn't breathe well

160

enough to move faster. And I looked up, but there was so much dust, it was like a snowstorm when the flakes get really big, just before it stops. It was just raining paper, and I couldn't see all the way through it.

"But then there was this—umbrella that spewed out from the South Tower and I knew it was coming down, I could feel the ground moving under me. And then this rock came flying toward me and I knew it would hit me, but I couldn't get out of the way fast enough.

"And then I could sort of see another—body coming down, and it just got bigger and bigger until it came down right beside me. It sounded like an explosion, the sound was so horrible . . ."

Ω Ω Ω

Oh, David. What you saw.

The 90th floor, where the first plane had gone in, was a thousand feet up. And there were twenty floors above it. The free-fall to the plaza below would take several seconds.

She counted out several seconds.

There were stories from eyewitnesses who said that some people tried to make parachutes from things on hand, to no avail. Some had jumped hand in hand. Others had spread their arms like wings. Skirts flew up; one woman, she'd heard, had tried to hold hers down, going to death with a last remnant of modesty.

Steel melted. Burned flesh hung in ribbons. One minute you're opening your briefcase, the next you're on fire. David had witnessed it from arm's length.

". . . and I remember thinking that this was a *person* who landed there, a human being, who got so desperate for a few more seconds of life that he tossed himself out a window when he could barely even see the ground, he'd be cooked alive if he didn't. I can see it in my mind, Gina, I can count it with my heartbeats.

"The guy's leg landed on me. It was all burned. I know it was a man because the other leg had pants on. He was wearing a tie, a blue tie."

All during this recitation, she held his hand, her eyes were closed, trying to see behind her own lids the things he had seen. The beep of the ICU equipment thundered in her head. She silently counted out nine heartbeats as she watched his chest rise and fall.

Ω Ω Ω

And now again he was at Bellevue. His tale of two towers lingered in her brain. *We still have each other,* she had told him. *We've got our life. We are so lucky.* Even more so, she knew, because as the stories began to circulate, she'd heard that not thirty feet away and two minutes later, a firefighter from their neighborhood house

161

had been hit straight on by another desperate jumper. Alone at his funeral, with David still hospitalized, she could not bring herself to speak to his widow.

She looked through the hazy glass of a two-way mirror into a small room with an empty bed. David was tucked into one corner, huddling with his arms wrapped around his knees, motionless except for the rise and fall of his chest.

She counted out nine heartbeats and watched his chest rise and fall.

The psychiatric nurse assigned to David for the day shift was a sturdy woman with scrubbed-looking skin, a throwback to disinfectant soap and the white shoe polish that came with its own dauber. There were awareness ribbons pinned on both sleeves, one pink, one red, white and blue.

"Is he asleep?" Gina asked.

"Not exactly," the nurse answered, "but he probably doesn't really realize he's awake. He was pretty agitated when he came in, so they gave him a load of Ativan."

"How long has he been in the corner like that?"

"Pretty much since it took effect. He's hardly moved." She flipped through the pages of David's medical chart, then scribbled a few words on the last page.

"How long did Dr. Richman stay?"

"He was here till about two, they told me. His wife was with him, and they said she looked *gorgeous*, and that big man, his attendant. Apparently they were all dressed up like they just came from some party."

Gina stared back through the glass again, then looked back at the nurse, her expression full of questions she couldn't bring herself to ask.

"I'll be back in a few minutes; he's due for another injection. We don't want any gaps in his sedation." She touched Gina's arm. "Don't worry, Hon, this is the best place he could possibly be, you of all people should know that. We'll take good care of him."

Gina had just been reminded of Bellevue's amazing history, some of it glorious, some of it not so pretty. But it was undeniably the best psychiatric hospital on Earth, with specific services for those who had been through the horrors of 9-11. And somehow, the ordinarily despised *Hon* didn't feel so deplorable coming from this caring and capable woman, who exhibited the exceptional skill level that was blessedly common at Bellevue.

She thanked the nurse, and as the woman walked away, Gina leaned up against the glass and remembered a day when she and David had gone to hear a concert in Battery Park on a sunny Sunday afternoon. They'd eaten a sinfully delicious lunch as music filled the air. Then they'd walked back uptown in the shadows of the towers. *A million years ago*, she thought. *A totally different lifetime.*

Oh, please, if there is a god, tell me what do I have to do to get that back.

Aaron's words cut through her like a steel blade. *Denial, anger, bargaining* . . . And though they no longer existed, she understood that she and David were still living in the shadow of those towers.

Ω Ω Ω

She heard steps behind her and turned around. Diane was there with two cups of coffee from the lobby cafe. She took the coated paper cup from her sister's hand and just held it for a few moments, letting it warm her.

Diane looked through the glass, then back at Gina. "How's he doing?"

"No change from the time he came in, and he's about to get another dose of Ativan."

"Yikes," Diane said, with bitter sarcasm. "Junkies all over New York are jealous."

There were moments when Gina would have been angered by her sister's flippant comment; this was not one of them. "*I'm* jealous," she said. "I could use a couple of good drugs myself right about now." She sipped the coffee. "Starting with caffeine."

She stared through the glass again. "I wonder what David thinks of all this. I mean the real David. The *before* David." She sighed wearily. "You know him, he was always thinking."

Diane put one arm around Gina's shoulder. "Not as well as you do, but I do know him." She gestured toward the man cowering in the corner. "And I don't see the David I knew in there."

"You're right. But where did *my* David go? I mean, a person doesn't just disappear, the essence doesn't just dissipate. It has to go somewhere. His soul is still in there. His *spirit*."

Her voice grew steadily louder, angrier. "He's not some kind of robot where you press a button and the personality disappears, one big massive deletion, and *click*, you're gone."

Diane stroked Gina's hair but said nothing. She imagined a huge remote in the Cosmic Hand. *Click, you're gone, Sucker. Take that.*

Ω Ω Ω

How long had she been awake? She tried to think. *Somewhere in the range of twenty-four hours,* she guessed, *four or five of it spent fucking my brains out.* She'd managed to squeeze in one or two quick nod-outs on a chair outside David's cubicle, and they'd softened her brittleness a little bit, but one good tap would have sent her shattering to the floor in a pile of jagged human shards, which, reassembled, would emerge as a Picasso of the woman she'd once been. She longed for her own bed, to get horizontal and to sleep until all these nightmares went away.

163

One more thing to do, she thought, *before I can go home.* As she walked slowly through the halls of Bellevue, too tired to tilt properly, she was jostled and bumped by the passing hordes who *were* appropriately angled. *Not today,* she thought. *I'll fall over if I tilt today.*

Given that it was Sunday, Aaron might not be in his office. Gina tried the handle on the outer office expecting to find it locked. "Oh," she said in surprise when the latch clicked open. She stepped inside; the door to the inner sanctum was ajar. She crossed the reception room quietly and gave the door a couple of tentative knocks.

Mike's face poked out in a few seconds. "Oh. Gina. I didn't realize I'd left the door open."

"Hello to you, too. I didn't know if you'd be here. I need to talk to Aaron. *Now.*"

"He has rounds, we're about to head out."

"*Please.* I need to talk to him about what happened with David last night."

"Hold on, I'll ask." He ducked inside the office again, but came back shortly. "If you'll give us about five minutes, he says he can see you."

"Thanks," she said with relief, "that's great. Wonderful. I'll just sit out here."

She sank gratefully into one of the chairs, her haunches aching all the way down, a reminder of the previous night's activities. *Haven't used those muscles in a while,* she thought. She looked down at her strange outfit: unzipped fur-trimmed parka, wrinkled black lace dress, torn black stockings, and white walking shoes with phosphorescent orange laces. *So they can see you at night,* she reminded herself as she wondered what had possessed her to purchase them. *For visibility.*

She closed her eyes and let the chaotic images that had gathered in her brain have their way with her. Floating in the mental soup were vague questions about what Mike and Aaron were doing in the inner room.

"Gina?" she heard Mike say as she was drifting off to sleep. "You can come in now."

Aaron was sitting behind the huge desk, looking, as he always did, like he'd just emerged from the cover of *Gentleman's Quarterly.*

She took off her parka and slipped it over the back of the chair, then flopped down ungracefully. She let out all her breath in one long sigh.

"Good morning, Gina," Aaron said. His cheerfulness sounded forced. "You look very, um, *unusual* this morning." He smiled thinly.

She sat up and leaned her elbows on the edge of the desk, then rubbed her eyes. "Aaron, if I didn't know you, I'd find that remark really insulting."

"Sorry," he said. "Just trying to be consistent. You've had quite a night, haven't you?"

"Yes. Quite a night. And day," she said, "and the evening before the night, and the previous day, week, month, year, decade, whatever."

"We'll talk about all that at your next appointment. Tomorrow, if I'm not mistaken. If it wasn't that soon, I think we'd try to work you in anyway," he said. "I want this stuff fresh in your mind."

"That's precisely why I'm here. It's pretty *fresh*."

He forgave the sarcasm. "As we discussed, one of the potential side effects of this study medication is insomnia. Last night David was wide awake and raring to go. The orderlies had a tough time keeping him from hurting himself."

He saw her look of alarm. "He'll probably have some bruises but nothing that requires treatment. But I'm guessing he's feeling even more ragged than usual inside. As you know insomnia will exacerbate that. You haven't mentioned sleep problems."

"There haven't been any that I know of. My sister Diane was with him last, she's the one who called you. It's the first time she's stayed with him since he started this new medication. Mrs. Miller hasn't said anything about him having problems sleeping. She looks after him when I'm at the center. Gives him dinner, makes sure he gets his pajamas on and goes to bed."

"But she's not there every minute with him?"

"No. He can usually make it through the night alone. At least until recently."

"Then she wouldn't know if David has been having trouble sleeping."

"No," she admitted. "He's only awakened her once or twice over the last year. Her number is programmed into the phone."

Aaron was silent for a few moments, cogitating. Gina could almost feel his gears spinning; his bright eyes twinkled with intense thought. "And have you found this arrangement satisfactory?"

She knew that what he wanted her to say. "It's been all right," she said quietly, "until now."

"I think perhaps when David is able to leave the hospital, you might need to reconsider it."

He had not said *come back home*. "How long do you think it will be?"

"That depends on two things. First, how long it takes to switch him back to his previous medication. We did have the best results with that, uneven as it was. It will probably take seven to ten days to get him stabilized again."

"When can he start taking it?"

"In a few days. I want his system clear of other psycho-pharmaceuticals before I put him back on it, except the sedative. We can phase that out as we phase the antidepressant back in. All in all, you're looking at a total of about two weeks of hospitalization."

"And the second thing?"

"How much care you're willing to arrange for. I'm not sure that David should be alone at all, at least for a little while. Maybe Mrs. Miller would consider sleeping on a cot in your apartment."

"I've already asked her. She doesn't want to."

Aaron sighed. "Too bad." He paused, seemingly in thought. "Well, you don't need to make a decision today. And probably shouldn't until you get some rest yourself. Your perspective right now will be colored by what's just happened. We'll figure something out."

She sat with her arms folded across her belly, almost hugging herself, and rocked forward and backward. "You know, we've started to talk about David as if he were some kind of object, something we can just—pick up and move around." Recalling the words that had passed between her and McCarthy that morning, she said, "I did that recently in another conversation. I wonder when we stopped thinking about his humanity."

"I haven't," Aaron said gently. "But I gather from what you've just said that you feel *you* have. David's position in my life is constant. He's my patient, period. He comes in here when it's scheduled. Yes, I knew him before he was hurt. And that colors my thoughts, no doubt. But he is my patient. Now this incident is an exception, but I don't ordinarily have to shift the patterns of my life to accommodate him. You do, every day."

Every hour, every minute, every second. The guilty wish for relief flooded through her and tears welled up. She wiped one away, the looked down at her nails, the foreign red things, two of which were badly broken from the previous night's exertions. She found none of the customary safety in staring at them, no place to hide.

Suddenly Aaron was speaking again, snapping her back to the moment. "You know how I make you recite your treatment goals every now and then? This is the reason why. There's been a change in your perspective on David's place in your life. Now is a time for you to think about what you really want."

She did not reply, and after a few seconds of silence, Aaron looked down at his computer panel. "Well, you've got some time to think. I've got to get up to the wards. I'll see you tomorrow, okay? Hang in there; you're working toward a resolution, and you're making progress."

"Am I?" she said. "I wonder."

"You are," he reassured her.

She stood up and slipped her arms back into her parka. As she turned to go, Aaron said, "And Gina? I didn't have a chance to say this at the banquet, you left so suddenly." His smile was full of unspoken implications. "Congratulations on your award. It was richly deserved, and long overdue. You're a real asset to this hospital and this community. And I have to say, you just glowed. Miriam noticed it, too. It was really nice to see it."

She smiled through her confusion and said, "It was really nice to *feel* it." *Really, really nice,* she thought.

Chapter 15
Omicron

The phone at her bedside buzzed. Gina reached out to grab it. Her hand knocked Aaron's copy of *The Bacchae* to the floor.

"Hello?" she yawned.

"Gina, it's McCarthy."

She sat up in bed almost instantly and yanked the covers over her nightdress. *As if he can see me*, she thought. Then she remembered that he had already seen that part of her, *sans* nightdress.

"McCarthy. Wow. It's so good to hear your voice."

"I hope you don't mind me calling you now. I mean, when you're not working."

"No, it's fine, really." After a brief pause she said, "First time for everything."

He chuckled nervously. "I guess you could say there is."

The conversation went embarrassingly dry until McCarthy finally said, "I woke you up. I could call back later if you want."

"No, it's okay. You did me a favor." She picked up the clock and looked at the back of it. "I forgot to set the alarm. I need to get up and get going to the center."

"It's not bad outside. No one's gonna freeze if you're a few minutes late."

She smiled into the phone. "Probably not."

"Listen, Gina, I, uh, was in the cop shop at Bellevue and I saw Miranda. She told me about what happened last night. With David."

Gina winced internally. Explanations would have to be made, and she was not looking forward to that. "How'd she know? I haven't seen her yet."

"She said your sister called her."

Thank you, Diane, for saving me the heartbreak of telling it all over again. "News travels fast."

"Seems that it does. Listen, I won't keep you. I just wanted to tell you how sorry I am. I mean, what a shitty thing to come home to. Especially after—" He was quiet for a few seconds, then added, "I mean, getting that award and all."

He was struggling to say the right thing; she could hear the genuine concern in his voice. *How incredibly sweet*, she thought, taking comfort. She thanked him, then said, "*And all*. I've never heard it described that way before."

It put him at ease. He laughed. "Well, like you said, first time for everything."

Then, with audible nervousness, he added, "I just hope it's not the last."

He'd phrased it as a statement, but she knew it was really a question. His cards were on the table, and he wanted her reaction to the hand he'd just played. She waited for a few moments before showing her own. "I hope not, too."

Ω Ω Ω

Freddie tilted his head to one side and listened. "Ah, crap," he said after a few seconds. "It's raining."

"A rare bit of unembellished truth," Harpo groused. "Congratulations on your perfect candor. Zeus knows you need more truth here, and less of this maddening wetness."

But Freddie would not be drawn into his box-mate's bitterness. "If it's rainin', maybe it means it's getting warmer. Maybe we won't have any more snow this winter."

"Yes," came the jaded reply. "The maiden Spring steps forward and vanquishes Winter, to take her rightful place at the Gate of the Seasons. Zeus can always be counted on to make the Earth warm so Spring will be pleased."

"The poor guy never gets a break, does he? Always doing stuff to please some woman."

"Indeed," Harpo said. "And he is most times successful." He frowned. "But it would seem that he has not passed that ability on to his son."

"Ah, come on, cheer up. This shit takes time, you know. You gotta be patient with women." He offered up the bottle of wine.

Harpo took a long pull, then grimaced and wiped his mouth on his sleeve. "This swill hardly cheers me," he said.

"Yeah, it's not so great. Best wine I ever had? The kind we used to put on the table at Sunday dinner. Oh, man," he said, reminiscing, "my mother used to put on a feed you wouldn't believe, rest in peace." He made the sign of the cross on his chest. "We'd start about four o'clock in the afternoon and the food just kept on coming till we were so tired from all that chewing we had to go to bed. It was great."

"It sounds much like one of our ancient Grecian feasts."

Freddie grinned. "We didn't eat no *goat*."

"No? Well, you are mortals. You may be forgiven. Perhaps someday order will be restored here to the point where goat is once again understood for the delicacy it is." He sighed longingly. "I suspect that you will be restored to *your* rightful place in this world before I am properly restored in mine. Gina will lose her heart and soul to this McCarthy, and she will be so consumed by his attentions that she will not find me in any way divine."

"Yeah, but McCarthy's a good guy," Freddie said. "He's done right by me a lotta times. Didn't throw me in jail when I split your forehead open. Coulda, though."

Harpo made a wistful half-smile. "Ah, yes, our inauspicious beginning, after my even more inauspicious arrival on this noble edifice." He tapped the box affectionately.

"You made an entrance, I'll give you that."

"Things have changed very much since then, have they not?"

"Oh, yeah. A lot. I gotta admit, you're not so bad. Weird, but not bad."

"And you have surprised me, my friend, by becoming a worthy companion and a capable helpmate. For one who knew so little about proper hospitality."

"Aw, shucks." Freddie waved his hand. "Better watch out, or I might get the idea you're trying to get *me* to believe all your crap instead of Gina." He laughed and winked. "Just kidding."

"But I do not jest when I say these things!" Harpo said. "You are a good man, on whom the Fates have played some despicable tricks. And despite your overall shortcomings, I find you mortals to be a far better lot than I expected. Even this McCarthy. Why, were it not for him, I might have met some other mortal woman before Gina. One who might have been far less—pleasant."

"See? He did you a favor."

"Indeed," Harpo said, "but a favor ripe to bursting with irony. Any decent Greek playwright . . ." He sighed in deep frustration. "By bringing me to her McCarthy has spared me lesser women, but directed me instead to the woman whose worship he *himself* wants. It is a paradox of such a sublime nature that even I, with the wisdom of a god, cannot begin to sort it out."

"Hey, you coulda ended up seeing some hooker before you saw her. Or maybe a dyke. Then you'da been in really deep shit."

"I—"

Freddie stopped him with a raised hand. "Just leave it that it's a good thing you ended up with Gina. You can't go wrong with a woman like that."

"She *is* a fine mortal. She has a good heart, and she knows what is fair. I suppose I can only expect her to give me the treatment she thinks I deserve."

He let out a weary breath. "And so I think I must go to her again and apologize for my behavior at the Museum, when she is not engrossed in her own concerns, though there hardly ever seems to be such a time." He glanced over at Freddie. "Perhaps she will understand if I explain again my unfamiliarity with mortal customs."

"It's worth a shot, anyway. You still got the chocolates?"

Harpo shook his head in guilt. "I disposed of them in a fit of anger."

Freddie looked momentarily miffed, then his expression relaxed. "Ah, that's all right. Easy come, easy go." He chuckled. "Story of my life. But we can get some more. No sweat. Us bums gotta stick together, right? And speakin' of that, I was thinkin' maybe I could talk to her for you. You know, smooth things out a little."

"You would do this for me?"

"Yeah. Why not?"

"You are too kind, my friend. You see? We have improved each other. You have become a fine host, indeed." Then he smiled. "And I have become a better guest."

Ω Ω Ω

The raindrops landed with a steady pitter-patter on the top of the box, and Harpo soon succumbed to the soporific rhythm by closing his eyes and drifting off to dreamland.

A short while later the rain tapered off, so Freddie pulled back the drape and took a look outside. Finding both the weather and the hour acceptable, he said softly, "No time like the present," and climbed over Harpo, taking care not to wake him.

He found Gina in her office, working intently at the computer. He observed her for a few seconds before making his presence known, and thought to himself that she looked worn and sad. Hat in hand, he knocked on the door frame.

"Hey, Freddie," she said, "come on in. What a nice surprise to see *you* in here." She swiveled her chair to face him, then pointed down the hall. "Bathroom's empty."

"Oh, yeah. Good. I'll be right back."

"Don't forget to wash your hands."

She chuckled as he shuffled down the hall. It was the hand washing she really wanted. He came back holding his hat.

"Have a seat," she said. "Take a load off. I'm completely honored that I didn't have to drag you here."

Freddie laughed nervously. "Yeah, uh, well . . ."

"Is everything okay?" Then, with more concern, "Harpo's okay?"

"He's back at the box sleepin. And I'm okay too."

"Because I know you don't like to come in. So, it makes me wonder why. Not that you need a reason. You're always welcome—"

He interrupted her gushing. "I, uh, wondered if I could talk to you for a minute."

Gina saved her data file, then closed the program and gave him her undivided attention. "Sure, Freddie. Any time."

"It's kinda personal."

170

"That's okay. Don't be embarrassed." She laughed a little, trying to put him at ease. "There isn't a whole lot you can say that will shock me, anyway. I've seen just about—"

"No," he said, interrupting her again, "I mean it's personal about *you.*"

She was momentarily caught off guard, but recovered quickly. "I want you and all the men who come in here to feel that you can offer criticism without worrying about it. It helps me to do my job better if you guys speak up. So anything you have to say—"

"No," he said again. "It's nothing like that. You're doing a great job here. I mean, most of us would be dead if it wasn't for you."

His blunt acknowledgment lifted her dark spirits. "Then what is it?"

"It's, um, about Dionysus. I mean, Harpo."

"I thought you said—"

"Oh, he's okay. I mean, sort of. He's not hurt or anything, but he's not too happy."

Neither am I, she thought cynically. "I'm very sorry to hear that. But you know as well as I do that everyone gets unhappy now and then. Me included. And I don't understand how you mean that it's personal for me if Harpo's unhappy."

He shifted uncomfortably. "Well, he's real sorry about what happened at the museum."

"He should be. He acted like a complete jerk."

Freddie came to his box-mate's defense without hesitation. "I think I finally got him convinced of that. I think he understands. You know, he's not from around here, and he doesn't know how to act sometimes."

He did not elaborate on what he had begun to believe about his companion's true place of origin.

"That's no excuse, Freddie. When in Rome . . ."

"Aw, Jeez, don't say anything about Rome to him, that sets him off like a freakin' rocket. But he's gettin' better about most of the other stuff. Doesn't get so mad all the time. The Rome stuff still pisses him off. But I guess you could say he's makin' progress."

He likes him, she realized with genuine surprise. *He didn't want to do it when I first asked, but now he likes the guy. And he's doing a good job of watching over him.*

What a world. "So, how do we go about making him happier? I mean, you're obviously doing your part, but what do you think I can do?"

His face brightened. "Well, you could tell him that you understand he's sorry."

She crossed her arms over her chest. "How would I know he's sorry?"

"You will, real soon. He already tried to apologize to you. We got you some chocolates, but you were going out, so we didn't get a chance to give 'em to you. You left kinda fast."

"When was this?"

"The other night." He smiled bashfully. "You looked real pretty, all dressed up."

They saw me all dressed up. They had followed her at least to Miranda's apartment. The conversation with Harpo on the stoop of her apartment building the next morning fell neatly and retrospectively into place.

"Thanks." She stared unfocused for a moment as she considered the disturbing implications of his revelation.

I'm probably not in danger, she finally concluded. *But what does this all mean? What is it with this guy?*

She turned back to Freddie. "Well, I guess I can cut him some slack, since he's not from around here. Has he said anything about where he's from yet?"

Freddie's gaze flinched momentarily, then he looked down at the floor before speaking. "No. He won't tell me."

The classic indicator of a lie, learned in Psych 101. *He knows. So why won't he tell me?* "I found out there's a guy who fits the same description who went missing just about the same time Harpo showed up here. He's a professor at Columbia. Has he said anything to you that might make you think they're one and the same?"

"A professor? Are you kidding?" Then he thought for a moment. "Well, maybe. He does get kinda preachy sometimes. I s'pose he could be a professor."

But by the furtive glance he cast in her direction, Gina knew that Freddie didn't think Harpo was anything of the sort. And he was protecting him.

"Oh, well," she said, trying to sound nonchalant, "We'll find out sometime. In the meantime, tell me what you think I should do."

Freddie looked immensely relieved. "When he comes to tell you he's sorry, act like you understand. Like everything's okay."

"Okay, I will. If you think it will help, I mean."

"Oh, it will. He'll be real happy."

"But he's going to have to behave better in the future."

"I told him. He understands."

She smiled broadly. "Okay, I'll do it. But just for you. I think you missed your calling, Freddie. You should've been a shrink."

He blushed, more bashfully than Gina would have imagined possible for such a man. "Nah, thanks, but I like doin' books."

And he shared with her a different time. "My father didn't think I'd amount to nothing, I was always in trouble when I was a kid. You know, stupid stuff."

"We all do stupid stuff when we're kids. It's just part of the deal."

"Yeah, well, I was pretty stupid. Not *challenged* at all, just plain stupid. A couple a times he called the cops on me and they took me out behind the overpass and smacked me around. The good old days, I guess. Except I wasn't stupid in math. I could do stuff in my head so fast, Ma used to take me shopping with her. So she'd know how much she could spend. She was so surprised when I wanted to go to school to learn accounting."

He was silent for a moment, as his smile gradually faded. She imagined him wondering how he got from there to here. It had happened way too fast.

"Speaking of math," she said, "why don't I bring my tax stuff in tomorrow?"

"*Really?*"

"Yeah. But I want you to stay with Harpo a little longer, if you don't mind. I'm still not sure he's ready to go out in the world on his own."

"Sure," he said excitedly. "I can do that."

"And depending on how the taxes go, maybe you can give me a hand with the books for the center. I can't pay you a lot, but I can give you something."

"*Really?* Wow! *Thanks.* I mean, anything's all right. Anything you got." He made a few nervous steps toward the door, then turned back toward her. "Okay, listen, I'm gonna go back and tell him. I'll come back tomorrow for your stuff." Then he ran out of the office, mumbling happily to himself.

Gina watched him depart, musing sadly about how little it took to make him happy, if only the world would trust him. She wondered how long it would take to get *him* to trust the world again.

She turned back to the computer, closed the program she'd been working on when Freddie came in, and spent the next half hour furiously poring over East Coast arrivals for the previous six months, entering every form of spelling she could think of. She came up with a big, fat, frustrating zero.

Ω Ω Ω

"Plan," Freddie said aloud, grinning triumphantly, "with a capital *P.*" He trotted along, humming to himself, keeping his eyes open for a corner with good traffic for a brief stint of panhandling. *Four or five bucks oughta do it,* he thought. He'd go back to the box and get Harpo, and they'd buy more chocolates. Then he'd drag his unhappy, godlike ass down to the shelter, where the apology would take place.

And then he'd get to do Gina's taxes, and if they came out all right, which he knew they would, he'd be doing the center's books. *And after that? Who knows! I get cleaned up. No more booze. A job.*

He set himself up on a favorite crosstown route, but after ten minutes, he'd only collected a handful of change, and was beginning to think about moving on to a more lucrative location, when a very happy-looking man came down the street, his hand full of crisp new bills, which he counted gleefully as he strode along. He peeled off a twenty and pressed it into Freddie's outstretched hand. As Freddie stared after him, the man grinned generously and said, "I just hit the number!"

Freddie shouted, "Hey, congratulations! And thanks! Thanks a lot!" He waved as his benefactor flagged a cab, hopped in, and sped away. Holding the bill up to admire it, Freddie laughed aloud. "Ha *ha*! Okay, Mr. di-O-nee_sus, I'm comin' home. You're gonna like mortals even better now."

He kissed the bill, stashed it in his pocket, and, whistling a happy tune, set off in the direction of the Freezer. So distracted was he by thoughts of his new-found fortune on the trek home that the gods would forgive him for failing to notice he had acquired another shadow.

Chapter 16
Pi

"Scoot over there and pass that bottle," Freddie said, "We're celebrating."

Harpo rose up on one elbow and yawned. "Ah, yes, the bottle," he mumbled groggily, "let me see . . ." He rooted around in the corner of the box and produced the half-empty bottle. "Here it is, such as it is."

Freddie took the bottle from him and set it down, then lit the candle and closed the drape. Humming happily, he unscrewed the metal cap and took a long drink.

Harpo rubbed his eyes and said, "Has some bit of good fortune befallen you?"

"You bet it has," Freddie said with a grin, "befallen *us*."

"Well, do not keep this happy news a secret!"

"Jeez," Freddie said, "I don't hardly know where to start." He pressed the bottle to his lips, swung it upward, and guzzled down a few good swallows. "You're gonna love this. I went down to the center to see Gina while you were sleepin', and I squared it with her for you. Told her you were real sorry, that you wanted to come down there and apologize, and that you said you were gonna behave better from now on."

Harpo sat up, jarred awake. "And how did she react to this?"

"Well, she seemed kinda skeptical at first. I'm thinkin' maybe she was just playin' hard to get, you know what I mean? Kinda angry and hurt. Women love all that dramatic shit. But I think I managed to convince her you mean it. I told her how you didn't understand the way we act around here, and she seemed to buy it."

"And she will hear my apology?"

"She will."

"She said this?"

"Yep, she did."

"Truly, this is marvelous!" Midas made a few *simpatico* yips.

"Pretty fucking marvelous, indeed, if I do say so myself. I think things are gonna go a lot better for you now. So, do you remember the apology?"

Harpo nodded his head eagerly. "I do!" He positioned his hands in dramatic supplication, furrowed his brow plaintively and recited, "Honey, I'm so sorry, I was a great big shit and I promise I'll never do it again."

Freddie clapped in approval. "Aw, that's great, if you do it just like that for her, she's gonna melt. You'll have her eatin' outta your hand. I guarantee it. Ain't no way she won't believe in you."

"Well, she need not go to such lengths to convey her understanding of my regret, but of course, she may eat out of my hand if she wishes to do so, for I am most anxious to please her, and if such an activity pleases her, though I am at a loss to understand its appeal, why, then, I shall not deny her."

His elaborated giddily. "After all, am I not the god of such excesses? Your mortal fetishes are often the first step toward achieving true *ecstasis*, and such a state would be a very great blessing for this woman." He smiled magnanimously. "She may eat out of my *navel* if it makes her happy! But I will be satisfied if only I can reenter her good graces."

"That's gonna be the minimum," Freddie declared.

"And this is what makes you so happy? This triumph on my behalf?"

"Hell, no, there's more. Lots more! Some guy who just hit the lottery gave me twenty bucks."

"I do not understand this lottery."

"Yeah, I didn't think you would. But no problem. OK. A lottery is a game where lots of people all put in a little bit of money and they each bet on a certain number. They put all the numbers in a hat and they choose one. Then the person who has that number gets *all* the money. You have to be really lucky, but someone's gotta win! Well, I ran into a winner tonight when I was panhandling. He gave me twenty bucks! And remember how Gina said I could do her taxes when I got through cartin' you around? Well, she's gonna bring her stuff in tomorrow so I can start on them right away! Oh, man, this is just what I was hopin' would happen—"

The candle flickered for a few brief seconds and Midas began to growl. Suddenly the drape was pulled up; the incoming rush of wind blew the candle out. A hand with fingerless gloves reached in and took hold of Freddie's jacket by the front of the collar. A frightening, unfamiliar voice hissed, "Gimme the twenty bucks, asshole."

Freddie started to push the hand away, saying, "Hey, let go of me, and who you callin' asshole, *asshole?*"

The metallic click of a blade cut the quiet air. "You," said its wielder, "*asshole.* Now shut up and give me the twenty bucks."

Still defiant, Freddie said, "Do I look like I got twenty bucks?"

The hand yanked him closer to the box opening. "Fuck, no. But I saw that guy give it to you. Too bad he got into a cab or I woulda got him. So I followed you.

And you didn't stop anywhere to spend it." The voice grew more jittery with each word, and the interloper poked the knife through the air a few times. "Now, come on, gimme the fucking money or I'll cut you."

Harpo leaned forward and hissed, "See here, Mortal, you are—"

The knife whipped through the air with a *whooshing* sound and Harpo found himself staring at its glinting tip, now a mere inch from the end of his nose.

"You wanna die?" the thief said.

"*Ha!*" Harpo said defiantly. "I *cannot* die, for I am—"

"Yeah?" The thief said. "Let's see." As the knife was thrust forward, Harpo tipped himself to one side. The knife cut clear through the cardboard of the box and was momentarily locked in its corrugated grip.

Freddie took that window of opportunity to pummel him with closed fists, and Harpo began kicking with his feet. But the thief was young and quick, and managed to get the knife free. He heaved himself against Freddie and pushed him down, the box rocking to the side as they bumped against one wall.

Then he slashed through the air with the knife, and Harpo understood from the dull, wet sound that the blade had connected with flesh. The smell of hot blood assaulted his nostrils.

There was a brief and terrible silence, followed by the frantic hard breath of the assailant and the crumpling of paper. Then the thief turned to Harpo, knife extended. "Gimme the necklace," he said.

His eyes wide, he clutched the vial. Midas growled.

"You wanna end up like your friend here?"

Harpo opened his mouth to voice his defiance, but before any sound came out, the thief reached up and tore the necklace free with one good yank, its broken cord searing the skin of Harpo's neck. Then the thief made one more slash through the air with the knife. Harpo recoiled into the corner, and watched as the young aggressor disappeared into the darkness.

He knelt over Freddie and in the dim light saw the long, gaping slit in his companion's neck. "Sweet Athena," he prayed in anguish, "guide his steps to Hades."

He pulled Midas out of the front of his toga and dropped him at Freddie's side. "Stay here," he said sharply, "Guard the mortal. I will return."

When he came out of the box, he caught a glimpse of the thief stumbling around the corner. He ran after him, splashing wildly through the mud.

He followed the thief for two long blocks of First Avenue, and then the young man turned and headed down a busy crosstown street. The pounding chase weaved through the bustle of evening: merchants selling their last of the day, customers buying for the dinner ahead, homeward-bound workers trekking through the maze of New York with dry-cleaning and afternoon editions.

Just shy of Second Avenue, a tiny Korean grandmother deftly hoisted a crate of grapes off a small table outside her store and set it down on the sidewalk. It caught the fleeing thief by the toe and he belly-flopped onto the hard, wet surface with a huge thud. The knife went clattering onto the sidewalk, out of reach. Within a few seconds, Harpo was straddling him.

Ω Ω Ω

The stranger who called himself Dionysus placed one foot in the middle of the stunned youth's back. His leaned over and whispered, so the thief alone could hear him. "It seems the Fates have decreed that you should be given to me."

He reached down and placed one hand on the back of the thief's head and pressed down hard. At thin stream of blood came out of the youth's nose. Harpo made a sinister smile. "What shall I do with you?"

"How about you get the fuck off me, for starters."

Harpo shook his head. "That would be a very ungodlike thing to do. You have done grave harm to my friend, and he must be avenged."

"I don't know what you're talkin' about, man. Get the fuck offa me."

"You mortals should not attempt to lie," he said, "for a god can always tell. As I can tell now."

"I ain't lyin'."

"Ha! *Another* lie, equally detectable. Now, while I decide how the murder of my companion will be avenged, you will give back what you stole." He extended an open hand, and pressed down harder on the thief's head.

"Let me up!" he blubbered.

"Perhaps I will when you have returned what you stole." Harpo ground his heel into the thief's back, and the youth shrieked. Finally, his face contorted with pain, he acquiesced through gritted teeth. "Back pocket."

Harpo reached down and fished around in the pocket, and easily found both the money and the necklace. The silver chord was broken, but the amulet was intact. He tucked it into his own jacket pocket.

"And now I will have my revenge." he said. Muttering a devout prayer, he reached down and turned the thief's head as far to the side as it would go. When his supplication was complete, he looked directly into his eyes. "This," he whispered, "is what you have earned with your treachery. Bid your sanity good-bye. And for you, it will not be the sweet blessing some others have known."

The young man looked back at him with fearful, bulging eyes. He began to scream and struggled to get up. But Harpo bore down on him, and soon the culprit was both still and silent.

The blaring of sirens grew louder as a patrol car neared the scene. It screeched to a halt at the curb and two uniformed cops jumped out. One trained his weapon on Harpo, who offered up his wrists in bitter compliance. The first cop knelt over the thief and restrained his hands behind his back. As he tried to stand him up, the thief began to thrash about wildly, hitting his own head repeatedly on the sidewalk.

"Shit!" the cop swore. "Get me a blanket or something! This guy's gonna crack his own head open!"

More cruisers arrived; a sea of blue-clad men and women began their practiced routine of managing bystanders and preserving evidence.

McCarthy and Stein made their way through the growing crowd. "Harpo!" McCarthy called out when he saw him, "what the hell is this?"

"This thief attacked me and Freddie in our box with a dagger and tried to rob us."

Stein looked around and said, "Where's Freddie?"

Hi head drooped. "Still there. Midas is protecting him, for I could not let this villain get away."

"Is he all right?"

His eyes shifted back and forth between Stein and McCarthy, his expression heavy with sorrow. He said nothing.

McCarthy looked around among the uniformed cops, then spoke to one he knew. "Get over to the Freezer. First box on the left." He looked back at the captive perpetrator, who lay face down on the sidewalk, his entire body shivering. A wadded-up blanket lay between the concrete and his bleeding head, and his eyes were glazed with a lost, vacant look.

McCarthy glanced around the crime scene and saw the knife, still lying where it had fallen. The blood had not yet dried on the blade. He looked at Harpo with a grave expression. He pointed in its direction. "Is this the knife he used?"

Harpo scrutinized it for a brief moment. "Indeed."

McCarthy's expression darkened even further. "You're nuts to run after a guy with a knife."

"Precisely! And what would you have me do? Allow this criminal to get away with his vile deed? Should I have allowed him to go unpunished after what he did to Freddie? And he tried to steal my very immortality from me! Such things must *not* be allowed." He cast a hard glance at the trembling youth on the cold concrete. "He should be chained naked to a jagged rock in a wet cave full of hungry rats."

McCarthy wanted to say, *I couldn't agree with you more.* "Yeah, well, you still shouldn't have chased him. And what the hell happened to him, anyway? What a mess. He's gonna have a hell of a headache."

"He tripped. And you are right, his head will ache most terribly, I am certain of it."

McCarthy surveyed the gathered witnesses. He turned to the Korean grandmother, who launched into a streaming explanation in her native tongue. "*Oy,*" he muttered. "We need a translator here." Stein took out his radio and began speaking.

McCarthy turned to a nervous-looking man who stood nearby. "Did you see what happened?"

The witness took a quick look at Harpo, then looked back at McCarthy. "Like that guy says, he tripped. The old lady put the crate down just before he got there. He musta not seen it."

A few feet away, he saw a cluster of grapes laying on the sidewalk. He bent over and picked it up. The firm, round fruits were unscathed. He walked back to where the thief was still lying, immobilized, and held a bunch of grapes in front of the youth's contorted face. "Looks like you got tripped up."

The youth's face took on an expression of terror. He opened his mouth and let out a long, frightened wail, then began to blubber. "Get them away from me, get those fucking things outta my face!" He hitched in another breath and started to scream.

"Okay, okay," McCarthy said, "Take it easy there."

"You see," Harpo said with a caustic smile of satisfaction, "I spoke the truth, why else would he react so?"

"No idea," McCarthy said. "I'm gonna take these cuffs off you, but I want you to wait in the car 'til I get through here. Someone's going to check on Freddie." He called the dispatcher for a wagon to take away the suspect.

Ω Ω Ω

There were several cruisers and an ambulance, all with their roof lights flashing, at the entrance to the Freezer.

"Stay here for a minute till I see what's going on," McCarthy said through the open back door.

"No! I will come with you." He sidled toward the car door.

McCarthy reached out and shoved Harpo back onto the seat. "Stay here," he said firmly. "You'll just be in the way."

The rain had returned, and each new drop that fell on the car window hooked up with one or two others. Soon small rivulets meandered idly down the outside face of the window, distorting further the already sordid scene beyond them. Flashes of blue light danced on the surface of the thick glass and were magnified until the cold stark brightness seemed so grating that Harpo wanted to close his eyes and be rid of the whole mess. But he found to his dismay that he couldn't tear himself away from what was happening in the alley.

McCarthy returned to the car, with Midas tucked under one arm. His little paws were tinged pink from Freddie's blood. He was wet and trembling. The cop opened the door and said, "Come on out." Harpo followed him.

"They found your dog next to the body, yapping like crazy. He tried to bite one of the guys." McCarthy nodded toward the cop in question. "I guess he was trying to protect the bod—the victim. The detectives are already here and they want you to tell them what happened before you started chasing the thief."

Harpo nodded. Then he lowered himself down and pulled aside the curtain. No one made an attempt to stop him. He saw Freddie laying inside the box in an arrangement of limbs that no living being would choose or tolerate.

"Ah, my friend," he whispered to Freddie's corpse, "You may have risen above *some* of the limits of mortality, but it seems the unavoidable one has claimed you." He dropped the curtain and stood up, then turned to face the two unfamiliar officers. "Soon the ferryman will row him across the Styx to greet Hades. His earthly journey is at an end."

One of the detectives mumbled a few sympathetic phrases, then began asking questions. Harpo listened carefully and responded as well as he could. McCarthy saw the difficulty he was having and said to the questioner, "How about we take him down to the precinct house? Maybe he'll feel more comfortable there." The detective agreed.

Several other homeless men, also Freezer residents, were gathered at the perimeter of the scene, observing the proceedings with cautious interest. McCarthy pulled Harpo aside when he saw them and said quietly, "You better make your mark on the box or one of these guys is going to try to claim it."

"How shall I make this 'mark'?"

McCarthy sighed. "This is no time to get cute, Harpo. You know, make your mark. Stand outside the box and take a piss. Empty your bladder."

Harpo gazed over at the box with disgust. "And by doing so I will claim this palace as my own?"

McCarthy nodded, his expression full of dark sarcasm. "Yeah. Quaint custom."

"Indeed," he said, and as McCarthy and the other cops continued to go through the routines of a murder scene, he stood at the side of the box, lifted his robe and urinated into the slush in full view of his gathered neighbors, who all withdrew, muttering discontent.

McCarthy planted Harpo in the back seat of the cruiser again and drove to the center, but before he got out of the car, he turned around and faced his solemn passenger. "Listen up, Harpo," he said sternly. "You do what I tell you now. Wait here, because I have to take you down to the station to talk to some more detectives. But right now I have to go in there and tell Gina that Freddie's dead. He has no family around here, so she's gonna have to identify his body, and she's not gonna be too happy when she comes outta there. So I want to you try to rise above your usual bullshit and be quiet."

He opened his mouth and began to protest. "But there is something very important that I must say to her—"

"Let it rest, okay? You'll get your chance later. She's not gonna be paying much attention to you, anyway. So button it up, and you'll be doing all of us a favor, but especially her."

Harpo closed his mouth and sat back. McCarthy gave him a bitter grin and said, "That's the ticket."

But as he watched McCarthy walk slowly down the steps into the shelter, Harpo could almost see the weight of the grave news the man was carrying. He leaned his face against the cool glass of the window and said to Midas, "It is a very difficult thing to be mortal, I think. They take death so hard! They fear that he will have nothing beyond its veil. How foolish they are. Freddie was a very fine mortal, despite his appearance, and he will not be turned away from the gates of Hades."

His *melancholia* was interrupted a few seconds later when a bedraggled-looking group of men came out of the center and dispersed into the night. McCarthy supported Gina as she walked up the steps and helped her get into the cruiser.

Harpo whispered to Midas, "For once I do not mind that he touches her."

When she got into the front seat of the car, she turned around; their eyes met for a few moments, and he could see the wet streaks of tears. He nodded gravely, and she looked away again, but not before he saw the bitterness in her expression.

She stared straight ahead into the gloomy night as they drove along, until something caught her attention. She sat up straighter and pressed her hands against the window glass.

"Pull over, McCarthy. Here."

McCarthy, surprised by the her vehemence, skidded to the curb. Before the car was even completely stopped, Gina threw open the door and leapt out, leaving it agape behind her.

She ignored McCarthy's plea to return to the car, and instead looked around on the ground for a few moments. She dug out a rock from the base of a sidewalk tree. With a huge grunt, she hurled it into the night. It whistled through the darkness and crashed through a second-floor window of a square, ungraceful brick building with a sign painted along the top floor. Harpo took in the letters he could recognize, but could glean nothing of their meaning.

Within seconds a blaring alarm sounded. "Yes!" Gina shrieked. She jumped up and down and clapped her hands together. Then she cupped her hands around her mouth and shouted, "Fuck you, DeMoula, and your ugly building, too."

McCarthy was about to retrieve her when she turned and got back in. "I'm gonna have to call that in, you know," he said softly.

She faced him and extended her two wrists. "Be my guest," she said. "I'm ready to go. Right now. I'll make a full confession." Her hands trembled with pent-up fury.

McCarthy's expression, when he took gentle hold of her outstretched hands, was full of sympathy. Her fists unclenched slightly.

"I feel so completely impotent," she seethed. "I just want to run out there and destroy that place."

McCarthy kept his grip on her hands. "Let it go," he said quietly. "The system's already chewed the whole thing up and spit it out. There's nothing more we can do to DeMoula that's gonna make it right. We don't need anyone else going down over that bullshit scam he pulled. Especially not you."

Gina squeezed her eyes tightly shut and hissed, "But it would feel so good to do something awful to him, to blow that place up, I just want to sit back and watch and laugh and gloat over it . . ."

"I don't think you can see that building from where they'd put you if you did what you're thinking about."

She raged in silence, her entire body shivering.

"Besides," McCarthy said gently, "he'll get his. I really believe that God picks up where we have to leave off."

"I wish I could," she said.

He let go of her hands and signaled the dispatcher. "Be advised that we have an alarm sounding at the DeMoula Liquor Warehouse." He recited the cross-streets. "Probable security on premises, likely armed." He hesitated for a moment, wondering how far he should go with it. *Fuck it,* he told himself. *Get the asshole back in here from his nice big house in Westchester.* He lied, knowing it would be impossible to prove. "I observed a gang of youths fleeing the scene shortly after the alarm started."

They sped away, and after a few more turns, McCarthy brought the car to a stop outside a large gray building and opened the back door for Harpo. Out of Gina's earshot, he said to McCarthy, "I do not understand what she did there."

"The guy who owns it pulled a real dirty trick on Freddie. That's why he ended up homeless."

Harpo said nothing. The cop's tale was a blunt, colorless little *precis* of what he'd heard, in more intimate detail, from Freddie himself. What Gina had done was to exact a small amount of retribution.

But he could see that it was not enough for her. It was merely an opening prayer to Nemesis, to be completed later.

"You mortals do not understand the importance of vengeance." He looked into McCarthy's eyes and proclaimed, "When I have power again, things will be very different."

Ω Ω Ω

A few times since they'd arrived at the 13th, he had seen McCarthy put his arm around Gina's shoulder and squeeze gently, then whisper something to her and stroke her hair. And despite his own jealousy, he was glad that McCarthy could comfort her. He had wanted to reassure her with explanations about Freddie's journey to Hades, but McCarthy had insisted, *quite* disrespectfully, that he be quiet, and he had complied.

Then the woman had done a remarkable thing to him—she had put her own arm around his shoulder and expressed her sympathy for *his* loss. "He was your friend, too, Harpo, I know. I'm really sorry."

She had apologized to *him*. He nodded. They were momentarily alone, McCarthy having stepped away. It was an opportunity he could not afford to squander. He looked around nervously, then turned back to Gina, and said, with an edge of uncertainty in his voice, "There is something I would say to you—"

But as McCarthy had predicted, Gina was not paying attention, and before he knew it, the big cop was back again, and with him, another man.

"Looks like the detective's here to take your statement, Harpo" Gina said. "Just write down what happened as you remember it, and then—" She halted, realizing the impossibility of her directive. "I'll tell him you're too upset to write it yourself. Just tell him the story, and he'll write it down."

She took the detective aside and explained. The man led Harpo to a small room, where Harpo recounted the night's awful events. The detective, without comment, dutifully recorded every crazy word. When they were through, he read it back, then said, "Sign here if you agree with everything in the statement." He offered a pen.

Slowly and carefully, the stranger who called himself Dionysus made the symbols of his name on the indicated line. When he was through he examined the pen carefully. "A fine specimen." He handed it back.

The puzzled detective took the ordinary Bic, then looked it over carefully himself, wondering if he'd missed something. After a few seconds, he shrugged, and handed the pen back to Harpo. "Keep it."

"Really?" he said.

"Really," the detective answered. They went out of the small room and found McCarthy.

The detective took him aside. "Could I have a coupla words?"

McCarthy shot a quick glance and a nod at Gina, which she understood immediately. "Harpo," she said, placing her hand on his shoulder, "why don't we wait over here until McCarthy's through?"

They stepped a few paces away and sat down on a long wooden bench whose ancient lacquer was worn away in a repeating series of buttock-shaped patterns, and watched as the detective and McCarthy engaged in a hushed but animated conversation. The detective cast a quick glance in their direction, then turned back to McCarthy and continued arguing.

Finally, McCarthy stomped away from the detective and came back to them. They stood up in unison, awaiting his word on what was next to be done.

"Everything all right?" Gina asked.

"As all right as it's gonna be under the circumstances," McCarthy said, frustration in his voice. Then his voice softened. "Listen, they're gonna take my ID of Freddie as a positive. You don't have to go look at the body. And the perp is completely whacked out, so they took him to Bellevue. Harpo won't have to hang around to ID him, either. Maybe later when the perp is himself again." He smiled, but it was bitter. "So you're both done here. I gotta stay for a little while to clean up a few loose ends, so I won't be able to give you a ride. I'll see if I can get one of the other guys to take you back."

"That's okay. We'll take a cab. It'll be fine." Seeing the worried look on his face, she hastily added, "So will I."

"Maybe I'll stop in later, or give you a call, Just to check, I mean."

She nodded. He kissed her on the cheek and walked back toward the waiting detective.

"Okay, Harpo, let's go," she said wearily. Her hand went to his shoulder. "I'll drop you off at the Freezer if you want to go back there. But you're welcome to come to the center. Maybe you shouldn't be alone right now." She looked at him, waiting for him to state his preference.

He shook his head slowly, declining her offer.

But he knew the apology still needed to be made.

As they stepped out onto the sidewalk in front of the police station, Gina stopped and stood still for a moment. "It's almost tranquil out here," she said. "It's so noisy inside, with all the telephones ringing like they do. They never seem to stop."

Now, he told himself. *Do not let the moment slip away.* "I would say something to you," he said, "about the museum." He sucked in a nervous breath. "Honey," he began, reciting the words with sincere precision, "I'm so sorry. I was a great big shit and I promise I'll never do it again."

He stood quietly on the sidewalk, waiting for her response. The look on her face was one of shock, and he feared for a few anxious moments that the moment had not been right.

But then she sighed deeply, and began to weep. She threw her arms around his shoulders and hugged him hard. With cautious tenderness, he closed his own arms around her and returned the embrace. A flood of confusing, terribly mortal emotions rushed through him.

And when the cab left him off at the Freezer a short while later, there was peace between them, and he was full of hope.

Ω Ω Ω

When she got back to the intake center, Gina took out her computer and powered it up, then opened Freddie's file and retrieved the California phone number.

After placing the terrible call, she sat at her desk for a long time, doing absolutely nothing. Then she took a few moments to read through Freddie's record, recalling wistfully each occasion on which an entry had been made. When she was through, she pulled down the FILE menu at the top of the screen and clicked on the command to "DELETE". The program, with cold clarity, questioned her intent. ARE YOU SURE YOU WANT TO DELETE THIS FILE? Her finger poised over the ENTER button, but she could not press it; she was not ready for the records of her work with Freddie to disintegrate into a random set of disconnected electrons.

Her phone rang. Her finger moved from the ENTER button to the phone's screen.

"Hello?"

The unrecognized voice of a woman came through. "Miss Bugbee?"

"Yes?"

"This is Judy Klein."

For a moment, the connection escaped her.

"You left a message with my housekeeper. I'm sorry I didn't return your call sooner, but I've been traveling."

"Oh! Mrs. Klein!" She sat up taller. "I was calling about your husband. I run an intake center for homeless men at Bellevue, and I have someone here I think might possibly be him."

After a few seconds of stony silence, Mrs. Klein said, "I already found him."

Despite her disappointment, Gina said, "Oh, I'm happy to hear that. But he's still listed as a Missing Person."

There was unmistakable disdain in the woman's voice. "Oh, really? I must've forgotten to notify the police that he returned."

What, Gina wondered, had the good Professor done to her? She'd never know. "Well, I'm glad to hear he's back, and I hope everything's okay."

There was a small, ironic chuckle, then Judy Klein said, "It will be when the lawyers get through with it."

There wasn't much more to be said, except, "I'm very sorry to have bothered you, then."

"Yes. Well, good night, Miss Bugbee."

She was about to return the sentiment, but stopped herself. "Good bye," she said, and disconnected. She could not bring herself to refer to this night as good.

Chapter 17
Rho

"I know you're coming in later," Aaron said when he called the next morning, "but I wanted check in and see how you're doing."

"Getting by, that's about it. What I'd really like is to crawl back into bed for about a week."

Quietly, Aaron said, "Depression, maybe?

"Yeah. Probably."

"So we'll talk about that later. But I also wanted to tell you that our friend Harpo is coming in today. I'm planning to play along with his Dionysus fantasy, at least today. I want to see just how far he'll go with it."

"It astonishes me how well he does it," Gina said. "Sometimes I actually find myself *wanting* to believe him."

Aaron laughed. "You could probably use a little god in your life."

"Really, Aaron? God talk from a shrink?"

"I've had patients for whom the power of their own faith in—*something*—was the only drug they needed."

After a few seconds, she said, "Good for them." She laughed quietly. "And all this time I've been looking for a terrorist. I could just have looked *up*. But seriously, I did manage to nail one thing down: I found out last night he's *not* a professor from Columbia. The wife finally got back to me."

"Oh, well, that sounded promising."

"Yeah. But listen, I'm glad you called, because there's something else I should tell you. About Harpo." She related the previous night's sad event.

"Aaron, he's . . ."

She couldn't complete the sentence.

But he understood. "I know. He's a pain in the ass that you've unaccountably grown attached to. I'll be gentle with him. I plan to push him, but not so far that he runs away."

"You never told me you could *read* minds."

"Only yours," he said. "You leave it wide open all the time."

Ω Ω Ω

The stranger who called himself Dionysus made his way through the lower east side, turning right and left and right again in a zig-zag path to his destination. Gina had told him how to navigate the streets, that when he traveled in one direction the numbers must go up: seventeenth, eighteenth, nineteenth, until he reached 29th. And when he went in the perpendicular direction, the numbers must go down: third, second, and then finally first.

And even more confusing, when he was ready to return to what was now *his* box, it must all be done in reverse.

It was so much easier when Freddie could guide him. And as he stared at Bellevue's gleaming façade, he realized with some trepidation that he had only gone inside with Gina.

He came through the front door and made his way to one of the benches, and sat down. He looked at his watch.

"Nine hours and thirty minutes," he said aloud. "Still thirty minutes until we are to arrive."

No one sitting nearby knew that Midas could hear him. But neither did they care. He watched the people come in and out of the building. Men, women, children, old people, all varieties of mortals passed by as he regarded them.

"None seem prosperous," he said, patting his chest. "Why, many seem no more prosperous than Freddie, may his underworld journey be safe."

The time passed in this manner until his watch read nine hours and fifty minutes. He stood and began his ascent.

Ω Ω Ω

The lobby receptionist smiled politely.

"We are to make our presence known," he said to her.

She looked around, and saw no one else.

"Mr. Isus?"

"Indeed. *Dionysus.*"

"Doctor will be with you shortly."

A few minutes later, Mike came out of Aaron's office and beckoned him in. And as before, when this patient took his seat, Mike stood guard.

"Ten AM, right on time," Aaron said.

Harpo held out his arm, turning the banded wrist forward. "I have this fine timekeeper, which Gina gave to me so I could know when I should do certain things."

Aaron made a show of looking at it. "Very nice, Dionysus. You can take off your coat if you want to. I have to keep it warm in here but you might find the temperature uncomfortable."

189

"I thank you," the patient said with a slight nod. "And I also thank you for using my proper name. You are a fine host. You see to my comfort in a most attentive manner."

"It is my pleasure," Aaron said. "I spoke with Gina this morning, and she told me about your friend. I'm very sorry." He paused, then added, "I hope his journey to the Underworld is swift and safe."

"Thank you. I am comforted by your sentiments. And I know that he will be well received." He leaned forward and asked, "You speak with knowledge of Hades; are you *quite* sure you are not Greek?"

Aaron smiled. "Quite sure, but if it will make you feel any better, I'll ask my mother. Perhaps she knows something about my ancestry she's not telling me. But last time I bothered to look down at the evidence, I was still Jewish."

Harpo looked around as if checking for nearby listeners. He whispered to Aaron, "You are circumcised, then?"

"When I was eight days old. By a Moyel."

Harpo looked puzzled, so Aaron explained. "That's someone who makes his living by circumcising baby boys."

"By all the gods, the man must have a firm hand."

"Oh, they all do, I assure you. They have Jewish mothers staring over their shoulders. It tends to firm up the hand rather quickly."

"You are mortal, so you must have felt much pain when this was done to you, no?"

Aaron chuckled. "I was too young to remember, but my mother said I wailed like a banshee for about five minutes."

"I do not understand this *banshee.*"

"I'm sorry, it's a Gaelic legend about a female spirit who visits a family and wails when one of them is about to die. It's from after your time, from the early middle ages. You come out of the time of Alexander, don't you, or maybe even a little earlier?"

"Well, my worship was very strong then, but I am much older than that, really. All the gods are very old."

"Interesting," Aaron said. "I'm very curious about something, regarding pain. I know that last night must have been very painful for you, seeing that you're half mortal. But what about the God half of you? I'm interested specifically in emotional pain, pain of the psyche, like sadness, anxiety, anger . . ."

Harpo sat taller. "Oh, very much yes. We *created* those things. Indeed, it could be said that we owe our very existence to the sort of pain you describe."

Aaron raised his eyebrows. "How is that?"

"Well, to be clear, we do not precisely exist *because* of pain, but because of qualities or—*characteristics* that might lead to it. Aphrodite often falls prey to jealousy. This must be a form of pain to her, no? Artemis is aloof. Hestia is shy. Hera is vindictive, Ares quick to ire. Hephaestus is ugly, and is therefore always ashamed of himself. Correctly, in my opinion, for his ugliness is *most* hideous. These are all pains of the *psyche*, are they not?"

"Yes," Aaron said, "all those things can be very difficult."

"And often, when mortals worship us, it is because they feel a certain pain, and would seek relief. Is this not so?"

"I hadn't thought of it that way, but I suppose you're right. So, what is *your* particular quality? What do *you* experience?"

Harpo sat back in the chair for a moment or two. "Because my mother was mortal, I experience everything. It can sometimes be a curse, I must say."

"I can see where it might be. Seems unfair. You must be angry that the other gods each really only have one quality to deal with, and you have the full range."

"Ah," Harpo said, "this is true. But you must remember that each of us has a realm of pleasure to rule, as well. And being half mortal, I have the unique ability to experience *all* mortal pleasure. Some of it is very fine, is it not?"

"I would have to agree."

"So it is not terrible to be half mortal, eh? Besides that, I am the son of a divine father who once had the power to do precisely as he wished. Zeus endowed me with a means of escape mortal pain. He gave me wine. And madness."

"A lot of my patients like wine very much, but I don't often hear them refer to mental illness as a gift. It can be very difficult for some people, life-shattering, even. Is it different for a god?"

"Ah," Harpo said, "finally we have reached the heart of the matter. *Everything* is different for a god."

Aaron sat in forced motionlessness, wanting so badly to engage in the captivating discussion with his full body, with dramatic gesticulations and purposeful pacing. The sparkle in his eyes intensified. "Tell me about your madness. I want to know everything."

"But it cannot all be told in one turn of the clock!"

"You can come back again. As many times as you need to. Just start. Anywhere."

Harpo saw nothing diabolical in Aaron's eyes, only pure interest. But could a mortal, even this brilliant mortal, fully comprehend his own divine madness?

"I will tell you of a madness I have *caused*, very recently." He leaned forward, as if confiding a secret. "I was surprised to find that I had the power to do it. Few believe any more, and all the power of *any* god has belief at its roots." He paused for effect. "Being an educated man, you should understand this."

Aaron felt strangely chastised. "You're right, and I do. But go on. Tell me about this madness you caused."

"It was not the joyful sort of madness. We spoke before about my mortal friend who crossed the river into Hades. Of course the mortal part of *me* is very sad. But the god part of me feels the sweetness of revenge, for I chased the thief and captured him."

"That must have taken a lot of courage."

"It takes no courage to do what is right, only resolve."

"Nevertheless, not many people would have done what you did. Though in our defense, I think most mortals would have wanted to."

"I am heartened to hear that," Harpo said. "It improves my opinion of you all. In any case, as he ran down the street, I followed him. He was fleet of foot—he might have been one of Hermes' finest athletes had he not squandered his gift on thievery. For some reason the Fates enlisted the help of an old woman, an Oriental, who set out a box of grapes just as the thief was passing. He tripped and fell, and it was then that I got hold of him." He let out a long sigh.

Incredible, Aaron thought. "That was an odd way for the Fates to stop a thief."

Harpo shrugged. "Indeed not. Grapes were appropriate, since I am the god of wine. And when I had this *daemon* pinned to the ground, I prayed to force madness upon him. Somehow, my prayer was answered.

He stood, gesturing. "Snakes writhing in his *psyche!* Explosions of dark confusion. The very opposite of *ecstasis*. And when he arose from his fall, that thief would scream in terror to see his own mother, thinking she was Medusa herself."

"You actually *did* that to him? It seems a bit extreme."

"If you require verification, you may ask the soldiers who came to take the thief away."

"The police officers."

"Yes," he said. "They were there almost immediately."

Aaron looked away and took in a long cleansing breath. "Was the thief injured any other way?"

"His face was bloodied, and his nose was quite bent."

Traumatic head injury from the fall. Aaron felt inexplicably relieved by this rational explanation.

"Then the soldier named McCarthy, the one who is enamored of Gina—"

Aaron made a mental note, but did not interrupt.

"—came and took me in his moving machine, back to the box, and there he showed me the remains of my friend. But I knew already that he was dead, for . . ."

Aaron interrupted him. "This McCarthy who brought you to the box—" *The man she danced with?* "He's a friend of Gina's?"

Harpo grew more somber. "Oh, yes. A very great friend. He visits her quite often. It was he who took me to see Freddie's remains."

"It must have been very difficult for you."

Harpo sighed again. "It was. I felt a great many mortal emotions. But what I felt most of all was a great desire for even more vengeance."

He sat down again. "Freddie was mad, though not as mad as the man David . . . though Freddie's madness was *also* not of his own making. He was forced into a terrible choice. And I am the protector of madmen. I should have protected him from further harm."

"So you felt guilty, as well, then, that you didn't do what you felt should . . ."

"More regret than guilt." Harpo said. "Guilt is not a useful thing to feel."

"You are very wise, Dionysus. I wish most of my patients could understand that about guilt."

"Vengeance, however, serves a great purpose."

"And that would be . . .?"

"Why, it clears the psyche, of course."

Aaron raised his eyebrows. "There are many people in this world who feel that vengeance is a wicked thing."

"Then they are fools," Harpo said.

"Perhaps." Aaron said. "At another time I would enjoy a conversation on that subject with you."

"Ah," Harpo said, "such a dialogue could be quite memorable, eh? We will call for a scribe."

Aaron smiled. "Good idea. But now that this incident is behind you and you've had a little time to think on it, are your feelings any different than they were right afterward?"

Harpo gave it a moment's thought, then frowned. "I feel things I am not accustomed to feeling." He looked up, his eyes sad. "With Freddie gone, I find suddenly that I am lonely."

Ω Ω Ω

The delicious crisp taste of apple lingered on Aaron's palate; he savored the little boost of energy the sweet fruit gave him. As Mike removed the napkin from his neck, Aaron said, "Four o'clock. Feels like midnight. Maybe we can move someone from tomorrow morning. Then we can both sleep a little later."

"Sounds good to me. I'll look into it." He wiped Aaron's face. "Okay, all set." A door in the outer office opened and then closed again. "That's probably Gina," he said. He disappeared through the door, leaving it slightly open.

"Well," Aaron said when she came in, "you look rested, almost."

"I could use a lot more rest, I think. And I just came from looking in on David, so I could use a little comforting, too."

"He's doing as well as can be expected, Gina. Before you know it, the two weeks will be over. You won't see much progress from day to day, but in eight or ten days . . ."

"It's gonna seem like eight or ten years, I think."

"Probably will. But today, we're talking about you, not David. I'm trying to be cautious, as much for my own sake as yours. I remember when you first started therapy I expressed my reservations about treating both you and David at the same time. I still have some reservations, although I think it's going pretty well. It *is* more efficient, but the ethics of it are sort of fuzzy."

"I'm all right with it," she said. "And I'll speak for David that he is, too."

"Good, so back to you. Tell me about McCarthy."

$$\Omega \; \Omega \; \Omega$$

She could not have been more surprised if Aaron had leapt up out of his wheelchair and throttled her. She felt the cold gut-stab of having been caught in what she considered, when all was said and done, an infidelity. "What about McCarthy?"

Instead of speaking, he gave her a knowing grin, and let *her* decide what she thought he knew.

"You saw us at the banquet."

"Yes. He's an impressive man, from what was said. I saw you two dancing; you seem to know each other rather well."

"It's not what you think, Aaron."

"What do I think?"

Her mouth was open but the words remained under construction. "Uh—I guess I don't really know what you think."

He didn't give her a chance to regroup. "Then what do *you* think?"

A few seconds went by. "McCarthy and I are colleagues . . . I've worked with him for years. I mean, I've always had a little crush on him, even when David was well . . . I can't imagine that would be hard to understand."

"He's quite a specimen. Tall, well-built, handsome, a good man, apparently."

"Yeah, he's all that, and he's been a good friend to me. I couldn't do what I do as well as everyone seems to think I'm doing it *without* him. He's always bringing men into the center, even though he could take them to worse places. Or leave them out there. He gives a lot of time to coaching teenagers in the summers. He's really just a terrific person."

"It would seem so. But you'll forgive me for observing that you and he were behaving like much more than friends that night. If your association was on that level until then, I'm wondering what influenced you to change it."

"Aaron, look, it's not what you think—I just—"

"Gina, *Gina*—" he said. "What I think doesn't matter. But I'll tell you anyway, just so it's clear. I think you are a very bright, attractive, deserving woman, and I stress *deserving*. And that you do what you do for reasons of your own. And my observations about what happens in your life are just that—observations, intended to help you clarify your own thoughts. I'm not judging you."

"It feels like you are."

"Are you sure about that? Are you maybe judging yourself and transferring the responsibility for that judgment to me? You looked like you were having a blast that night. Frankly, I think it's nice that you had such a good time. But as I said before, it's what *you* think that matters."

When Gina did not respond, Aaron pressed. "So, in view of all that, what *do* you think?"

Her answer sounded more like a question. "I think it was nice that I had such a good time . . ."

"You did, then, I mean, have a good time."

She wrapped her arms tightly around the front of her body, as if she could shield herself from Aaron's probing questions. "A *very* good time," she said softly. "A better time than I've had in a very long while."

"Elaborate."

She eyed him suspiciously. "You mean did I have sex with him?"

"Well, I wasn't going to ask that directly, but if you're comfortable going there . . ."

After a long sigh, she confessed. "Yes, I did."

"And how was it?"

She glared at him. "This is beginning to feel a little weird."

"Forgive me, I should have been more clear. I'm not interested in the lascivious details. I want to know how you felt about the fact that it happened. Not how *it* felt."

She turned away from Aaron's gaze and stared off into the distance, then surprised him by saying more than the "good" or "satisfying" he'd expected. "It felt positively cosmic," she said. Her expression was one of curiosity, as if she were looking to *him* for answers. "I don't know, Aaron, there was just something about it that went way beyond anything I'd ever done before, even with David, and I thought David was my soul mate. Like I'd taken some kind of aphrodisiac. Everything was heightened. I had a lot to drink, but I've been drunk and had sex before, and it wasn't anything like that. I almost felt like it was my first time again, but I somehow knew how to do everything anyway."

"You must have wanted to be there, then."

She concentrated, wanting to be clear on what she was saying. "I did. I *wanted* to be there. But that wasn't completely it. He's a regular, daily part of my professional life. We've been through some tough situations together. He's been very honest about his interest in me, though he knows about David. At least, he knows what I've told him so far. He lost his wife at Windows on 9-11. There's been this unspoken understanding between us—*wait and see*—until the other night. Then I almost felt like I had no choice. You know, like the devil made me do it. But that would be too simple an explanation."

"Does the explanation really need to be complicated? Maybe you were just *ready* for it, finally."

She gave him a hurt look. "You *know* my relationship with David isn't resolved yet."

There was a moment of silence while Aaron waited to see if Gina would say anything more. When she didn't, he said, "It may not be resolved, but I think you and I both know that it's finished. At least your relationship as a couple."

Her mouth opened, as if to speak, but nothing came out.

Aaron kept his voice steady and calm. "Maybe this fellow knows and acknowledges something that you know but *won't* acknowledge. Maybe you've been sending out signals without realizing. And maybe that's why this McCarthy, by your own account a good, ethical man, felt okay about pursuing you. Because he's clearer on your own situation than you are. What happened between you and him was right, natural, and appropriate for a woman who's not involved in a relationship."

She had her hand over her mouth and was trying desperately to hold back a sob. *Bargaining, depression, acceptance.* "But—"

"There *is* no relationship between you and David, Gina. He's no longer capable of it. It's terrible what happened to him; I know better than most what a long climb it is to an internship at Bellevue. He had a lot of promise. A great future. It would have been a wonderful life for you both."

Tears were pouring down her cheeks. "I didn't even get to be a widow," she whispered.

"That's *precisely* what you are, David's widow. You're behaving in a manner that says you know that your *marriage*, though it was never legal, is over."

Regretting that he could not reach out and place a sympathetic hand on her arm, Aaron reached out with his most sympathetic voice. "I know it's hard to move on. To give up. I'd be the first to admit that optimism is a healing attitude. Just like faith can be a drug. But realistically speaking, in my heart of hearts, and my mind of minds, I know that David isn't capable of loving you back the way you *need* him to. The way you deserve to be loved."

Ω Ω Ω

She'd been summoned south down the Jersey Turnpike to have dinner
with her parents, another of her mother's *we want to talk to you girls about something
important* dinners. But she was not unhappy or perturbed; escape from First Avenue
could not have come at a better time. As she pulled Miranda's borrowed Accord
into the driveway of the saltbox house where she'd grown up, Gina wondered what
the topic would be. Health? Finances? Retirement plans? Distribution of the family
silver when the inevitable finally happened?

She paused a moment and looked up at the twilight sky; darkness hovered
over the fading light of the horizon. She had gazed upward to the heavens so many
nights as a child, with her father and Diane, looking for identifiable objects and
constellations.

Not far from a crescent moon was a bright object that had to be a planet.
Mars. A Roman god.

A few minutes later, standing in the cozy kitchen of her girlhood home, Gina
watched the comfortable interplay between her mother and father with a mix of
satisfaction, embarrassment, and envy, wondering if she herself would ever get to
the place they were now, and if so with whom.

Her father was carving a turkey, and while he stood there with a knife in one
hand and a long fork in the other, all greasy and defenseless, her mother reached
over and patted him lightly on the *derriere.*

"Sexiest thing on two legs is a man in an apron," her mother commented with
a devilish smile. Then she turned to Gina and said, "Don't you agree, Honey?"

Gina remembered David in an apron, showing her a sticky oatmeal pan. The
pleading look of helplessness on his face. With more affection than rancor she
said, "Not entirely, Mom, but would it do me any good to disagree with you?"

"I speak from long experience," her father interjected, "and I can tell you that
it will do you no good whatsoever."

Her mother poured a small glass of wine and offered it in Gina's direction.
It was a good Cabernet Sauvignon, heady and aromatic. "Yeah. Thanks. Put in
another inch," she said, "but no more than that. I have to drive later."

"Oh, can't you stay, just once?" her mother asked, as she poured an inch and a
half. "You don't have to go home to take care of David tonight."

"Nobody knows that better than I do, Mom."

"Oh, dear, I'm sorry, I didn't mean to upset you." She smiled sympathetically.
"You must miss him."

Do I really? "I miss who he used to be."

There was stiff silence in the white kitchen for a few moments, until her
mother broke it with a change of topic. "Well, everything's ready and your sister's
late again." She made a show of looking at her watch. Then she looked up, her
authoritarian gaze settling on one of the *objets de cuisine* that had been brought out

for placement on the dinner table. "Oh, I forgot. The pepper mill needs to be filled." She picked it up and offered it in Gina's direction. "Would you do it, dear?"

Gina took it, and was grateful for the distraction. She went to the familiar place without thinking and found the jar of peppercorns. As she held the polished teak vessel in one hand while dropping in peppercorns with the other, she tried to recall if she had ever seen another pepper mill in this house, perhaps on holidays when a more fancy piece, maybe silver or cut crystal, might have been appropriate for her mother's beautiful table settings.

No, she was sure of it; this was the only pepper mill. There had been a never-ending stream of coffee makers, none of which had ever completely satisfied her mother, one of which a very frustrated David had thrown across the kitchen early in the aftermath of his brain injury. Butter dishes had come and gone, as had toasters, but the pepper mill seemed to be immortal.

She wondered as the solid weight of the teak rested in her hand if her mother had known when she bought it that it would be her one true pepper mill. She glanced around the room looking for other such singletons. The obvious ones surfaced. Her mother had had only one house, one man, and one pepper mill. But how had she known they'd be *The Ones*? *Had* she known?

"Where's the carving fork?" her father said.

Her mother's face tightened. "Right there. To the left of the platter. You just set it down there."

In her mind, Gina finished her mother's sentence. *Remember, Dear?*

Of course her father's memory was not what it had been. There were times when she caught *herself* walking into a room and wondering why. But that was caused by distraction, not disease.

He picked it up, turned it over. For a moment he looked confused. Then he started carving again, as if nothing had happened.

Gina glanced lovingly at her mother, knowing only too well what she would face, but wanting so badly to say, *at least you're getting a warning*. With David, the disappearance of his memory had been abrupt. They would all have time to learn, to cope, to adjust to her father's inevitable decline. Advantages she had not had.

She set the replenished mill down on the countertop, as she heard the sound of her sister coming in. Her signature luminosity restored after the dark incident with David, Diane strode through the back door into the kitchen, a great big bundle of joy in hiking boots and leggings. She passed out hugs and kisses like lifesavers, each one the correct flavor for the recipient.

Gina was surprised to see her sister alone. "Where's Rick?" she said.

"He had some work to catch up on."

After hanging her jacket on a coat tree near the curtained back door, Diane went to the kitchen sink to wash the grime of the journey off her hands, a habit which always infuriated their mother.

"That's why we have a bathroom right over there," she said, pointing. "Really, Diane, can't you wash your hands in there? We wash food and dishes in that sink."

Ignoring her mother's remarks, Diane committed an even more heinous kitchen crime by drying her hands on a dish towel. "I love you, too, Mom. Sorry I'm late, everybody."

"That's all right," Gina said. "Your reputation precedes you. But we're two glasses of wine ahead of you, and you missed out on a few good opinions."

The sisters chuckled in conspiracy as their mother scowled.

"How *will* I live?" Diane asked. "But you all need to loosen up anyway, so it's a good thing you got a head start. And as always, I have a reasonable excuse for my tardiness. I had *such* a day, let me tell you . . ."

As the events of Diane's day were recounted to nods and murmurs of interest, the assembly of kin entered into a practiced state of autopilot, each one taking a dish or utensil to the table. The comfort of the family sit-down settled over Gina like a quilt on a featherbed. She snuggled into the warmth of it, and it brought her back to a time of pigtails for herself and bowl-cuts for Diane, when the terms of life were defined by the unquestionable and loving authority of her parents. There were no decisions, no gut-wrenching emotional conflicts. Everything was simple and clear.

Forks clicked on porcelain as they chatted about Grandma, eliminating the cantankerous old lady from the list of potential family pow-wow subjects. Then they talked about Dad's impending retirement, and Gina thought for sure that the conversation would turn to retirement finances, another strong contender. Or his memory, though it was a discussion no one seemed ready to begin. Gina thought, *three down*. She wondered how many topics they would run through before getting to *the one*.

She waited for her mother to say, "We wanted you girls to come here tonight so we could discuss something very important . . ." but the anticipated lead-in never materialized. The coffee was already brewing and dessert was on the table before her mother turned to her and said, innocently enough, "So, Gina, tell us what's going on with David."

She looked around the table at the faces of her family and the conspiracy became clear. She understood the true reason why Rick had not come. Tonight was an intervention, and she was the object of their intended manipulation.

The previous warmth evaporated and was replaced by stomach knots. She was being ambushed, defenseless, by people who claimed to love her. She gave each one of them a look of knowing disappointment, saving the most pointed one for Diane. Of course Diane would have told their parents all the gory details of the incident. It felt like a violation of sisterhood.

She faced her sister and said, "*Et tu*, Diane?"

Diane was silent and stared down at her dessert plate, the guilt spreading slowly across her face. She looked up at Gina with eyes full of apology. "I'm sorry. I know you don't want to hear this, especially from us, but I can't keep quiet any longer. It's really time to start talking about it."

Gina picked up her napkin and wiped every last crumb from her mouth, as if unburdening it in preparation for a terse speech, all the while staring at Diane. "Didn't we already establish that this is a very complicated situation, that there are subtleties you can't understand if you're not involved in it? And as it happens, I'm—"

Diane cast off all evidence of having inherited the painful graciousness that, until now, kept her mother from speaking with candor on the delicate matter of David. "Oh, come on, Gina," she interrupted. "Spare me the shrink rap. The situation's not complicated, it's a wreck! There's nothing subtle about it. David runs your life, or at least his—*condition* does. David gets *everything* he needs before you get *anything* you need. When was the last time you even thought about what you need?"

McCarthy shot through Gina's mind, and she quickly pushed him out. She said nothing.

Diane continued her diatribe. "You're too close to it to be objective. I can't believe how helpless he's gotten since the last time I've seen him. For God's sake, he's like a two-year-old! How long is it going to be before you have to start diapering him?"

Her hands clenched angrily, Gina pushed herself slightly up from her chair and loomed forward in her sister's direction. From somewhere to her right, a hand came out of the confusion and settled gently on her arm. She did not need to look down to see that it was her mother's hand that had firmly but lovingly grabbed her wrist. Seconds ticked by, the air full of anger and resentment, and for a few moments Gina thought she would not be able to contain herself. But her mother's touch was like a lightning rod, drawing off just enough rage to quell the pending explosion.

She looked around at her family again. Their faces all showed pained, undisguised worry. Their opinions she could battle with some hope of winning, but their loving concern was unconquerable. She sat back down again, and her mother let go of her wrist, then took hold of her hand. As Gina wept into her dessert plate, her mother, father and sister sat silently by.

Seconds, then minutes passed, and Gina gradually began to feel connected to herself again. When she felt safe to speak, she said quietly, "It's already been decided. His doctor is working on some arrangements. For a place."

Diane got up from her chair and came around the table; she hugged her weeping sister fiercely from behind, cradling her with comfort. She whispered in

Gina's ear, "It'll be all right, Gina, you're doing exactly the right thing. This is the best thing for David and the best thing for you."

Ω Ω Ω

In a nightgown she always left there, *just in case*, Gina slipped between the cool pink sheets of her childhood bed and replayed in her mind the afternoon that she and David, visiting for some holiday, had screwed themselves senseless on that bed while her parents ran a few last minute errands before the rest of their extended family arrived. She touched herself all over, her fingertips wandering, as the emotions flooded through her, trying to bring back the sensations as well, but it was a frustrating and ultimately incomplete exercise. She tucked it all away for one more night and slipped into an uneasy sleep.

Chapter 18
Sigma

The sidewalks were a sea of colored umbrellas, all bouncing in crazy rhythm as the people beneath them wound their way home. Occasionally, from his locked down chair in the back of the van, Aaron would glimpse the brave bare head poking up; often there was a telephone held to one ear of that head. It was hard, he imagined, to balance an umbrella and a cell phone at the same time. The cell phone always seemed to win.

Maybe someday, when the neurosurgery made that craved leap, he would have the movable limbs to confirm that notion.

But for now, and the foreseeable future, he depended on others to be his arms, his legs, his everything. Miriam had managed with some daytime help at first, but he soon saw the toll it took on her. Despite her protestations that it was her job to care for him, he knew that their marriage, his most precious asset, would inevitably suffer.

As Miriam set their dinner on the table, Mike wheeled him to his place at one end, tucked an over-sized napkin into his shirt at the neck. The large man with large hands gave Aaron a soft pat on the shoulder, one of the few places he could feel the sensation. Then he sat down directly next to Aaron, folded his hands, and prayed silently for a few moments.

Mike picked up a knife and fork, and began cutting Aaron's food into small pieces. He fed Aaron one bite, then took a bite from his own plate. And so it went, with bits of cordial conversation slipped in, until their repast was complete.

Mike became his patient when, after two years of nightmares, cold sweats and flashbacks, he had tried to end his life, but the knot had given way, and he'd broken an ankle in his fall to earth. His downstairs neighbor heard the thump and called the police.

He'd tried to take the gun out of a cop's holster. In the holding cell at Bellevue, when asked what he intended to do, he had said he wanted to use it on himself.

For that full month Aaron saw Mike every day in the Bellevue psych ward. He listened to his horrific tale, as many times as Mike would tell it. Sometimes Mike would cry, sometimes scream. Sometimes he would stare at the floor in silence. Always he was confused.

He went back to his mother's home, refused to see his brother firefighters. He took to wandering the streets all day. But always he came back to Aaron.

Aaron's eyes darted back and forth behind closed lids as Mike began to undress him after dinner, transporting him back to that time when he'd come fully into their lives. It had been a bit of a mental leap, an all-too-neat solution to a problem that seemed otherwise unsolvable.

I really think he's one I can save, he'd said to Miriam.

As Gina had said about Harpo.

And now Aaron needed *another* mental leap, to solve the dilemma Gina's situation presented. He let images, sounds, thoughts all float freely through his mind. The program he'd found was ideal for David; close supervision, personal care, affordable within the limits of his means, the kind of attention that might satisfy Gina and allow her to *let go.* The call had produced the good news that a bed would be coming available, and the bad news that there would be a week-long delay between the time David would likely be discharged from Bellevue and the time he could enter the facility.

David would still have to live in their apartment; there was nothing to be done about that on such short notice. But he needed to get Gina—at least partly—out of the mix.

The answer came to him like a jack-in-the-box, popping to life, surprising him, pleasing him immensely. He opened his eyes and smiled, prompting raised eyebrows from Mike. It was a simple and elegant solution, almost too simple, and for that reason he questioned himself. It was sure to meet with resistance, perhaps on both ends. But he thought it could work. *I'll give her a little time to recover from the shock of the last few days,* he thought to himself. *Then I'll call her.* He wondered how she would react.

Ω Ω Ω

Well. That was unexpected. Staring at her phone, Gina wondered how it was that such an innocuous object could turn her life around by doing nothing more than carrying a seemingly crazy idea from one person to another, in this case, from Aaron to her.

Incredible, she thought. *Just when I figured I was running out of options . . . along comes THIS.* "Keep an open mind," Aaron had said at the start of the call, an appropriate prologue, for had she not, she would have dismissed the things Aaron suggested as unimaginable.

"I've come to the conclusion you're not really going to let this guy Harpo go," he'd said, "so here's how I think you can keep him. But you have to set aside your concerns about who he is and where he comes from, or this won't work."

She laughed aloud and shook her head. *What a crazy place this world is.* She wondered if it would ever again seem sane to her.

She heard steps coming down the long corridor.

There in the doorway, looking entirely too big and fine for the world in which he lived, stood McCarthy. And though he was never very far from her consciousness, the sight of him standing there, within touching distance, took her breath away.

"Hey," he said softly, "it's good to see you."

"Yeah." It was all she could manage.

"I probably should have called," he said, "but I was afraid you might tell me not to come. I was upstairs in the cop shop and Miranda had some mail that got sent to them by mistake. She said she would have brought it later, but I figured it would be a good excuse to stop in for a minute."

"Thanks," she said, her heart pounding mercilessly. "Saves me a trip up into the world of *really* crazy people."

"Because you do want to get away from all these normal guys down here every now and then," he laughed, "just for a change."

For a few seconds their eyes were locked in a wordless embrace, beaming back and forth a volley of excited and hopeful what-ifs. And when McCarthy finally broke the spell by exhaling, she felt it as if the air he let out was rushing into her own lungs.

"Plus," he said quietly, "I have this." He held out a large manila envelope, separate from the rest of her mail.

She took it, saw his name written across the front of it. She gave him a curious look, as if seeking permission to open it.

"Go ahead."

Inside were two photographs, taken the night of the banquet. In one, she was leaning against him, her cheek on his shoulder, his arm around her waist, and they were both smiling directly into the camera. His face wore a wide grin of unqualified happiness, hers a small, bashful smile. A nice couple, having a good time. *No wonder they're all teasing us,* she thought. How could anyone miss it?

The other one had been taken with a closer lens, and in its unlying eye they'd been caught in a more personal moment. She was gazing with undisguised adoration into McCarthy's sparkling eyes; that adoration was reflected back. She studied this stark evidence of their mutual affection for a long, quiet moment, and then looked up at the man in blue who had given it to her.

"They're wonderful."

The clumsy silence that followed was broken by a solitary cough from one of the center's current occupants, magnified by the surrounding stillness into something more like a thunder crack. When they both finally tried to speak, their words collided in midair.

"Gina, I . . ."

"McCarthy, I . . ."

They laughed, the sounds mixing happily. Gina thought with surprise how comfortable and familiar that mixture was beginning to feel.

McCarthy made a flourish of his hand, indicating that she should speak. "Ladies first," he said.

"Coward."

"Yeah, but I'm a polite coward."

"I'll give you that," she said. "Okay." She took a deep breath. "Wow. Okay. Here goes." She laid the photographs on her desk and then clasped and unclasped her hands. "I can't even begin to tell you how good a time I had with you . . . I mean, I felt like a teenager again, and ever since that night there's been this wonderful undercurrent of—"

She faltered, then her face softened. "I guess I would have to say it's *joy.*"

"You're so good with words," he said. "I've wanted to say something to you, but sometimes I feel like it's just not gonna come out right, and I didn't want to scare you by coming on too strong . . . I'm still slapping myself to see if it's all some kind of dream. I mean, I never thought . . . I hoped, but I never thought it would actually happen between us."

"Yeah, I know what you mean," she said. "I feel like I was sort of *touched,* almost. By what, I couldn't say."

McCarthy put on a theatrical face and began to sing into an imaginary microphone. "Cupid, draw back your bow-ooh-oh . . ."

Gina covered her eyes with one hand in feigned embarrassment. She peeked out from between two fingers. "Don't let Harpo hear you say Cupid. It's *Eros.* But whoever it was must've been packing surface-to-air missiles that night." When she finally took her hand away from her face, her cheeks were hot and red. "I spent all this time trying to explain to Aaron how I felt. And all I had to do was sing him that song and he would've understood."

McCarthy crossed his arms on his broad chest. "You told him?"

"No. He asked."

"Does all of New York know about us?"

"I don't think all of New York cares," she said. "Miranda and Stein can't help themselves. Aaron is usually careful about boundaries, but he waded right in on this one. He was there that night. I was talking to him and his wife just before we started dancing."

"So what *did* you tell him?"

She reached out and took hold of one of his hands, and played with the tips of his fingers. "I told him how totally amazing the whole night was, how I felt almost like I was drugged, like I couldn't have resisted you if my life depended on it."

"And what did he say when you told him that?"

She let out a long breath. "He said a lot of stuff, but the basic gist was that you were probably seeing my situation more clearly than I was. He said it was a *good* thing."

"*Whew*," McCarthy said. "That's a relief to hear. I was hoping you wouldn't say that he said you should wait, or anything like that . . ."

She tried to reassure him. "Basically, he says that what I—we—did is what we should be doing."

McCarthy's anxious look lessened, but there was still uncertainty on his face. "So what *should* we do now?" he said.

She felt wonderfully happy, sharing his eagerness to define their relationship. But reality had to prevail. "Go slowly, I guess. I have to learn to feel all right about some of the stuff that's happened. Truth is, there's probably stuff I'm never gonna feel all right about, no matter how much time I give it."

"Such as?"

"Knowing that I won't ever get to finish things with David, for one. I feel like I should tell him with some hope of him understanding. He doesn't know what I know about him. About us. He *can't* know right now. And I know that I'll never stop going to see him. I'm still his best friend. I worry that he might 'wake up' someday, like Rip Van Winkle, and wonder where I am, why I'm not with him. When this all started I was a part of his life, I was there that day, I spent some of it at his side. And I don't know what's going on in his head now, I mean, maybe he's fully cognizant of how to live life, and he just can't get it out. He might still expect that I'll be with him. But I won't be."

"One day at a time," he said gently. "One foot in front of the other. You have no idea what the future holds, and you can't control it. I know it's unsettling; I see that in the kids I coach every time I'm with them. They all feel robbed, and some of them have moments when I know they just don't trust anything."

He took a step closer and placed his hands on her upper arms. "I have an idea of what I'd *like* the future to hold for me, and every day I try to work toward it. But you never know if it's gonna work out. That proverbial Mack truck might come screaming around the corner and do me in, you know what I mean? And being a cop adds a whole other layer. Some jerkball with a new toy gun could come along and turn any one of us into a puddle on the pavement."

A chill went down her spine. "Don't tempt fate."

"Hey, you know what?" he said. "I think we make our own fates. And I think the Universe is leaning toward the good side on the meter. That's what keeps me going. I tell myself every morning that it might be my last. I mean, with all the shootings . . . So I try to spend at least part of each day being happy. I learned a long time ago that you can't be too hard on yourself."

"I wish there was an immunization against bad stuff. And a skin patch for after it happens."

McCarthy smiled. "Like I said, worry about tomorrow when tomorrow actually comes."

She laughed softly. "Philosophy in blue. In addition to being good looking and a fabulous piece of ass, you're a pretty smart guy. Are you sure you're a cop?"

Pointing with a proud grin to the medallion on his pocket, he said, "Got a badge here, don't I? And a gun. I guess I must be a cop." Then he took a guilty glance at his watch. "Speaking of which, I'd best get back out there and start behaving in a coply manner."

"Listen," she said, "while you're out there, could you do me a quick favor?"

He went down on one knee, placed one hand on his chest, and raised the other up in a gesture of adoration. "Only name it, Fair Damsel."

She smiled and extended a hand dramatically toward him. He dutifully kissed it. "Would you go by the Freezer and tell our buddy Harpo I'd like to talk to him? And try to be nice. I need him to do something for me."

Her hand still in his, he stood and bowed deeply. "Anything for you," he said. "Even being nice to Harpo."

As he turned and walked out of the shelter, his stride long and firm, she watched him with an uplifting sense of anticipation. She thought, with cautious happiness, *it's going to be a very different life.*

Ω Ω Ω

While Stein waited in the cruiser, McCarthy carefully traversed the obstacle course of mud and detritus in the Freezer. He tapped on the top of the box.

"Harpo? You in there?"

A dark mass of curls poked out of the front drape. He eyed McCarthy suspiciously. "I greet you."

"I, uh, greet you, too," McCarthy said. "Listen, I need to talk to you."

I must offer this man hospitality, Harpo thought with annoyance, *though I would rather turn him into a spittoon.* He made a welcoming gesture with his hand. "Enter, please."

"No, it's all right, I can stay out here while we talk . . ."

"I insist," came the reply.

"No, really, I just need to ask—"

"I will not hear of you standing out there unsheltered. That would be a most ungodlike act of inhospitality."

She said be nice to him, McCarthy thought dismally. He sighed and bent down. Harpo moved to the back of the battered box and made room for him. McCarthy *scootched* in on his buttocks, wishing for the ability to levitate.

"You may close the drape if you are cold."

"That's all right," McCarthy said. "I like a little fresh air."

Harpo held up a half-full bottle. "Then I would advise you to leave this city. May I offer you some wine? I have just finished creating it . . ."

McCarthy eyed the dark liquid suspiciously. He held up his hand, signaling polite refusal, thinking that he would have sooner drunk Drano. "Rules. No drinking on duty, but thanks, anyway."

"As you wish. Nevertheless, I welcome you to my humble abode, even if you insist on refusing my offerings."

McCarthy looked around at the inside of the shabby box. It was lit by the flame of a single candle, and in the glow he saw the "Home Sweet Homeless" on the brown wall, scant improvement. "Nice picture, very *homey*," he said.

"It is adequate," Harpo said. "But I must admit, it is not the same here without Freddie." He raised his bottle in salute. "He was a fine mortal, if downtrodden. He was cruelly treated by the Fates."

"Rest in peace," McCarthy said. His eyes were beginning to water. "But listen, I came by to tell you Gina wants to talk to you. She wants you to come down to the intake center."

Harpo almost dropped the bottle. He moved abruptly closer to McCarthy and grabbed hold of the front of his blue shirt. "Did she say why?"

"No. Just that she wanted you to come by."

Harpo let go of McCarthy, who moved away from him gratefully. "I must bathe and see to my garments . . . I am not properly prepared . . ."

McCarthy remembered what she'd said. *Be nice to him.* "I can give you a ride in the cruiser if you want to come along right now, but I don't have a lot of time to wait around. And don't worry. You look all right."

Though Harpo could not help but wonder why McCarthy was treating him so nobly, he accepted. "You are too kind. I am grateful to you."

As he followed McCarthy down the alley toward the cruiser, he whispered to Midas, "These mortals have the annoying habit of turning out to be *good* when we least expect it, eh?"

Ω Ω Ω

"Just hurry up, McCarthy," Stein said, "and don't get all caught up in any 'deep' conversations like the last time."

McCarthy got out of the cruiser. "I'll do my best, but I'm not makin' any promises." He opened the back door, then made a sweeping motion with his arm, inviting his passenger to alight.

Harpo took the lead and strutted divinely into Gina's office ahead of McCarthy. He expected that she would rise and greet him. And so he was quite surprised to find her slumped in her chair with arms crossed in front of her, a look of utter disgust on her face.

On the desk in front of her was a single sheet of paper next to a torn envelope.

He stood there staring at her, his expectations dashed, his hopes on hold, as McCarthy rushed past him, already asking questions.

"Gina? What's with the *face?*"

She looked up at him, ignoring Harpo. "They didn't renew my grant." She picked up the letter and handed it to him.

He scanned it quickly, muttering the words. "Regret to inform you . . . fiscal restraints . . . duplicate services . . . consolidation of agencies . . . what kind of bullshit is this?"

"Official bullshit. Bureaucratic bullshit. Of the *Noo Yawk* variety."

She stood up and stomped around, coming to rest next to McCarthy. Harpo stared in dismay as McCarthy put his arms around Gina and embraced her.

"Jesus Christ," he heard her say, "they give me an award for service then they shut the service down. I don't get it. I mean, what kind of assholes are in charge of this stupid City?"

"Big ones," McCarthy sympathized, "Immense ones."

McCarthy saw Harpo gawking outside the door and reached out with one hand. He gave the door a gentle push and it swung slowly shut. Harpo was forced to wait outside the office while his rival, the one to whom he always seemed to owe some gratitude or another, comforted the woman. He could feel the tenderness right through the closed door.

Ω Ω Ω

McCarthy came out a few minutes later, visibly angry, and shook a stern finger in Harpo's face. "She's ready to talk to you now. Go ahead in. But you do anything to upset her more and I swear to God you'll be one very unhappy wino.."

Harpo watched McCarthy stomp up the stairs, filled with bitter envy over whatever it was that drew Gina to the man. He turned back toward the office and poked his head in, then entered cautiously.

"Oh, Harpo," Gina said, "thanks for coming. I apologize for that little explosion you just witnessed. I got some bad news earlier."

"What was the nature of these tidings, that they could anger you so?"

After a long, weary sigh, she explained. "Well, it seems the City is not going to give me money to run this center next year. When my money runs out this year, that'll be it for this place, I'll have to close it down. Unless I can find some other source of funding, which will probably happen right about the time the Hudson dries up. Anyway, I apologize for keeping you waiting."

He gave her a sympathetic look. "I will wait for you forever, if you like."

She didn't seem to hear him. "Listen, I asked you here for a reason. I want to offer you a job, sort of."

"A job? Do you mean work?"

"Yes, I guess you could call it work."

"Impossible. A god does not work."

Hmm. She began to wonder if Aaron had been right about him. "Well, it would only be temporary, a week maybe . . ."

"Seven days?"

"Yeah," she said. "Seven days. Maybe a little longer, but not much."

Perhaps if I do this thing she asks, he thought, *she will cast her eye favorably on me.* "What sort of work is this that you require?"

"You remember David, my—uh—boyfriend? He's in the hospital right now, upstairs. He had a, um, bit of a, uh, *breakdown* a little while ago. The night the ambulance came and took him away. He'll be here a little longer, but he'll have to leave in a few days. Aaron—uh, I don't know if you know this, but Aaron is David's doctor—has arranged for him to go to a residential treatment facility for a while after he leaves here, just until he gets better, of course, but he can't get in there until a week after he has to leave Bellevue. He shouldn't be by himself any more. So I need someone to look after him for the week that he'll be back in our—"

She paused, then corrected herself. "*My* apartment. Aaron said you have a, uh, a special way with people who are mentally ill."

"Indeed. I am the ruler of *all* madness."

She smiled and nodded. *Ruler, rule thyself.* "I'd pay you, of course."

He had not expected anything of this sort, but he was almost jubilant to know that David would soon cease to be a distraction to her. And with payment, he would no longer need to beg for his sustenance.

His expression darkened. *But by taking on the care of him,* he realized, *I will free her to be distracted by the other one!*

Gina stumbled on bravely. "Aaron also said that you're under an *obligation* to help people who are—uh—*mad.* Maybe this would help you with that obligation. He thinks it would be a very good thing for David and that it would help you to get over feeling useless and lonely."

He searched her face intently, looking for evil purpose or deception. But he saw nothing base in her expression, only hope and anticipation.

What if I refuse? He wondered. *Will she despise me for turning her away when she needs help? And what of my obligation to protect madmen?* Self-reproach flooded through him. *I failed with Freddie.*

He rubbed his forehead to soothe out the growing tightness. "I would like to see him."

"No problem," she said. "I can take you up there right now if you want to go. He's upstairs."

Ω Ω Ω

This time they took the elevator, since Harpo was no longer afraid. Unlike in Macy's, he fit neatly into the throng of people getting in and out of the packed car. Gina was buzzed into the locked ward, and signed Harpo in with herself.

David sat stiffly on the edge of the small metal bed, muttering something only he could hear and understand. He counted, touching one hand with the fingers of the other in second-by-second rhythm. Harpo saw the expression of resignation on Gina's face as she looked through the glass.

"Don't be sad, he is only speaking the language of madness," he said in his kindest tone. "Many in his condition do so. I myself know this language well."

Gina inhaled slowly through her nose, needing an infusion of oxygen. "Then you two should get along just fine."

Harpo stared briefly at David's rigid form, then turned to Gina. "You mortals treat your madmen most terribly, caging them like animals. Think how he must feel to have these prying eyes on him all day. It is no wonder that he has turned inward."

"The other side of this glass looks like a mirror to him. He doesn't know we're here right now."

Harpo touched the glass lightly with his fingertips. "Remarkable," he said as his gaze wandered over it. "But why can he not roam the Earth, experiencing its many pleasures? It seems unusually cruel and punitive, his incarceration. Do you mortals not understand that freedom is as precious to the mad as it is to the sane?"

Gina felt almost ashamed at having no good answers. Of course, she could give him the clinical answer, a Latin diagnosis peppered with legalese. She started to open her mouth, uncertain of what would come out, when the floor nurse came by and rescued her. The woman looked Harpo up and down with jaded curiosity.

"With you?" She said to Gina.

"Yup."

"Well, hello," the nurse said, and before Harpo could "greet" her, she turned back to Gina. "He's doing pretty well today. Small improvements."

Knowing that "improvements" meant David had made the quantum leap from the floor to the bed, Gina said, "Thanks," very quietly as the woman walked away.

"Is she his keeper here?" Harpo asked.

"During the day. She takes care of a number of patients on this ward. She's been awfully good to David."

"But she will not come take care of him when he leaves."

"She already has *this* job, Harpo . . ."

He looked in at David again, and considered the man's deplorable state. He felt a strange anger building inside of him.

"My father Zeus spoke at great length to me about my divine calling just before I left Olympus. He pointed out that I have been remiss in my duties of late." He looked over at Gina and said, "He was right."

Their gaze was drawn to the inside of the small room, for David had stood up suddenly and walked to the barred window. After a few moments of agitated hand movements, he took hold of one of the bars and tried to pull on it. Then he just stood there, staring down at the street below.

Harpo was filled with discomfiting compassion for the man. At the same time, he felt resentful. But any potential path to her belief in him must be explored.

"I accept your offer of this 'job.'"

She put an arm around his shoulder and hugged him. "Oh, Harpo, thank you! You don't know what this means to me! I really believe you'll do well. You won't be sorry."

She had said the word *believe*. All he needed was for her to carry that farther. Looking back through the glass, he was already filled with doubts about the wisdom of the arrangement he had accepted. He sighed very deeply. "It is the only godlike thing to do."

Chapter 19
Tau

Gina arrived home with David to find Harpo sitting on the stoop of her building. As they emerged from the cab, he rose up proudly, in full regalia, a ratty refugee from the Bizarro World.

For a few moments, she wished she could take it all back.

"I greet you," he said. "This time I was even more able to find the entry to your abode."

"Good. That's—reassuring." She drew David toward the stoop. "Look, David, Harpo's here."

Harpo turned to David and nodded. "I greet you, as well."

David remained stiff and unresponsive. His eyes darted back and forth between his two companions.

Quietly, Harpo said, "He is frightened."

Gina looked at David briefly, then back at Harpo. She took a big hopeful breath. "Let's go upstairs, shall we?"

She handed one bag to Harpo, took the other herself. The elevator barely contained them. David kept his eyes fixed on the floor indicator over the door and nodded every time the next level was reached. When the door finally opened on twelve, he stepped out and robotically led the party of three to the apartment door.

Gina flipped through the keys on her heavy key ring. Deadbolt first, then knob. "This is it," she said when they were finally inside. "Home sweet tiny-little-apartment. It's not exactly a colonial in Westchester, but we get by."

"What is this colonial—"

"A big house, with lots of room." She sighed. "Something I'll *never* be able to afford."

She took his ratty jacket and hung it beside her own in the neat closet.

"Go ahead, take a look around if you want to."

He nodded, then advanced cautiously through the living room and peered into the adjoining rooms. Though small, they were airy and bright, with high ceilings and light-colored walls. Everything was immaculately clean. He turned to Gina and smiled. "It seems a comely abode. Suitable for a woman such as yourself."

"Thank you, Harpo, that's a nice thing to say."

David headed straight for the couch and sat down. He picked up the remote and began pressing buttons. Gina automatically followed him there and sat next to him. "Oh, okay, I guess you want to watch TV, it's been a while." She went to the entertainment center and spread open its bi-folds. "You have to open the door before the clicker will work, remember?"

He looked up at her in confusion, raised the remote, pressed buttons. His movements were slow and uncertain. She took the remote from his hand, pressed, and a picture flashed onto the screen. After adjusting the volume, she returned to the couch.

Harpo leaned in and whispered. "I have seen these devices in the windows of merchants and in the Bellevue building, but I have not seen one so close before." He moved nearer to the screen and squinted. "It is truly an amazing device."

He'll say whatever he has to say to maintain the assumed personality. Aaron had reassured her of this in their phone call. *And he functions perfectly well if you just play along with it.*

So despite her disbelief that he'd never gotten close to a TV, she played. "Yeah. It *is* amazing. My mother tells me there was a time when they had to get up off the couch and physically turn the knob to change the channel. But there were only three or four channels they could get then, and depending on the weather, they didn't always come in clearly. We get about a hundred, every one of them clean and sharp."

As if on cue, David began surfing through the channels.

"I knew it would come back to you," Gina said, patting his shoulder.

Harpo watched the flipping images with intense interest. "*Astonishing.*"

"Lots of people would use a different word. 'Irritating' comes to mind for me."

Gina glanced toward David, who had settled on one program and was magnetized to the image on the screen. "Listen," she said, "while he's occupied, let me show you a few things."

He followed her from room to room, each one no more than an arm's length from the next, and listened politely as she described their functions. "This is the kitchen," she said, showing him the long narrow space. "It's pretty cramped, but I don't do all that much cooking, at least not lately." She opened the refrigerator and pointed out the stored items to him. "It looks pretty empty in there. I guess I'd better do some shopping."

A blast of cold air came out. Harpo stepped back. "You have brought the outside in." He peered closer. "But it is not empty, I see many vessels inside it."

Gina smiled. "Yeah. *Vessels.* Mostly condiments." She poked around. "Maybe we should have ketchup for dinner tonight."

"What is this ketchup?"

Play along. She closed the fridge door. "You've never had ketchup? Oh, you'll love it. We put it on practically everything. French fries, hamburgers and hot dogs . . ."

He stepped back and clutched his chest. Midas started to growl. "You eat *dog*? That is an *abominable* practice."

"No, Harpo, of course we don't eat dogs. That would be *disgusting*." She made a face to illustrate her distaste. "Well, some people do, in other countries, but mainly because they don't have any other meat. Hot dogs are long tubes of meat stuffed into—" *intestines?* "casings, and they're made of beef or pork or chicken. Turkey, sometimes."

"Then why are they called hot *dogs*?"

It was a reasonable question, even for a madman. "I really don't know," she said. "I suppose I should know." She almost said, *I'll google it*, but caught herself, knowing that *Google* would be a challenging and protracted explanation.

She settled on, "I'll try to find out. Hey, tell you what, let's have hot dogs for dinner tonight. David loves them, but we haven't had them in ages. What do you say?"

He could sense that she was trying very hard to please him, as well as David. "You are a most amiable host," he said with a slight bow.

"Oh, please—" she said, "it's *nothing*, really." She closed the refrigerator door and put one hand on his shoulder. She looked into his eyes and said, with great sincerity, "I'm so grateful that you're willing to help me out. I'm not sure that I'll ever be able to repay you. Dinner seems pretty insignificant."

Only tell me that you believe in me, and all debts will be erased, he thought as he followed her into the bedroom.

His eyes widened when he saw the bed. "It is wonderfully sumptuous!" he said. "And so *large*! Why, it is almost fit for Zeus himself."

"It's a king," she said, beaming. "I don't want to tell you what we went through to get it up here." She patted the bed affectionately. "This is where I sleep during the day, and where David will sleep at night when I'm at the center. And you can sleep on the couch."

He scowled. "Ah. In the Roman style."

"No. Not really." Then, quickly, "I understand that would offend you. The couch folds out into a bed. I'll show you how to do it just before I go tonight. David may want to watch TV for a while after dinner, so we'll leave that for last."

They looked at the bathroom, opened all the closets, turned the taps on and off, operated the intercom, and played the radio. "Well, that's it," she said when the tour was complete. "Do you have any questions?"

"There is so much to know if one is to live here! I hardly know *what* to ask. But there is one thing that truly puzzles me." He looked at her with a sad expression. "Though he explained his plight to me, I am still wondering why it is that Freddie lived where he did when others have such good Fortune."

"I'm afraid that one's above my pay grade." She sighed deeply. "Now, about lunch . . . offer David anything he wants. But he won't think of eating on his own. He's gotten accustomed to eating at about one o'clock at Bellevue, and it's probably a good idea to keep that up, at least until he settles into his own rhythm."

He nodded his head. "As you wish."

"Good," Gina said. "Now please, *please* wake me if anything happens that you think I should hear about. I know this is new to you."

"All will be well, I assure you."

"I hope so, Harpo, I hope so. Well, I need to get some sleep now because I have to go to the center later." Her expression grew somber. "To start packing it up." She looked at the clock on the wall. "It's ten now; I'll set my alarm to wake me up around four. Then we can all have dinner together before I go. Hot dogs, like I said." She turned to David. "What do you think, David?"

David said nothing; he continued to stare hypnotically at the television.

Harpo said, "Your hospitality is most gracious. Sleep well." He smiled.

As she slipped between the sheets, Gina thought nervously that it would be a wonder if she slept at all.

Ω Ω Ω

The hum of the city rose up from the streets; Harpo heard it clearly through the closed window. It served as a droning background to the crashing, banging and blaring of the television. Gina had closed the door when she disappeared into the bedroom earlier, shutting out the sounds. When Harpo pressed his ear to the door, he heard nothing. *She sleeps,* he thought.

He went to the couch and sat down at the opposite end from David. "To sleep during the sun's time," he said with a sad shake of his head, "is not right. It must be a terrible way to live. Don't you think?"

But David would not be interrupted; he picked up the remote and increased the volume on the television.

"I think perhaps it is not good for her to do this, eh?"

This time David looked at him. He locked eyes with his perplexed caretaker for a few moments, then looked back at the television again.

"Have you nothing to say, my friend? If we are to be companions as the woman wishes, we must talk, no?"

David turned back to Harpo and said, "No."

"Aha!" Harpo said triumphantly. "So you *can* speak after all! This is very good, very good."

But David was already deeply engrossed in the black rectangle again. He stared forward, his gaze never wavering, and though Harpo made persistent attempts to engage him in dialogue, he could not entice his charge to connect.

Finally, his frustration was so great that he gave up. He went back to the living room window and looked outside. The sun was at its height, casting only minimal shadows, and its rays reached down between the tall buildings to touch the pavement below. He saw people scurrying as they always seemed to do in New York, jostling and bumping each other in passing on the crowded noon-day sidewalks. He saw the ubiquitous pale, dark-clad women slinking by. *What are they always carting about in their sacks? I want to know these things!* Yellow moving machines sped down the street from one red light to the next, surging then slowing, then surging again . . . loud dirty trucks rumbled by, some decorated with images of familiar fruits and vegetables.

He looked back toward the couch. There sat David, absorbed in the small world before him. "You must come to the window," he said, "for there is much to see below."

But David did not stir from his seat. He turned his head very slowly toward the window and stared at Harpo with his mad blue eyes, then raised one finger up to his mouth and said, "*Shhh!*"

Ω Ω Ω

The clock ticked loudly on the wall, each second feeling longer than the last. Harpo whispered to Midas, "I am beginning to understand just how terrible an eternity on Earth could be . . ."

When the desired configuration of the clock finally occurred, he let out a sigh of relief and turned to David. With a big smile, he pressed his hands together and said, "Now is the hour for taking nourishment. The woman says it must be done at one on the clock."

He went to the couch and took one of David's arms with the intention of guiding him to the refrigerator. David looked up in surprise and pulled his arm away.

"No, really, you must come with me now, for the woman says we must take nourishment." He pulled again.

David shrank back, a fearful, uncertain look on his face.

Harpo threw up his hands. "I do not understand your refusal." He retreated to the narrow kitchen, where he spent a few minutes reconsidering his strategy. As the minutes after one o'clock ticked by, his sense of frustration mounted, and he grew increasingly peeved at David for resisting.

"There must be some way to reach this mortal," he said to Midas. "What will tempt him?"

David likes ketchup, the woman had told him. "Eureka!" he said, rubbing his hands together. He opened the refrigerator and poked around, and took out the bottle of red food that Gina had identified. He went into the living room and tapped David on the shoulder. When David turned to face him, he held out the red bottle.

"We must take nourishment now, for it is past one o'clock. The woman will not be pleased if we do not eat, so you must break free of this noisy distraction that so captivates you. Look, I have brought you ketchup."

David looked curiously at the proffered bottle for a few seconds, then tentatively took hold of it. He set the remote on the table and ran his fingers slowly over the plastic surface, examining it carefully. Harpo quickly picked up the remote and started pressing buttons; the images changed in rapid progression, the volume increased and decreased, the picture grew faint and then sharp again. But none of the buttons seemed to put an end to it entirely.

"Please, if you would show me, how does one get this cursed machine to stop working?"

David took the remote from his hand and pressed one button. The image disappeared, and the room was blessedly silent. "Off," he said. "O-f-f."

"Praise Zeus!" Harpo said. "Yes, *off,* indeed. *Off.* I shall remember that."

He glanced up at the clock again; it was closing in on one-fifteen. An hour before, the hands of the clock would not move fast enough.

Now he fervently wished to slow them.

"We must eat." He took the red bottle from David's hand. "We shall have this for our mid-day meal."

He grabbed hold of the white plastic top on the bottle and pulled, but it would not budge. As he was cursing and swearing at the uncooperative container, David reached up and took it from his hand. With one efficient flick of his thumb, the cap was up and the viscous red liquid finally attainable.

David handed the bottle back to him. Harpo placed it in David's hand again. "No, it is for you. You must eat it, as the woman says."

Again, David handed it back to him.

Fuming with frustration, Harpo said, "It seems we are at an impasse. Perhaps you do not understand. You are to *eat* this."

Then he saw in David's eyes something he hadn't seen before: a *desire* to understand. "You do not seem to know what to do with this," he said sympathetically. "Very well, mad one, I shall show you."

He went back into the kitchen where he had seen the assortment of ceramic vessels and shiny metal implements the woman kept. After a few noisy moments of opening and closing drawers and cabinets, he returned to the dining area with two small bowls and two spoons.

"Here," he said, setting the lot on the table, "you must come and sit. We shall take our meal together. This is a very fine thing to do." He went to the couch and took David by the arm. This time there was no resistance. He led David to the table and pulled out a chair, then guided him into it.

He seated himself across the table from David and took the bottle of ketchup from his hand. He flipped the top open as David had done, and said, "Ingenious!" as he held the bottle upside-down over his own bowl. He waited for the liquid to pour out, but it stayed precisely where it was, in the now-inverted bottom of the bottle. He shook the bottle up and down, but still nothing came out. He tapped it on the bottom.

"This is a most disagreeably mulish concoction! It will not budge!" He plunked the bottle down on the table in disgust.

Wordlessly, David reached out and picked up the plastic bottle. He turned it over his bowl and squeezed hard. Spatters of ketchup oozed out and plopped into the bowl accompanied by the airy sound of squeeze-bottle farts. David looked up at Harpo and grinned.

Harpo roared in laughter; he tipped back his chair and slapped his knee. "A delightful noise!" He took the bottle from David and turned it over his own bowl. "Let me try now . . ." He gave the bottle a sharp squeeze. Ketchup splattered out all over his bowl, straying onto the flat surface of the surrounding tabletop.

"Oh, see now, I have made a mess," he said. "Well, what can one expect? We are eating. This is by its very nature a messy thing to do. You should see what happens when one eats a goat." He dipped his finger into one of the red splatters then stuck it in his mouth. "Great Demeter!" he said. He looked up at David. "It is wonderful to taste! I understand now why you like it so much!"

David in turn stuck his finger into his bowl of ketchup and then licked it off. He smiled and smacked his lips in satisfaction, then did it again.

"Eh? Do you see?" Harpo said. "The woman is right! It is a very good thing to take nourishment. Now take more, and she will no doubt be very pleased with us both."

Disregarding their spoons, they dipped and licked, slurping and smacking until their bowls were nearly empty. Had Gina arisen from her uneasy sleep and walked out into the dining area, she would have thought herself unawake and dreaming. For there at her dining table over their near-empty bowls, were John Lennon and Harpo Marx, smiling, laughing, and exchanging their exquisite genius.

The clock read one-sixteen.

$$\Omega \; \Omega \; \Omega$$

She heard the sounds of their laughter before she came out of the bedroom.

As she pulled on her jeans, Gina listened intently, hoping for some truth in what she was hearing. When she'd finished zipping, she leaned up against the bedroom door and pressed her ear on the painted wood.

Their gaiety was unmistakable, David's little chuckles, Harpo's animated words. Laughter was something that sounded almost foreign coming from David; she had not heard him laugh with real pleasure in a very long time. It was muffled and dampened by the bedroom door, but it sounded delicious and sweet. She quickly buttoned her shirt and, praying for good news, opened the bedroom door.

The two adult beings sat cross-legged on the living room rug, the small white dog between them. David had one bare foot, while the other still sported a red-and-gray argyle sock. Pulling on its mate was Midas, who snarled and growled and tugged while David, the food-stained corners of his mouth curling upward in a smile, teased him with it. Harpo cheered them both on like a ringside announcer, extolling the brave moves of one participant, then applauding the skill of the other, exhorting them both to new heights of sock-pulling.

A deck of cards was strewn haphazardly across the coffee table, and a few had fallen off, small visual insults camping out on Gina's otherwise pristine floor. Naked and uncapped on the dining table she saw an assortment of bottles and jars. Ketchup, mustard, strawberry jam, all empty. Soy sauce and red vinegar, both still partly full. Two bowls, the colorful evidence of their former contents splashed here and there on the surface of the table. Two clean spoons.

She could feel the corners of her mouth actually drooping. "What is going on here?" she said sharply. "Harpo, what *happened?*"

The sock-play stopped immediately and both David and Harpo looked up at her. Midas let go of the toe of the sock and scampered into Harpo's lap. David lowered his eyes and looked guiltily at his sockless foot.

After tucking Midas back into his toga, Harpo stood up. "Why, we are—uh—engaging in sport."

One hand on her hip, she pointed to the sock on the floor with the other. "This is a sport?"

Sensing that she was upset, he cleared his throat nervously. "Why, yes, it is, after a fashion. You see, in Greece we used to pull ropes in a similar manner and I thought—"

She interrupted him in mid-explanation. "And why are all these condiments out? What happened to all the ketchup and the mustard?" She picked up the empty Smuckers jar. "This was almost full this morning."

"Why, we ate it, naturally. We took our midday meal at the hour of one, as you instructed us to do. Well, it was a bit later, actually, but—"

Her tone of voice was suspicious and accusatory. "You mean you made sandwiches?"

"We simply ate the foods."

"You didn't put this stuff *on* something? You just *ate* it? Good *Lord*." She picked up one of the spoons and examined it. "This spoon is clean." She looked over at David's smeared face, her eyebrows furrowed. "David, did you eat with your fingers?"

Harpo answered for his ashamed-looking charge. "Naturally we did. It seemed the most sensible thing to do. We did use the vessels, however."

Gina let her arms flop to her sides. "I don't believe this," she said angrily. "What can you have been *thinking*—what can *I* have been thinking?"

"I did not expend a great deal of thought on it. The only part that seemed to require any real thought was getting David to eat in the first place. He was reluctant, as you said he might be. So I considered what should be done, and I remembered that you said he likes this ketchup. And it seemed only logical that if I were to convince him to take nourishment, it must be of an enjoyable nature."

She stared at him, speechless, realizing that it was all perfectly true. And perfectly nuts.

"Do you deny that you yourself said he enjoyed this?"

Defeated in logic, she sighed. "No, Harpo, I don't. But it's totally insane to eat a bowl of ketchup for lunch."

Harpo gave her a sage little nod. "Precisely," he said.

Ω Ω Ω

Gina was terribly confused; there were so many things that neither she nor Aaron had anticipated, and she wanted more than ever to know, *who is this crazy guy?*

It was proving to be an unnerving arrangement, but she kept telling herself that Aaron had said it was a safe thing to do, and that if she played along with the delusions, everything would be fine. So, with fingers crossed, she left Harpo and David alone in the apartment and went across the street to the corner grocery. When she returned twenty minutes later, everything did seem fine. They were seated on the couch watching something noisy on the television. Harpo looked bored, and David was predictably engrossed, but nothing was out of place, or spilled, or broken.

Whew, she thought to herself. *Finger-crossing must actually work.* The foods she now removed from the bags were not much different from the ones she had tucked into cupboards, stretching on tiptoes, as a little girl. Kid foods: peanut butter, pretzels, potato chips, packaged cookies. Tasty, loaded with salt and sugar, all highly grabbable foods. Sliced bread, strawberry jam, and Oreos. Toaster tarts.

Shaking her head, she chuckled aloud. *Tonight, with a "guest" in my home, I'm serving hot dogs on those plasticky white rolls, canned baked beans, and frozen corn. And ketchup,*

221

lots of ketchup. Too bad Ronald Reagan isn't here to see this.

The saving grace of the whole meal was the gourmet ice cream she'd bought for dessert. Double-Fudge Chunky Sundae; rich, full-fat chocolate ice cream loaded with boulders of dark chocolate, the whole sweet brown mess laced with viscous rivers of *more* chocolate. It beckoned from her freezer, a quart of gooey depravity, promising sweet salvation.

As the food warmed, she set the table with her company best, and then added the finishing touches: a *new* bottle of ketchup, a jar of mustard, and a two-liter bottle of Diet Coke. She lit the candles then went to the stereo cabinet and selected Bach's "Air in G" to accompany their repast. Soon its soothing progression of chords floated through the small apartment.

Harpo was fascinated by her preparations. "Are we engaging in some sort of ritual?"

"Family dinner, we call it."

He gestured toward the assortment of steaming platters and bowls on the table. "But this looks to be nearly a banquet. There are so many foods here. These are foods indigenous to your country?"

As she set the napkin on David's lap, she said, "Native delights, all."

Observing what she had done, Harpo unfolded the light blue cloth and placed it over the lap folds of his now-ratty robe. Midas poked his nose up out of the front and sniffed the air, prompting his master to tap him back down again.

"Now, this is what you're supposed to do with ketchup," Gina said. She held the bottle upside-down and squeezed a long line of the red stuff first onto David's hot dog, then her own. She offered the bottle to Harpo, who did precisely what he had seen her do, adding a squeeze at the end to create the coveted farty *splurt*.

Then Gina picked up the whole rolled assembly in her hands. She shoved one end of it into her mouth. "Hmm," she said, chewing the big bite, "I forgot how good hot dogs are."

Harpo agreed wholeheartedly. "Delicious!" he said. He set his partially eaten hot dog down on his plate and picked up a few baked beans in his hand, then tipped his head back and dropped them into his open mouth.

"No, Harpo—" Gina said with a small gasp, "use a fork for the beans!"

He quickly licked the brown sauce from his fingers, then wiped his wet fingers on the hem of his filthy toga. "Oh, Zeus forgive me, I have offended you! May the stench of—"

"No, no, it's okay. You can use your napkin to wipe your hands, like this." She demonstrated the proper technique with her own napkin.

"Yes, of course . . . my apologies. I am most ashamed to have besmirched your fine hospitality."

"Really, it's all right. You didn't know."

He doesn't know, she thought. *He really doesn't know. He knows about Alexander the Great, but he doesn't get forks.* She stared at him for a moment, then shook her head. *No. Impossible.*

The meal continued in quiet congeniality, and when everyone was finished, Gina removed the dirtied plates. When she came back from the kitchen she said, "I have a special treat for dessert. Another American classic, ice cream. In honor of your presence tonight, Harpo, I splurged and got the good stuff. Would you like some? I know David loves it, right, David?"

At the touch of her hand on his shoulder, David looked up at her. His expression did not change.

"Okay, I'll get you some," she said. "So how about you, Harpo? It's chocolate."

Chocolate! He saw again the beribboned box, sailing into the night. Freddie had died for the paper money he had collected to buy another box. The idea of having anything more to do with the accursed stuff was abhorrent to him.

But I can hardly refuse, he thought, *considering that she has obtained it in my honor.* "It would be my pleasure to sample it," he said quietly.

"Great." She went back to the kitchen and returned with three bowls, a serving device of some kind, and a roundish carton with a thin layer of frost on its surface. She removed the carton's flat cover and tiny shards of ice spilled onto the tablecloth. She served out three bowls and placed one in front of each of them. Then she picked up her spoon and took a small mouthful.

"*Mm,*" she purred, closing her eyes in rapt enjoyment.

Harpo did as he'd seen her do. He pressed the spoon into the firm pudding, incorporating a chunk, which he consumed in his first bite. As the cold ooze melted on his tongue, and its flavor released, his eyes began to widen. He looked down at the contents of his bowl.

"Great Zeus," he whispered, "there is nothing else in all of the Cosmos that tastes like this."

"Yeah. It's good, isn't it?"

He grabbed his amulet. His voice was shaky. "This is *chocolate?*"

"Yes," she said innocently. "I love chocolate. It just makes me—oh, I don't know—*happy* to eat it." Smiling, she held up her spoon with a full glob of ice cream on it.

It makes her happy . . . he thought. "I think it is perhaps the most delicious thing I have eaten since arriving on Earth." *Chocolate* . . . he thought as he took another mouthful. *What a strange thing to call it. They do not even know what they have.*

Ω Ω Ω

"Mrs. Miller is just next door," Gina said. She handed Harpo a piece of paper.

"You remember I showed you about the phone, how you just press this number, the one with the M next to it . . ."

"The letter which has the same appearance as *mu*," he said. "If I need to contact this Mrs. Miller, I have only to press that number."

"Right. And here's my number at Bellevue," she said, handing him another slip. "I put a B next to that one."

"*Beta*," he said. "And this *delta* is for your sister."

"Good," she said. "You really picked this stuff up quickly. Okay, this is a bit more complicated." She handed him another scrap of paper. "This is the number you dial for a real emergency. You know, like a fire or a burglary or if either of you gets hurt. Just dial these three numbers and you'll hook up to Emergency Services. 9-1-1. Tell them you're in apartment 12C. They'll already know the address from their computer."

"But how will they know?"

"Just trust me, they will," she said. "Well, that's it, I think. I've got to get down to the center. It's supposed to be cold tonight and I think we'll have some traffic. And I've got a lot of packing up to do. Anyway, you've got plenty of food, there's all sorts of stuff on TV, and my sister Diane is going to stop by around eleven to make sure David gets ready for bed. She has a key. I told her you'd be here with him. Your sheets and blankets are already on the couch, you just need to pull it out like I showed you. I'll be back about nine-thirty in the morning."

She'd already unplugged the stove. There were no matches within reach. She looked around the apartment, finding nothing more she could do to insure their safety. She turned and headed toward the door, but hesitated. She turned back. "I'm a little nervous about this. Stay inside. And please make sure you call for help if you need it. You know, if David gets upset."

He smiled. "All will be well, I assure you."

"I hope you're right," Gina said. "And Harpo, I really appreciate your help. I mean that."

She checked the clock, then looked at her phone, saw that they were out of sync. *Slow*, she thought. *Time for a new clock battery.*

Ω Ω Ω

By nine PM, he was so sick of the noise from the television that he was ready to pick it up and throw it across the apartment. "Perhaps I will change it into a mule," he said to Midas. "The braying will be far more pleasant. Let it be done . . ."

And curiously, he heard braying coming from the black box. He stared at the picture, but saw no mule, only a series of other assorted animals. *But still, I am certain I heard it . . .*

He shook his head and went to the window. The night sky was clear, and he saw a sliver moon above the buildings, felt its pull.

"Ah, fair Artemis, I hear your call."

He turned to face David, whose unwavering gaze was glued to the bright screen. "It is no wonder you are mad," he shouted over the din. "The worst kind of drivel leaps from those images and pours into your psyche."

But their previous gains in communication had been dampened by Gina's earlier displeasure, and every time Harpo tried to engage David in some sort of activity, he retreated inside himself again.

"There is much to see out there," Harpo said.

Stay inside, she had told him. But what would be the danger? He had wandered those streets with Freddie; it was only within his box that he had come to harm.

"Why do we not go out to see it all?"

David said nothing.

Finally, in exasperation, Harpo picked up the remote, and pressed the "off" button. The screen went blank. Before David was aware of what had happened, he dropped the remote into the front of his robe, and quickly folded his hands behind his back. He was standing there, all innocence, when David finally looked away from the blank screen.

"It's off," he said.

"Indeed," he said, rocking back and forth on his heels. "I can see that it is."

David began to look around for the remote. "Where's the clicker?" he asked.

"I'm sure I do not know," Harpo said. "But come, my friend, let us not be concerned with that just now. Let us go out to the streets, where we may observe *real* mortals in their activities." He went to the closet where he'd seen Gina hang his coat and took it out. He made a great show of putting it on. After a moment, David arose from the couch. Harpo handed him his jacket.

Smiling, he said, "Now, let us see what is out there," and they went out the door.

Chapter 20
Upsilon

"You see?" Harpo said. "There is so much to observe!" Perambulating at a pace David could manage, the escapees came upon a storefront filled with brightly colored toys stacked floor to ceiling in a tortuous balancing act. Enchanted by the rainbow tower, Harpo came to a sharp halt in front of the display. "Why, look at these—*Oof!*"

David bumped hard into his protector and the two went down on the sidewalk in a jumble of arms and legs. The walking traffic around them took little notice of their mishap and adjusted by oozing out in curved paths of avoidance.

Harpo let out a string of mild curses as they disentangled. "By all the gods, my friend, did you not see me stop?"

David said nothing.

"No, I think you did not," Harpo answered himself. "I think perhaps you are not seeing much of anything, eh?"

He stood up and brushed off. He offered a hand to David, who took hold, then compliantly allowed himself to be hoisted. Once they were both on sure footing again, Harpo led David back to the window, in front of which he'd attempted to stop.

He pointed to a bright yellow box with magenta polka-dots. Out of the open lid protruded a tightly coiled spring painted bright blue. At the top of the spring, a striped cloth clown beamed out his joy at being freed from the confines of the box and, with widespread green felt arms, offered an embrace to passersby.

"Look," Harpo said, pointing. And when David did not, he took gentle hold of the quiet man's face and turned it in the proper direction.

"Look," he said again, and David's eyes finally settled on the colorful object before him.

"He is happy, this little cloth mortal, eh? He has been let out."

David turned his head slowly away from the jack-in-the-box and came face-to-face with Harpo. They locked eyes for a moment. Harpo smiled. "*You* have also been let out, no?"

After a brief, shiny-eyed moment of searching his escort's face, David nodded.

"You must try to be happy. To be mad and sad at the same time is not a good thing. There must be joy in it, or madness will do you no good. You must believe me, for I know of these things."

They set off on their quest again, traversing streets and avenues, and soon came upon the Freezer. As they turned the corner, Harpo put out his arm and stopped David's forward progress. "Wait," he said, "for we must be certain that no one has overtaken my abode in my absence. We shall offer a prayer to Hera that all is well." He opened his hands and looked upward into the night sky. "Lady Hera," he whispered, "ruler of all hearths, let no intruder rest there, as I did when Freddie first came upon me."

A pang of grief stabbed his heart. "There. Now we must see what awaits us."

He took David by the arm and led him through the stuff of the alley, and soon they were standing in front of the box. It was miraculously intact, void of occupants, and ready for entry in all its corrugated glory.

"You see?" he said happily. "My prayer has been answered. It is as I left it. It seems that there is honor among the mortals who live here."

He bent all the way down and crawled inside, then motioned to David to follow. "Welcome," he said with a flourish, "to the temple of a god."

David sat down tentatively, settling himself against one side of the box. Harpo took the blanket from the corner and spread it over their knees. "I regret that my hospitality is so thin," he said. "But perhaps my circumstances will be better someday. I could try to make some wine, if you wish."

David shook his head no.

"Well, perhaps another time." Harpo held out his empty hands, demonstrating plainly his lack of means. "I have nothing else to offer, expect some entertainment. I will tell you the story of how I came to be here," he said. "It is a very long tale, but quite interesting, I think. Only Freddie has heard all of it, and it held him quite rapt." He leaned closer to David and said, "But you, being touched by the moon yourself as well, may have a similar appreciation. Would you like to hear it?"

At David's nod, Harpo grinned. "Very well. This will pass the hours nicely. It all started in Olympus one day . . ."

Ω Ω Ω

At two minutes after eleven, the phone rang in Gina's basement office. Her first thought was *Oh God, what's wrong* . . .

"Stop it, Gina," she said aloud. "Everything is fine."

Then she thought *McCarthy.* She reached over and picked up the phone. On the other end of the line was her sister's voice, frantic with worry, and when Gina hung up a few seconds later, she dialed the Bellevue Police Office.

Ω Ω Ω

Miranda's rich voice came through the phone line. "Bellevue Police, Sergeant Rasp—"

Gina didn't wait for her to finish the legally required greeting, which would have concluded with the revelation that the call was being recorded. Neither did she bother to identify herself. "Miranda," she said, her voice panicked, "Diane just called me. David and Harpo are *not* in the apartment."

"Calm down, now, I'm sure there's a perfectly logical explanation." She had kept her own reservations about the situation in apartment 12C to herself, and this moment didn't seem to her a particularly good time to reveal those doubts. "Don't panic," she said. "I'm sure nothing's wrong. They'll turn up."

"Oh, God, I don't know what to do—should I go out and look for them?"

"Gina, get a grip! It's a big city out there. Do you have *any* idea where they might have gone?"

"No! None whatsoever. David doesn't wander around outside; the only place he's been going lately is the bookstore. And he hasn't been there in a month. I can't imagine he'd remember how to get there."

"What about Harpo? Where does he go?"

"He used to hang out with Freddie until Freddie died. I guess he went where Freddie went. I don't *know*."

"The Freezer. Maybe that's where your boys went."

"But David would never go there!"

"Maybe he's not leading," Miranda speculated. "Do you want me to see if McCarthy will take a look? Anybody else finds them, they'll have to be processed."

There were just no plausible explanations for their situation, at least none that a stranger official would buy. Her voice took on a thin veneer of hope. "He's on tonight?"

"I'll see if I can raise him, then I'll call you back and let you know."

Ω Ω Ω

"Tell her I'm on my way," McCarthy said when she found him. "Also tell her that if they're not there, I'll go check out the area near her building again, see if they're hanging around outside. I'll call back in, one way or the other, so tell her to stay at the center. And tell her not to panic."

"I already have. Didn't do any good. She's a wreck."

"I figured as much."

He replaced the radio handset and looked at over Stein with an *oh-shit* expression on his face.

"Well, well, well," Stein said, "the lady in distress calls her knight in shining armor."

"Zip it, Stein, this is real for her."

They'd been strategically positioned nearby on First Avenue when Miranda's radio call came and it took them only a minute to reach their destination. McCarthy left Stein in the car again and stepped carefully down the alley. When he neared the box, he heard Harpo's lively, accented voice pouring out in a continuous stream. Then he heard the familiar thin growl of the small white dog.

He bent over just outside the box. "Harpo? You in there?"

Harpo stuck his head out and looked up at McCarthy with undisguised disdain. "I greet you," he said, frowning.

McCarthy took note of the resentful tone. "Yeah, I'm thrilled to see you, too." He saw a long-haired man he took to be David tucked in beside Harpo, and took a moment to absorb his image.

So this is what he looks like now . . . he thought to himself. *Not what I expected.* "I hope I'm not interrupting anything," he said, "but Gina—"

"As Fortune would have it, you *are* interrupting, but please—enter."

Shit and a half, he thought. *The hospitality thing.* He crouched further down and looked inside the box. "I don't think I'll fit. It looks a little crowded in there."

He looked at David. "How ya doin', David?" he said.

When David failed to respond directly, Harpo answered for him. "He is well." He tapped David on the arm. "Are you not well?"

David looked at Harpo and said, "Well."

Harpo gave McCarthy a smug look. "You see? He is well. I am well."

"Everyone's well, then," McCarthy said, "me included, in case you should happen to be wondering. But listen, I have to interrupt your little party here. I have to take you guys back to the apartment. Gina's a little worried about you."

"She need not worry. I am telling David a story."

Exasperated, McCarthy said, "Well, she *is,* and you can tell him the rest of the story back at the apartment. So let's go, because I don't have all night. And Gina wants David to go home."

"But—"

"Trust me, Harpo, you want to go back to the apartment. She's not very happy right now."

"Very well," he said with resignation. He gently nudged David in the direction of the opening. "We must return to your abode now," he said.

David got out of the box and stood up next to McCarthy. As he clambered out himself, Harpo silently compared them, one so huge and strong, a stalwart with power and purpose and conviction. And seemingly, a good heart. The other pale and quiet, a beautiful man whose soul was the captive of a rare and sweet insanity, which the world did not appreciate.

"Follow me, boys," McCarthy said, leading the way down the alley toward the cruiser. "Your chariot awaits."

Ω Ω Ω

McCarthy left his two captives in the cruiser with Stein while he went into the basement to talk to Gina.

"They seem all right," he said, "but you might want to come out and take a look."

"No." She shook her head. "I'm afraid I'll blow up at them if I do. But they look okay?"

"A little wet, but otherwise fine. And I have to tell you, they looked like they were having a good time."

"In a box?"

"Hey," McCarthy said, "I remember having some good times in boxes when I was a kid."

She sighed. "Good point."

"If you want to give me your keys, I'll get them back to your apartment and get them inside, and I'll put the fear of god in them so they won't go out again."

"Are you sure you don't mind doing that?"

"Protect and serve, remember? Anything else you want me to tell them?"

"Yeah," she said, fishing in her purse for the heavy key ring. "Tell them that I expect to find them both sound asleep when I get home in the morning."

He smiled. "Will do. I'll bring your keys back before my shift is over."

"Thanks, McCarthy. Once again, you've been a real prince."

"No problem." He leaned over and placed a light kiss on her forehead, but before he could move away again, she had her arms tightly around his neck, and was clinging like a frightened child.

He was surprised by the intensity of her grasp. "Hey, Gina . . ." he said softly as he enfolded her in his own arms. "Hang in there. Everything will be fine. Really soon." He stroked her hair. "All this will seem like nothing pretty soon. I promise."

Ω Ω Ω

Gina was sitting on the floor with her back leaned up against Aaron's office door when he and Mike came around the corner early the following morning. When she heard the hum of the wheelchair, she opened her eyes and stood up.

"Good morning," Aaron said. "What a pleasant surprise to find you here."

"I am *not* pleased to be here."

While Mike was unlocking the door, Aaron said, "Come inside, tell me why."

As he motored across the waiting room, Gina walked beside him and launched into the harangue she'd been rehearsing in her mind as she waited for him to arrive. "Harpo took David outside last night. Apparently they walked all over the lower east side."

"Really?" Aaron said. "That must have been a treat for David after being stuck in that hospital for so long. How did it go?"

"How did it *go*?" She was almost shrieking. "It shouldn't have *gone*."

"Why not?"

"Because they're both *nuts, that's* why. Who's supposed to be in charge? And if we hadn't found them, who knows what could have happened. David might have ended up out there on the streets . . ."

Aaron winced from the shrillness of her voice. "Gina, I can hear you. You don't need to yell. Now, was anyone hurt?"

She lowered the volume of her voice obediently, but its intensity remained. "No. But I had to send McCarthy out to look for them. He found them in Freddie's old box."

"Which Harpo now considers to be *his* home."

"Yeah, I suppose so," she said, still fuming. "McCarthy said they looked okay. But I haven't been home yet, so I don't know what to expect. As you well know, David doesn't usually communicate too much about his condition. He might be hurt and not say anything about it."

"He'd find some way to show his distress, believe me. Did McCarthy say if they'd been in any kind of trouble?"

"No, but—"

"Don't you think he would have mentioned it if they had run into any difficulties?"

She let out a perturbed sigh. "I really don't know. He might have thought it would upset me."

"A reasonable assumption, based on what I'm seeing right now."

"Well, why shouldn't I be upset? I woke up yesterday and they were eating ketchup, for God's sake. And mustard. They ate *condiments* for lunch, Aaron, no bread, no fillings, just condiments. Then they just took off last night like a couple of happy wanderers."

Mike opened the inner door and Aaron motored through. He took his usual place at the far side of his desk and Gina sat down, without invitation, in the chair opposite him. "I don't know, Aaron, maybe this wasn't such a good idea, I mean, *one night* and they're already out of control. I can't go to work knowing that David's not safe, and I don't have anyone else who can take care of him."

"One unsolvable problem at a time, please." He took a cleansing breath. "I wouldn't say they're out of control. They just went outside. They didn't get hurt, or in trouble, or cause any damage that we know of. So tell me what's wrong about them going out."

She began to sound flustered. "It's just wrong, that's all. David's not well, and Harpo's only working on half a tank himself. All sorts of things could happen to them."

"None of which did."

"Not last night, but—"

"What makes you think that they're not going to be able to avoid trouble? Harpo spent a lot of time with this man Freddie. He probably picked up a lot of street-smarts from him, don't you think?"

"If Freddie was so street-smart, how did he end up dead?"

The psychiatrist hesitated before speaking. "I don't have an answer for that," he said. "But if you pushed me, I'd have to say that it was probably just bad luck. If anything, Harpo's going to be a lot warier after that experience."

"You're rationalizing. You know it's dangerous out there just as well as I do."

"Of course it's dangerous, Gina, it's dangerous in lots of places, many of which happen to be inside. Statistically, the inside of your own home is the most dangerous place you can be."

"I'm not worried about one of them sticking his finger into an outlet, I'm worried about muggers and trucks and that kind of stuff."

"Reasonably. But don't panic. Lots of *kids* come home alone while their parents work. Some certainly go outside. I'm not saying I'm especially in favor of that arrangement, but my point is that David and Harpo are grown men, and not necessarily as vulnerable. Harpo may *appear* to be delusional, but that's his *schtick*. The truth is he's one very smart fellow. And if you simply can't bring yourself to trust him, you can close the center earlier than you have to and stay home until David is situated. Or you can take David with you when you go there."

"I don't think I should do either of those things."

"Right. I know. You want complete control over every aspect of your life and David's, and now that's extending over into Harpo's life, too. But you can't have it, and you're going to have to stop setting yourself up in situations that can't possibly work out. What are you going to do in another week when David's in his new life and completely out of your control?"

She was quiet for a moment. "I don't know."

"You're going to need to give it some hard, fast consideration."

She stood and paced.

"Here are some suggestions for the meantime. First, be very clear with Harpo about what the rules are. He'll respond to clear limits."

"He didn't last night."

"Then be more forceful about it. Give them a set of keys. Give them some money. Suggest destinations, movies, a park, things like that. Tell them when to come home. Try preparing lunches ahead of time, or be very specific about what they should eat. And then just *let them go!*"

"Oh, God, Aaron, I'm just so scared something terrible will happen to David . . ."

"You can't keep bad things from happening, Gina, no matter how hard you try. You can't be *every*where in every moment. And in case you haven't noticed, Harpo is pretty desperate to please you. He's going to go out of his way to make sure David's all right. Not to mention he thinks it's his 'divine mandate'. Give it at least another couple of days. I don't think you'll be sorry."

Ω Ω Ω

There was no one on the other side of the door to assault her with questions, and though it was a welcome change from the way David once greeted her, she found the calm unsettling. She wondered for a moment if her two vagabonds had sallied forth, unpermitted, on another great adventure.

She found them on the couch, sound asleep and innocently leaning against each other, like Eeyore and Tigger in a Pooh dream, their unconscious expressions accordingly sweet and benign. She sat down on the chair opposite the couch and stared at David, the man who'd once been nearly the king of witty sarcasm, a brilliant young intern who could rip a Gray's Anatomy in half with his bare brain, the same sweet, extraordinary man who'd somehow managed to find something in her *ordinary* self that was worthy of his own worship. Where was the well-honed sense of irony, the gift for caustic understatement?

Where did that luminosity go? She felt more bewildered than sad.

Maybe he will *do better somewhere else.*

Denial. Anger. Bargaining. Depression. Acceptance?

David suddenly shifted in his sleep, turning so his own back was up against that of his companion. Then Harpo shifted, and his eyes fluttered open. Slowly he came to consciousness, as if he had been awakened by some subliminal awareness of Gina's observation.

He sat up. Remarkably, David did not slide down into a horizontal position on the couch. "I greet you," Harpo said sleepily when he saw her.

The list of questions she wanted to ask about the evening's escapades whizzed through Gina's mind like a fleet of Ferraris. She would likely get a protracted explanation, splendidly embellished with cultural cross-references. *In Greece we did this, in Greece we did that . . .*

Wisely, reluctantly, Gina decided to forgo her inquiry.

"I greet you, too," she said with a wan smile. "I understand you and David had an interesting evening."

His expression was downright confessional. "Yes, and I am sorry that our leaving upset you, but—"

"It's okay, Harpo. I'm not mad."

He gave her a curious look, which warmed gradually to a smile. "Of course you are not," he said. "You are vexingly sane."

His astute summation of her entire life blasted right through her crust of indignation. "I mean I'm not angry," she said. "I guess it's okay that you went out. I just didn't like the idea at first; it sort of scared me that you two were out there in big old Manhattan by yourselves. That's why I sent McCarthy out to find you. But I guess it was okay after all."

She took in a big, brave breath and held out her hand. "Here," she said, "This is a set of keys to the apartment. That way you can go in and out without having to worry about whether or not I'm here."

She showed him how to slip in the keys and turn them, and told him that one of the keys was for the main door to the building. "Don't ring the buzzers," she admonished him. Then she took out a full change of clothing for David. "When he wakes up, he should change into these. Make sure he washes up first, you know, his face and hands, and tell him to brush his teeth. I'll leave the toothbrush out on the counter with toothpaste already on it. His dirty clothes should be put in the hamper." She pointed to a tall wicker basket squeezed into one corner of the bathroom.

"Then you and he can both have some breakfast. You should both eat cereal." She led him to the kitchen, where she extracted a large and colorful box from one of the cabinets. "Pour some of this in a bowl," she said, demonstrating, "then add a little milk." She held up a spoon "And eat it with these."

"Can we not have chocolate to break our fast?" he asked.

She smiled. "Chocolate tastes wonderful, but it's not a good idea to eat too much of it. We usually have it as a special treat."

"Aha," he said, clutching his amulet, "you use it ritually, and take only minimal amounts. This is very sensible for such a powerful food."

"Hmm. I hadn't thought of chocolate as precisely being powerful, but I guess it does hold a kind of power over some people," she said jokingly. "I know when I feel lousy, I head right for the stuff."

"So it has medicinal uses, then," he noted.

She found his interest in chocolate curious. "I suppose you could say that. But I think it would just be a good idea if you had cereal."

"We shall eat cereal, then," he said.

"Good. Oh, and here," she said, "I almost forgot." She pulled a small slip of paper and twenty dollar bill from one of her pockets. "Here's the address of this apartment. If you get lost, just show it to anyone, and ask for directions. I wrote

David's name on it, and my name, and here's the phone number. Oh, and here's money in case you need it. If you do leave, make sure the upper lock is locked on this door up here, and that the outer building door closes behind you. Take your watch, because I want you to be back here by four-thirty at the latest."

He nodded, then took the paper and money from her and pulled out the front fold of his toga. As he tucked it all away, he said to Midas, "See that you do not chew on this. We shall need it for later."

Oy, Gina thought. With one last look at David, who seemed perfectly, maddeningly okay, she went into the bedroom. "I'll see you in a few hours," she said, and closed the door.

Chapter 21
Phi

They descended the steps in the bright, warm sunshine. Harpo took off at a brisk pace, leading the way, with David stumbling behind. Heading roughly south and east, they meandered in a zigzag path through the wondrous folly of lower Manhattan, seedy enough to be ignored by predators, too absurd looking to be feared themselves. They progressed unhindered on a journey toward no particular destination.

They came upon Battery Park when the sun was in full reign over an unimaginably blue sky and there, just outside a stone wall, they encountered a pretzel vendor. The warm, yeasty smell drew Harpo in like a magnet, so he bought one of the big twisted wonders for each of them. He handed over his twenty dollar bill with great ceremony, as if the transaction had some sacred importance beyond ordinary commerce.

"Hey, pal, you got something smaller?"

"This one is not the correct size?"

The vendor said, "I'll have to give you back fives. Got no tens."

His eyes widened in surprise when he got back four bills in place of the one he had put forth. "There are four," he said, looking directly at the man.

"Yeah, the pretzels are two apiece, so that makes four bucks, and twenty take away four is sixteen. I gave you three fives and a one." Then the vendor looked away toward another customer, so Harpo led David off to one side, shaking his head over the twisted fortune of getting four back for one.

They stood on the sidewalk and ate their pretzels, crowds of people passing around them with pointed indifference. Tiny nuggets of salt exploded on his tongue, and Harpo proclaimed, "What a delightful sensation!"

"Delightful!" David parroted.

Harpo smiled on hearing David speak. "Yes, my friend, delightful." He took another bite and chewed languorously, savoring the warm yeasty dough. "Delicious!" He looked all around at their surroundings, soaking up the sights with great curiosity. "I must admit," he said, "that I grow more heartened every day by the goodness and beauty of some of the things I find here."

He ran his tongue happily over his teeth. "When I first arrived here, it seemed a terrible place. It lacks the transcendence of Olympus, but it will more than suffice, at least temporarily."

David looked at him, clearly not understanding.

"Oh, well, we have a few minor defects there. I myself am no longer the image of perfection I once was." He grinned and grabbed hold of his small paunch. "But it cannot be avoided, so I have given in to it. It is Fate," he said, "nothing more."

A pigeon fluttered down and settled at their feet in search of a handout. Harpo eyed it with frank disapproval. "We had these birds in Greece as well. A noteworthy imperfection." He shook a finger angrily in the bird's direction. "I wish I had my powers back," he said, "for I would deprive you of your disguise by making all your feathers fall off. Then you would be exposed for the rat you really are."

Midas poked his head up and sniffed the air, so Harpo took him by the scruff of his neck and put him down near the pigeon, which flapped its wings and hurried off, skimming a few inches above the sidewalk in its unworried escape.

"Well done!" Harpo said. Then he and David walked toward the entrance to the park with the little dog at their heels.

He did not notice the trail of newly-shed feathers on the gray cement.

Ω Ω Ω

They were seated on a bench inside the wall. "But I must also say," Harpo added, "that many of the things I have seen here *do* offend me. Why do the widows not sweep the walkways? There are surely enough of them." He pointed toward a scurrying black-clad woman. "You see? There goes another now.

"But on the whole, I am not displeased. You mortals have done some very ingenious things with what we gave you." He held up what remained of his pretzel. "I am most taken by the foods! I have tasted many delicious things. Ketchup, and hot dogs! Potato chips. Ice cream. All very wonderful." He elbowed David lightly and said, "But your most incredible food is chocolate, eh?"

David thought for a moment, then said, "I like chocolate."

"Three words! Marvelous. It is understandable that you like chocolate." Harpo's eyes sparkled. "Any wise mortal would. And you are very wise, no?"

"No," David said with a grin.

"Say, *no I am not*. Four words. But truly, you are."

David rocked back and forth on the bench. He met Harpo's eyes and laughed.

They walked on through the curved pathways, the spring sun warming their shoulders. They passed through the deciduous glory of the park, tantalized by near-bursting buds, all promising bright new leaves. They came to an open area where two groups were setting out their gear, the bats, balls, bases, and gloves that would kill off the last vestiges of winter. Off to one side was a playground with swings and climbing gear where children scampered noisily over the equipment, with watchful mothers nearby, trading stories as their progeny worked out the kinks of a long winter confinement.

On the pathway was a bench. In the shade behind it was a defiant patch of snow, with a crop of crocuses poking through. Harpo said, "Let us rest there for a while and observe. There is much to be seen in this spot."

They headed toward it just as a new vendor appeared around the corner, pushing his cart of goodies toward the baseball group. When they crossed paths with the vendor, David hesitated briefly, then turned back toward the cart and said, "Chocolate."

Harpo stopped abruptly. "Where?"

David pointed to a box of Hershey bars.

"They are chocolate?" he asked.

"All the way through," the vendor answered. "Two bucks apiece."

Harpo reached inside his toga and pulled out his remaining sixteen dollars. He handed the bills to the vendor.

"You want *eight*?"

"I want as many as this paper money will buy," was Harpo's reply.

"Eight it is, then." He counted out the bars and handed them over.

Harpo took them eagerly. "Thank you!" Then he turned to David. "Come, my friend, we will sit and partake of this blessing. But we will not tell Gina, eh? She will not approve."

They sat on the bench, observing the goings-on, unwrapping bar after bar. Squares of chocolate disappeared into their mouths with astonishing speed. "You must tell me about this contest," Harpo said. He pointed a chocolaty finger in the direction of the players.

"Baseball," David said. "A good game."

Pleased with this small but significant elaboration from his charge, Harpo said, "Four words! Marvelous. Indeed, the game looks to be quite intricate. You will tell me about it, please. And then when you are through, I will finish my interrupted tale of how I came to be here." He tucked a square of chocolate into his mouth and let it melt on his tongue, then smiled, smears of chocolate curling upward on his cheeks. "You see, we have many stories to tell each other. This is very good."

"Good," David agreed, a very small smile showing on his lips. And slowly, haltingly, he brought forth what he could remember of pitching and runs and outs. Harpo commented on the brilliance of it all, how sublime and ingenious and intelligent it seemed.

They remained on the bench for a while, as Harpo told his tale. When at last they left the park, their progress was true north, and not far along their route, they came upon a large construction site.

David stopped altogether.

"What is it, my friend?"

But David remained frozen to the spot, and would not speak.

Harpo surveyed the vibrant scene before him. He saw a vast pit, surrounded by four thick walls.

"A castle, perhaps? For many warriors."

But set deep into the earth rather than atop it. On the opposite side was a large gleaming edifice made of glass. The sun reflected off the new building so brightly that he had to shade his eyes from the glare. He took David by one hand and tugged him along to the pit's southern wall.

With David at his side, he leaned over and peered down, taking in the scene. Not far to their left he saw a long ramp-road that started at the top of the wall and sloped down into the pit, ending roughly in its center. Everywhere were construction vehicles, cranes, trucks and piles of materials. The noise was deafening as vehicles moved forward, reversed, picked up loads, and redeposited them elsewhere. Workers in uniforms with bright yellow helmets and wide belts bore objects that he took to be weapons, though there was no apparent conflict.

Megáles michanés, he whispered. "I have never seen such monstrous devices!" He turned to David. "Truly, these are—"

David's eyes were squeezed tightly shut. His hands were clenched at his sides, trembling.

Harpo turned away from the scene and put one hand on David's arm. "What is it? Again you are frightened."

Finally David opened his eyes. He slowly raised one arm and pointed toward an area near the end of the ramp.

"There," he said.

"What?"

Halting, pained words came out of him. "There. I. Was. There. *Right there.*"

And he sank down, turning so his back rested against the wall. He put his hands to his face and began to cry, quietly at first, and then with bitter ferocity. Tears streamed down his cheeks as he wailed out his anguish.

For a long time.

Ω Ω Ω

The stranger who called himself Dionysus sat next to the troubled man and held him close.

"Tell me," he said. "I am the protector of souls such as yourself. Tell me what sorrows you so."

"The towers," David whispered. "They were there."

"Ah." And for a long moment, Dionysus was quiet.

"Now I understand. My friend Freddie told me of this. He told me there would be a new one, this must be it, eh? He was there on the day this thing happened. It was very terrible for him. And I think you were, too, eh?"

David nodded *yes*. And then he spewed forth everything he could remember, leaving Dionysus in disbelief, for once stunned to silence.

Finally, his keeper whispered, "By all the Gods . . .this was very terrible for you, and so many others."

Dionysus closed his eyes. He held David and rocked him until the man's tears finally abated.

"All will be well," he said. "You must embrace this sadness you feel, become one with it, then conquer it with *enthusiasmos*, or your madness will be troubling to you. As I see that it is now."

"*Why?*" David whispered. "Why?"

"Even as a god, I cannot answer. Freddie thought it was because *their* god has many, many believers and they have made him strong. Perhaps this god falls prey to the same flaw as *our* gods often do. We have power, and we use it. *Too often*. And not always to the benefit of those we reign over."

His voice darkened. "But someday, some other deity will arise, and you will have your vengeance. I cannot offer this to you myself. And for that I am truly sorry. Perhaps it will come from your Christian god Jehovah who has so many believers now. Or Yahweh of the Jews. They will direct their mortals to do what must be done. That vengeance will be *sweet*. It will purify."

He rubbed David's shoulder. "But now you are clearing your psyche, vengeance or no. So all will be well, you will see."

He stood and helped David to stand. With one last look at the pit, he guided David around the wall to the east. They continued homeward, arriving just as Gina was coming awake from her daytime sleep. By then all evidence of David's tears had vanished.

Ω Ω Ω

Just as she was clearing the dinner dishes off the table, Gina's telephone rang. She balanced it on her shoulder as she scraped the crumbs of macaroni and cheese, glazed carrots and pineapple upside-down cake into the garbage pail.

Aaron's familiar voice came through. "Just checking on how the day went," he said. "I figured I'd better get the report now so you wouldn't have to camp out in front of my door again tomorrow morning."

"I'm sorry about that. It was brazen."

"It was fine," Aaron said. "And if that's how you define brazen, I'd advise you to get out a little more. You *were* pretty agitated, though. Frankly, I'm surprised you didn't take the door off the hinges before I got there."

She chuckled. "I was tempted. But I don't think you'll find me there tomorrow. We had a pretty good day, all things considered."

"Define 'a pretty good day.'"

"Well, for starters, I slept all the way through undisturbed. Our boys wandered around some and ended up at Battery Park. From what I can gather, they watched a pickup ball game and ate Hershey bars for lunch. After that I guess they just kept—wandering around."

"Interesting," Aaron observed. "The mythical Dionysus was said to have wandered Earth. He's still right in character." Then he chuckled. "Sounds like my kind of day, though. And very good for David, to get outside in the fresh air."

"And you know what? Harpo said David actually talked to him. About baseball. Harpo gave me a good run down, and he says he got it all from what David told him."

Aaron said nothing for a moment; it was entirely possible that Harpo was already familiar with baseball.

"David hasn't talked that much in a very long while, has he?"

"No. So you were right. It *is* good for him to go out."

She paused, put the trash pail back into the cupboard and closed the door. "And there's something else. I don't know quite how to put it. David just seems, I don't know—calmer. At peace. Like he's moved on."

She could almost hear Aaron smiling. "Not that this was a race, but I think he beat you."

"Yeah, I think he did. Wow."

"I'm very relieved," Aaron said after a short pause. "Though I have to go on record here by saying I'm not surprised. But that's as close as I'll get to saying 'I told you so.' Now all *I* have to do, *not* you, is figure out what Harpo's going to do when David goes into the facility. He's going to be facing some big changes in the structure of *his* life."

"Is there any reason why Harpo can't visit David there? I mean, if you clear it with the people who run it first, couldn't Harpo take David out every now and then? It seems to be so good for David. He's the liveliest he's been in a long time. He actually seems to be engaging with the world. Not with me, but . . . well, anyway, Harpo seems to be enjoying it, too."

"I don't have any specific objections to it. I know they do encourage residents to go outside, under controlled circumstances of course. But about Harpo. He won't be able to stay with you after David goes. He'll have to go back to his box to live unless we find him something else."

She was quiet for a moment, then said, "For once I wasn't thinking about bums."

"I took him off your hands, remember? I'm sure I can find him something better. You, in the meantime, just worry about yourself."

She sighed reluctantly. "Okay, Aaron. I'll try," she said. "But taking care of people is a hard habit to break. It's what I do for a living."

"This situation is a little different, Gina."

Don't I know it, she thought. "But it's still hard."

Ω Ω Ω

As she was getting ready to leave for the center, Gina remembered that David and Harpo would need money. As she rooted around in her purse to find the ever-elusive wallet, her hand came to rest on the circular band Harpo had given her on his first night at the center. She had put it there a few days before when she was emptying out the safe. She stifled a small gasp. *I've had this in my bag all this time . . .*

She pulled it out and turned it over in her hands, examining it carefully. Ounces of gold. A hundred or more carats of fine gemstones. *Hundred thousand, I bet,* she thought, dreaming for a brief moment. *What I couldn't do with that much money . . . Where on earth did he get it? And why is he loose in the world with it?*

He wanted her to keep it, though he understood its value. *What if I didn't give it back?* It could be used to pay for a placement for Harpo in the home where David was going, if another room came up, at least for a while. There'd need to be a lawyer, and a judge who was willing to declare him incompetent. *Maybe I could serve as his legal guardian . . .*

She stopped, chided herself. *Give it up, Gina. Time to let go.*

She looked into the living room. There she saw the two men sitting on the floor, happily creating a house of cards.

"Harpo," she said as she entered, "Here's money." She handed him another twenty, wishing a smaller amount would suffice.

He accepted it with a slight nod of his head and tucked it into his toga. "Thank you," he said.

"You're welcome," she said. "Also," she added reluctantly, "there's this." She held out the collar. "I want to give it back to you."

He stared at it for a moment, then looked up at her. He got slowly to his feet.

He knew she was the sort of mortal who understood and respected the obligations of safekeeping. *So why is she giving it back to me now?* He did not reach out to take it. He looked at it, then looked back at her. Her face wore a vague expression of sadness.

Finally, he said, "I would be glad to have you hold it for a while longer."

She kept her hand extended. "I appreciate your trust in me, Harpo, but I can't do that. It's yours and you should have it. And I'm not worried about you like I was when you first came into the center. Why don't you put it back on Midas?"

He took it from her hand, making no attempt to hide his confusion and sadness. "When this work of mine comes to an end, may I come to visit with you?"

She gave him a warm, genuine smile. "Of *course*. I would be very happy to see you. You're almost like a member of my family now. I'm very grateful for the way you've helped David. You can come to see me any time."

Ω Ω Ω

When she was gone, Harpo pulled Midas out of his hiding place and put the collar back on his scruffy neck. The little dog became very excited and bounded happily from Harpo's lap to David's. In one particularly enthusiastic leap, he bumped into the elaborate card house that the two men had constructed on the living room floor. The structure fluttered quietly to the rug, demoted by the swipe of a tail to an ordinary pile of cards.

An immediate look of distress appeared on David's face. He looked forlornly at Harpo, who was busy scolding Midas for his clumsiness.

Harpo tucked the dog away, and, setting aside his own preoccupation with Gina for that moment, said, "Oh, don't worry, my friend, another one can easily be made. I shall do it." He laughed. "Let me see if I can do this with my godly power, weak though it is. It will go back together much—"

Before the sentence could be finished, the cards leapt up off the rug and reassembled themselves into a house.

He stared down at the reborn paper palace, momentarily speechless, and then whispered, *"Sweet Zeus . . ."*

And as Harpo sat and stared at the small miracle, uncharacteristically quiet, David knocked the cards back down with a sweep of his hand. Grinning with excitement, the happy madman said, "Do that again."

And after a moment, Harpo did.

Ω Ω Ω

The stranger who called himself Dionysus passed the evening and the early part of the next day in celebrating and testing his newly reclaimed power. *Overnight,* he thought giddily, *I have gone from grape juice to fine, sweet wine.* He amused himself with small bits of mischief: locking and unlocking doors, stopping and restarting the clock, turning the television on and off. *Why, I have* become *the god-cursed remote!* He was enthralled.

But still, he was cautious. *I must satisfy myself that it is true before I use it to claim her. There is no doubt,* he assured himself, *that she will join my worship when she finally sees the truth about me. And then when my full powers are restored . . .*

He tested himself over and over, practicing, honing, and clarifying what he could accomplish. It became easier with each attempt.

Why, I need only wish something, he thought, *and it comes about!*

It was a gloriously warm afternoon, so with excitement befitting a god restored, he set out with David, intending to conquer yet another piece of Manhattan. They wandered south and west, their journey sweetened by walk lights that unaccountably changed in their favor at the curb, and passersby who smiled and stepped politely aside as they approached.

He reveled in the wonder of it all. "This city seems so beautiful to me now," he said to David. "Indeed, the same might be said of the entire Earth!"

As they passed a florist he said, "Look at this!" He stopped and picked up a tired-looking bunch of flowers, and through his wish, restored it to plump freshness, leaving the astonished proprietor staring in disbelief and calling for him to come back. They walked further down the block, and a fruit vendor became his next beneficiary as he erased the bruises on a full crate of forlorn-looking peaches.

He skipped down the sidewalk, with David hurrying along beside him, and released all his pent-up joy into the New York spring.

He stopped suddenly and grabbed hold of David's arms, pinning his elbows to his sides in an excited grip. "This is because of Freddie. He *believed.*"

David offered no comment but smiled back at his excited protector.

"*Someone* must believe!" he said, staring into David's eyes. "Is it you?"

David shook his head.

"Then it *must* have been Freddie!" He let go of David's arms and threw his hands up gleefully. "He must now be across the river, and well into Hades, where he is greeted with much jubilation! This is very fortunate for him. Great Zeus," he shouted into the sky, "he was the most unfortunate of mortals, but he has left me the finest legacy!"

He was swimming in the delirium of his good fortune. All around him, things were awe-inspiring and new. Everything he touched seemed to glow. Colors came alive as his glance grazed over them. Everything he passed buzzed and hummed and vibrated with the heat of his presence.

But as they rounded a next corner in their blissful romp, he was struck by sudden familiarity, and he came to an abrupt stop. Though he could not recall having been on that corner before, he was filled with a sense of *knowing* about a building across the street. He shaded his eyes with one hand and scrutinized it. Its dirty brick walls bore the obligatory six vertical feet of tagging, defiant sloped letters with soft edges, some of it unaccountably beautiful. On the second floor, there was a sheet of wood covering what he took to be a broken window. He looked up and picked out some of the letters he recognized from the sign. *Delta, epsilon, mu, omicron* . . . but they were not enough for him to know what it said or meant.

"It seems that my new powers do not extend to deciphering these letters." He tapped David on the shoulder and pointed up toward the sign. "Can you tell me what they mean, my friend?"

David looked up and said, "DeMoula Liquor Importing Company." Almost as an afterthought he added, "Incorporated."

And Harpo recalled the rock Gina had thrown through that boarded window on the night that Freddie had begun his journey across the river.

Ω Ω Ω

It must have been Freddie, he thought. He lay on the couch in Gina's apartment and stared up at the ceiling, knowing that it would be many hours before his eyes closed. He could hear David's snoring through the open bedroom door, and knew that his charge was soundly wrapped in a quilt of dreams.

The immediate joy of his rebirth had begun to wear off as a better understanding took hold. *I have power again, though I do not know how much, or what it can do for me.* Who knew how long it would last? He was convinced that his logic was right, that Freddie had somehow come to believe in his divinity. But Freddie was gone, and the effect might therefore be temporary.

He had prayed to Zeus for an answer, and anxiously waited for some sign that he'd been heard. Thunder had come in the late evening, but it was weak and unfocused, and he was still uncertain. He tossed and turned, counting out each successive hour on his watch, which now seemed less a gift and more a curse. He pondered every possibility with divinely meticulous care, seeking Cosmic guidance in formulating a plan.

But the Cosmos ignored him; there were no bursts of divine inspiration.

Finally, realizing that he would not sleep, he sat up on his elbows and threw off the blanket. He patted Midas until he felt the small dog stir. "I need your counsel, Small One. You are my only advisor." He clutched the vial at his neck. "These mortals already *have* ambrosia here. It works only *slightly* to improve their situation. I am afraid that mine will not work as my father intended. So I may need this other power to go back."

Midas whined in sympathy of his master's dilemma. "And what if I try and

245

fail? Then the ambrosia *must* work, or we shall be here forever."

It was a sobering, melancholy quandary. He sat in the darkness and let his warring thoughts have their way with him, and, after much internal turmoil, reached a decision. "I will try *once* more to make her adore me. I will use this power to give her something she wished for."

The burden of indecision lifted, he lowered his legs to the floor and stood up. Rubbing Midas through his toga, he said, "It is the only godlike thing to do, eh?"

Ω Ω Ω

After making sure once again that David was deeply asleep, he slipped out and headed at a quick pace in the direction of the edifice he had seen earlier. He regarded the square brick building through the midnight murk from a stoop across the street. He watched the building for a few minutes from his post, then arose and slipped through the darkness, crossing the street in a few swift steps. He made a complete circumnavigation, taking in all the building's details, then returned to his stoop.

As he prepared himself to begin, he whispered to Midas, "There are wines worthy of Olympus in there, I can sense them through the walls. A pity to destroy them. Some will never be known again. But Freddie has led me here for just that purpose! And this is what the woman wished for, a great revenge, so we must give it to her."

The small dog whimpered. "I know. It is troubling what I must do. But be still, for now I must concentrate."

He closed his eyes, envisioning the quarter million deep green bottles laid neatly on racks inside the walls, and concentrated his thoughts in their direction. His silent will swirled within him, a shapeless miasma, seeking form, striving toward articulation.

Finally, his will solidified. It grew and expanded into a maelstrom, building up force and pressure, until he felt that his own divine cork would pop.

Ω Ω Ω

The head watchman of the night crew at the DeMoula warehouse let his canine sidekick lead him through the long rows of shelving on the ground floor. The young Doberman bitch stepped lightly just ahead of him, straining at the end of her leash, searching the air with her nose for rogue molecules. He stayed in her good graces with a pocketful of liver treats, about which his wife complained endlessly on laundry day.

The floor trembled slightly under his feet. He stopped; the dog's ears perked up. *Subway*, he thought, *or maybe a truck rumbling by outside*. He patted the dog's head and said, "Good girl," then fed her a liver bit. They walked on, his footsteps echoing on the concrete floor.

Then it trembled again, this time harder. He heard the tinkling of glass on glass as the bottles in the stacks vibrated.

Very big truck, he thought, his concern growing.

Somewhere in a distant corner of the ground floor, he heard a cork let go, the familiar dull *pop* of champagne being set free. The dog strained hard on her leash and growled.

Oh, Christ, these guys get bolder all the time, he thought as he followed the dog in the direction of the sound. *Now they start celebrating before they even finish the heist.* He pulled a radio off its clip on his belt and spoke quietly into it, directing all his men to join him in a specific area of the ground floor. He heard another *pop*. He quickened his pace, the dog pulling him faster.

And then there was another pop, and another and another, and before long the stacks were trembling violently back and forth, pushed as if by a gale. Bottles crashed to the floor, exploding red, gold and green all around him. The acrid smell of boiling vinegar assaulted his senses.

"Holy shit!" He abandoned all stealth and screamed into the radio, "Everyone get out *now!* Evacuate!"

As he ran out of the building, he grabbed the master switch on the main alarm box and yanked it downward. Bells went off inside and outside the building, and the sprinkler system sprang to life. The last few men rushed out of the building drenched in wine and water, bloodied from flying shards of glass.

Flashing lights and blaring sirens awakened the neighborhood. A crowd of onlookers gathered to witness the chaos, many clad in robes and slippers. *Terrorist* was whispered from one hushed observer to the next. Confusion reigned.

From his stoop across the street, Dionysus watched with delicious satisfaction as a bright fire erupted. Midas poked his head up from the folds of the toga, sniffing the air, his tongue hanging out.

"You smell the female dog," his master said, then sniffed the air himself. "I do, as well." He patted Midas reassuringly on the head. "You forget, my small friend, that you are a bull and she is a dog. I cannot recommend such a match. But do not be concerned. We shall find you a lovely cow when we return to Olympus."

Spent, satisfied, and for the first time on Earth unconditionally joyful, Dionysus began to laugh. He saw the moon up above, slim and white, smiling back down at him. Across the street from the chaos he created, he bellowed and wailed, shuddering, twirling, dancing in mad joy. He caught no suspicion, for observers of the disaster were too engrossed in what unfolded before them. When he had exhausted himself, he left the stoop and stole away, darting furtively through the shadows until he reached the apartment again.

Safely inside, he looked in on David. The gaunt man's limbs were positioned exactly as they'd been when he left. In a divine mood, Dionysus lay down on the couch, slipped the blanket back over himself, and, smiling sweetly, fell into a dream of Olympus. In it, his father Zeus was looking down on him, beaming with pride.

Chapter 22
Chi

The call from Aaron came only seconds after she'd stepped through the door and found them both still sleep.

"The room is available now."

Already? "Wow."

"They want us to bring him at twelve-thirty".

She sat down on a chair and breathed deeply to calm herself. The future had once again arrived.

So no sleep today. Quietly, taking care not to awaken them, she put herself to the unsettling task of organizing David's things. She ignored the growing tightness in her belly as she filled and taped and then stacked each box. She detested each small decision she made, on his behalf, as she downsized his world. Would he want this? Will there be room for that? What items would he need around him to make this new place feel like home?

And what should I keep here for him, just in case?

All his accomplishments and accolades, everything that was *David*, was being reduced to a smattering of shitty little boxes in a pile by the door.

She looked over at the couch and saw David's confounding caretaker still sleeping there and thought to herself that he would be gone soon, too. But where would he go?

I'm working on some things for him, Aaron had said.

She nudged him gently on the shoulder. "Harpo? Rise and shine."

He rolled over.

"Good morning," she said. "I let you guys sleep late, but you should probably get up now."

"*Ugh*," he said as he rose up, "I have been dreaming *viciously*. My heads pounds as if Alexander's chariots had been driven through it."

Gina chuckled. "I can relate to that. I've had a couple of *killer* hangovers."

Rubbing his forehead, he said, "I do not understand this 'hangover.'"

"Let's hope you never do." Then her voice took on a more somber tone. "Listen, I wanted to talk to you for a few minutes before David gets up. Aaron just called me to say that the room in David's new house is ready for him. I'm going to take him over in a little while."

Panic gripped him. He stiffened. "When?" he said, his voice suddenly shaking. "Twelve-thirty."

He studied his watch for a few moments, muttering as he counted out the hours and minutes. He looked up at her, his face full of alarm. "But that is too soon!"

She smiled sympathetically. "I know. I feel the same way. But we've known for a while that he was going to go *somewhere*. And look at it this way—now you won't have to take care of him anymore."

"But—"

"I mean, you didn't really want this job in the first place, right? Now it's over, and you're free to do what you want again."

"You don't understand, I . . . I . . ."

But the thought would not complete itself. Words deserted him, so he just stared at her with a stricken face.

"What don't I understand?" she said.

He stammered out his answer. "Th-there is something I must show you, something very important . . ."

"What?" she said.

"I must show you—"

"Can't you just tell me what it is?"

"I cannot explain in words, it must be seen—but it is very, very important that you see it, and I must take you there personally. It is not far, just a few minutes' walk . . ."

She felt annoyance bubbling up inside her. *With all this stuff swirling around me, you want me to go see something?* "Harpo, I usually love surprises and under ordinary circumstances I'd be happy to see what you've got to show me, but I'm gonna be sort of busy today. Can it wait 'til tomorrow?"

David will be gone by tomorrow, and with him, my usefulness to her. It is now or never, he thought. *My fate will be decided on this day.*

"No, it is very important, you must see it today . . ."

She threw her hands up in exasperation. "Oh, for crying out loud—"

"Please!" he begged her, in a tone was so desperate that she stood still and listened. "I beseech you to trust me. I promise that what you see will not displease you."

She stared at him, perturbed, for a few long moments, and then said, "I'm *already* displeased. But I'll go with you after David gets settled." She wrinkled her brow in obvious unhappiness. "And whatever it is you want me to see, it better be good."

She turned away from him and picked up the telephone, but he had more to say. "Please, Gina . . ."

250

It was so unusual for him to address her by name that she put the telephone down in mid-dial and turned to face him again. "What?"

"May I go with you when you bring David to his new home? I would like to know where it is."

And with the thought, *just when I want to drop-kick him back to his precious 'Olympus'* . . . she said, "Yes. Of course. But you can't interfere with anything."

"I will not. You have my divine word."

"I'm going to hold you to that. Now would you go wake David up? I have to make a phone call, but he needs to start getting ready."

He nodded. As he went into the bedroom, he heard the soft beeps of numbers being tapped out on the phone. By the tone of her voice, he knew who she'd called.

Just outside the door, he listened. There was a short pause, and then she said, "Okay, I guess. But I think this is the official crappiest day of my life. I'm packing everything for David, and then at the shelter. I want to get it all over with. Then I'll be able to think straight again."

Then she listened for a few moments. "Well, assuming everything goes well, I should be back here around three or so, and then Harpo has something he absolutely, positively has to show me. *Today.*" Pause. "I'll probably get over to the center no later than six." Long pause. "I'd love some help. And some company. I'll see you later."

Harpo moved quickly to the bedside and shook David, a bit more roughly than necessary. David sat up almost immediately, wide eyed, as if he had been awake already. "You must arise now, my friend," he said. "This will be a trying day, I think. For both of us."

He sat down on the edge of the bed, trying to shake off the knowledge that as David departed from her everyday life, he would, too, and McCarthy would enter. *Ah, well, it is Fate,* he thought eventually, *nothing more, nothing less.* Fate had decreed that he would make his final plea to her that afternoon. It could not happen on a worse day. He cursed his luck.

Ω Ω Ω

It was painful for Gina to watch David disappear into a welcoming party of his new house mates, some of whom were far more social than she would have expected. *It's a mixed-level house,* Aaron had told her. *There are some folks there who will draw him out, if it's going to happen.* So Gina stood quietly to one side, swallowing the hurt, suppressing the separation anxiety that had crept in over the last week. It was something she would have to shed, though it would surely not depart willingly.

She watched the odd-looking group of residents troop down the hallway to the room he would share with one of them. She turned to Aaron and with a sad smile, said, "They must have been told to expect him."

He nodded. "They do this with every new arrival. Give them kind of a welcoming party. Most of the residents will be here for a long time, and they try for a good start."

She looked around. "I don't know why, but I thought this place would be a lot dingier. It's very nice."

"It's a gem," he said, motoring forward into the common room. "We could use about a hundred more of them in Manhattan alone."

"I guess I should feel pretty fortunate that we were able to get David in here." Her voice trailed off sadly.

"But you don't."

"What?" she said, looking up.

"Feel fortunate."

"Oh, Aaron, of course I do. It's just—"

"—so hard to *accept?*"

Gina shrugged and sighed. "Acceptance," she said wearily. "My last frontier. I guess I'm getting there. Just like you said I would. But by God it's hard. Is it written all over my face? I thought I was so good at stomping it down."

"I'd be out of business if people didn't stomp all over their own feelings."

And as their soft laughter dissipated, Harpo came into the common room with the last of David's boxes in his hands. Gina took it from him and disappeared down the hall, heading for David's new room. He started to follow, but Aaron called out to him.

"Dionysus," he said, "wait a minute."

He stopped short upon hearing his real name, and turned back to Aaron. "Yes?"

"I was wondering if you could stop into my office later so we could have a visit. At four o'clock. I have some ideas that I think might work well for you, about where you're going to live, that is."

He stiffened slightly. "I am sorry," he said, "but I cannot accept your hospitality today, though I am most grateful for the kind offer."

Expecting an explanation from his usually florid patient, Aaron waited. When it failed to materialize, he said, "Really?"

"Indeed, really."

"That's too bad. I was hoping we could talk. Well, perhaps you could come sometime tomorrow."

Zeus alone knows what lies in wait for me tomorrow. "I am not certain where I will be on the morrow."

Aaron was perplexed. "I'm sorry, I guess I don't understand what you mean."

"I mean that only the Fates know what is in store for me. I could be anywhere in the Cosmos by then."

"Are you leaving New York?"

"I do not yet have a definite plan, and as I said, the Fates will decide. But I think perhaps they will determine that it is time for me to wander on."

Aaron found himself in the unusual position of feeling perplexed. "And if you *are* fated to start wandering again, you have no idea where you might be going?"

"No."

"Dionysus, why don't you tell me what's going on? We've become—friends, you can confide in me, but you seem very distant and unsettled all of a sudden. I get the feeling that you're having some difficulty that you don't feel comfortable discussing. I want you to know that if I can help you in any way, I'd be happy to do so."

Harpo inclined his head very slightly. "I am most appreciative."

"Has something happened that we should talk about? You seem to have changed rather abruptly. I'm a bit concerned."

He gave him a wistful smile. "You need not be. While I am truly grateful for your kindness, there is nothing you can do to change my circumstances. Everything is in the hands of the Fates now."

Aaron sounded almost perturbed. "Where are you going to sleep tonight?"

"I have a very good home, which I inherited from Freddie, along with a few other things," he said. "He was a very good mortal. The legacy he left me is greater than you can imagine. And I will not be alone. I have a wonderful companion." He patted Midas. "You are a kind man to give such thought to my comfort. I will commend you to my father Zeus upon my return to Olympus."

Aaron hesitated for a few seconds, then said, "So you're planning to go back there soon?"

"There are a few tasks I must attend to before I can depart. Now, please, I must be about them, so I cannot speak with you any longer. If you would tell Gina that I will wait for her outside, I would be most grateful."

He left Aaron staring after him.

Ω Ω Ω

Gina emerged into the sunlight a short while later looking as if the life had been sucked out of her. Dionysus arose from his seat on the steps to greet her. "Okay," she said, "I guess that's that. We'll take a cab back to my apartment now and you can get your things."

Such things as I have. She had given him some clean clothing, none of which he wanted to take. The watch he would keep, for it served a purpose. "And then you will come with me? To see what I must show you?"

"Yeah," she said, leaning back into the seat. "I'll come with you."

He waited a few seconds before speaking. "You will be pleased."

"I hope so, Harpo, I hope so."

Ω Ω Ω

They stood across from the remains of the large building, on the same stoop where Dionysus had sat the night he turned the rain red. He pointed toward the building and grinned expectantly.

This is what he wanted to show me? "I already know about this," she said. "An explosion. Someone thought it was terrorism at first. They were talking like it was another tower." She looked across the street and said, "I suppose I shouldn't say this, but I was secretly happy—for a minute, anyway—when I heard. This guy really deserved it. But it's really bad. For the neighborhood, the employees . . . and I don't understand, why did you want to show it to me?"

"Because I thought it would bring you joy to see it."

"Oh, I does, a little, I mean, that it happened to DeMoula. He deserved it."

But her face was somber, not alight with the glee he'd hoped for. "Then why do you not seem pleased?"

"Because for a lot of other reasons, this is a terrible thing. It was a crappy old building, but it's been part of this neighborhood for a long time. I feel sorry for the people who worked there. They'll all have to find other jobs. And it's difficult for the businesses he sold wine to. They'll be hurting if they can't find another wine supplier. It's gonna be hard for those people for a while. And people were hurt in there, I heard. Flying glass."

Scratches and pimples. He thought of the gash in Freddie's neck, and of David's deep sorrow.

"But what of your wish for vengeance?"

"Vengeance? *Wait.* You—"

His voice was angry and impatient. "On the night when Freddie died, you spoke of vengeance. That you really wished for it."

She looked hard into his face for a moment. "I hope you didn't think I was asking for—" Her expression grew more worried. "I was talking more about doing something directly to DeMoula himself."

"Is not the destruction of his property a very direct injury to a man who so adores money that he would ruin another man to acquire it?"

"Yes, but—"

"And would it suffice if the deed was done specifically on your behalf?"

"I guess so but—"

"I did this," he said firmly, "for you."

She stared at him in shock. "*What?*"

"I did this. For vengeance. For you. You must believe that it was me. That it was my divine power."

"Harpo, what are you talking about? You didn't do this. The newspapers said there was a problem with the building trembling from some sort of vibration. Someone was even talking about a mild earthquake—"

"Poseidon did not shake the earth. It was entirely my doing. No other gods were involved."

He smiled proudly. It was obvious to her that he expected to be praised.

Instead, she glowered. "You're insane, you know that? You're carrying this god thing way too far. You couldn't *possibly* have done this."

"Please," he said, taking her by the arm. "Come with me, and I will show you." And before she could protest, he was dragging her across the narrow, crowded street in mid-block. As they stepped out from between two cars, a speeding taxi bore down on them.

Her entire life flashed before her.

But he put out a hand, and it screeched to a stop; she stood there for a moment, frozen in fear, until Harpo dragged her forward again. Dazed, she allowed herself to be pulled, and soon found herself in front of a yellow-taped door.

"We shall go inside," Dionysus said, "and I shall show you my work."

She resisted. "No, Harpo, we can't do that. This is a police barrier and we can't cross it, or we might be screwing up evidence. We shouldn't be trespassing in this building, and anyway it's gonna be locked—"

His hand reached out toward the door. She heard a soft click, and then he gave the door a push. It swung effortlessly under his touch, and soon they were standing inside the dark building. Gina heard a steady distant *drip drop* and smelled the residue of fire-fighting chemicals. Her eyes began to water, her throat burned. Crumpled shelves lay on the floor, surrounded by shattered bottles.

"This is an—apocalypse."

"Indeed. *Apokálypsis.*"

"I can't stay in here . . ." she said, and she turned toward the door.

But Harpo grabbed her by the arm. "*I did this. For you.*"

She began to feel frightened. *He'll turn on a dime.* "Harpo, this had to have been an explosion . . ."

"It *was* an explosion. Of bottles of wine." His voice was urgent and forceful. "It was I who made them explode."

Her eyes widened. *God my ass,* she thought wildly, *he IS a fucking terrorist, disguised as a homeless guy, and now he's obsessed with me. No wonder I couldn't find him anywhere, he's probably buried so deep that his own people can't find him.* It explained the middle-eastern accent, the cultural misplacement, the total lack of personal history.

And he's been in my home, while I was asleep . . .

"Did you put a *bomb* in here?" she asked in a near-whisper.

"A *bomb*? Of *course* not. I used my own power!" His voice was high-pitched and shrill. "I am the *ruler* of wine, and I have reacquired my power because Freddie began to believe in me. Do you not understand? This was a *good* thing to do, avenging his death! I did it because—because—"

His voice softened, and he let go of her arm. He looked downward, his face stricken with despair. "Because I would have you believe in my divinity. I *need* you to worship me."

"What?" she whispered.

"I would have you truly believe that I am a god," he repeated. He looked pleadingly into her eyes and saw not the hoped-for sympathy but shocked disbelief. Unbridled rejection, disdain and anger. "For if you will only believe in me, the curse will be lifted." He grabbed the vial hanging from his neck and held it out for her to see. "I carry in here a gift from my divine Father, a vial of ambrosia, and when you believe in me it will enable me to return to Olympus."

Her response was pure reflex. "Harpo, I don't believe in you. I'm not *ever* going to believe in you. I don't really even believe in the *regular* god." Then she, too, looked down unhappily and said, "I'm sorry." When she looked up again, her expression had hardened. "I would *never* have wanted this to happen. This was terrible."

She turned and walked away, leaving him to ponder the things she had said. When he finally looked in her direction, she was disappearing out the open door. She did not look back.

"Well," he said miserably as he stroked Midas with a trembling hand, "it seems that the Fates have spoken."

Chapter 23
Psi

The god named Dionysus sat in his box with the drape closed. With eyes squeezed shut, teeth clenched, and hands balled into tight, angry fists, he concentrated with every ounce of his determination. But no matter how hard he wished, the force of his will seemed inadequate, for the vial remained cold. And when he opened his eyes again, he was still in the box, still on Earth. Still in the abyss of mortality.

Seething with frustration, he yanked open the drape and roared his bitterness out into the night. Without a blanket of snow to absorb it, his rage echoed off the adjacent walls, bouncing crazily around the alley. But with each reverberation, it lost a little of its power, and soon his angry cries were swallowed up and spirited off by the gentle winds of spring. Tonight, no matter how much noise he made, no moving machine would come with soldiers to whisk him off to Gina's center. And tomorrow there would be no center.

As if he could sense his master's despair, Midas whimpered inside the folds of his toga and shifted upward, then stuck his head up and nuzzled him sympathetically.

"We are lost, Small One. My act of vengeance seems to have distanced her even further. Curse Aphrodite for requiring that a woman believe! Could not Freddie have been enough? I wonder what Freddie must think, down in Hades, of how I have frittered away his fine legacy on a useless effort."

The dog began to whimper. "I know, I know," Dionysus said, patting the dog's head affectionately. "You wish for the sweet fields of Elysium. I do, as well."

He shifted around in the box, muttering miserably, finding little comfort. He moved into another spot, one he hoped would be more compatible with the shape of his buttocks. "Cursed eagle-pecked liver of Prometheus," he whined, "I *know* there are places more welcoming than this, for I have wandered to such places before. Why could I not have landed in one of them at the start of this journey?"

Midas yipped. "Ah, yes, you are right. The Fates have sent us here for their own purposes. I daresay we may never know what those purposes might be."

A light wind blew in through the opening and Dionysus hugged Midas closer to him. "But," he said, "I do not think it is wise to remain here. What do *you* say?"

Midas let out two decisive barks of accord.

"Ah, Midas, I can always count on you to refrain from arguing. A fine quality, indeed, especially in a bull! Very well, we shall leave here. But where shall we go? This California place where there is no snow? It seems as good a choice as any. Freddie said it is a very long journey. We will leave tonight, eh? The stars are bright, and the heavens smile down on us. This bodes well for traveling, does it not?"

He crawled out of the box and stretched, and felt a small bit of his frustration melt away in the cool night air. "Time to shed all of this unhappiness," he said, "and to acquire joy in its place. In time, we shall know *ecstasis* again. Far away from here, I think."

He looked back inside the box one more time, then patted its creased and spattered top affectionately. "Now you shall be *my* legacy."

Facing into the length of the alley, he cupped his hands around his mouth and shouted, "I am leaving now, and I shall not come back." He turned, and as he walked toward the street, he heard the sound of someone running.

"But there is one thing yet for us to do before we go," he said when they reached the street. "The woman is very angry at me, and I would be a fool to leave such enmity to fester. Who knows, perhaps there will come a time when McCarthy is no longer her lover. When she is an old, gray mortal, I will still be virile and handsome. Well, mostly. Perhaps we will catch her at the right moment. She is a good mortal, and someday she might be convinced to set aside her earthly concerns and assist me with the more cosmic one I have presented. But she will never do so if she is angry, eh?"

He turned onto the sidewalk, considering the eternity before him. "I must go back to her and apologize one more time, though the notion of it galls me. Oh, well, even a god must prostrate himself every now and then. Now, what were the words Freddie taught me? Ah, yes! I remember. 'Honey, I'm so sorry, I was a great big shit, and I promise I'll never do it again.'"

Midas yipped his approval, and Dionysus laughed. "Perhaps we will spend the rest of *her* life apologizing to her. Ah, well, I suppose it would not be so bad if that were to happen." He scratched Midas's head and said, "After all, we *could* be chained to a rock . . ."

Ω Ω Ω

This day would be forever etched in Gina's consciousness as the Day of the Boxes, and she vented her accumulated spleen on the shabby ones in which she was packing up the minutiae of the center. She drew the tape machine viciously over each corner, flap, and seam, applying layer after layer without mercy, until there was almost no cardboard visible on any of them.

The distress of her afternoon encounter with Harpo still lingered. Terrorist, professor, God, plain old ordinary whacko, she was through with him. He had, through his behavior, managed to do what Aaron could not do with words: he had rendered himself un-savable.

She had had the phone number of the closest FBI field office already entered into her phone; Miranda had questioned her pointedly about why she needed it, and it had been hard to escape without revealing the reason. But she had never dialed, and she didn't really know why. So much for *if you see something say something*.

As Professor Poulos had predicted, the games had become dangerous. Just walk away, she told herself. Play no more.

But what if . . .

She called the thirteenth precinct and asked for the lead detective on the DeMoula case.

Without giving him a chance to ask her name, she explained why she had called. Told the detective about the strange middle-eastern man who had privately revealed his responsibility to her, *assured* her he had blown up the building. For more than a minute, she expounded on his intimate knowledge of the disaster.

Finally, the detective stopped her. "Ma'am, first I want to thank you for calling with this information. But I need to let you know you that what you're telling me doesn't fit with the evidence. There *was* an explosion. And so far it's still officially unexplained, but we do know that there wasn't a bomb.

"None of the security videos show anyone suspicious near or inside the building. The dogs went all through what's left of it, they didn't point on anything. Maybe you didn't see that in the *Times* today. The fire marshal did already say there was no obvious incendiary device. So it really looks like the cause could be electrical. And it's possible that some bottles of wine were under enough pressure to blow and start a chain reaction. We also gave that to the *Times*."

A bitter thought crept into her head. *Maybe a little tiny airplane crashed into it*. She thanked him, quietly said goodbye and broke the connection. She went back to the boxes, feeling bitterly frustrated.

She stacked them on the floor of her office and was amazed by the sheer volume of social service flotsam she'd managed to corral. Only the medical equipment had any value at all, and what little there was of it was sadly outdated. Soon the boxes would be assigned to anonymous invisibility in Randy's basement, perhaps to be forgotten for all time, and if Randy ever got around to selling the bookstore, Gina knew they'd be discarded. Some of her files were perhaps the only ones ever accumulated for each client. Many had gone to Potter's Field, in unmarked graves. It was as if they had never existed.

But *she* would never forget them.

She glanced at her watch. *Six-thirty. McCarthy should be here any minute.*

Giving in to her excitement, she allowed herself to smile. Sweet salvation, tender bliss, unconditional *sane* love were all heading her way. She couldn't wait to wrap him around herself.

Ω Ω Ω

McCarthy whistled *Everything's Coming Up Roses* as he made his way down the street toward Gina and her waiting boxes. He'd switched his night with another cop, so that guy could have a day to do something with his wife and kids. He was still in uniform, except for the vest and the gun belt, which he had secured in his locker at the station. In one hand he carried a bouquet of flowers, the first he had ever bought for Gina. *Not gonna be the last,* he thought to himself, a smile cracking onto his lips.

He headed down the familiar side street and was almost sad to think that this might be one of the last times he walked its tawdry length. I would always hold a special place in his heart.

He passed by the doorway of the adjacent building, his senses piqued, feeling rather than seeing a shadow. There were shuffling sounds, and then a few soft and halting steps. Light steps, like a child's. He slowed his pace and listened, then looked back over his shoulder, but saw nothing out of the ordinary.

He picked up his pace again and resumed his whistled tune where he'd left off. But the steps returned, and all his senses went on full alert.

"Hey, Cop," he heard. "Turn around." The voice was surprisingly thin, way too high.

Well, well. I was right. McCarthy came to a stop, then turned around slowly, more casually than he felt, and found himself staring into the business end of a large gray gun. It was gripped in the trembling hands of a boy who seemed barely able to hold it. The boy bounced back and forth from one foot to the other, an angry bee, nervously buzzing its intent to sting.

"Gimme your badge," he said, his young voice shaking.

"Just a minute," he said quietly, his hands raised. "What do you think you're gonna do with a badge? Even if you had my ID, you don't look anything like me."

"I don't need the ID." The gun was trembling even more. The boy held out one hand, fingers fluttering, waiting for his prize. McCarthy saw that his finger was poised on the trigger; the gun's weight caused it to waver in his small hand. One wrong squeeze and it would be all over.

"I just need the badge. Come on. I gotta get a badge so I can get in."

Looking down the barrel of the gun, he understood the cold reality: he was a gang ticket to this child. He willed himself to remain calm, went to his training.

Think this through carefully, he told himself: *young kid, inexperienced, scared to death and all hyped up.*

He dropped the flowers to the ground; the kid flinched. He slowly raised his hands up to shoulder height in a gesture he prayed would seem submissive. He cursed the vanity that had made him remove his vest and leave it in his locker.

"How ya doin', kid?" he said.

He had a small handgun in an ankle holster, but he knew with certainty that before he would be able to free it, there would be a hole in his chest. More likely the top of his head.

And this is a boy, a child. Eleven, maybe twelve. The same age as some of the kids he coached. He knew in his heart that if it came to it, he would find it hard to pull the trigger.

"Shut up. Gimme that badge," the boy repeated. He waved the gun downward. "Or I'll put you down on that sidewalk."

"Take it easy, now," McCarthy said. "I'm gonna give it to you. But I want you to stay calm, and don't do anything crazy. He kept his voice soft and level. He needed a stall, more time to think this through. *Ask a question, engage him.*

"Why do you want to be in a gang, anyway?"

The boy's grip tightened. "Because—what the fuck do you care?" The pitch of his voice rose. "Give me the fucking badge."

"Just take it easy," McCarthy said, "I'm gonna give you what you want, and then we'll both walk away from here in one piece."

Ω Ω Ω

Up ahead, Dionysus spied the silhouette of a large figure. He saw the uniform and the familiar cadence of the man's step and knew it was McCarthy.

He cursed angrily. "Even in the hour of my departure, the man must torment me!" he said to Midas.

"Lord Zeus," he whispered in disgust, "could you not just rid me of the gallstone that is McCarthy?"

There was a roll of thunder.

And then someone came out of the shadows, following McCarthy, and before they had gone too far he saw McCarthy stop. Dionysus ducked into the dark hollow of the same doorway where he and Freddie had concealed themselves on the first morning they'd followed Gina, the one from which the follower had just emerged.

He poked his head around the door frame; he saw McCarthy drop the flowers and raise his hands.

"By all the gods," he said quietly. "The man has never shown himself to be supplicant before."

He heard angry words. He came out of the doorway and pressed himself into the shadows along the wall. He moved forward slowly.

Midas made small growling noises. "*Shhhh,*" Dionysus warned him. "*Keep still. Do not make a sound.*" He flattened his body against the cold hard bricks, then inched himself along the wall until he was close enough to hear what was being said. He heard McCarthy's calm pleas for reason, and his promise of compliance, and thought to himself, *truly this is not good.*

He moved closer still, until he reached the edge of the shadow; to go any farther would bring him into the light. He heard McCarthy's voice, negotiating, stalling. Straining to hear the assailant's response, Dionysus leaned forward and tilted his head.

The knot in the cord of his ambrosia necklace let go. It fell to the sidewalk with a loud *clunk.*

He gasped, then reached down quickly and picked it up. The boy turned his head toward the sound and stared for a half second at Dionysus. McCarthy lunged his arm downward toward his ankle as the boy looked away. But the boy whirled back and fired before McCarthy could pull his own weapon free.

The blast of the gunfire reverberated in his ears and Dionysus clamped his hands over them, screwing his eyes shut in pain. When he opened them again he saw McCarthy staggering backward, a dark stain spreading in his blue shirt. His knees buckled and he struggled for balance, but managed to remain standing. "Oh, Jesus, you didn't have to shoot . . ."

The hot-wired boy shot again. A second hole appeared in his shirt. The big man, now helpless, went down fully. The boy ran forward and pulled the badge off the uniform shirt.

"*Great Apollo,*" Dionysus whispered. He rushed toward them.

The boy turned the gun on him and squeaked, "You. Stop. Move over there." He gestured with the gun, indicating a position near McCarthy's fallen form.

"Now turn around and put your hands on the wall."

Reluctantly, Dionysus complied.

Holding the gun on Dionysus, the boy searched McCarthy's pockets for his wallet, fumbled for what money there was, then tossed it away, as if it were radioactive. He was about to bolt when his eyes settled on the gleaming silver cord that hung from one of Dionysus's hands.

"Gimme that," he ordered, waving the gun toward the necklace.

Dionysus took his hands off the wall and turned around slowly. "Never," he hissed. "I will spread my buttocks to a *Roman* before I comply."

McCarthy groaned in agony, and Dionysus took one step toward him. "Move aside . . ." the god ordered.

The boy shifted his weight but held his ground. "I said give it to me!" He extended a trembling hand and wiggled the fingers expectantly, the other hand still holding the gun, now only a few feet from its intended target.

Dionysus head the sound of Gina's footsteps flying up concrete stairs. The boy whirled, gun ready, toward its origin. She stopped at the top of the stairs, gaping in horror at the scene before her. Midas began to bark, and the boy whirled again. Then Gina wailed, and he whirled back again, the gun wavering precariously in his frightened grip.

Gina rushed toward McCarthy. But what the boy saw was Gina charging forward in his own direction. Dionysus watched in horror as the gun was pointed and aimed. He heard the grate of metal on metal.

She must not die tore through his brain. He directed his will toward the gun.

It exploded into a million pieces of gray glitter and floated, in a slow shimmer of sparks, to the sidewalk.

The boy screamed and fell to his knees, wailing in pain. "Fuck! My hand!" He staggered up and then ran away, clutching his bloodied wrist.

Gina stopped in her tracks and stared down at the gleaming bits of metal on the sidewalk. Eyes wide, she looked up at Dionysus for one brief moment, her incredulous stare demanding an explanation. *"Oh, my God . . ."* she said.

Then McCarthy groaned, and she brushed aside the unfathomable event she had just witnessed. She was kneeling at his side before the gun dust had completely settled.

"Oh, sweet Jesus, McCarthy . . ." she moaned, her hands frantically searching for something to use to stanch the bleeding. She pulled up the red front of his shirt and looked at the massive wounds from which the essence of his life was leaking at a terrifying rate.

She looked up. "Harpo," she pleaded, "please help me here . . ."

He ran over to her and knelt at the other side of McCarthy's body. "What shall I do?" he asked frantically.

"I've got to run up upstairs to get help, but I need you to stay here with McCarthy. Oh, Christ," she moaned, "he's bleeding so badly! Give me your jacket—hurry—"

He tore off the jacket; she wadded it up and pressed it on McCarthy's chest. "Stay here and hold this in place so he doesn't bleed out! I'll be right back with help . . ." And with one brief, loving stroke of her hand on McCarthy's forehead, she got up and ran off.

As he pressed down on McCarthy's chest, Dionysus gazed into the stricken man's face. Beneath his hands he felt the life oozing out of the shattered chest.

Ω Ω Ω

By the time the EMTs arrived Dionysus had already tossed aside his blood-drenched jacket and applied the bottom of his own toga to McCarthy's chest, pressing down as Gina had instructed him to do. One of the EMTs tugged on his shoulder, shoving him back. "Step aside, please, sir, we'll take it from here."

He stood, a streak of bright red down the front of his garment. Gina looked at him and said, "Dear God, all the blood . . ."

"Gina," the second EMT said, "hold up the bag." As soon as she freed his hands, he pulled out a radio and spoke into the mouthpiece. "We're coming upstairs, ETA one minute, white male, forties, cop. Repeat, *cop*. Two gunshot wounds, one to the chest, possibly through the lung, the other to the thorax, possible damage to the liver, gall bladder or spleen . . ."

Standing over the grim and confusing scene, Dionysus heard, "gall bladder . . .", and the words his own wish came back to him.

Dear father Zeus, rid me of the gallstone that is McCarthy . . .

The two EMTs struggled to lift McCarthy, but he was too heavy for them. "Sir," one of them said to Dionysus, "could you give us a hand over here . . ."

He barely heard them. *The gallstone that is McCarthy . . .*

"Sir?" the EMT said sharply. "We need your help *now.*"

"What?" he said softly, emerging from his fog. "Oh, yes . . ." He bent down again and helped them lift the man onto the stretcher. Then with the flip of a button, it sprang up and they rolled it away, with Gina running alongside, still holding the plasma bag.

Dripping with mortal blood, shamed to the very bottom of his divine soul by his cruel wish, he trailed behind them, hanging back in dismay, trying desperately to remember anything else he might have wished.

Chapter 24
Omega

He stumbled into the trauma room, with McCarthy's blood still dripping from his toga. A triage nurse rushed forward to question him.

"*Sir.*"

So loud; could she not understand that he heard everything with brutal clarity?

"Sir, are you hurt?"

He managed to mutter, "No." His own voice sounded lifeless to him; the words were thick in his mouth; he stumbled over them. "No. I am—at least I think I am—uh, well. But my friend . . . I fear for *him.*" He gestured at the dripping red streak extending down the length of his toga. "You see, he is—*not* well."

The nurse stared at the blood. "Is he here?"

He nodded. "McCarthy," he mumbled, his eyes darting around the room.

"The cop?" she said quickly.

Dionysus nodded again.

"Good lord." She watched another red drop fall to the floor. She grabbed a cloth from a nearby cart and wiped it up. But another drop just took its place. She let it lay. "He's in that room over there." She pointed toward a glass-enclosed cubicle.

He nodded his somber thanks, then made his way numbly through the injured multitudes in the triage area, barely seeing them, but hearing every breath, every cry, every moan.

He found Gina staring intently at a frantic scene; beyond the glass he saw a small army of green-gowned mortals hovering over the table on which McCarthy lay, casting their chrome-and-tubing spells in a whirling, rhythmic rite.

Gina turned to him with a look of such terrible pain that the mortal half of his heart almost broke. He had done a most ungodly thing. It had all gone so terribly wrong, and he wanted to explain, apologize again, beg forgiveness, but this time from the very depths of his *divine* soul, in the sweet words of his own language, so the sublime nature of what he wanted to say could shine through and touch her heart.

Ímoun énas megálos vlákas kai poté den tha to kánoume aftó kai páli.
I was a great fool and I will never do this again

She held the key to his eternity in the tight confines of that frail and troubled organ, and he, the supposed ruler of joy, had failed to wrestle that key free. He had done everything he knew how to do, but had failed to bring her to *ecstasis*. His vengeance for Freddie had not cleared her psyche. *I did this for you, To win your soul. To bring you to belief. Because you said you wanted it. I did this for you.*

Now she stood watching her lover die, and of that tragic event, he could only say, I did this *to* you.

Guilt swirled inside him like Charybdis; he felt himself drowning in her depths. He leaned against a pillar and breathed deeply of the dry Earth air, staring up at the ceiling, wondering miserably how his existence had come to be so thoroughly *undivine*.

He knew there was a time when he would have shrugged and walked away, to come back when she would be more open to him, when she could not remember so keenly the tragedy that was unfolding.

For there could be no doubt that the mortal would die. He had wished for it, in careless disregard of the possibility that he might actually have the power to make it happen. He had set the Fates in motion, and the Cosmos, in its eternal ruthlessness, had responded with movement of its own. At his wish, a man had been struck down.

But this is only one! he told himself. One grain of sand on an unending beach! It is the Fate of all of them, to die, sooner or later. Was that not the very essence of mortality?

Then Great Zeus why, he pleaded silently, *does it pain me so?*

Because, he knew, his own mother had blessed and stained him with just enough humanity to experience their struggles.

Gina was weeping into her hands beside him. How could he comfort her, when he himself had been the cause of her misery? He looked through the glass again and watched a man shove a tube into McCarthy's nostril. McCarthy's hand jerked and then clenched as the tube assaulted his insides. His hand was the cold white color of sculpture.

He suffers. But it will not be for long. He tore his eyes away from the glass room and looked around the waiting area at the chaotic jumble of mortal suffering. He wished with all his might that the child whose arm hung at an odd angle would not have fallen down the stairs, that the old woman with gray skin and shallow breath could regain her strength. But time would never turn back. It marched inexorably forward, and nothing changed.

A bloodied doctor came out of the small room and approached them, one of the residents, whom Gina did not know.

"Mrs. McCarthy?" the woman said.

Gina winced, and shook her head no. "I'm just his—best friend."

"Is there a Mrs. McCarthy?"

"No." Then, more tentatively, "Not now. But if there was, it would be me."

That seemed to satisfy the young woman. "He's stable, for the moment." She yanked off her mask and wiped her forearm across her brow. "One bullet is lodged in the pericardium about a centimeter away from his heart. It's not moving, so we'll watch it for now, take it out later. The other one passed right through his abdomen just below his liver, nicked his gallbladder, which we'll have to remove. The bullet didn't do too much damage going in, but there's a bad exit wound. We're having a tough time closing it up."

Gina wrung her hands together. "Oh, God, why did this happen?"

The doctor placed one hand gently on Gina's arm. "*That* I can't answer. But he's a tough guy, from the looks of him. The surgeon's ready to go, but he wants his vitals more stable. Right now, he's still leaking all over the place, and it's a ten-steps-forward, nine-back kind of situation. We keep pouring blood in, and he keeps losing it. But he's retaining more than he's losing, that's a good sign."

Gina managed to stifle her sobs long enough to ask, "So what's the bottom line?" Her voice trembled. "Do you think he's going to make it?"

The doctor sighed; she was still new at answering this question. And Gina should have known better than to ask, but could not stop herself. "That's in the hands of fate. It's going to be touch and go over the next few hours. He's fit and strong, that works in his favor. We just have to make sure he doesn't spring any new leaks. We're going to move him to a separate room off the trauma area away from all this—" she glanced wearily around "—bedlam. There'll be a nurse checking on him every few minutes."

Gina reached out unconsciously and took hold of Dionysus's hand, her eyes still locked plaintively on the doctor's face. "Can we sit with him?"

"Of course. He's not responsive right now and he may not be aware of your presence. But if he is, it'll probably help him to have you there."

Suddenly there was noise at the ambulance entry, and the physician turned away as a stretcher came crashing through the swinging doors into the emergency room. A coterie of EMTs began shouting out the details of the new arrival's injuries and vital signs.

"Damn, another gunshot wound," the doctor said. As she retreated backward in the direction of her new case, she called out to Gina, "They'll take your man to the side room in a minute or two . . ."

Ω Ω Ω

Gina called both Diane and Miranda from the waiting room; an orderly rolled McCarthy's gurney past her. She followed, and, without thinking, dragged Dionysus with her. A nurse walked alongside steadying the intravenous hanger.

Encased in a network of tubes and bandages, McCarthy seemed smaller. The monitor beeped out his thready heartbeat and displayed his blood pressure; thin tubes in his nose fed oxygen into his lungs. She imagined him—glorious and strong—in the tuxedo he wore the night of their tryst, and could hardly believe they were one and the same.

Miranda set the cop network in motion. Word spread quickly, and soon legions of cops began arriving to keep a blue watch in the crowded waiting room. In and out of uniform, they lined up in the hallway to donate for their fallen comrade. Reporters gathered outside, as much in vigil as duty. Even they were quiet. The air reeked of unknown outcome.

In the small room down the hall, Gina and Dionysus waited in numb shock and watched over McCarthy, whose torn chest somehow managed to rise and fall, if erratically. Every few minutes a worried-looking nurse came in and scrutinized the digital displays on the monitor, checked his bandages, then sighed and ran out again, leaving them in bewildered silence.

The clock on the wall ticked thunderously. Harpo thought he could even hear McCarthy's heartbeat, beyond the monitor. He put his hands over his ears.

Gina touched his arm. He took his hands away.

"Yes?" he said quietly.

"What you did out there . . ."

He hung his head in shame. "I am truly sorry."

"No," she said, struggling for words. "Not the building. The gun—I've been playing it over and over in my mind . . ."

He rose up slowly, then walked to the window and peered out between the dusty slats of the blinds.

"Guns just don't disintegrate, I mean, I know sometimes they explode, but . . ."

He said nothing.

She stood and came up next to him. "It wasn't just the gun exploding, was it?"

He looked into her eyes but found her expression unreadable. He shook his head *no* and watched with anxious concern as she groped her way back to the chair and sat down, one hand clutching the armrest.

Staring blankly into the space in front of her, she whispered, "Oh, my god . . ."

He gave her a small, ironic smile and said, "Indeed. A very contrite one."

Then she stood up again and looked straight into his eyes. "And what you showed me this afternoon at the DeMoula building, you really did that, didn't you?

And it wasn't a bomb."

He sighed. "I did."

"I just don't know—*what* to think . . ."

He looked at her, eyes pleading for understanding. "But I thought it was what you had wished for! You spoke of it so vehemently on the night Freddie began his journey. And I had just found my power again! Freddie himself brought it to me, I know he did! I thought you would be so *pleased*, and that you would adore me as so many others have, that you would believe in me . . . I—I—was a fool, and I wish with all my divinity that I had never done it."

"No, *no*. It *was* a terrible thing you did—but I understand now. *Why*. I—wish I'd understood then."

She paused and drew in a breath. "That's not right either. I'm not even sure what I'm trying to say. Maybe I did understand, but I couldn't really accept it. All these stories, about Olympus and knowing gods and your father being Zeus and having statues made of you—it's all so, so crazy, so *hard to believe*."

He gave her a small, sad smile. "Believing is not so terribly difficult. You must simply decide that you will do it."

"Is that all it takes, really?"

He spoke very gently, for she seemed confused. "Many mortals throughout the ages have believed simply because they wished to."

"It's not that simple *these* days. I wish it was. The world is just not the same as it was, before . . . a lot of us lost what faith we had that day, it disappeared with the towers."

"And yet you mortals have enough faith to raise another one."

She turned away from him and looked out the window. "And may it please the Force that it stands forever."

She turned back again. "And what you said about me saying I believe in you and then you can go back to Olympus . . ."

He sighed. "It is the truth."

She was silent for a few moments, then said, "You made that gun just vanish. You saved my life out there. And—maybe—McCarthy's."

After I nearly took it. And were you to die, he thought bitterly, *how should I ever get home?*

"Yes," he murmured, "I did."

But should I reveal how McCarthy came into danger, through my casual and unthinking wish?

"You saved my life," she repeated, "and all you need from me is '*I believe in you*.'"

"Yes," he whispered. He looked down at the floor.

There was silence for a few moments, then Gina said, "Harpo."

He looked up again. "Yes?"

"I believe in you. I think you're who you say you are."

A startled look came over his face. He grasped anxiously at the vial of ambrosia. *It will become warm, and then you must consume it . . .* Zeus had said.

The seconds ticked by and he tightened his grip on the small vessel, his fingers searching desperately for any change of temperature. But the vial remained cold. Minutes passed, and finally he looked up at her. He let go of the vial and shrugged sadly.

"It's not working?"

He shook his head *no* and sighed.

"This afternoon you proclaimed to the Cosmos that you would never believe in me. I think you spoke what you thought to be true. And moreover, it was heard. Things have changed since then, but not that much, eh?"

"Maybe not," she said quietly. "God help me. I don't know."

"So what the Cosmos understood is that you do not adore me."

"I'm sorry," she said. "Oh, Harpo, I'm so sorry . . ."

He sat back down and slumped into the curve of the chair, then stared up at the ceiling with a bitter look on his face. After a long, deep sigh, he said, "Ah, well, it is in the hands of the Fates, eh? They seem not to like me much lately."

She sat down beside him and placed her hand over his. "I wish there was something I could do to make this up to you . . ."

"There is nothing," he said sadly, and closed his eyes.

But after a few moments, he opened his eyes again and turned to her. "There *is* something you could do that would please me."

"*Anything.*"

He shrugged and smiled and said, "You could call me by my proper name. Somehow, I think it would make me *feel* as if you really believe."

She gave him back a sad smile and said, "Of course. *Dionysus.*"

Ω Ω Ω

They listened for another hour to the erratic beep of McCarthy's monitor. Dionysus drifted in and out of an uneasy sleep. The half of him that was mortal *ached*, craving rest. A sharp noise from the hallway outside jarred him awake, and he thought to himself, *I wish they would be quiet out there . . .*

And suddenly there was silence.

He sat up. *I wished for it, and it happened.*

He looked down at his watch. *I wish it would stop.* The glow of the phosphorescent crystal faded and the second hand stopped moving.

He stood abruptly and looked down at Gina dozing in the chair next to him.

Great Zeus! he thought, his mind racing, *of course!*

He stared at his watch again and compelled the hands to rock back and forth. The venetian blinds opened and closed at his wish.

And then he stopped testing himself. *This time,* he vowed, *I will not waste this power.*

His arms raised in praise of this turn of Fate, he propelled prayers toward Olympus. *Great Hermes, may your winged sandals ever be swift. Pure Artemis, may your arrows find their targets. Proud Athena, may your wisdom never fade. Sweet Apollo, may your golden light shine for all eternity.* As these prayers left his lips, he knew in his heart that they had been heard, and it filled him with joy. He said to Midas, "Wake up, Small One, we are going home!"

Midas poked his head up from the folds of the toga. "Yes, home!" Dionysus said. "Where there is no cold wind or maddening rain, where there is true ambrosia to be had, and where you can once again be the bull you were born to be!"

He sat down on the floor, cross-legged, and closed his eyes. Thoughts of Olympus drifted pleasantly through his consciousness. He imagined the sweet smell of honeysuckle, the caress of a soft breeze on his skin, and the gentle sounds of water flowing through the sacred streams. Peace permeated his soul, and he thought of nothing but his desire to go home.

But the *beep beep* of the monitor intruded on his concentration, and try though he might, he could not get it out of his head.

"Sweet Apollo," he whispered, "Rid me of—"

He stopped. It was his wish that brought about the need for that monitor. "By all the gods, what irony," he muttered, "for I *am* chained to a rock. A very *large* one."

He got up off the floor and went to the bedside. Standing over the pale man, he understood why he was still bound to the rock called Earth. *It is this mortal guilt that holds me,* he realized.

In a pained voice, he said aloud to Midas, "I will have to answer for this misery I have caused."

He placed his hand on McCarthy's chest, and felt the unevenness of the flesh, the terrible hole that the projectile had made there. He focused, sending pulses of warmth into the torn tissues.

Behind him, he heard Gina stir. She came to the bedside. "What are you doing . . ."

He ignored her and concentrated on his task at hand, for it must be done before the Fates discovered his disregard for their will. "Sacred Zeus," he murmured softly, "immortal patriarch, grant that this mortal shall be heal—"

"You're trying to fix him. Oh my God."

"Please, allow me—"

Then thunder boomed, so loud it seemed to originate from within the room itself. There was a brief hiss of electricity, a few blue sparks, and then the room went dark. As did the lights in the hall beyond. The alarm on the heart monitor sent a shrill whine into the ozone-scented air. An emergency generator kicked into action, restoring the reassuring *beep beep*.

When her senses returned, Gina looked around in the dim emergency light, not seeing Dionysus, but found him a few seconds later, on the floor, unconscious.

"Oh, Jesus," Gina whispered as she hovered over the fallen god. "Harpo? Oh, Christ, I—*Dionysus?*" She patted the side of his face.

He came out of his trance and opened his eyes.

"What happened?" she said.

He sat up slowly and mumbled, "A message from Olympus . . ." He shook his head to clear it. "A forceful one. I think my Lord Father is trying to summon me home."

Then the lights came back fully.

"Tell him not to," she cried. *"Tell him.* You can't go yet, at least not until you finish."

He hoisted himself onto his feet and came back to McCarthy's bedside. "I shall try again."

He closed his eyes and drifted into a sort of trance. The clock stilled. The irregular beep of the monitor was the only thing he heard. He allowed himself to become filled with the sound of it, and slowly, gradually, he took hold of the heartbeat that drove it. Through the force of divine will, he matched the beating heart to his own. Then he opened his eyes and clasped his hands together.

Great Apollo, healer, physician, in honor of Hippocrates, answer my prayer that this mortal shall live . . ."

And when his prayer was finished, he forced McCarthy's heartbeat to separate from his own, then slumped to the floor exhausted. The beep of the monitor became steadier and more rhythmic, and a few moments later, McCarthy's eyes fluttered.

Gina touched him, needing to feel the truth of what her eyes could not believe. She ran her hand over his chest, felt its renewed evenness. "You're here," she whispered, "you're still here . . ."

His eyes moved around the room. "Water," he croaked. His voice was barely audible.

She grabbed the glass and angled it so the straw just touched his dry lips. After a sip, she pulled it away. "Not too much yet," she said.

He managed a small nod, then squeaked, "Kiss."

She wiped away tears with her sleeve. "You can have as many of those as you want." She leaned over and brought her lips to his.

Then she pulled herself away and turned to Dionysus. "You did it . . . he's awake again . . ." Her voice was full of—

Joy. He had done what he was supposed to do, finally. He had brought her joy. A deep calm settled over him.

Gina took him into her arms and gave him a long, hard hug. She blubbered out a string of thank-yous, then let go of him again and took hold of McCarthy's pale hand. She leaned closer to his face and whispered, "I hardly even had you and I thought you were already gone . . ."

McCarthy moved his lips, but the sound was weak. He wanted to tell her something. She leaned down, desperate to hear him. "Say it again."

It came out so thin and quiet that she could barely understand.

"Ambrose."

She pulled back and looked at him curiously. "What?"

"The A," he croaked. "My name. *Ambrose.*"

She laughed through her tears. "You're telling me *now*? Jesus Christ, McCarthy, you almost died, and I didn't know your first name. What's gotta happen before I get the Z?"

"Never," he said weakly.

Dionysus leaned in. "I know what it is."

"What? Tell me."

"Zeta. For Zeus."

"No." She looked at McCarthy. "Really?"

He only smiled.

Ω Ω Ω

They sat in silence for a few moments; the monitor was steady and rhythmic, and Dionysus knew that he had accomplished his task. The man McCarthy would live, heal, and fully claim the heart of the woman.

"Well," he said quietly to Midas, "I have brought them *ecstasis*. It is too bad that Aphrodite will not accept that alone as a means of my return."

For a short while, Dionysus watched the two shaken mortals reclaim the sweetness of having each other for yet another day, a day that *he* had given back to them.

"They get so few days," he whispered as he stroked Midas's neck. "Ours are not so precious, eh? Too many of them, truth be told. I think perhaps I am a bit jealous."

Ω Ω Ω

McCarthy grew stronger with every passing minute. Gina came away from the bedside and sat in the chair next to Dionysus.

"There's something I want to ask you, but I'm almost afraid."

He turned to her. "Speak. Please. Without fear."

She drew in a deep breath. "Can you fix David? His brain, the injury. Like you fixed McCarthy's chest."

Her eyes were full of hope, searching his, as he considered the implications of her request.

Finally, he said, "But he is already fixed."

"No, his brain—

He held up a hand to stop her. "I speak of his heart. What truly matters. And that is already fixed."

"But—"

He cut her off again. "David has been let out. His psyche has been cleared. He *accepts* his fate and has found joy."

She went quiet.

"As you must do, too, no?"

He stood up slowly and went to the window again.

"Yeah," Gina whispered from her chair. "As I must do. After all, you're the god, and you would know."

He turned back to her. "Accept your joy, and let it rule you. Let it clear *your* psyche." He glanced toward McCarthy. "You have in your heart all the means to do so. Do not squander this power. For when it is gone, it may not come back again."

She stood. "But David—"

"I will protect him, no matter where I go." He smiled. "It is the only godlike thing to do, eh?"

Gina could only nod. She sat quietly for several minutes, then rose. "I should go out and tell the others about McCarthy, they'll want to know he's doing better . . ."

She stepped forward and took hold of the door handle, but hesitated. She turned back to Dionysus and hugged him with all her strength. "I don't care about the warehouse. I care about this. And I believe *you* did it. That's the truth. No matter *what* the Cosmos thinks." Then she went out into the hallway to deliver the good news to the waiting blue army.

Ω Ω Ω

I believe you did it, that's the truth. It echoed in his ears like all the sweet music of the ages, put the wings of joy on his soul. And soon his most precious hope was realized, for within a few seconds, he began to feel warmth glowing out from the vial, spreading into the depths of his flesh. He grasped the necklace with trembling hands, and felt the heat intensify.

"Home. I am going home. Midas, we are—"

"Harpo," he heard. The voice was weak and thin.

He rushed to McCarthy's bedside. "Yes, my friend? Speak quickly, for I must leave."

"Thank you."

He smiled divinely. "It was nothing, eh? It was the only godlike thing to do. And now you shall have great good Fortune! Surely the Fates have many marvelous things in store for you! You will join with Gina, and have many children, and you will know great prosperity—"

McCarthy laughed very softly and said, "From your lips to God's ears. I'm just glad to be alive. Everything after that is a bonus."

Dionysus smiled broadly. "You are thinking like a mortal. In this case, the message came from a god's lips to *your* ears. This is the proper way of things, no?"

"Hey, I'm happy either way."

"Then you are a very wise mortal to accept joy in any form. Now, I must be off."

"Don't go yet, please . . . Gina will want to say goodbye."

He glanced at the door through which she'd disappeared, and for the first time since his arrival on Earth, felt no urge to follow her. He turned back to McCarthy. "This may be my only opportunity!"

"Just—" the mortal said, "do you want me to tell her anything for you?"

"I do not know what I should say, my friend, at a time such as this . . . for once, words fail me."

Midas whined and tried to crawl up out of the toga. Dionysus pushed him back in place. It was then that he felt the smooth metal under his fingertips, and he looked down at the collar. *They value such things,* he thought to himself. He patted Midas on the head and slipped the collar off his thin neck, then put it into McCarthy's hand.

"Give her this," he said, "for a new center."

He uncorked the vial, threw his head back, and poured the sweet, delicious ambrosia into his mouth.

Then with fine, mad joy in his heart, Dionysus swallowed, and was gone.

Epilogue
Epilogis

The god Dionysus lay back in the soft clouds of the Ether and rested his head on his cupped hands. A butterfly floated overhead; he stared up at it, then let his focus drift off into nothingness.

"There is no end to the Cosmos in sight, praise all Gods," he said to Midas. The magnificent white bull, who stood nearby in a patch of lush grass, let out a long low of accord, then swished the butterfly away with his tail. He lowered his massive head and tore off a few green tufts, then chewed lazily.

Dionysus arose and stretched, loving the light touch of the Ether on his skin. He wrapped his arms around the bull's thick neck and embraced him, then stroked his fine strong horns. He fingered the braid of honeysuckle that replaced his jeweled collar.

"Perhaps someday Aphrodite will once again look on me with favor and will give you another collar worthy of your magnificence."

He breathed in the scent, then let it out in a long sigh of contentment. "There is much to be thankful for! Already you have your horns again. And my own are returning!" He bent over and parted his hair to display his own budding protrusions.

He heard the sound of rumbling thunder; the air grew electric. The clouds parted, and there appeared Zeus in radiant glory. With each step, bolts of lightning crackled into the Ether around him. When he came to a stop, he stared down at his half-mortal progeny, who bowed low.

"You have recovered from your journey, my wayward son," Zeus boomed. "Arise and let me look on you. I was worried that you might have been damaged on Earth."

Dionysus stood and faced his all-powerful father. "Is that why you tried to bring me back?"

Zeus's eyes narrowed.

"I felt the tug of your summons, you pulled at me when I was attempting to fix the mortal man. Their earthly light and energy were disrupted. You forget how unmistakable your glorious presence can be."

"Then why did you resist? The Fates had already spoken. The power was there for you to return. The woman believed, and you could simply have ridden that belief home!"

"By my stupid wish for the mortal man's death, I set the Fates on a course of action that would have brought her to harm! I did not have it in me to leave things that way."

Zeus gave him a hard look. "Then I fear you *have* been damaged. You have never fallen prey to such concerns before."

Dionysus sighed. "These mortals now are different than those I have known in times past. You would have to know them yourself to understand. But I assure you, I am quite sound, and I am ready to resume my divine duties."

Zeus slapped his thigh and laughed, and thunder boomed throughout the Cosmos. "Things turned out well enough! You are back. One mad mortal has found his place among his kind, and he knows peace. The other mortal man is fixed, and because of this, the woman knows joy. All that is left is to determine what will happen in the remainder of their short time. Come; join me. We will consult with the Fates, although I am not sure They will receive your recommendations with complete enthusiasm."

"I do not understand why. By my actions, I have kept them very busy, indeed."

Zeus began to walk again. Dionysus followed through the parting clouds.

"Now, let me see . . ." the patriarch said, "What shall we suggest for these mortals?"

"Oh, many good things, Father, for they richly deserve them. It is the only godlike thing to do."

"Very well, let us try this: long lives, perfect health, and many children."

"Ah, yes!" Dionysus cried happily. "This woman loves to care for others, that is the essence of her very soul, and she will feel quite blessed." Then he furrowed his brow. "But these days it is very difficult to find sustenance on Earth. It was near to impossible for the man Freddie who befriended me. Some among them have much, but more have so little. If they are to have long lives and many children, they will need certain things."

"Of what sort?"

"Well, to begin with, a very large moving machine to carry them all around. The mortal Aaron spoke of something called a 'minivan.' And the woman now resides in a very small abode; surely they will need a more substantial one. She once mentioned a particular sort of domicile called 'a colonial in Westchester' . . ."

"But how shall all of this be accomplished? Our influence has waned!"

"Ah! Very simple—we need do only one small thing, completely within our power! There is a game they engage in, that Freddie told me about, something called a lottery . . ."

ACKNOWLEDGMENTS

My deepest thanks to all my wonderful critical/editorial readers: Spence Frazee, Pat Sanders, Deborah McVeigh, Mary Christine Ormond Kjellstrom, Renee Frost, Paula Lehmann, Anna Eddy, Christine Seaquist, and my agent Deborah Schneider of Gelfman Schneider/ICM Partners.

Profound admiration and awe go to Edith Hamilton, whose pioneering works on mythology have touched me from my childhood to my God-knows-when.

Special thanks to Tim Carlin of SSN Studios in Brewster, Massachusetts, for his incredibly professional help in recording the audio.

Sincere thanks to my wonderful daughters Meryl and Ariel Glassman who encouraged me through this entire decades-long process.

To my husband Gary Frost, no words can express my appreciation for his patient tolerance of a wife who simply cannot be idle.

Ann Benson is the author of the three historical novels of the Plague Trilogy: *The Plague Tales, The Burning Road,* and *The Physician's Tale,* as well as the stand-alone novel *Thief of Souls* (Random House). She is also an internationally acclaimed designer/teacher of beading and fiber arts and is considered the leading authority on beaded crochet. Ann has published eight books on beading and needle arts and holds over one thousand copyrights for fiber and beading design. With her husband Gary Frost, she winters in Port Orange, Florida, and summers on Cape Cod. She is the mother of two fabulous grown daughters and adores her many wonderful grandchildren.

Visit annbenson.com for more information

CPSIA information can be obtained
at www.ICGtesting.com
Printed in the USA
LVHW051550041119
636245LV00002B/197